THE HEART THIEF

ROSE GREY

THE HEART THIEF

Rose Grey

I am a fiction writer, which means I lie for a living. The characters and events in this book are imaginary. Any resemblance to actual persons living or dead, businesses, events or locales is purely coincidental.

This book is written for your personal enjoyment only and may not be reproduced in whole or in part without my written consent, except for brief quotations in critical reviews. Thank you for respecting my hard work.

Editor, Judy Roth
Cover Designer, izabeladesign@Fiverr

Simply Romance Press
26 Homestead Ave., Apt. 5
Warren RI 02885

For David. Always and Forever.

THE HEART THIEF

Chapter 1

"RAIDERS. COMING FROM THE NORTH." Old Rank bent over at the waist, wheezing.

Interim Marshal Poe Lancaster had never been fond of Tuesdays, and this was just proving his point. He snatched a handful of cartridges from his desk drawer. Normally when it came to law enforcement in Sector 1065, the threat of arrest was all he needed to keep the peace. Failing that, an actual stint in one of the two cells in his office did the trick. But Raiders were a different matter. Poe loaded his weapon and kept it out of his holster as he brushed past Old Rank and stepped onto the sidewalk. His boots made hollow sounds on the planks. A chilly spring wind tugged at the brim of his hat and the shadows of the buildings lengthened as the sun descended toward the southern plains.

The Raiders were still pinpoints in the sky to his right over the northern mountain range, but they were approaching at speed. Main Street was unnaturally empty. Darius, who owned and managed the Farmers' Mercantile, was framed in the display window as he draped the glass with burlap to obscure the stacked goods on display. Rank's General Store nearby was designed with smaller windows, but Sandok, Old Rank's youngest son, had already raced outside to close the shutters and was likely hunkered down inside behind a barred door with a club at the ready.

The open-air farmers' market between the stores was deserted too. Most of the farmers and their customers had prudently taken refuge inside the buildings, although Poe thought he saw someone's leg clad in the telltale orange of a Melchior miner's coverall sticking out from underneath one of the stalls. Chevalos at the hitching post near the market stalls whinnied, rolling their eyes and tugging at their tethers and even those who were hobbled, harnessed to wagons along the sidewalk, noses comfortably in feed bags, perked their ears and shifted uneasily in their traces.

Poe stepped down onto the street and strode across it until he was dead center facing the incoming Raiders. There were three, diving and whooping as they approached. Young, then. The more experienced Raiders knew the value of a silent approach and to focus on the steal.

The leader's helmet was emblazoned with a jagged streak of lightning, and his swooper looked nearly new. Two more Raiders followed him on older vehicles, but the smooth metallic fenders of their swoopers were also polished to a shine. Raiders' traditional jagged helmets and bulky armor contributed to their fearsome aspect and made them look larger than they were, but Raiders weren't any bigger than the average citizen, just a little meaner. The leader hunched over his handlebars and bared sharp teeth in a parody of a smile as he dove close to the surface of the road, his thrusters kicking up a thick cloud of dust.

Swooper fenders were designed to deflect weaponry, but the headlights were a point of vulnerability Poe had exploited before. One power stream aimed correctly could bore through the light right into the engine. It just required a steady hand. Poe set his feet shoulder width apart and lifted his weapon into position. Before the dust obscured the lead swooper entirely, he squeezed the trigger.

The swooper spun away out of control, tossing its rider toward the ground and nearly hitting one of the chevalos as it slid to a stop in front of the Mercantile. As the Raider fell, his armor curled around him in a smooth metallic ball, protecting him from injury on impact. Poe had always admired that feature of Raider gear, but in a fight, it could be a disadvantage. Raider armor automatically performed a wellness check before unfurling, which meant Poe had a moment's grace.

He squinted, willing his eyes to pick out the remaining swoopers in the cloud of dust. He could just hear their mechanical whining over the alarmed neighing of the chevalos, and he caught a glimmer of a headlight on the left near the deserted market stalls. He couldn't afford to take the shot. Hitting a Raider would be bad enough, drawing attention to or even hitting the hidden miner would be even worse.

He chanced a glance at a nearby wagon. The bovoquin net the farmer had used to hold his produce on the way to market now lay loose and empty on the wooden wagon bed. Keeping his weapon trained on the swoopers, Poe stretched his free arm toward the wagon. He hadn't worked with bovoquin since the summer of his fifteenth year. That experience had convinced him tending live-stock was not his forte, but the muscle memory of swinging a net had stayed with him. The tips of his fingers hooked around the edge, and in one smooth move, he pulled the net toward him and flung it, feeling that old satisfaction when it wrapped around the silver ball. Instantly he tugged the draw-cord, winding the loose end around his arm to pull the net shut. Just as he dropped the cord to the ground and slammed his boot onto it to hold it in position, he heard a scream from the market stalls.

One of the remaining two Raiders had continued to kick up their signature dust cloud, but Poe could see the source of the screaming just fine. The third Raider had found the cowering miner, hooked him by the back of his coverall and was now dangling him above the cloud. Perfect. Poe had never been fond of market days, and this was just proving his point. Market days were problems waiting to happen.

Keeping his movements large and dramatic, he lowered his weapon to the road, and in the same motion picked up the net's draw-cord. He didn't speak Raider, but he was fairly confident he could make his point. Trading was trading in any language.

The miner abruptly stopped screaming and struggling and now dangled quietly high above the street, his face a pale oval in the distance. Poe hoped the coverall held up. Melchior's miner uniforms were durable, but they weren't intended to withstand this sort of usage. Poe gestured broadly toward the miner and then toward his own captive.

The Raider who had been stirring up dust brought his swooper to rest at a hover just above the surface of the road. He glanced up at his partner and then back at Poe's captive, whooped again and followed the cheerful noise with a barrage of chatter. The silver ball in Poe's net unfolded. Poe was keenly aware of the weapon at his feet as his captive turned to look at him.

The net wasn't much of an obstacle—a more experienced Raider might have attacked. But this one simply grinned and let out a shrill whistle. His companion overhead and slowly lowered the miner halfway to the ground. Poe released his hold on the draw-cord. As his prisoner wriggled out of the net, Poe picked up his weapon again. He made a point of holding it with a relaxed grip, but the threat was clear.

The thin cable holding the miner released more quickly now, and Poe caught a glimpse of a pair of townspeople scurrying out of a storefront to pull the man to safety. But Poe's main focus was on the two mounted Raiders as they swooped forward, one to pick up the wrecked swooper and the other to allow their friend to leap onto the saddle behind him. A moment later they were pinpoints on the horizon over the Northern Mountains, flitting like black wasps against the clear blue sky.

"You should have shot those yenxers." Sandok's face was flushed with fury.

"Not sure that miner would agree with you." Poe kept his tone mild.

"I don't care what a kekkin' miner thinks. Miners come and go. But those of us who live here, who run businesses here, deserve protection."

"That's right," Darius chimed in. "How are we supposed to make a living if we have to worry about Raiders showing up whenever they feel like it?"

"Shoulda killed 'em," a farmer said. "That'd send a message."

The steadily growing crowd poured from the various stores they had taken refuge in. To Poe's relief most of the citizens seemed more interested in finishing their shopping than in arguing about Poe's methods. The farmer and the two shopkeepers scurried off too, their irritation forgotten in their zeal to make up for any sales they might have missed.

Poe folded the net into a neat packet and was returning it to the wagon bed when the unfortunate miner hobbled by.

"You hurt?" Poe asked.

"Nah," he replied cheerfully. "I was like this before I got here."

Chapter 2

"DILARA ELIAN?"

"Present."

Mrs. Onkelson glanced up, paused for a split second, and looked back at her attendance list without comment. She wore a pair of tortoiseshell glasses that slipped down her nose whenever she glanced at her tablet. A cuff on each of her wrists meant she probably suffered from space sickness when traveling at hyper speeds. Dilara had been feeling mildly ill too, but she hadn't felt sick enough to put up with the inevitable stares and whispers from the ship's gift store clerks to buy cuffs for herself, even if she had been able to afford them.

"Good morning, ladies. Welcome to the final week of our obligatory Sector 1065 orientation course. It's been a long journey, and I know you all must be eager to step onto solid ground, especially after the last solar windstorm. But you can rest assured that sort of trouble will be behind you once we have arrived safely in Valora's orbit."

Dilara stared absently at Mrs. Onkelson's shock of white hair, strands of which had sprung free from the tightly wound bun. They waved about gently in the breeze from the air vent as if they had minds of their own. The solar storm had been unexpectedly turbulent, but since the crew had not seemed alarmed, she hadn't been either. This was Dilara's first experience with interplanetary travel, and despite the circumstances, she had had a childish sense of glee when they blasted off. The entirety of her world had shrunk slowly to a pinpoint in the distance and then, when she blinked, disappeared into the void. Now though, she missed natural light. Even with just one central star, Valora would have been a welcome respite—too bad she wouldn't have a chance to enjoy it.

She looked around the room that had been designated as a classroom due to its unusually large size. The SS MacLaren was built as a luxury vehicle, and the wealthier passengers probably enjoyed a bit more elbow room, but what was roomy on a spaceship would have been cramped anywhere else. How the crew had managed to cram twenty-eight chairs into the space was a minor miracle. Most of the chairs were filled with the women of the twenty-ninth class of Well-Wed. Additional attendees trickled in as Dilara watched from her perch in the back row.

She glanced toward the portholes, but windows made no difference when all you could see on the other side was the occasional distant star in the black emptiness. Still, feeling trapped was relative. If suffering stuffy cramped quarters was the price of escape, it was a price worth paying. She dragged her attention back to Mrs. Onkelson who alternated teaching the classes with her husband, the equally dull Lieutenant Onkelson.

Out of sheer boredom, Dilara had already read everything the small onboard library had to offer about Valora, which wasn't much. The obligatory classes taught by the Onkelsons were designed to orient the women to life in Sector 1065, a small frontier town in North Union, the largest continent of Valora. Even so, Dilara had forced herself to pay attention during the classes—any extra nugget of information about life outside her home planet of Caron 5 could prove useful.

"My husband always asks me to teach this particular class because of the sensitive subject matter. Our topic this morning is Finding Love on Valora."

A titter and some whispers flitted through the classroom. All the women seemed restless today, shifting in their seats and giggling at odd moments, excited or uneasy, depending. Guerenne and her band of three acolytes sitting in the front row fell into the former category. Dilara guessed anyone sitting in the back, herself included, fell into the latter.

"Has anyone here ever been married before? Nothing wrong with that, ladies, as long as you are single now."

Three hands went up.

"What about engaged?"

Another five hands rose.

"Boyfriend or girlfriend?"

More hands waved. Dilara carefully kept hers down. There was a peculiar satisfaction in keeping at least one shame private.

"These things happen, dears. But I think you'll find men on Valora meet a higher standard than the men you left behind. Remember, many of the fellows on the planet, especially the ones in Sector 1065, are eager to settle down and start families."

Dilara kept her face expressionless. She wouldn't remain on Valora, but the other women would, some of them for the rest of their lives. Those were the ones who were listening intently as Mrs. Onkelson described the International Quilting Society meetings and the monthly poetry readings at which Mrs. Onkelson had herself occasionally shared a lyrical work or two. Who hung onto Mrs. Onkelson's descriptions of the fine examples of manhood Sector 1065 had to offer. And who dreamed of falling in love, making a home and a life with the perfect mate.

So it was unnecessary to learn what a woman's obligations to her man would be on Valora. It wasn't going to be an issue. She broke her own rule and let her attention wander.

Despite Dilara's steadfast resistance to socializing, she had learned most of the other women's names over the past two weeks since she joined the group. Ngendo, tall and willowy, smiled gently and nodded at something the instructor said. But Dilara had noticed Ngendo's ability to maintain a polite veneer while undoubtedly thinking about something completely different. Blonde, shapely Susanna tapped on her tablet, probably sending a message to her boyfriend back home. The application materials had been specific about having no current romantic attachments, but Dilara suspected Susanna had lied.

Kiko didn't bother to pretend. Her face was turned away toward the window as she stared at the distant view of Valora. Her sleek waist length black hair was twisted in a single complex braid.

Dilara watched her silhouetted face as long as she dared. Kiko didn't want to be on the SS MacLaren either, but unlike Susanna, Kiko seemed more angry than upset.

And then there was the group of six missionaries who were included in the orientation classes but who were not members of Well-Wed. All of them wore brown habits, and except for Cella, Dilara found them indistinguishable. Dilara had wondered upon first seeing how Cella kept a constant, if slight, distance from her companions whether she had been forced into missionary life. It happened. But over time, she had come to the conclusion Cella was ostracized because she was unpardonably beautiful. The irony of it had almost made her laugh.

Mrs. Onkelson droned on, waxing enthusiastic about the civilizing influence the women would provide for the frontier town. The expectation that twenty-two women could infuse a bunch of hardy pioneers with culture and social graces was unrealistic in Dilara's opinion. She might have studied art songs in school, but she had no illusions about the kind of music she'd be singing if she were to stay on a planet like Valora, or where she'd be singing it.

"Mrs. Onkelson." Guerenne waved her hand. Dilara took a deep breath and stared at the floor, willing Mrs. Onkelson to announce a break. But the woman loved to talk, and Guerenne and her three friends seemed to get a certain degree of pleasure in extending the torture of the classes. "Can you go into detail about what a wife's duties might be depending on the type of man she marries?"

Carefully muffled snorts rippled through the class. But Mrs. Onkelson nodded, oblivious.

"Certainly, dear. A beautiful and educated lady can hope to achieve great social heights on Valora. A woman who marries an executive at the mines, for instance, would be expected to host dinner parties, run fundraisers for good causes like the art museum or the library and generally be an asset to her husband as he climbs the corporate ladder.

"Marrying into a farm family is unlikely. The farm community tends to marry their own. But should the opportunity arise, I recommend you take it. Because Valora began as an agricultural colony, most of the farming families are well situated socially.

"Some of you are perhaps a little less accomplished and might have to satisfy yourselves with a miner or a shopkeeper. If any of you feel you fit into that category, I recommend you enroll in our on-planet cooking and finance classes so you will be prepared to take on household management and even helping with the store or running a side business."

"What if you only had one hand? Wouldn't a wife like that be more of a burden than a help?"

Dilara whipped her head up, but Guerenne and her friends sat in the front row with their backs to her, and she couldn't be positive who had spoken. Reflexively she jammed her stump deeper into her skirt pocket and cupped it in her left hand for good measure.

Mrs. Onkelson sighed gently. "Some challenges are bigger than others. But I was brought up to believe there is someone for everyone. It takes all sorts, you know. Some years back…"

She blathered on, recounting success stories of previous graduates of the Well-Wed program. Dilara stared at her desk, hoping her long hair covered her face sufficiently so no one could see her flushed cheeks. Once the ship landed, she would never have to see any of these people again, she reminded herself. She almost missed the announcement.

"Ladies," Mrs. Onkelson said, "the captain has confirmed we are scheduled to dock Tuesday, a week from today. When we arrive at the colony, we will mark your new beginning with our traditional disembarking ceremony. Each of you will stand at the top of the gangplank as your name is announced. Once you have descended to the dock, the lieutenant will escort you to the wagon that will transport you to the hotel.

"A good first impression is critical to a match," she added, "so I know you will want to look your very best when you are introduced to the welcoming crowd."

Dilara's neck tingled, and she made an effort to keep her expression calm. The moment Mrs. Onkelson announced a break before the final lecture Dilara rose and headed for the door. Once out of the classroom, she strode faster, avoiding the curious glances of passersby as she headed deeper into the center of the ship.

There was no privacy to speak of on the MacLaren. First class passengers had cabins and their choice of dining options. But the women of Melchior Intergalactic's Well-Wed program were assigned one long table in the second-class mess hall. At least they had a table. Early in her first week, Dilara had accidentally stumbled on third class quarters and knew she should be grateful she didn't have to eat MREs while sitting in a shared berth.

Nights weren't any easier. She had a berth to herself but since it was only two feet away from the next snoring woman, it was hardly a panacea. The only place one could find a kind of privacy was in the communication center. There, when Dilara clapped on a pair of headphones and focused on the screen in front of her, she could pretend for a moment she was alone. And often she was.

Most of the Well-Wed women had traveled from parsecs away, so it made sense for them to have invested in cheap disposable tablets with which to keep in touch with family and friends during the long journey. But once the ship entered Valora's atmosphere, they would have to rely on hard wired devices. The timony ore that veined the substrate on Valora made wireless communications impossible. On Dilara's first day onboard, Mrs. Onkelson had handed her Melchior manuals filled with details about life on Valora and in particular in Sector 1065. In the section about communications there were images of clunky computers and an odd-shaped object called a telephone Dilara had only seen used once in a copy of an old two-dimensional film from Earth.

But the founding farmers of Valora had been delighted at the opportunity to create a less technologically based society than the one they had left behind on Earth. Adherents of the "back to the land movement," they had flocked to the newly annexed planet, bringing seed packets, farm animals and little else. The oxygen laden atmosphere, plentiful water and temperate climate had made farming in the old way more practical than other destinations closer to home and the second Homesteading Act of Earth Year 3004 had sweetened the risk. Now, seventy-six years later, smaller rural settlements like Sector 1065 still clung to the old ways even as the cities on Valora struggled to find a balance between the planet's founding philosophy and the realities of Earth Year 3080.

They even still used paper on Valora. The precious sheets she had brought with her from Caron 5 had cost her dearly. If she had been able to wait and buy them here, they would have been far less expensive. It was intriguing to imagine a society that still communicated using pen and ink. In a way, that sort of communication was more private than e-communication.

Even if she had been foolish enough to steal a tablet and bring it along, Dilara couldn't have used it. Unlike the ship's communication center network, which was secure-locked for safety reasons, a tablet's communications would have been traceable. She couldn't afford the risk.

Still, she couldn't resist checking her inbox on the secured computers every so often. She hated the desire even as she acknowledged its power. It was like touching a sore tooth—the kind of thing you did to reassure yourself you hadn't imagined the ache, as though agony was somehow preferable to losing one's sense of reality.

Two unopened communications sat in her inbox, one from Aleksandr Lekin and one from her mother. There was nothing from her younger sister, Saskia, naturally. Dilara's hand froze over the screen. Opening the communications would only cause her pain. Besides, it wasn't as though she was planning to reply. She should delete them unopened. She *would* delete them, she decided finally. She reached a finger toward the screen, but the motion was too quick for the aged computer and instead of disappearing, Aleksandr Lekin's letter opened. She caught her breath at his expression—the polite mask of a stranger.

"Greetings Dilara, soon-to-be elder sister." There was the merest flicker of uncertainty in his eyes, but then he blinked and it was gone. *"I was surprised and delighted to hear of your upcoming nuptials to Mart Henkelor. Congratulations!"*

She watched, waiting for it.

"Initially I thought you and Mart might like to hold a big double wedding with us, but Saskia assures me you would prefer

something quiet and understated. Perhaps you would consider a brief private ceremony on the morning of Saskia's big day? Of course you and Mart would be more than welcome to share in the festival week to follow.

"On a personal note, I remain deeply grateful for your discretion regarding our friendship, such as it was. Surely you will agree there is no need to hurt Saskia's feelings or to make her think she's anything but first in my affections."

As a declaration of intent, it was hard to beat. Aleksandr had made his choice, and he was not going to let a pesky thing like morals get in his way. He was ambitious and a flawed wife would have stood between him and the leadership position he had yearned for his entire life. She had known this about him, she reminded herself. If she had thought with her brain instead of her heart, the end result would have been obvious. But she had allowed herself to be played, used, until she had no choice but to accept it had always been Saskia he wanted—beautiful, covetous, perfect Saskia.

There should be an app that allowed one to crumple an email, or twist it, to make the edges of the margins glow and turn to ash at the touch of a flame, or tear each screen shot into teeny tiny fragments to toss into the wind. Dragging the message to the virtual recycle bin was not nearly satisfying enough. She shrugged and jabbed her finger at the message from her mother—might as well drink all the poison at once.

Wraya Elian was dressed formally for whatever state event she planned to attend after leaving a message for her errant eldest daughter. Her face was a mask of civility, but her tone was firm.

"Your father and I just returned from the Summit Conference. I sent Tok to look for you, but I must say I find it inappropriate that you were not home to greet us when we arrived. I did not give permission for you to wander and certainly not to leave the estate.

"Dilara, Henkelor is ready to sign a marriage agreement. And it couldn't come at a better time. Saskia's wedding plans will require a substantial outlay. I don't have to tell you what a marriage

into the Lekin clan would mean for us in the long run, socially as well as financially. Our initial investment in the festival week could prove vital in cementing those relationships.

"But peacetime is never good for business, and your father has suffered reversals this year. So Henkelor's bride payment is critical. Call me as soon as you read this so we can finalize our plans. It would be selfish to make Saskia wait any longer than necessary."

Dilara froze the screen and stared at the image of her mother. Her own face reflected back from the shiny surface, and for a moment she caught the likeness—long thick dark hair, tawny complexion. But there the similarities ended. Wraya's face bore an air of entitlement Dilara could never hope to achieve, even if she had wanted to.

The screen flickered a little. That meant the ship was passing through the outer zone of Valora's atmosphere. They would be docking soon. And once Dilara was within the bounds of Valora, even though she wasn't going to set foot on land, she would have taken an irretrievable step. It was one thing to run away from a betrothal. It was another thing altogether to leave the solar system. Still, she considered the threat of marrying Henkelor would be a mitigating factor if she was ever caught.

Calling Mart Henkelor a pig was an insult to pigs everywhere. Dilara knew for a fact the rumors about him were true because she had bandaged his second wife's head after the couple had a particularly tumultuous argument. There had been a lot of blood. She shuddered at the memory.

If there had been a way to use a false identity when she had signed on with Melchior Intergalactic Industries, she would have done so. But she had neither the funds nor the connections to pay for a new universal identification code. She would have to rely on Melchior's promise to protect the anonymity of the women and the sheer numbers of ships leaving Caron 5 every day to cover her tracks. Not to mention the bribe she had paid the recruiter who had been pleased to pocket the bulk of her remaining cash in exchange for a promise of a new life.

At least the communications gave no indication her family knew where she was or even that she had left the planet. She sat back and closed her eyes. She inhaled and caught the faint scent of mint from a candy someone had tossed unfinished in the trash receptacle. It was good to feel safe for a moment. There was a muffled quality to the communication center, silent except for the tick of the ventilation shaft and the occasional hum of a computer fan.

On Caron 5, everyone knew the Elian clan. They were closest to the Supreme Ruler and the weight of the clan's fame was a constant part of daily life. It was what made appearances so critical and what made her imperfection even more glaring than it might have been on a civilian.

But if her plan succeeded she would be nobody, a nothing, for the rest of her life. The thought of anonymity was intoxicating. Guerenne and her crew could have all the social status they wanted in the town they would now call home. But Dilara would travel far farther and would be happy with the shadows. All she had to do was manage to stay in them. Rising quickly she shoved her chair aside and strode back toward the classroom, her shoulders tight with tension. It was hard to be comfortable with purposeful disobedience, but there was no choice now.

Chapter 3

POE SHOOK RAINDROPS FROM HIS DUSTER AND scraped mud from
his boots before striding into Glory Ann's Coffee and More for
breakfast. It had rained sporadically in the week since the Raider
attack, which had cut down on any real risk of a recurrence. Raiders hated wet weather. With any luck they had started their annual
migration, and he would be able to turn his attention to other pressing matters, like sleep and regular meals.

The food at Glory Ann's was mediocre but the "and More" to
Poe's mind stood for information that made it the restaurant of
choice for a discerning marshal. There might not be screen news
in Sector 1065, but between the newspaper and the rumor mill at
Glory Ann's no one missed out on current events for long. Gossip
might be morally wrong, but it was an awfully useful tool for law
enforcement.

"Hey, Poe!"

Emilio Linh, one of Poe's two deputies, waved cheerfully from
a table in the far corner. Snappy red suspenders peeped out from
under his brown woolen jacket and his collar was slightly askew.
Poe wove through the crowded dining room to join him.

Emilio waggled his eyebrows and grinned. "Going to the port
later? I hear the MacLaren is docking this morning."

Poe grunted but didn't respond until he had squeezed his legs
under the table and the waiter had brought his coffee. He had forgotten. Or maybe he just hadn't wanted to remember. He busied
himself with the menu as if he didn't always order the Morning
Glory Special.

"You should get yourself a woman," Emilio persisted. "There's a whole bunch of them gonna be coming off that ship this afternoon. They're not all going to be like Lenette, you know," he continued earnestly. "If I wasn't on desk duty this morning, I would head over there myself. There's bound to be a lot of competition, so it's good to scope out the options—"

"Not interested, Emilio."

Emilio, momentarily subdued, occupied himself with studiously scraping up the last bits of oatmeal from his bowl as Poe's meal arrived. Two rubbery eggs, soggy fried root vegetables, chewy pancakes and remarkably dry wheat toast, same as last time and the time before.

Poe didn't have a problem with the women arriving per se— he might not want another woman in his life, but he understood why other men did. The real issue was the extra hours Poe would have to put in as a result of those women. The marshal's job description meant keeping order, which Poe defined as defusing bar fights, chasing down poachers, and keeping the peace between homesteaders, miners, and the indigenous community of Mnoani. That could be challenging enough, but when there were women involved everything got worse. Bar fights were more frequent and for higher stakes. Poaching and general theft increased because lower-level guys who didn't make much money working in the Melchior mines still wanted to impress a woman with a bauble or two.

And then there were the Mnoani. Inevitably one of the new women would catch a glimpse of a Mnoani man and fall head over heels for his long blond hair and pointy ears. Not an issue for Poe. People loved who they loved. But some of the miners would take offense because Melchior shipped the women as an employee benefit. And while the farming community had plenty of women available, they hated the Mnoani as a matter of course.

"Morning." Stig sank into the chair next to Emilio and snagged a piece of toast from Poe's plate. "It *is* morning, isn't it?"

Dr. Stig Haugen had lived in Sector 1065 almost as long as Poe had. His parents had moved to the colony when Stig was five, and he and Poe had been fast friends from the time the Haugens had arrived to homestead the abandoned farm next door. Of course even though Stig had lived most of his life in the sector, among the founders, Poe's great-grandparents' generation, Stig would never be a true Sector 1065 native. Unless you were born in the colony, you were always considered "from away." But Stig's healing skills made a big difference in how he was perceived by the farmers. There was nothing like having your fingers reattached after a harvester incident to build a rapport with the guy who sewed them back in place.

The miners appreciated Stig's willingness to treat them on credit. And the Mnoani had made him an honorary member of their tribe after he saved the chief's grandson, Orioldo, from near certain death from Conch Fever. It had been good luck, Stig told Poe later, rather than skill. Definitely good luck, Poe had responded. If Orioldo had died, Stig probably would have lost the trust of the entire tribe.

Stig waved a weary hand to the waiter who scurried to fill his empty mug and take his order for a berry muffin.

"Next time I tell you I want to become a doctor, shoot me."

Poe smiled. Stig had been a doctor in the making since boyhood. He pushed the sugar toward his friend and watched as Stig poured a heaping spoonful into his mug of coffee.

"Bad night?"

"The worst. Five miners with the bends and a midnight call to Bellemar Farm to deal with food poisoning. Whole damn place was vomiting. Remind me to never eat goulash again."

"Probably better not come back to Glory Ann's for lunch then." Poe gestured at the chalkboard on the wall. Goulash was the Monday Special.

Stig paled slightly. "Now I'm not sure I want breakfast." He glanced at Poe's plate and then shot his friend a curious look. "No appetite? It must be serious."

Emilio snorted. "That's my fault. I reminded him the Well-Wed women are docking today."

"Oh." Stig raised a brow. "I can see why that might put a person off his food."

"I'm just saying the boss has a better chance than most,"

Emilio protested. He turned to Poe. "I'm on duty, but there's no reason you shouldn't go. You're a good-looking guy. Tall, big muscles, black hair down to your shoulders and those eyes—not as good looking as I am, of course, but not ugly. And you're the marshal." He grinned. "What's not to love?"

Poe raised a brow. "Nice sucking up, deputy, so points for that. But it doesn't change my mind. These women are not here looking for love. They're just looking for the main chance—a rich guy with a big farm or a Melchior executive."

"Not all of them." Emilio grinned and rose, jamming his hat onto his head. "Some of them are missionaries. The more pious they are, the easier they fall. Usually I just tell them I'm a sinner, and they can't resist trying to save me from the depredation I live with on a daily basis."

Poe laughed. Emilio's optimism was infectious. Still, it wasn't infectious enough to convince Poe to agree. Stig took his muffin to go and left with Emilio while Poe used the last piece of toast to wipe the last bit of egg from his plate. He sipped his coffee slowly. It was pleasant here in the warmth and hubbub. The four men at the table next to him talked cheerfully about someone named Bren who had picked a fight with a Melchior shift manager named Saur Fanko and won. Poe had never heard of Bren, but Saur was a regular problem. Mean SOB, so kudos to Bren, whoever he was.

"Good morning, Marshal. I see you're taking a little break from your duties." Mayor Teamue settled into the seat across from Poe. Teamue's hair was glued down so firmly across the top of his head, not one strand moved when he raised his brows. He even wore a satin show kerchief in the pocket of his suit jacket to go with the satin lapels. All he needed was a medal hanging from a striped ribbon resting on his plump belly to complete the picture of a self-satisfied politician.

Poe's stomach knotted. He had checked for Teamue when he entered the café and had assumed the mayor had simply grabbed a cup of coffee at his desk. Now he wished *he* had done that.

"I hear you had a run in with some Raiders a week ago," Teamue said with a tight-lipped smile. "Next time, perhaps you'll let me know before I hear it from a citizen."

Poe's brow shot up. "Sir?"

Teamue frowned. "I should be apprised of issues when they occur, not days after the fact, especially when there is any sort of controversy. Sandok told me one of the miners could have been killed, and you did nothing to prevent it. We issue you a weapon for exactly this sort of situation, and Sandok tells me you just surrendered it."

"The swarm is due to start their migration north for the summer. These three were just young stragglers—not a real threat."

"That's not how that miner sees it, and the merchants aren't happy either. Profits were down last week because people didn't feel safe, and that's on you, Poe. Your performance review will reflect this I'm afraid."

The feigned disappointment on Teamue's face was a cover. Poe was pretty sure nothing made Teamue happier than the thought of firing him. When Poe's predecessor, Marshal Jackman had died of a heart attack over a year ago, Teamue had anticipated filling the spot with one of his own picks. But the board had overridden him and chosen Poe, then the most experienced deputy in the marshal's office. Poe had been an interim marshal for thirteen months now, and since he was subject to Teamue's increasingly negative performance reviews, it was only a matter of time before Teamue got his wish and Poe lost the only job he had ever wanted.

Being a marshal's wife had been Lenette's dream once too, although she wouldn't have been content with it long. For Lenette, the position would have been just one step on the long path toward the mayor's mansion. Throughout their yearlong marriage, Lenette had hosted dinners and chaired committees with the ruthless persistence of an army general. She had walked out on him to return to Earth just a month before he had finally gotten the job.

"You're right," Poe said. "I'm sorry. It was a full weekend and the week has been busy too, but that's no excuse. I should have kept you informed. I'll try to be better about that."

Teamue gave him an assessing look but didn't pursue the topic. "I assume you are headed to the docks this afternoon?"

"Actually, this afternoon I'll be working on the annual budget," Poe said. "I should be able to get it to you by our meeting next week as you requested. But I'm glad to shift Emilio off desk duty and send him down to the docks."

Emilio would be thrilled, Poe thought sourly.

"No," Teamue said. "You can work on the budget some other time and still get it to me by next week. I need you at the docks today. The statue of Mayor Winslett is arriving on the MacLaren, which means it's your job to make sure the Mnoani remain peaceful. The welcoming ceremony is an important community event, and Melchior expects us to provide a pleasant and secure environment for these women. They are not accustomed to the rough and tumble ways you grew up with, Poe. These are refined creatures that deserve our protection and care. And brush off your coat before you get to the docks. You look like a dust cloud."

Poe breathed in carefully. "I can be at the docks this afternoon," he said. "And I'll get you the annual budget by next week."

"Good man," Teamue said, rising, Poe already an unnecessary distraction. "No need to be up on the deck of the MacLaren with me. Just keep an eye on the crowd on the docks. Make sure there isn't any trouble."

Teamue left, shaking hands with constituents as he went. As the door closed behind him, Poe looked down at his hand and carefully loosened his grip on the handle of his mug. It was lucky Glory Ann's mugs were sturdy. He waited until he was breathing steadily again and then he dropped his dishes off at the counter, waving at Glory Ann as he did so. She smiled and waved back before turning back to the busy grill. It was good to have some friends who liked you the way you were. Or, at least, the way they thought you were.

Chapter 4

THE FINAL WEEK ON BOARD THE MACLAREN had moved surprisingly fast. Because the women were in a flurry of packing as they prepared to disembark, it wasn't until late morning that Dilara managed to be alone in the dormitory. Directly across the hall there was a staff supply closet. The door was often left unlocked by the crew members who serviced this particular level—she knew this because Kiko had plundered it for bath soap once when they had run out in the dormitory. Still, she felt a surge of relief when the handle turned.

Checking once again to make sure the hallway was deserted, she slipped into the closet and turned on the light only after she had shut the door behind her. Hastily she grabbed a loose black coverall and a dull looking pair of scissors from the shelves and retreated to the deserted dormitory. She pulled the bulky garment on over her clothing, doing her best to smooth any telltale bulges underneath the coarse fabric. It was too big, but it would work well enough to fool anyone who wasn't looking too closely. She hoped.

She had known her hair was going to be an issue. All the staff she had seen so far conformed to what were probably rules for MacLaren crew—short-cropped hair. Still, she had hoped there would be a way around the problem. She would find a way to return the coverall to the MacLaren once she was safely past the outer reaches of the galaxy, but there was always a punishment for even the most inconsequential of lies, a kind of balancing of the scales, even if you didn't realize it at the time. Maybe cutting her hair was that penalty.

Five minutes later, she strode toward the "crew only" staircase, her knapsack bumping against her back. The rough fabric of the coverall scratched against her thighs as she walked, and her head felt weirdly light. She resisted the urge to run her fingers through her hair, to let the uneven blunt strands brush against her palm. Instead, she rested her hand gently on the handrail as she descended. The designers must have felt the carved wooden stair rails that adorned the passenger areas would be wasted on the crew. This one was metal—unpleasantly chilly to the touch.

The diagram of the ship she had been given when she boarded had only included the areas passengers were expected to access. But like every child, she had studied the basics of ship construction in school, so she knew where the engine rooms were and therefore where the hold was likely to be. She arrived at the end of the long flight and shoved through the swinging doors, trying to look as if she belonged.

The hold was a hive of activity and noise as workers maneuvered crates and trunks toward the open hatch. Quite a few passengers, including the Well-Wed women, were disembarking on Valora, so some of the steamer trunks and boxes were theirs. Plus, there were packages of all sizes filled with goods ordered by the colonists. She could hear good-natured cheers from the colonists below as pallet after pallet of crates descended from the straining ropes and safely touched the dock.

Quickly she pivoted toward the back of the hold. The amount of baggage being dropped off on Valora was negligible compared to the quantity of shipping crates traveling on to the farther reaches of the galaxy. Trying to look both competent and boring, she strode away from the activity, down the vast aisle that ran between the stacks of crates and boxes, leaving the noise behind her. She turned down one of the feeder aisles and squeezed between two crates, hugging her knapsack close as she crouched. No one would find her here, if they even cared to look. By the time she ran out of food in a day or two and had to reveal herself, the MacLaren would be another thousand parsecs away from Valora and there would be nothing the crew could do about it.

The combination of fear and excitement was heady. She felt a mad desire to laugh aloud and pressed her palm against her mouth reflexively to prevent any sound escaping. The boxes around her were labeled in Frin, in Slak, in Boningen, languages she recognized by sight but had not studied. The colors of the labels were deep, vivid, and warm. She wondered if the contents of the boxes reflected their societies in the way Caron 5's script, with its exacting silver curves, reflected its own focus on cold perfection. Perhaps she would have a chance to find out—if she didn't die in the process. She shivered and reached a finger to trace the orange and burgundy curves of the label on the crate nearest her.

She barely registered the approaching clatter until it was upon her—two baggage handlers and a foreman approached, their automated forklift following in their tracks like a pet. She shrank farther back among the crates, peeking through a crevice. The foreman checked his clipboard, rattled off a string of garbled orders and gestured in her direction as the forklift began removing crates. He hadn't seen her, he couldn't have. But if she didn't move quickly, he would. In her hurry to avoid detection, she nearly stumbled over a moderate-sized crate behind her, hidden amid the behemoths around it. A corner of the top panel was out of kilter, damaged in transit perhaps. There was a rope tied around it, the knot pulled tight.

She crouched and forced herself to focus. She knew this type of knot and was grateful whoever tied it had been in too much of a hurry to do it right. Silently she held it still with her stump while she manipulated the center with her hand, feeling for weaknesses. Then, when she felt the give, she tugged and the knot fell open. She considered removing the rope altogether, but there wasn't time, so she did her best to poke the ends out of sight under the edges of the crate.

The baggage handlers were too busy arguing over whose fault it was that the item they were searching for had been left off the list to notice the squeal of the tacking nails as she forced the top farther askew. Whatever was in the crate was cushioned with great quantities of straw. Quickly she tossed her knapsack in, clambered into the crate after it and tugged the lid back into position. The label on the box had been scrawled in Slak, so it probably wouldn't be offloaded for weeks. She wiggled her fingers into the outer pocket of her knapsack and pulled out the packet of protein bars and the flask of water. If she ran out, at night she would climb out of the crate and drink from the employee water dispenser. If she rationed, she would be able to make the food last for several days. She snuggled into the straw between what felt like two large porcelain vases and couldn't help feeling a bit smug as the grinding gears of the forklift came closer.

"Here it is. I told you it had to have been mislabeled." This in the supervisor's nasal tone. "And fix that lid, it's loose."

Her breath froze, heart paused. They would open the lid, discover her. She would be sent back, and this time there would be no escape. But instead there was a scraping sound and a sharp rapping as the thin line of light above her disappeared and the baggage handlers nailed the lid shut. The straw further muffled sound, so she couldn't make out what the supervisor said next, but it didn't take long to figure it out. The growl of the forklift came closer, and the crate tipped onto its prongs, her added weight shifting the balance toward the machine. She squeezed her eyes shut. This couldn't be happening.

Chapter 5

OCCASIONALLY WHEN HE CLIMBED INTO THE electric vehicle Stig had dubbed the marshal mobile, Poe felt the lack of a chevalo with an almost physical pang. But he reminded himself, he didn't have time to take care of an animal, and since he had access to the marshal mobile, he didn't have to incur the expense either, not that he could afford one on an interim salary. The yearning was persistent though. He guessed when you were a member of a founder family, it was in the blood.

On the upside, a battery powered vehicle was quieter than a creaking wagon and a clopping chevalo, so he had silence on his side when he crept up on the bad guys, not to mention speed. And if he ever really needed a chevalo, he could rent one from Ansel's Livery or borrow one from Pop. In this case, since he was running late, he could hardly complain. He should have been at the docks ten minutes ago.

At least the rain had done a good job washing the vehicle off. It looked almost clean in the sunlight, which was convenient. At his last weekly meeting with Poe, Teamue had passed on a complaint about the state of the vehicle. If the mayor saw it today at the docks, it would look as if Poe had taken the complaint seriously. A brisk wind flapped at the canopy above him, and a few residual raindrops plopped onto his duster as he climbed onto the bench and flicked the engine on. Pulling out from the parking area behind his office, he waited for a space between wagons to drive onto Main Street. As he waited, he glanced toward his office. The window shade was down, which meant Emilio must have gone out

26

on a call. Poe's other deputy, Zela McGilliam, would be on shift tonight.

Zela was the only reason Poe didn't completely hate the US Spaceship MacLaren. Zela had arrived on it three years ago and like a sensible woman had decided to stay single and raise her son, three-year-old Jebbie, on her own. He thought she might have something going on with Glory Ann, but she wasn't as outspoken as Emilio about her private life and Poe hadn't probed. He guessed Zela would tell him when and if it came to an engagement. He hoped whatever she decided wouldn't change her career path. No offense to Emilio, but Zela was the far more focused deputy. If Poe got fired, he had no doubt she could pick up the reins and run the marshal's office without a hitch until Teamue's stooge took over.

Rank's General Store was hopping, as was the Mercantile, and the farmer's market in the empty lot between them was doing brisk business too. This time of year it was mostly young greens and radishes, but the fresh crunch would be welcome after a winter of soups and stews. He would have to stop by on his way back and pick up some fresh produce just the way the miners did. He didn't grow his own anymore.

Stig's office, next door to his, was quiet, but morning wasn't prime injury time. That was usually reserved for payday nights unless there was a problem at the docks. Last time the MacLaren had actually arrived on a Melchior payday, so there had been a large crowd of men, about evenly divided into farmers and miners on the dock, and things had gotten out of hand. Today the crowd was likely to be mostly farmers, along with a faction of Mnoani protesting the statue. Of course some folks would be there just to satisfy their curiosity about the Well-Wed women.

Across the street at Joseph's Barber Shop a line of waiting customers snaked along the sidewalk, but the crowd looked cheerful and no one was pushing. Poe waved to Levi Yellowknife, who stood in the window of his deserted tailor shop rearranging some fabric draped over a settee. Levi smiled vaguely and waved back. Probably the sun's glare made it hard to see. On the other hand, Poe had a sneaking suspicion the eighty-year-old was losing his sight. This was a catastrophe for a haberdasher, but Levi had made Sunday suits for every boy who had grown up in Sector 1065, so no one had the heart to mention it.

The theater looked tired, but the new owner, Yan Tavol, was putting everything he had into the equipment. As a result, the peeling marquee boasted almost current films and even holographic versions of several Earth productions. Occasionally there was a live show, usually presented by traveling troupes of actors from off planet. The theater was deserted at the moment, but tonight it would be hopping.

Not a lot of activity at Roland's place, but the photographer got most of his walk-in trade on Sundays when people were already nicely dressed. Roland Cross was probably off with his easel and canvas catching the early morning light unless he was in his back room filling out an order for a wooden sign.

The hotel's porch was deserted. That wouldn't last. Once the MacLaren disembarked, the hotel would be booked solid and so would many of the brothel's rooms, whether occupied by friendlies or not.

Traffic, such as it was, had ground to a halt as three farmers stopped their wagons to chat, blocking the road. Poe shook his head and turned the marshal mobile back the way he'd come. He accelerated as he passed his office but slowed again as he realized the intersection ahead of him was stalled as well, this time by a wagon with a broken axle. Quickly he took a left down a narrow cross street between the wheelwright's workshop and the brothel. Poe spent a lot of time in that alley.

BangBang, the tavern that functioned out of the first floor of the brothel was a trouble spot in general, and it was likely he would be back there tonight to deal with at least one fight. The bar was harmless enough in the early morning light, but on payday nights it was always a problem. If he cut through the alley quickly enough he would be able to make up some time on Second Street.

He maneuvered past a trash bin, congratulating himself on not having scratched the finish of his vehicle, but Bang Bang's big red door opened and a wash of filthy water spewed out, splatting over the top and sides of the marshal mobile. Poe jammed on the brakes.

The mop and bucket looked like toys in Porky Lummon's hands, but the man was a peaceable enough fellow when he wasn't breaking up bar fights. The way the big man shrugged, a guilty expression on his face, reminded Poe of the little boy he remembered going to kindergarten with. No point in holding a grudge, he decided. He nodded at Porky.

"I thought you were the bouncer. Carntel making you clean too?"

Porky stood a little straighter. "Carntel doesn't own BangBang anymore. As of yesterday, Rudolph and I do."

"Yeah? Congratulations," Poe said. "I think."

"Thanks." Porky beamed. "We're our own bosses now. Been saving for years and the bank finally gave us a loan for the rest. We're gonna doll it up real good, hire Roland for a new sign, make sure our friendlies get their health checkups on time."

Every time Poe stepped into BangBang in the past, the floor had been tacky with spilled beer and the smell beyond description. And the brothel was, well, a brothel. The friendlies who worked there rarely got into fistfights, which he guessed was all he could ask. In that respect, the brothel was one of the more law-abiding establishments in town. He suspected Porky's aspirations would be choked out by the reality that was Sector 1065. Still, there was no point in being the one to dash his hopes. Life would do that soon enough without Poe's help.

"That's great, Porky. Congratulate Rudolph for me too."

"I will," Porky said. "He's out picking up supplies or you could tell him yourself."

"I'll let you get back to your cleaning then," Poe said.

"Thanks. I've got to hurry if I'm going to make it to the docks in time," Porky added. "Bride boat's coming today."

"Yep, headed there myself," Poe replied.

"Nice," Porky said. "I can't afford a wife yet, what with the bar and all, but it's fun to look. Sort of like window shopping, you know?" he added wistfully.

Poe nodded. He did know. That was how he had made the worst mistake of his life.

"Well." Porky stood awkwardly, empty swaying bucket in one

hand and wet mop in the other. "Sorry about your vehicle. Want me to throw some clean water on it?"

Poe considered the offer, but it would take time for Porky to refill the bucket, and if he was much later Teamue would notice.

"No need. The next rainstorm will take care of it."

He looked at his watch as he turned onto Second Street and frowned. With luck he would still make it to the docks in that sweet spot after the ordinary passengers disembarked and just as the cargo was being unloaded. The women always made their appearance on deck last, and Teamue would be speaking as they did so. Melchior insisted on a welcoming ceremony, and by now it had become a tradition of sorts. On special occasions it didn't turn into a riot.

Chapter 6

POE COULD HEAR THE RUMBLE OF THE CROWD as he neared the main docking area. He left his vehicle and strode toward the looming structure, maneuvering between off-duty miners and farmers with their families until he reached the dock itself. To his relief, the crew had just begun unloading cargo.

Six muskuli hitched to a large flatbed wagon snorted uneasily amid the milling crowd. While some citizens had gathered to collect personal items or shipped purchases, others had come to witness the arrival of a statue commemorating Oregon Winslett, the first Mayor of Sector 1065. A cheer rose up as a vast crate was lowered by crane to the wagon.

Not everyone was a fan of the putative hero. A group of Mnoani, their green and brown clothing luminous in the shaded building, stood silently, holding signs and a banner. "It's Not Heroism When You're Stealing" read one sign. The banner said "Winslett: King of the Land Grab." A number of farmers shot them angry looks, but there was no indication of any real trouble yet, so Poe walked toward the weighing station and turned his gaze back up to the loading door high above.

Crew members in black coveralls stood far above in the open hatchway. They hitched straps around loaded pallets, attached a crane hook to the straps and signaled to the crane operator. When the pallets reached the dock, more crew members unstrapped them and waited for the recipient to appear before weighing each individual box. Shipping fees were never final until both parties had viewed the scales and approved the result.

31

As the rest of the cargo was unloaded, and the Winslett statue was carted away, some of the crowd dispersed, including the protesters. The remaining spectators seemed cheerful enough, but Poe stayed alert. Sector 1065 was no longer the easygoing society he remembered from his youth. Of course his childish perception of the colony had been formed by growing up as a member of a founding family. He now understood that the Sector 1065 of his memories had never actually existed for the less privileged, especially not for the Mnoani.

Even allowing for old wounds, there was a persistent underlying unease in the colony that was new. He could feel it as a kind of underlying hum all week long but particularly when large crowds gathered for any reason, whether somber or celebratory. It was the sort of tension that could change a happy crowd into an angry mob in an instant. The catalyst didn't have to be anything major—even a fight over a woman would do it.

The ceremony welcoming the Well-Wed women had begun, and Poe kept his eyes on the cargo. He tried to tune out Teamue's speech, the mere sound of the man's voice ratcheted up Poe's irritation, and besides, he had heard the speech enough times to know it never varied. Teamue's voice rose toward the end, and Poe mouthed the words with him.

"Even in a mining town like Sector 1065, built by the hands of our founders, we can all agree that love is the most precious gem one can find, the heart the most beautiful flower one can discover. Welcome. Welcome to all!"

It was a relief when Kurt Lendl, CEO of Melchior's Sector 1065 Division started his own welcome speech. Poe might have paid more attention to what Lendl had to say if he hadn't heard raised voices by the scale a few yards away.

"Impossible." Poe recognized the man near the sole remaining crate. Leo Chen was building manager for Melchior's local corporate headquarters. "The weight is wrong. You must have unloaded the wrong container."

The cargo master frowned, scrolling through his database. "This is the number that matches your order, sir. And it is a large crate, which is why it's so heavy."

"It is a large crate, but it only contains two decorative porcelain vases and straw to keep it from breaking in transit," Chen insisted. "It cannot possibly weigh that much. Perhaps there is something wrong with your scale."

Several bystanders drew closer, first simply curious and then increasingly invested in Chen's plight. Most of them had also received packages at one time or another, and whether the shipping prices were in actuality fair or not, they always seemed suspiciously high. It didn't help that ships often provided their own scales. Shipping companies usually argued that the goods they carried were so heavy and odd shaped they would break standard shipping scales.

Lendl had finished formally welcoming the women and was now calling out each one's name to the appreciative cheers and applause of the audience at the foot of the gangplank. But Poe kept his attention fixed on the dispute. The bystanders were already muttering, and Poe knew it was only a matter of time before someone threw a punch. He pushed his way into the center of the circle, tapped the rattled employee on the shoulder, and pointed first at his badge and then at the crate in question.

"Open it."

"We're not supposed to open packages. That's for the customer to do, after he has paid the fair shipping rate."

He had to give the man credit for sticking to the company line despite the steadily growing crowd of scowling onlookers. He might be foolish, but at least he had guts.

"Open it," Chen agreed. "If it's not mine, you can close it up and put it back on the ship. If it's my vase, I'll pay. All these people are my witnesses."

The cargo master pushed through the crowd, glanced at the scowling faces and nodded at his underling. "Open it."

The crew member, looking relieved, jammed the end of a crowbar under the lid and levered it open with a mighty screech. Poe blinked and several bystanders cried out in surprise. There probably were vases in there under all that straw, but what mattered was what was on top of the straw. A young woman, a crew member by her apparel, sprang up and hurdled over the edge of the crate, hauling a knapsack with her as she raced into the crowd.

Poe's first thought was to wonder why a crew member would hide in a crate when it would have been simple to just lose oneself on the crowded dock and simply not get back on ship when it was time to leave. It wasn't legal, technically, but it happened all the time. He glanced back at Chen and the crate, but the cargo master was rechecking the scale, and Chen seemed satisfied with whatever the cargo master was saying.

Poe didn't wait for the conclusion but followed in the direction the absconding crew member had taken. He kept his pace deliberate, and the crowd opened a path for him as he strode. He glanced from side to side as he went, watching for disturbances. She wouldn't be running now, he thought. Even a foreigner would realize that running through the crowd would attract too much attention.

If he had whistled an alert, the crowd would have participated in the hunt. But there was a certain pleasure in doing it himself. Besides, he could tell from the body language of some of the bystanders that someone had hurried by them—a stranger, by his guess, or they wouldn't have been murmuring to each other and gesturing. He felt a click of satisfaction. Once in a while he remembered what had drawn him to being a marshal in the first place. There was nothing like having your hunch play out and then there was that triumphant feeling in actually catching someone.

Best he could tell she had stumbled against one of the miners who had taken advantage of the moment by grabbing her. It wasn't acceptable behavior, but in a mining town it wasn't unusual either. Most of the few women the miners had access to were friendlies, and friendlies didn't mind a guy who took liberties. He guessed this woman had minded though. Looked like she had smacked the offending miner over the head with her knapsack—the guy's friend was laughing so hard he could barely stand. But the woman was gone.

He climbed onto a handy pallet and surveyed the crowd. The docks were filled with gawkers, newly arrived business travelers, pushcart venders selling everything from clothing to unidentifiable but appetizing smelling food, and the burly stevedores who lumbered by with their barrels and crates of goods.

All attention was focused on yet another Well-Wed woman who was making her descent down the long gangplank. Poe ignored the show and kept working his way toward the back of the dock. There were crates back there a fugitive could use for cover. The crowd's noise grew to an approving roar, and he glanced up despite herself. He just caught a glimpse of the wagon filled with Well-Wed women leaving to the cheers of the crowd when he saw her striding toward the crates using a stevedore carrying a roll of carpeting as cover.

He caught up with her as she slid between a sticky bun vendor and his customer. Poe got a firm grip on her shoulder, and despite the looseness of her coverall he held firm as she tried to slip out of his grasp. He flicked his duster open so she could see the five-pointed star pinned to his shirt. It had the words *Interim Marshal* etched on it along with the town's emblem, a fibulin tree.

"Marshal Poe Lancaster, ma'am. Come with me, please," he said.

He had expected defiance, maybe even an attempt to rally the crowd of spectators near her to her defense. Instead, she froze. She was thinking hard—he could practically see the cogs turning. While he waited for her to respond, he checked her face against his internal list of Wanteds. He didn't really expect a match. Criminals didn't spend time contemplating, they either ran or caved. He could feel his lips curving to a smile and forced them back into a firm line. It had been a command, not a suggestion. He opened his mouth to tell her so, but she spoke first.

"If you wish."

He blinked. Compliance was always better, and he was just as glad not to have to chase her through the noisy crowd, but he didn't care for the noblesse oblige attitude. Still, he released her, his fist oddly reluctant to unclench.

The remaining spectators milled around the dock aimlessly now the welcoming ceremony was over, and he would just as soon not be the entertainment they were looking for. It occurred to him as he gestured toward the entry, she might have had the same concern. Interesting. She wouldn't be the first crew member of a spaceship to have a problematic past. Probably not breaking and entering though. If her performance with the cargo was any measure, she was too clumsy to make a living doing anything surreptitious.

He kept close to her side as they walked in tandem. Poe was tall, six foot five. But the woman was nearly as tall as he was. Slimmer though. She looked a bit younger than his thirty-two years, but not by much. Brown eyes and brown curly hair and her skin had a warm golden tinge. She moved with a kind of gawkiness as though she had only recently reached her current height and was still getting used to it. She didn't limp, but there was something uneven about her gait. He glanced at her again but couldn't identify it.

The crowd was beginning to dissipate, and he and the woman joined the flow toward the parking area. The train's timely arrival at the station stop near the dock meant the remaining bystanders had somewhere to go, so he tapped her on her shoulder and pointed toward his vehicle. But she also noticed the train and paused. Again he watched her consider her options. After a split second, she must have dismissed the possibility of making a run for the train because she turned away from it and strode in the direction he had indicated. He didn't like the way she considered everything he told her to do before doing it.

He had thought she might need a hand up into the seat. Lenette always had insisted wagon seats were too high for her, and the driver's bench on the marshal mobile was nearly the same height. But when he saw her grimace at the messy residue from Porky's bucket, he changed his mind. She was a criminal, not a date. Without looking back at him, she slung her knapsack onto the floorboards and pulled herself up onto the bench.

He shook his head and climbed up himself. Normally he put suspects in the back, but she had been cooperative so far and anyway, he wasn't convinced he was going to arrest her in the end. Mostly as a marshal he relied on evidence, but there was no question gut played a role in the job, and he had learned to listen to his. It rarely steered him wrong. And anyway, where was she going to run?

She looked around her curiously as he started the engine, and as she did her hair swayed with her movement. He watched out of the corner of his eye, fascinated. She might or might not be a felon, but her barber should have been placed under lock and key. Or maybe there was some new fashion trend that called for incredibly uneven hair with a touch of scalp showing. He wouldn't know. Sector 1065 wasn't exactly fashion central. Lenette had complained about that a lot in the last months of their marriage, but then returning to Earth in triumph had always been her long-term goal, and he had been the one standing in her way. He veered away from the thought and focused on his passenger.

"Want to tell me your side of the story?"

She stared out the windshield and tapped her foot with an impatient air. "I just need to get back to the ship."

"Oh?" He kept his tone mild. "It's a rarity to find cargo crew so dedicated that they climb into crates to check the contents for damage. Or maybe it's just you. In either case, they should award you "Stevedore of the Year" for your meticulous attention to detail."

"I'm not—" She stopped abruptly.

"Right. You're not an employee. So now I'm wondering why you popped out of a crate disguised as a crew member." He leaned forward and gazed pointedly at the embroidery on the lapel of the coverall. "I assume your name is not Martin O'Dare."

She sniffed and stared out the window again. It was fine with him if she didn't want to talk yet. Better, in fact. He turned onto the road into town and took a deep breath of the warm flower-scented wind that puffed against his cheek and made the canopy above him flutter.

Spring was deceptive. Winters in Sector 1065 were snow laden and the summers could be downright miserable, but spring and fall—they were the ones that tantalized with possibility and then broke your heart. The worst part was you were complicit because they were so damn enchanting while they lasted.

Chapter 7

AFTER THE FILTERED AIR ONBOARD THE MACLAREN, the breeze was so sweet she could almost taste it. And the moment the gentle heat from the spring sun had touched her skin, a tightness she hadn't known she had been holding onto released. The canopy on the marshal's vehicle shaded her now, but she could still see the way the sun dappled the tree trunks as they passed through a wooded area.

"Is it far, where you are bringing me?"

A tiny part of her hoped it was far, the part that had hated being confined to even as large a vessel as the MacLaren. But she knew that was foolish. What she should be hoping for was a speedy return to the ship, a safe space to hide, and a long time before she was discovered.

"No," he said.

"How long will this take?"

She could see the moment she said it that he was taken aback by her tone, but she needed to know, and she wasn't sure there was a more politic way to phrase it. He steered the vehicle to the side of the road and slowed to a stop. Her heart sank. Not only was he a jerk, he was a pedantic jerk.

"Are you in a hurry?"

He was looking directly at her now and she shifted uncomfortably. He wore a leather duster that brushed the tops of his dusty boots. His broad brimmed hat cast a shadow over his face, so at first glance all she had been able to see of it was his jaw line, sharp and straight. She tried to keep her expression bland and only vaguely curious, but it was difficult because she could see his face now. He had the most extraordinary eyes, one green and one brown. Both looked distinctly unfriendly. Her heart thudded, and it felt as if her rib cage didn't want to expand to let in her next breath.

"It's just...I need to get back onboard before the ship leaves port. It's important."

"Important, huh? You can tell me all about it when we get to my office. Of course the longer we sit here by the side of the road, the longer it will take to get there."

She pressed her lips together and looked away. He chuckled and started the vehicle moving again. For a moment, she hated him. She kept her gaze fixed on the horizon ahead and meant to keep silent, but when she saw the greasy looking black cloud of smoke suspended in the distance, curiosity won out.

"What's that?"

"That's the Melchior mines. Melchior opened a division here in Sector 1065 when a scout discovered a vein of timony. Since then they've discovered lots more, so the mine has become a big part of the town's life."

Dilara already knew this. Since the Well-Wed program was sponsored by Melchior there had been lots of Melchior related information in her study materials. But all of it had stressed the advantages the company brought to the tiny homesteading colony. Melchior hadn't gone into detail about the impact of their industry on the environment.

"'Course not everyone loves them," he continued. "In other territories, Melchior has been involved in using its political sway to grab land from locals. Even though that hasn't happened here, farmers are worried about the possibility."

"That seems hypocritical," she commented, reluctantly intrigued. "The farmers are originally homesteaders from Earth, right? Isn't homesteading a type of land grab? Someone must have been living in this place before the homesteaders came along."

He shot her a look and then turned his attention to avoiding a wide wagon pulled by a pair of muskoli hauling a load of logs. His lips twitched and despite the fact she still disliked him, the approval felt good—novel, actually.

"That's right. When Earth took dominion of Valora, all the indigenous peoples lost their rights to their land. The Mnoani were local to this portion of our continent, North Union, and they still have maintained a presence in Sector 1065. You may have noticed the protesters on the dock when the ship landed."

She shook her head. She had been nailed inside the crate at the time, but it seemed prudent to avoid reminding him of that. He moved one of the levers sticking up from the floor between his feet and the vehicle turned left. She could see a jumble of wooden buildings ahead in the distance she guessed was the town.

"The Mnoani created a new village in the woods past town on land Earth assigned to them," he said. "Mostly they keep to themselves. Still, there's no love lost between the farming community and the Mnoani, that's for sure. This is Melchior housing for the miners."

He gestured at the cottages crowding the road on either side. They were small, and she guessed whether they were well kept or not depended on the resident. Most were tidy, and many of the small yards had garden plots with young plants poking up from the soil. Ahead she could see larger buildings, although none taller than two stories.

The marshal pointed out the Higher Power Worship House, which stood across a greensward from the town hall. There were clocks on both buildings, but they were not in accord, which made her uneasy. She couldn't afford to let too many hours slip by, and now she wasn't exactly sure what time it was. At least the distance they had traveled wasn't impossibly far. If necessary, she could walk it.

At the green the marshal turned left again, and they drove down the center of what seemed to be the main street. Unlike Caron 5, there appeared to be no order to street and sidewalk travel. Pedestrians and drivers simply went wherever there was no obstacle. It was surprising no one collided, and she wondered whether there was in fact some sort of system of order she couldn't see. She was too busy marveling at several near misses to notice the businesses they passed except to notice the hotel where no doubt her fellow classmates were already settling in for their six-month stay.

She thought she caught a glimpse of some of the Well-Wed women on the veranda and turned her face away so they wouldn't recognize her. She didn't look much like she had yesterday, but still, one couldn't be too careful. No one called out as they drove by, and she breathed a sigh of relief when the marshal turned down a narrow lane and parked his vehicle without incident.

She felt a little hum of excitement now. No one knew her here. In Sector 1065, she was just another unfamiliar face, which meant she was marginally safer than she had been in some time. Daughters of good families didn't have adventures, but she guessed in all the ways that mattered she didn't have a family anymore. She watched him as he jumped down from the vehicle. All she had to do now was convince him to bring her back to the MacLaren before it left the dock.

Feeling energized at the prospect of getting her plan back on track, she clambered down from the bench and reached for her knapsack, but the marshal grabbed it before she could do so and led the way toward his office. There were some stairs up onto the raised wooden sidewalk. She paused halfway up to gaze at the busy street once more and was struck by the lack of women. There was one woman helping a man, who was probably her husband, load a wagon, and another farther away sweeping the entrance to what looked like a restaurant. But all the other pedestrians in view were male.

It went a long way toward explaining why Melchior needed to import brides. Lieutenant Onkelson had implied there was an issue, but he hadn't made clear the full extent of the problem. Now she was doubly glad she wasn't going to stay. It was bad enough to be stared at because of her flaw, but it would be entirely different to be stared at just because she was female.

The marshal's office was one part of a long, single-story building that also housed a clinic. She followed him into a generously sized room. It was furnished with a large wooden desk placed so the marshal could survey the street through a multi-paned bay window on his left or keep an eye on the two jail cells on the opposite wall. There was an additional table too, set up as a second desk, presumably for his deputies to use if he had any. She walked past it and studied the display of wanted posters on the wall. Many of them were curled at the corners, and she wondered whether the marshal was just disinclined to clean out the detritus or if the people in the pictures had managed to escape capture. The rest of the office seemed tidy, so she guessed it was the latter. Her mood lightened a bit at the thought. It was good to know fleeing people weren't always caught.

Chapter 8

POE WATCHED THE WOMAN AS SHE SCANNED THE collection of curly edged wanted posters on the wall. Her left hand was on her hip, but her right arm hung at her side and the right sleeve hung loose and empty. He had missed it, maybe because she had been to his right from their meeting on the docks until now. At least he hadn't tried to cuff her. He felt a flush of discomfort at the thought. He had been sloppy, primarily because he had been too busy noticing the way she moved, the flash of her dark eyes and her imperious manner, to consider the basics of his job. She had seemed compliant enough at the time, but even a one-handed woman could fire a weapon, which made him all kinds of foolish. At least he had had the presence of mind to relieve her of her knapsack when she got into his vehicle.

"You got clothing on under that coverall?"

She raised her brows. "Of course."

"Good. Take the coverall off."

"Why?"

"Would you prefer I search you for weapons?"

As she toed off her boots with an impatient huff of breath, he shook his head and watched to make sure she didn't reach into her pockets. Watching her wriggle out of the coverall reminded him of a calf breaking out of a sac, all limbs and angles. Then she held it out to him, her arm extended.

"And the boots."

She nudged them toward him with her stocking feet and then stalked back to sit in the chair next to his desk. She perched on the edge of the seat, her left hand cupping her right wrist. If he hadn't caught a glimpse of her stump when she was pulling off her boots, he might never have noticed it. She was good at hiding things. Because Sector 1065 was filled with farmers and miners, there were often accidents, so he had seen his fair share of amputations. Even with medical advances, there was only so much a doctor could do. But there was no scarring on her stump so she might have been born that way.

Her back was ramrod straight, leaning forward slightly as though at any moment she might leap up again. Her gray dress suited her better than the black coverall had, but not by much. He wondered why she had chosen a color that made her skin look sallow. It fit her too snugly to conceal a weapon. Still, he had learned to pay attention to his gut a long time ago, and his gut told him something was off.

He reached for the boots and shook them, checking for hidden compartments in the thick soles before handing them back to her. Then he checked the pockets, seams and hems of her coverall. Setting the garment aside, he sat at his desk and grabbed a pen and an intake form before sliding his tablet closer.

She scowled as she pulled her boots back on. "I thought you didn't have mobile devices here."

"Originally they were forbidden," he agreed. "The colony of Sector 1065 was founded on the back to the soil movement of the 2050s, so when I was growing up here, there weren't any electronics at all. And forbidden or not, cell phones are useless on Valora. The layer of timony ore below the surface of our planet interferes with radio waves. So, if you want to communicate, this is it."

He gestured at the phone on his desk and grinned at her skeptical expression.

"Then what about that?" She jutted her chin toward his tablet.

He reached for the cable coiled on his desk and plugged it into the tablet's socket.

"Like I said, no radio waves on planet," he explained. "But we got a satellite in orbit a few years back, which means we can connect to GalacticPol via cable. You're from Earth, I assume." He tried to keep the sneer from his voice but suspected he was unsuccessful.

She paused. "Caron 5."

He looked up in surprise. Caron 5 was a small planet and off the beaten track. The residents were known for their intricate work with gold and for their insular society, hence the phrase "discrete as a Caronite." A ferry ship making a weekly stop on Caron 5 would be a big event there.

She nodded as if she had followed the incongruity without his speaking aloud. "Normally the MacLaren would have shot right by," she added, "but they needed to stop for an engine repair."

"And your name?"

There was another telling pause before she responded.

"Dilara Elian."

He raised a brow.

"Sure about that?"

She clamped her lips shut, her eyes defiant. He tapped the information into the search function on his tablet. He might not know her real name or origin, but he did know one thing about her. She was a liar. There was a Dilara Elian who lived on Caron 5, a trust fund babe from an upper echelon family. A sister Saskia was all over the society pages, which meant Dilara Elian probably was too, but he wasn't going to waste time digging any deeper. The woman in the worn dress perched in the wobbly chair next to his desk was no princess-in-waiting.

"Try again."

"That's my name!"

He leaned back in his chair until it creaked and shook his head.

"You should give up while you're ahead. You'll never make it as a grifter. See, now you're coming off as angry, when you should be conciliatory. This would be the moment to tell me about how you could only afford a cheap false ID and you realized after it was too late that the guy used a celebrity's name.

"Oh, and give me a sob story about how you're on the run," he added, "I love sob stories."

She shot to her feet and glared down at him. "My reasons for travel are none of your business. My name is Dilara Elian. My completely legal ID, which will confirm that, is in my knapsack."

"Okay, for now let's call you Dilara," he said, hauling the knapsack onto his lap and unfastening the buckles. "Before I look, any chance there are any more stolen goods nestled in here next to that 'completely legal' ID?"

"I don't steal. If you hadn't hauled me off the docks, the coverall would already be back on the ship."

She watched him defiantly, cheeks slightly flushed, as he opened the bag and tipped the contents onto his desk. He slid his hand inside the empty bag to confirm. It was mostly clothing and not much of that. There were a pair of shoes, a comb, a thick leather portfolio, a pen, and a small coin purse containing a few credits and an ID card.

If the ID was a forgery, it was an excellent one. But excellent forgeries cost a lot of money, and this woman didn't seem well off, although given her manner he could believe she had been once. The clothing and shoes were well made but also well worn. He put them back in the knapsack along with the pen, the coin purse and the ID.

He could hear the intake of her breath as he opened the portfolio, so he scanned the sheaf of papers methodically. Unless there was a sheet music theft ring he hadn't heard about yet, he guessed she was in the clear. He replaced the papers in the portfolio and tried to slide the leather case back in the knapsack, but it wouldn't fit without some persuasion.

She rose quickly and snatched the portfolio from him, muttering a string of what sounded like curses.

"What's that mean?"

"It means *don't bend it*," she said through gritted teeth.

"That's a long way to say it," he said. "I heard at least two sentences there, maybe even three."

Her eyes flashed but she didn't respond. Instead, she pulled the knapsack toward her, spilling out most of the contents of her bag onto his desk before repacking it to her satisfaction. She swung the knapsack onto her shoulder.

"If people on this colony are all as offensive as you are, it's no wonder travelers only come here if they have to. Since you haven't arrested me, I assume I am free to leave."

His chair creaked as he leaned back in it. "You would be if you weren't here illegally."

"Take me back to the ship, and I'll be out of your hair as soon as it leaves port. I can walk, but I'll get there faster if you take me in your vehicle. And the sooner I get back onboard, the sooner I can return that coverall."

"Not sure I trust you to do that."

She looked offended, which was amusing under the circumstances, but he also found it irritating. There was something about her high-handed attitude that rubbed him wrong, and he didn't like her secretive air.

"Fine," he said finally. "I'll take you back to the docks. You probably have that sob story, but I don't need to hear it now. If GalacticPol is looking for you, they'll find you quicker once you are in open space anyway."

The blood drained from her cheeks, and her glance flicked toward the window looking out onto Main Street. Following her gaze, he too scanned the busy pedestrians and then turned back to meet her eyes. He felt a flicker of curiosity, but then his eye fell to the thick pile of papers in the inbox on his desk and decided her problems were none of his business. Besides, Sector 1065 didn't need another social climber with delusions of grandeur. One had been plenty. He would bring her back to the MacLaren and let the crew deal with her.

Chapter 9

"WHEN IS THE SHIP SCHEDULED TO LEAVE?" He stared straight ahead as he drove past the mismatched clocks on the town green.

"I'm not exactly sure," she admitted. "I didn't expect—"

"You didn't expect to be unloaded and discovered." He shot her a wry look, and she refused to meet his eyes.

"I didn't see a ticket in your knapsack," he added. "What makes you think they'll let you back onboard?"

She opened her mouth and shut it again. There was no good answer to that since Mrs. Onkelson had collected the women's travel documents for safekeeping. Getting back onto the MacLaren would require subterfuge and possibly lying, neither of which was likely to meet a lawman's approval.

"Why is the clock on the town hall set at a different time than the one on the worship house?" It was as good a way as any to deflect, she decided, and she did want to know.

"The town hall clock is close to the correct time," he said, "although it tends to run slow. But the worship house was built by missionaries from Earth, and when they came here, they wanted the clock to run on Earth time."

Incredulous, she shifted in her seat to stare at him. "You're kidding, right?"

He shook his head and steered right. They had made good time traveling through the miners' cottages and now the road was quiet, surrounded by woods. Through the occasional gap, she caught fleeting views of plowed acres. Occasionally there was a fallow field, bursting with wildflowers in joyous disorder. For a moment, she wondered what it would be like to stay in Sector 1065, to watch spring turn to summer, to see the light green of the new plants turn dark and lush.

"There were seven missionary women on the ship," she said. "Four planned to disembark in Sector 1065, but the rest were traveling farther. Will the four women who stay here work at the worship house?"

"Not likely," he responded. "They've given up on the Mnoani, so nowadays they head off into the mountains to try to convert other tribes."

"Are the Mnoani dangerous?"

"No more or less than anyone else. But they didn't take kindly to being told that a wise, ancient religion they have revered for over ten thousand years is wrong and maybe a bit foolish. The missionaries didn't stand a chance."

She nodded and thought about Cella. "Is it dangerous in the mountains?"

"If you don't know how to live in the wild, it can be," he said. "There are predators, both human and animal, and the law is more a suggestion than a command there. But most of the missionaries I've met have done their homework and have the fortitude to survive. Course, once they go over the mountains, I rarely see them again, so who knows."

Dilara bit her lip. She wondered if Cella had a clear understanding of the dangers she might face, especially given the lack of friendliness Dilara had observed in Cella's fellow travelers. If Dilara were with the Well-Wed women at the hotel, she might have had a chance to warn Cella of the dangers. She shrugged and tried to let go of the idea. It wasn't likely Cella would take her warning seriously anyway. In Dilara's experience, one could not argue people out of their beliefs. Still, she felt a pang of conscience as she saw the docks looming ahead.

The moment the vehicle stopped, she jumped down, swung her knapsack onto her shoulder and waved a farewell to the marshal. But instead of driving off, he climbed out too and strode ahead of her into the wide doorway. For a moment she refused to see it. There was a casual cruelty inherent in the empty dock, the vast space where the SS MacLaren no longer was. Her knees weakened and darkness edged her vision.

HE HEARD HER GASP AND TURNED BACK TOWARD her, leaping to catch her before she hit the ground. The sudden paleness of her face made his heart stutter. He scooped her up and carried her out of the building at a run, figuring he would drive her to Stig, but as he neared his vehicle, she stirred and opened her eyes. For a moment he could imagine what she might look like when she had just woken of a morning, still caught in dreams, her lips soft and warm. She struggled out of his arms and stood, frowning at him accusingly.

"What happened to me?"

He shook his head. "We walked onto the dock and you fainted."

She hissed in a breath. "Is the MacLaren really gone?"

He nodded. She sank to sit on the ground, her back to the spoked wheel. He slid down next to her. She didn't edge away, but she didn't seem comfortable either.

"Tell me," he said.

She paused and he could practically hear the gears clicking.

"I'm part of the Well-Wed women's group. But on the way here, I changed my mind."

"So you're one of those foolish women who come all the way to Sector 1065 from Earth dreaming they are going to improve their own lives by making some poor guy miserable for the rest of his."

"No!" she snapped and then amended, "My contract with Melchior doesn't obligate me to marry anyone. If it had, I wouldn't have signed it. Marriage is for idiots."

He cleared his throat to avoid laughing at her frankness. "So you misled the recruiter just to get the free trip?"

He was pleasantly surprised to see this last had stung her.

"That was wrong of me," she acknowledged, cheeks flushing as she spoke. "The group was short one woman and Lieutenant Onkelson was so persuasive for a moment I convinced myself it would be right to come, to help the group out. It was only once I signed the contract onboard the MacLaren that I realized he had not understood, had not seen." She gestured toward the stub end of her right arm as though her point was self-explanatory. "But by then we had taken off and it was too late."

He shook his head but decided not to pursue it. "So, if you're not here for marriage, how are you planning to support yourself?"

She sniffed. "I'll get a job. I'm quite capable."

"I don't doubt it, but it'll still be a challenge," he responded slowly. "Not a lot of job openings in Sector 1065. I don't know what you do for a living, but Melchior's hiring freeze has been all over the news for months, the merchants tend to keep their stores family run and the farmers don't hire outside help except for when it's time to harvest. Unless you're a licensed friendly, prostitution is out."

She scrambled to her feet and glared down at him.

"I'm not a friendly."

"Be nothing wrong if you were," he said mildly.

"Well, I'm not."

She sounded so self-righteous, he couldn't resist a grin. Her lips twitched in response, but she turned away to pick up her knapsack and when she turned back to him, the moment was gone.

"I don't know what to do now," she admitted. "Nothing went according to plan."

That sounded familiar. It was the story of his life.

"Why don't I drop you off at the hotel and you can rejoin the Well-Wed women until you can figure out a new plan, preferably a legal one. Who knows," he added, "you might find some miserable, lonely rich old man to con into a loveless marriage."

She flinched but climbed back into the vehicle without further comment, and he was momentarily sorry he had said it. For some reason he couldn't quite put his finger on, her comments about marriage had bothered him. She was right, of course, and he agreed with her in principle, but for a ridiculous moment he had been sorry to hear her say it so adamantly.

Still, when he dropped her off at the hotel and drove back to his office to do battle with the kekkin' budget, he felt unexpectedly lighthearted. He wasn't in the market for another woman—he never would be. Lenette had seen to that. But it might be fun to cross swords with Dilara Elian every so often.

Chapter 10

HE DROVE AWAY WITHOUT A SECOND GLANCE, and Dilara decided that was just as well. It was hard to know what the protocol was for thanking someone and at the same time blaming them for one's predicament. If he hadn't detained her, she was sure she would have found a way to re-board the MacLaren, but there was no denying that the hotel promised a more comfortable place to sleep than the crate had.

The white wooden building was fronted by a broad veranda. Flowers spilled out of urns near the stairs, their carelessness so perfect they had clearly been arranged with great care. Etched glass tulip-shaped lamps framed the wide entrance and twinkled in the afternoon sunshine. The doors were open to the breeze and as she neared them, a fussy looking man with a pristine knee length white apron wrapped tightly around his waist stepped out to greet her.

"Would you be Miss Elian?"

She nodded, feeling a flush of gratitude for Mrs. Onkelson's efficiency. Obviously either she or the lieutenant had provided the hotel with a list of the women's names. There was a little guilt there too, for the several occasions she had mentally laughed at the Onkelsons. They might be self-important, but Dilara owed them something for having given her a way to flee safely and in relative comfort and now for providing her with a lifeline when she had treated their program so cavalierly.

"Welcome to the Alarite Hotel, Miss Elian. I am Jenkson, the hotel manager. I assume you have additional baggage." He raised a brow at her knapsack. She swallowed a grin and gave a non-committal nod.

"All the steamer trunks have already arrived and yours should be in your room already. I expect you'll want to freshen up before supper."

In her hurry to flee to the hold unobserved that morning, Dilara had skipped breakfast. Then, in her hurry to escape the crate, she had left her packet of sandwiches behind. Now she felt a bit faint at the prospect of solid food. She was going to have to come up with a new plan, but she would be able to think better with a full stomach. Besides, she was going to have to get used to taking advantage of free things when she happened on them. She flashed on the image of her thin coin purse resting like an accusation in the marshal's palm as he sorted through her meager belongings.

The fare to Sector 1065 had been free—it was Melchior's attempt to entice women to sign on with the program—but each woman was expected to come up with a large sum to cover her hotel stay and meals during the six-month program. As an additional incentive, if the woman married a Melchior employee during that six-month period, Melchior would return her expenses in full.

Dilara hadn't had the funds, of course, but it hadn't seemed to matter. The Onkelsons had been so eager to fill the unexpected vacant spot in their group they had neglected to press the point before leading her onto the MacLaren. She suspected it had slipped their minds since then. Perhaps each one of the couple thought the other had taken the payment. Or maybe, as long as they filled their quota, they didn't care. She hadn't thought it mattered at first. But now that she was in Sector 1065, instead of in the hold of the MacLaren, it was going to matter a great deal. She probably had enough coins for three more meals and nowhere near enough for a hotel room.

Small groups of Well-Wed women were scattered across the generous lobby, exclaiming over the size of the crowd on the docks to welcome them, speculating over whom they might be introduced to at tomorrow's introductory tour of the town and admiring each other's elegant clothing. This was exactly what Dilara had been hoping to avoid, and now she was stuck here. And it was all Marshal Poe Lancaster's fault.

She ignored the other women, took the ornate key, and headed up the elegant staircase to the second level, trying to look less despondent than she felt. The hotel rooms would be more pleasant than the ship's dormitory, but they would still be shared. Many of the women had planned to room together ahead of time, but Dilara, having no intention of being part of the group any longer than necessary, had not joined in that discussion with anyone. Now she wished she had engaged in the pretense a bit more energetically. As she slid her key into the lock for suite 217 her shoulders tightened at the prospect of seeing curious faces, answering eager questions tinged with malice.

The sitting room was deserted, but two of the three beds in the attached bedroom had already been claimed although currently unoccupied. She recognized one of Ngendo's colorful tunics spread casually across the first bed and Kiko's distinctive blue cloak draped over a chair near the second and sighed with relief. Kiko was too engaged in her own problems to be interested in Dilara's, and Ngendo was off in a world of her own most of the time. Neither would be likely to gossip. Both women were probably already downstairs, so she hurried to wash her face and to brush the dust off her clothing. Then she carefully tucked her knapsack out of sight under the unclaimed bed before heading down to join them. The lobby was even more crowded now with women cooing over the elaborate furnishings and exclaiming over the elegant carpets. It took a moment to pick out Kiko in the crowd. She and Ngendo stood next to each other near a tall window. Dilara made her way toward them, flicking a watchful gaze from side to side as she went. It wouldn't have occurred to Wraya to hire a searcher yet. But it was important to develop a habit of alertness now, before it was necessary.

When she arrived in front of the two women, there was barely time for a polite nod before the great gong at the doorway to the dining room rang. Relieved, she mingled with the other women as they streamed toward the buffet set up against the long inner wall of the room. Although sufficient, meals on the MacLaren had not been generous, and she hadn't seen fresh produce since she'd left Caron 5.

Some of the offerings were easily identifiable, others less so. There was fisken, a type of fish chowder common on Caron 5, along with fresh bread and butter. She had heard of papin, a mélange of roasted root vegetables and duck, considered North Union's signature dish, but had never had the chance to try it. But there were other foods she didn't recognize. One labeled larlar consisted of rubbery looking tubules in a slick shiny sauce. She also passed on the pressed protein patties with an accompanying turquoise colored relish. She didn't recognize most of the greens in the salad bowl either, but they looked crisp and appealing, and she added them to her already filled plate before turning to look for a place to sit.

Most of the chairs near her were already occupied, perhaps for business dinners—the men wore suits and were engaged in serious discussions punctuated by forced laughter at the jokes of the man at the head of the table. Across the room along the great floor to ceiling windows were four large tables with vases of flowers on them at which the women were slowly settling.

Dilara tightened her grip on her brimming plate and paused. She didn't like the openness of the setup, the way anyone passing would be able to see her through the panes. Still, one of the women's tables was set between two windows, and if she sat against the wall, she would be less visible. She headed in that direction, weaving between the tables of men when one of them pinched her rear.

She whipped her head around to see who had done it, but no one met her eye. Then, as she turned away, her foot caught in a chair leg and she nearly fell, catching her balance in the nick of time but spilling her plate of food onto the lap of the executive nearest her. He leapt to his feet, shooting her a venomous look as his coworkers guffawed.

The urge to run from the room was strong, but her need for food was stronger. She went back to the ravaged buffet table and refilled her plate from the remains, even including one of the pressed patties. She couldn't bring herself to sample the larlar even though there was still a lot of it on the platter. This time she walked around the outer edge of the room without incident and was pleased to find no one had taken the seat she had hoped for.

She settled into the crowded spot between Kiko and Marielle. Marielle, one of Guerenne's friends, made a show of ignoring Dilara except for shifting her chair as far away as possible when Dilara sat down. Kiko flashed Dilara a rare smile.

"More space for you."

Nodding, Dilara took a bite of her food and tried to remember to savor it the way she had been taught, but she was too hungry to do so properly. It was embarrassing. A few minutes later, she wrenched her attention away from her plate and forced herself to speak.

"Our room is generously sized and well appointed. This room too is beautiful."

Crystals dangled from the massive chandeliers above and were reflected in the long rectangular mirrors adorning the walls. A vast patterned carpet covered the length of the burnished wood floor. She wondered how many people and how many hours it had taken to weave the complex design and had a pang of guilt over the food that had spilled on it when she dropped her plate. That was the problem with perfection—it was so easy to mar.

"They use children to make these carpets. Did you know that?"

There was no anger in Kiko's tone now, only a kind of weariness.

"In my country on Earth, some poor parents still apprentice their children to carpet factories to pay off family debts. Carpets like this require tiny knots, thousands upon thousands of them and children's fingers are small."

Dilara frowned. Surely if a travesty like that was common knowledge on Earth, someone would have done something about it. Child labor was illegal on most planets, so maybe it was a myth. Admittedly Caron 5 was a prosperous planet, and Dilara's family was both powerful and successful, but their financial stability was nothing compared to the fabled wealth of Earthers.

"I thought Earthers were wealthy."

"Many are," Kiko said, "but not all."

Kiko stared at the carpet as though looking for an answer to an unasked question in the twining stems of the flowers it depicted. Dilara watched her. This was more than she had ever heard Kiko speak at one time.

"You know the worst thing about poverty?" Kiko said.

Dilara shook her head.

Kiko frowned. "It limits your dreams," she said.

Dilara opened her mouth to ask more but closed it again without speaking. There was a depth to Kiko's silence that made asking seem like an intrusion. Still, it was surprisingly pleasant talking with her. Even though they came from different places, they had Well-Wed as a commonality, and it was nice to be with someone who had a shared experience no matter how short or unpleasant.

"Are you looking forward to finding a mate?" It was a neutral sort of question and to her surprise she was interested in the answer. Kiko met her eyes now with a rueful look.

"No. For one thing, I dislike the process. I hate parties, and I'm no good at polite conversation."

Dilara laughed. "What skills do you have?"

"None that would make me a good match for a Melchior executive."

Marielle shot Kiko a disapproving look and rose from her seat. She walked off without a backward glance, and Dilara felt her shoulders ease. As she turned back toward Kiko, Ngendo slid into the newly emptied seat.

"What did I miss," she asked.

Kiko grinned. "I'm explaining to Dilara why I am Mrs. Onkelson's supreme challenge."

Ngendo smiled gently. "I doubt it. Remember, she won't have an easy time with me either. My skills aren't much of a selling point in an agrarian community."

Dilara turned to Ngendo. "Why? What are your skills?"

"I am an artist," Ngendo said, "a sculptor."

Dilara fumbled for a response. Sculptures were common on Caron 5. Her parents had commissioned several of themselves both together and individually, and Saskia would be sitting for her first now that she was engaged. Sculptures were a way to capture perfection in perpetuity.

"Then you bring beauty into the world," she finally said.

Kiko looked at her with a surprised expression. "Not any more than anyone else does."

"But beauty is the point of art."

As Dilara said it, she knew it wasn't quite true. The song she had been working on most recently had been harder to write than any of her previous attempts. She had struggled with the harmony for days until she realized it needed to be less pretty, less sweet. Coming to that understanding had been a revelation, but it had also been frightening.

"I don't mean that," she said abruptly.

"No," Ngendo agreed. "Art is about truth, I think. And some truth is not beautiful in a standard sense. It is just beautiful because it is true. There was a poet, Keats I think, who wrote *Beauty is Truth, Truth Beauty*."

"That's wrong," Dilara said.

She flushed at Ngendo's curious look, but she didn't take it back. Some things that were true were not beautiful, and some things that were beautiful were lies. The truth about her stump was that it was not beautiful while Saskia's beauty simply served to cover a slew of lies.

"What about you," Kiko asked. "What is your selling point?"

Dilara shrugged. "I sing."

"That's funny," Ngendo said. "I didn't imagine you as a performer."

Dilara kept her tone light. "I don't need two hands to sing."

"And are you looking forward to finding a mate?" Kiko echoed her question back.

Dilara paused, unsure how best to respond. Honesty was all very well, but until she had a plan in place, she couldn't risk her place in Well-Wed women. She suspected Kiko was unlikely to chat with the Onkelsons about their conversation, but she didn't want to bet her life on it either. So she nodded and smiled politely and spoke of inconsequential things until the two women excused themselves to attend the evening event. Dilara watched them go,

Kiko walking in her precise measured way, Ngendo's bright colored tunic fluttering with each step, and tried to dismiss her own growing sense of unease.

Sounding casual had taken unusual effort. On Caron 5, she had become accustomed to being an "other" even though it was like having to lug an enormous invisible stone around at all times. That stone might have been a burden, but it was a familiar one, and it required a kind of constant diligence. But on the ship and now in Sector 1065, Guerenne aside, no one seemed to care much about whether Dilara was flawed or not. At first, it had been a relief to let go of that constant weight, but now she understood how dangerous that release could be because those muscles had atrophied from lack of use.

That weakening was evident and she couldn't afford it. Friends were dangerous, not only because they were a potential risk of exposure but because betrayal by a friend was both debilitating and unavoidable. It would be better if she kept her distance from the other women. She would make sure she was out of her room until nighttime to reduce the possibility of further conversation with either Kiko or Ngendo. She couldn't afford to avoid meals yet. But if she found a way to earn money, maybe she would be able to avoid some of them.

At home a job hadn't been an option—she was enough of an embarrassment as it was. But here she could search through job listings and apply without anyone on Caron 5 being the wiser. Then, as soon as she earned enough to pay the fare, she would buy a ticket on the next ship out. But this time she would be able to afford a berth instead of hiding in a crate, and this time she would get far enough to be out of searching range. Rokh would work, despite its lousy climate, or even Dilphin.

In the meantime, she would keep her distance from Marshal Poe Lancaster. Although it occurred to her that in small doses he could be useful, much like the foul-tasting medicine she had to take once for a fever. For instance, she wasn't going to betray her heart again. But if she ever forgot that basic rule, his astonishing capacity to irritate would be an excellent reminder.

She stopped a passing waiter to ask if there was a

communication center in the hotel, and he directed her to the town post office just up the block. There were computers there, he assured her, along with more old-fashioned means of long-distance communication, and they were open for another hour. As a hotel resident she would have complementary access, he added.

The post office was on Main Street just past the photography studio. In the lighted window, she could see there was one customer, so she waited until the old man had left before entering. No point in being memorable to two people.

She felt even better about her caution when the postmaster greeted her, his polite nod accompanied by a curious gaze. Probably each of the new women in town would be subject to that same scrutiny, but in her case, curiosity was a risk. Curiosity led to gossip.

She glanced at the small room beyond him and her heart sank. There was a wooden desk, which was likely his, a scale and a set of tall wooden shelves filled with neatly stacked stationary supplies.

"I'm staying at the hotel," she said. "They told me you have a communication center here."

He nodded and beckoned her to follow him to the back of the room. Behind the row of shelves, a narrow path led to an equally narrow corridor lined with doors on either side. He opened the first on the right and flicked the switch for the gas light fixture on the wall.

A small carved desk and a delicate uncomfortable looking chair took up most of the floor space. The surface of the desk was completely filled with a communication unit. It boasted the clunky muscular look of a previous generation of devices, and when the postmaster clicked it on, the internal fan juddered loudly, but she felt a wave of relief when the screen flickered to life.

She thanked him and a shy smile lit up his face. Still, she waited until he had left the corridor before closing the door and beginning her search. It took a while to find the local job advertisement site, primarily because whoever had established the site originally had spelled it "addvertisment" and no one had bothered to make the correction.

Most of the listings were from farmers looking for short term help planting or taking care of animals. She flicked through them slowly at first and then faster as she became more and more discouraged. Perhaps there had been some truth to the hurtful comments Guerenne had made about her uselessness—Dilara would be of little help to a blacksmith, a farmer or a carpenter looking to hire.

But when she read the twenty-ninth ad, her pulse sped up. This she could do, as long as the position hadn't already been filled. Despite its placement on the list, it was dated four days previous, so she felt a breath of hope. She tapped on the response button and began to key in her information. Once she had completed the application, she sat back and breathed. She shouldn't expect a response right away, she reminded herself, and even if she did get a response, it might not be positive. Still, hope was a rare commodity, and she decided not to waste the unaccustomed sensation.

She headed back into the hotel in the cool of the evening with an unexpected spring in her step. She would return tomorrow and resume her search. The thought of having a job, of being financially independent for the first time in her life, was so liberating she was nearly skipping as she climbed the stairs to the second floor and turned back for a moment to look down at the quiet lobby below. Nothing had changed yet so there was no real reason for more good cheer than before, but there was something energizing about having a new plan.

Chapter 11

POE SHIVERED IN HIS DUSTER AND GLARED AT the sky. Compared to last night's balmy temperature, which had smelled of the promise of new growth, the wind this morning was downright chilly, and a thick gray mantle of clouds covered the newly risen sun. Figured.

The farm was well situated. From their front porch, on a clear day Sven Borin and his family could see all the way across the valley. But today the rolling green fields of wild grasses were steeped in shadow and the house that overlooked them looked more neglected than triumphant. The paint on the clapboard above the porch was beginning to peel and the wagon wheel on the chimney was so far askew, no self-respecting stork would consider nesting there. The boards on the porch floor sagged slightly under his feet as he raised his hand to knock at the door. It looked like Sven hadn't put any money into repairs since his wife had left three years back.

The door creaked and juddered as it swung open.

"Why are you here? I called for Marshal Jackman." Sven Borin peered over Poe's left shoulder as if Poe's predecessor might magically appear if he looked hard enough. Poe wished he would. He missed the old coot more than ever, both for his experience and for his perspective.

"Marshal Jackman retired nearly a year ago. I'm the interim marshal."

"I pay my taxes. I want a real marshal."

Borin hitched his overall strap higher on his shoulder with an accusing air, but his shoulder was so thin the strap slid down again almost immediately. Borin might be scrawny looking, but Poe knew any weight he did carry was straight muscle—anyone who raised bovoquin had to be strong. The big animals were uncooperative at best and at worst could be dangerous. Still, because their meat was considered a delicacy on Formax, the return on raising them was good. Given the condition of the farmhouse, Poe wondered where Borin was putting the money.

Borin snorted and waved dismissively as he turned away from the door, his slippers scuffing on the worn floorboards. Poe figured that was invitation enough and followed him into the house. Borin reached for the knee-high boots leaning against the entryway wall and jammed his scrawny bare feet into them.

"I haven't seen Erik since the Midwinter Festival," Poe said. "He sure can play the trumpet."

Borin grunted as he fumbled for his coat amid the jumble on the bench. "About the only thing he's good at. Bunch of lazy yenxers, my sons. Take after their mother."

Poe raised a brow. Complaining about the laziness of one's children was a time-honored tradition among farmers, right up there with complaining about not enough rain, also about too much rain. Still, there was a mean quality to Borin's tone that made Poe feel an unwonted sympathy for Sven's sons. Erik had been a classmate of Poe's, and the two younger brothers hadn't been far behind. Poe didn't remember them being lazy, and the remark about their mother was simply uncalled for. Still, there was no point in arguing. If he argued with every yenxer he met in the course of his work, he wouldn't have any voice left. That included with his boss.

"Interim." Borin stopped buttoning his coat and glared at Poe, his left eye ticking as he spoke. "Teamue's an idiot, otherwise he'd never even have made you interim. But he isn't stupid enough to keep you on for the long haul. You'll never be marshal."

Borin hawked up some phlegm, spat it on the floor and stumped back onto the porch toward the stairs, shoving past Poe in the process. Poe stood for a long moment, but then took a breath and followed the miserable old man down the path leading around the house. As they walked, large drops from the dark cloud above splattered onto Poe's shoulders. The path was so hard packed from years of foot traffic the drops remained on the surface of the dirt for a moment before being absorbed. Poe walked faster and caught up with Borin as they passed the house and headed toward the stables.

"My deputy tells me you had some vandalism. 'Graffiti,' she said."

"You would probably call it that." Borin glared up at him. "Me, I'd call it a threat. I got some paint to cover it, but I figured I'd wait to fix the damage until a real marshal got around to showing up."

Poe decided not to mention that he had been digging his way out of paperwork until midnight last night and had stumbled out of bed before sunrise this morning to deal with Borin's grousing. Poe wasn't complaining. It was, as Mayor Teamue would no doubt have reminded him with a smirk, his job. And for the most part, Poe enjoyed the work.

"That's what I'm telling you about." Borin pointed a bony finger, his too loose boots scuffing the dirt as he neared the barn. The rain was falling faster now, and water rippled across the path like veins. "If you were worth the money we taxpayers pay you, you'd go arrest the yenxer who done it now."

Earthers = Trespassers

The rust-tinged red letters stretched across the broad face of the barn, lurid against the faded gray of the old boards. Rivulets of red that had run downward like blood as the paint was applied were dry now. An adult had done it, he thought. In Poe's experience, kids usually tagged with clever phrases, or jokes, or even, if they were particularly stupid, with their names. He ought to know. He had been one of those kids once.

He turned to look at Borin. "Any idea who might have done this? Anyone you had a disagreement with recently?" Given the past few minutes, Poe was hard put to think of anyone who wouldn't have a disagreement with Borin, but he had to ask.

"Some damn Mnoani kids came around looking for day work recently," Borin said. "I sent them packing. Don't like their kind around. Turn your back for a moment, and they'll steal your boots while you're wearing them."

Given the quality of Borin's boots, Poe thought, a thief might be doing him a favor. He pulled out his notepad.

"Any suspects in particular?"

Borin nodded. "That Orioldo kid, the chief's grandson—he was one of them. You put him in your lockup and he'll come clean. I never met me one of those Mnoani who wasn't a weak-willed coward."

"That hasn't been my experience." It popped out before Poe could stop it.

"That figures. Everyone knows the Lancasters are a bunch of Mnoani lovers—" He broke off and reddened under Poe's steady gaze.

"Well, it's got to be him," Borin whined. "There ain't no one else."

Chapter 12

DILARA WAS BATHED AND DRESSED BEFORE either of her roommates awoke. In stocking feet, she tiptoed to the lobby where she sat on one of the couches only long enough to put on her boots. The hotel was quiet although she could hear the clank of dishes in a distant kitchen and the swish of a broom on the floor of the veranda through the open front doors. She guessed it was the calm before the storm since Friday nights were likely to be busy at the hotel.

She selected a roll from the coffee bar set up for early risers and tucked it into her knapsack before setting out for the post office, waving a cheerful greeting to the man wielding the broom as she passed. The early morning clouds were beginning to burn off, and the brisk breeze gave the empty street an energetic air of possibility. The post office was still shuttered when she arrived, so she sat on the bench under the window and ate her breakfast. It felt delightfully unconventional to eat outside, kicking one's legs and watching the town wake up.

Shortly after she had brushed the crumbs from her lap toward a tiny black and white striped bird, the postmaster returned. He nodded at her politely, smiling the same shy smile he had bestowed on her for the past three mornings, and hung his hat and jacket on a wobbly coat tree before turning back toward her with an inquiring look.

A few minutes later she was once again ensconced in the tiny room waiting for the computer to finish waking up. Once again she opened the job site and began reviewing the listings. As far as she could tell, no new advertisements had appeared overnight and the farther down the list she read the older and more unlikely the listings became. When she came to several that were looking for help at the previous season's harvest, she clicked the site closed, discouraged.

Out of habit, she clicked on her mailbox. It had felt liberating to trash the communications from her mother and from Alexandr when she had read them on the MacLaren. Now she almost wished she hadn't deleted them so thoroughly. It was amazing how painful an empty inbox could be, worse even than an inbox with communications that hurt when you read them. She hated herself for believing her family and Alexandr might change and yet, stupidly, she kept doing it.

She reached a finger to click the mailbox shut when a new communication popped up on screen from an address she didn't recognize. Suddenly tentative, she hesitated. Then, feeling cowardly, she tapped it open.

The communication was only written words, with neither audio nor video options, and it was formal as though the sender had learned communication skills from a primer.

Dear Applicant Elian,

I am most delighted to accept your application for the job of singer at my new dining establishment. Your qualifications are excellent.

BangBang is a destination for all the good citizens of our town who wish to enjoy first-class entertainment while indulging in fine food and drink.

I know your talents will add to our clientele's enjoyment while providing the cultural enrichment we so appreciate in Sector 1065.

As a new resident on Planet Valora, Continent North Union, Town of Sector 1065, you are required to obtain a work permit from the town hall before I can officially hire you.

Please bring the permit with you on Saturday night, your first evening of employment, so I may keep it on file.

Yours, etc.

Stanley Lummon, Proprietor

She leapt to her feet and read it a second time just to be sure she hadn't misunderstood. Even in her most optimistic dreams, she hadn't envisioned getting a job offer today. She looked at the clock and winced. The women were scheduled for an obligatory tour of the town this morning, but the afternoon would be free time, and she intended to make the most of it.

Because of her travels in the marshal's vehicle, she was already familiar with the basics of Sector 1065, but she paid careful attention to Lieutenant Onkelson's explanations anyway. It was interesting to learn how the town had grown over time, but more important, the tour included areas she had not yet seen.

In addition to the post office and the marshal's office, Main Street boasted a lively collection of storefronts, a clinic, a café and a livery service. When the wagons turned right onto a cross street, she noticed a bakery and a newspaper shop. But as the road continued east, there were fewer buildings and the land seemed to open up, lush farmland spreading all the way out to the rolling foothills in the distance. The scent was lush too, a combination of earth and vegetation warmed by gentle sun.

She took a deep breath and was surprised at the tears stinging her eyes. It wasn't beautiful in a Caron 5 sense, the order of the fields was not, could not, be precise. But it had its own kind of beauty, she thought fiercely. Maybe the kind Ngendo meant. She glanced toward the other wagon, but Ngendo was focused on something Mrs. Onkelson had said.

A few minutes later they turned right again, passing a school and a number of elegant houses before they reached the town hall and alighted for lunch at the hotel. The tour had not included Melchior's mining compound even though the group was sponsored by Melchior. Nor had it included the miner's cottages, although they were not unattractive per se.

This made sense because the tour was designed to show off the most attractive attributes of the little town. Still, she was puzzled as to how there had been no mention of a restaurant named Bang-Bang. It was probably because the restaurant was so new, she decided.

As soon as she finished lunch, she headed out to the town hall. The big green lawn that stretched between the town offices and the worship house was deserted except for a workman removing bunting from a bandstand. Allegiance Day had taken place a week ago, and the celebrations on Earth colonies usually involved community picnics and fireworks.

The thick door into the town hall was heavy and the hallway within was cool and smelled dank. Her boots tapped on the marble floor as she approached the directory. Lummon hadn't advised her which office to go to, so she decided to start with the town clerk.

"Help you, Miss?"

The old man had a shock of white hair that seemed to be unaffected by gravity, but his blue eyes were placid and kindly.

"I'd like to apply for a work permit, please."

"Well, now," he said, "it's been a while since anyone asked. The Melchior folk handle their own permits, and I can't remember the last time I had to put my hands on one. Give us a minute, will you dear?"

He busied himself behind the counter, pulling out files and just as quickly shoving them back into their slots, muttering as he did so. He seemed so frazzled she was almost sorry she had brought it up. But just as she was about to tell him so, he popped upright again.

"Here we are!"

The form was so old the edges had yellowed, but he was so enthusiastic, she couldn't help but smile back at him. He handed her a pen and she filled in the blank spaces as best she could, although the box for specifying race was a puzzle. In the end she just wrote "second place" because despite her flaw she had always been a good runner, although not quite as good as Aurelia who was the fastest in the neighborhood. When she handed the pen back, the clerk pointed a stubby index finger at a single line printed small at the bottom of the page.

"Now all you need is a criminal check and you'll be all set. You can get that at the marshal's office."

Chapter 13

POE LEFT HIS VEHICLE PARKED AT THE OPENING in the trees and
headed down the track toward the Mnoani settlement. He thought
Borin's theory was unlikely to prove true. Young folks looking to
earn a few coins for a day's work would see no purpose in alienating the farming community. But he couldn't ignore the charge
no matter how unfair it probably was.

As Poe approached the Mnoani settlement, he could hear the
reedy tones of a wood flute. Another flute joined it, and then another, their harmonies twining as the melody revealed itself. The
music teacher sat with his class of elementary age children in the
shade of the last tree before the clearing around the school building. Over the years there had been numerous attempts to incorpo-
rate the Mnoani children into the central school system, some well
meaning and some probably less so. But the tribe had refused.
Given what Poe remembered of the standardized history lessons
offered in school that was probably a good decision on their part.

The curriculum neglected to mention the Earther theft of
Mnoani lands when waxing enthusiastic about the glorious deeds
of the founders. But one had only to grow up in Sector 1065 to
know that something terribly unfair had happened on the same
land the farming community now harvested. There hadn't been
much violence when the Earthers arrived with their homesteading
papers. The temporary military complex that had accompanied
them had presented overwhelming force, and the Mnoani took a
long view. "When your perspective on history is measured in thousands of years," Chief Manzarin had told Poe once, "a few decades

of injustice are a drop in the bucket by comparison." Still, Poe thought some of the tribe's youth might be less patient.

The arrival of the homesteaders had both an economic and a societal impact. Initially the tribe had been about equally divided between hunters and farmers. The Mnoani still farmed, although the soil was nowhere near as good up here in the foothills of the western mountains as in the valley below. But many more sub-sisted through hunting—mostly the wildlife that lived in the woods around them and in the mountains above, but there had been occasional complaints from homesteaders about livestock going missing too.

A group of hunters nodded politely as they passed him, head-ing home with their catch dangling from poles they propped care-lessly over their shoulders. He nodded back but tried to look like a busy man on a mission. Despite the successful haul, food was sometimes scarce in the early months of spring. If Poe met any of their gazes, the unlucky hunter would feel obligated to invite Poe to an evening meal, it would be considered rude for Poe to refuse, and then he would be taking food from that hunter's children's bellies. He speeded up a bit.

Chief Manzarin's house stood adjacent to a small brook, a prime location by any measure, but then Manzarin was part of a long line of Mnoani leaders. Like most Mnoani homes, the house was round, the outer walls were daubed with clay and the conical roof covered with sod. As he turned toward it, Manzarin's wife shuffled past the front door, hauling a brimming bucket of water in each hand. Poe clicked his tongue and hurried forward to relieve her of them.

"Didn't the doctor tell you not to do any more heavy lifting?"

Pretie's eyes lit up and her face crinkled into a smile. She had the typical lithe build and coloring of the Mnoani. Her long, straight blonde hair, tucked behind the peaks of her ears, had re-cently begun to turn gray, further accentuating the brilliant green of her eyes. Her skin glittered in the sunlight as though she had been sprinkled with silver dust.

"Doctors don't know everything," she said. Then she gestured at the flower beds at the base of the house. "These also will be good for my heart."

Poe shook his head but kept his thoughts to himself as he watered the pointed spears poking through the soil. Even Chief Manzarin knew better than to argue with his beloved wife, although Poe guessed the old man secretly worried. But when eighty-three-year-old Pretie made up her mind to do a thing, there was no point in trying to talk her out of it. Once the buckets of water had been distributed to her satisfaction, Pretie patted him on the shoulder.

"See? No matter what else happens, you did something good today."

He blinked and then cleared his throat. "Is Chief Manzarin able to see me?"

It always surprised Poe how large Mnoani dwellings felt on the inside. It wasn't just the breadth of the wooden floor, built with the wide boarding the Mnoani harvested from the local Jinja trees. The ceiling, painted a limpid blue, soared to a peak. Poe knew at night the light would not reach that far up, and it would seem as though the darkness above was a simulation of a night sky. Chief Manzarin sat on a cushion at a low table near the empty fireplace. He was flipping through the pages of a ledger with an irritated look on his face.

"I know I put a note in here somewhere," he grumbled. "I'm sure I didn't leave it in my office. Are you sure you didn't..."

He looked at Poe and raised his brow.

"Welcome."

Poe grinned and after a moment Manzarin did too.

"Pretie cleaned up again?"

"Eh." Manzarin shrugged. "I always find what I lost, and most of the time it was me who lost it."

He gestured toward the jug on the table. "May I share tea with you?"

Mnoani tea wasn't Poe's favorite drink, and the ritualized conversation around it took more time than he would have liked, but refusing wasn't an option. He smiled politely and settled onto the cushion across from Manzarin. As they sipped, the chief asked after the welfare of Poe's family in detail. In return, Poe asked after the chief's family and was treated to a lengthy description of the beauties of being a grandparent.

Poe knew hospitality was a hallmark of Mnoani behavior, but he was also well aware that his own small strain of Mnoani blood bought him something in Manzarin's world. Poe's great-grandfather had fallen for a Mnoani woman, and Poe bore the proof with his one green eye. It gave him a little extra leeway with Manzarin, but like Borin, some of the founding families still talked about the union with shocked tones, as though it had happened yesterday.

Only when they had finished drinking did Manzarin allow the conversation to turn to work matters.

"How is it in the marshal's office? Are there matters in which I might be helpful?"

"There is a man named Borin who raises bovoquin. His farm is to the north on the great hill overlooking Sector 1065."

"I do not know this man," Manzarin said. "I do know of him."

Poe noted the careful phrasing. Manzarin was careful to avoid speaking ill of people so when he had nothing good to say, it was worth paying attention to.

"Borin called me to look at some damage on his barn. Someone had painted 'Earthers = Trespassers' on it in red paint yesterday evening."

"I am sorry to hear this news," Manzarin said politely.

"Borin says some Mnoani youth came by looking for work the other day. He says they were angry when he turned them down. He thinks they might have done this damage."

Manzarin did not respond immediately. He took the jug of tea and refilled their cups, watching the liquid rise in each vessel and then returning the jug to its place.

"Marshal, you and I have had occasion to disagree occasionally," he said finally, "but I know you are not a lazy thinker. So I wonder why you are telling me this story."

Poe took an experimental sip of the tea. Each time he did so he kept thinking this time he might like it better, and each time he was disappointed.

"I'm guessing there is a reason why Borin's suspicions could not possibly be true."

Manzarin nodded approvingly. "After Borin turned them

down, those boys came to me and asked for work. I hired them to paint the community center."

"What color was that paint, Chief?"

"Red."

Poe opened his mouth to respond, but there was something in the chief's expression that stopped him.

"Then we honored the volunteers who built the building," Manzarin continued. "I hired those same boys to attend and to help serve food at the banquet that followed. All three were in my sight until we finished our celebration at midnight."

There was no way Manzarin could be mistaken. The community center was a big deal for the Mnoani and had been in the works for at least a year. Poe already had the dedication date marked on his calendar since it was likely to include visitors from neighboring tribes as well as a full complement of local and not so local dignitaries.

Chapter 14

POE HAD JUST HUNG UP HIS HAT WHEN Dilara walked in. She looked different, and it took him a moment to figure out why. She wore the same gray dress, the same scuffed boots, but the defeated air she had carried when he dropped her at the hotel was gone now. Not that he was interested in her, but she was a good-looking woman—obstinate and obscure as Jude, as his mother would say, but some guy might like that in a mate. Some crazy guy, he amended silently.

"How's the search for a rich sucker going?"

Her eyes flashed with annoyance, but she didn't respond, and he felt a twinge of remorse for having goaded her.

"I've found a job," she said, "and I applied for a work permit, but they won't stamp the permit until I pass a criminal check."

"Okay," he said. "I'll need to take your fingerprints."

Her lips tightened. "I can't imagine why that would be necessary. I have weaknesses, but a criminal nature isn't one of them."

Now he laughed. "So far as I know you are a thief who planned to stowaway on a major vessel."

She flushed. "Marshal, I am asking for your discretion in this matter. I'm not a criminal, I promise you, but I don't want to give you my prints."

"It's a quick, painless process. I'll run them through the GalacticPol database right now, and you can be on your way with a signed permit. If you haven't done anything wrong, you have nothing to worry about."

"That's not true," she said quietly. "Even your order to run the fingerprint check will be recorded on the database. If nothing else, it will be a mark against my reputation. I won't do it."

Watching her silently he ticked off the possibilities in his head. Caron 5 was into perfection, so that might be her issue. Of course that argument was a great cover if she had in fact committed a crime. If he didn't sign the permit, he would have no legal reason to investigate her, but the more she objected the more he thought there was probably something to investigate.

It was annoying but not unusual in the world of law enforcement. People were rarely forthright, even when it would have been to their advantage. That was okay. Two could play at this game. Nodding agreeably he reached for his pen and pulled the permit application toward him.

"I doubt the MacLaren has reported the coverall you stole yet, so if you haven't committed any crimes before arriving on planet, you should have a clear record at present. On the other hand, Melchior may have something to say about you taking on a second job. Aren't you supposed to be focusing your time on making yourself agreeable to the locals?"

She glared at him and looked as though she planned to spit out a reply, but then she coughed instead.

"It should be easy for you to fit in here," he added. "Many of the folks who settled Valora initially had a checkered history. Some of them were even outlaws and fugitives."

She coughed again.

"Want some water?" he asked. She tightened her lips but nodded. He headed toward the sink and filled a tumbler, making a show of wiping the surface of the glass clean with a cloth before setting it on his desk near her. She would leave a nice clear set of prints whether she liked it or not. They wouldn't be admissible, but at least he would know what or who he was dealing with.

While she drank, he checked the coffee pot. Zela must have made some this morning before she left, but it was barely lukewarm now. He shrugged and poured some in his mug anyway. The mug had a Star Marshal logo—Lenette had given it to him on their first month anniversary. Back when she was still trying to please him. He added a spoonful of sugar, but the crystals resisted melting and grated against his teaspoon as he stirred.

Dilara cleared her throat and spoke again.

"Thank you for the water. And for the record, I'm not an employee of Melchior exactly. Melchior paid my passage, and they'll give me a bonus if I stay in Sector 1065 for six months. It's part of their employee morale initiative to bring more women to the colony. But unlike the other women, I have no funds to live off of while I'm here. So after you left me at the hotel on Tuesday, I answered a help wanted ad, and today I received a communication telling me I got a job in a restaurant. It's called BangBang. Do you know it?"

He wheeled around to face her, coffee sloshing over the side of his mug onto his boots.

"Say what?"

Her eyes raked him from head to toe dismissively. "It's probably not your style. You look more like a bar and grill guy. Bang-Bang is an intimate upscale establishment for discerning diners. It's owned by a Mr. Stanley Lummon. Perhaps you've heard of him?"

Carefully he set the depleted mug on his desk and used the dry mop in the corner to wipe off his boots before responding. Despite her arrogance, she didn't deserve the sort of treatment she would receive on a Saturday night at BangBang. Nobody did.

"Yeah, I know Porky. But I had no idea he was such a good fiction writer. Sector 1065 is a typical mining town, so upscale establishments are few and far between. Probably the closest you'll get to class is the hotel dining room you've already eaten in and even then, it depends on the night. Still, if you were to rate the hotel dining room as a five-star restaurant, by comparison, Bang-Bang would be negative twelve stars."

"You are mistaken," she said. "Mr. Lummon's letter was gentlemanly, and his name is definitely Stanley, not Porky. He told me he is trying to upgrade the sort of clientele he attracts, and he felt I would be a good fit for his needs. I think it's quite rude of you to imply otherwise."

She shook her head and rose. "If you have no more questions, I'll thank you to sign my permit. I have to turn it in to the clerk by the end of the day if I'm to start work tomorrow night. And please be assured, once I receive my first paycheck, I will mail the coverall back to the SS MacLaren."

He waited until she had left with her signed permit before he brushed her glass with powder and loaded the images onto GalacticPol. Legally he had every right to do so—the Revised Code for Colonies was clear on that point. He had been honest with her about Valoran history—some of its most established cities had begun as penal colonies. For that matter, Sector 1065 was still a rough and tumble frontier town. Still, if Dilara Elian was a criminal, he wasn't sure he wanted to know. The less time he spent with her, or even thinking about her, the better.

Chapter 15

PACKING THE GOWN IN HER KNAPSACK HAD seemed foolish at the time—an irrational impulse. A guest at one of her parents' balls had left it behind. It had needed repair and was too out of fashion for Saskia to want it, so no one had cared when Dilara had volunteered to mend it. She hadn't worn it, of course. There had been no occasion for her to do so, nor had there seemed any prospect of such an occasion arising.

But now that Dilara had secured the job at BangBang, it seemed providential she had decided to bring it after all. She smoothed fabric, enjoying the sleek feeling against the palm of her hand. It was a rich burgundy silk, cut to flatter. It made her feel confident—as though she were the sort of woman who wasn't afraid to sing in front of a large crowd of strangers. She gave the mirror one last look. There wasn't much to be done about her hair—maybe the audience would think it was some new fashion.

She was surprised and a little concerned to feel the corners of her mouth turning up at the thought. Happiness led to sloppiness and she couldn't afford any errors. Besides, there was a real possibility this evening would be a disaster. She checked the directions she had copied from Lummon's communication. She hadn't caught a glimpse of BangBang yet because Thursday, Friday and much of Saturday morning had been devoted to classes and to more guided tours of the town, and none of those tours had included Mr. Lummon's establishment. But now she would see it because it was her first night of work, her first night to sing in public anywhere. Her heart squeezed a little at the thought.

She tightened her shawl so it hugged her snugly. It was

designed to disguise her flaw, so she'd intended to leave it behind on Caron 5 as a kind of signal of her liberation. But in the end, she hadn't been able to bring herself to do so. Now she was glad of it and not just for the shawl's welcome warmth in the nippy chill of the evening. At least even if the audience guessed something was wrong with her, they wouldn't have the burden of actually seeing her stump.

The source texts she had searched for and studied surreptitiously on Caron 5 described shockingly lax standards when it came to aesthetics on other planets, like Earth. So even given Guerenne's nasty comment about her stump, Sector 1065 ought to be a place where a flaw would be less significant. But now, as the time came to test her theory, she was less sure. There had been no one to ask aboard the MacLaren, and at any moment, she would find out for herself.

It was dusk as she headed out of the hotel. Gaslights already shed pools of kindly yellow light on the cheerful groups of citizens out for an evening of entertainment. Many of them had started their celebrations already, joking loudly and singing hoarse renditions of pop songs she had never heard before. The party mood was contagious, and despite the reality of her situation, some of her anxiety began to morph into anticipation.

She had always lived in Capital City and no matter how late at night, Capital City had glittered. But she had never associated that glitter with fun. Here everyone was equally small under the vast thick blanket of stars just beginning to emerge in the velvety expanse above. It felt good to be just another member of a crowd, insignificant and also, in an odd way, equal.

Stepping down off the sidewalk, she dodged between revelers and headed up the street. Light shone from the marshal's office, but it was deserted. Rank's General Store and the Farmers' Mercantile were dark, the silent farmer's market lot was a darker pool of shadow between them, but Glory Ann's was lit up and she could see cheerful diners within as she passed. At the corner, just past the livery stables, she crossed the lively intersection toward the wagon repair shop. Just past it was the narrow street where, if the map she had drawn was correct, she would find BangBang.

It was a strange location for an upscale restaurant, but perhaps that was how they did things here in Sector 1065. In any case, from her perspective, the more obscure the better. If BangBang had been hard for her to find, it would also be hard for a searcher to pinpoint. Besides, because she had only formal training and no performance experience, she was unlikely to get much notice. Also good since becoming a household name in Sector 1065 would make her an object of gossip, which would also result in catastrophe.

She paused a moment. The passageway that ran behind the repair shop and the building her directions told her must be Bang-Bang wasn't a narrow street so much as an alley. In the few moments since she had left the hotel, dusk had become darkness and the comforting light of the gas lamps behind her didn't penetrate the shadows beyond the first few paces. Instead she had to rely on the few rays of moonlight that managed to slip between the looming buildings on either side in order to pick her way between obstacles. About halfway, she stopped with a sinking feeling. Ahead there were crooked stacks of crates, squishy things she didn't want to identify and a few heaps of what appeared to be fabric but might have been men curled up to sleep off their early celebrations. This couldn't be right.

Before her on the right, a door opened to a flow of curses as a young man stumbled out into the dark. Beyond him, the massive proprietor was silhouetted in the light, hands on hips.

"I told you last night not to come in today for work, and I meant it. That was one fight too many, Titch. You're banned for two weeks."

"Give me a break, man. Hannon is a kekkin' Winslett Supporter. You're telling me you want to serve drinks to someone like that?" Titch growled.

The big man folded thick arms over his stained apron.

"I serve everybody. That's why your job is serving everybody too. Two weeks, Titch."

Muttering, Titch turned on his heel and headed down the alley toward Dilara. But the moment he saw her, he turned back toward the open door, his hand to his heart.

"Tell me you're seeing this angel, 'cause if not I think I'm dying. Still, what a way to go."

Dilara took a step back into the shadows. Her heart sank. There was no way this business could ever be the fine dining establishment she had imagined when she read the advertisement and Mr. Lummon's response. Even in the dark, she could see that much. Still, Lummon hadn't lied to her exactly. She had believed what she had wanted to believe, and not for the first time, she was getting what she deserved.

Nonetheless, it struck her as singularly unfair that Poe should have been right. And it was probably more unfair that she was angry at him for it. After all she could hardly expect him to lie to her just to make her feel better. But right now, the heel of her boot sliding unpleasantly on what might have been a dead rat, she was consumed with a childish desire to take out her fury on him. If only he had been nearby.

"Leave her alone, Titch. She's on staff, and if I'm lucky she won't be picking fights with the customers. Dilara Elian? Is that you?" The man squinted into the darkness. "Come on in."

She considered waiting silently in the shadows until he closed the door and then sneaking off to go with plan B, but this *was* plan B. Besides, he had pushed the door open wider now with a welcoming gesture, and he could probably see her anyway. Trying to look nonchalant, she slowly pulled her boot free from whatever it was stuck in, forcing herself to ignore the sucking sound that accompanied the motion. Maybe she could wipe the leather clean before she got up onstage. As she stepped into the light, the man's eyes widened and his mouth opened in an O.

"Wow," he said finally as she strode by him through the door. "Welcome to BangBang."

He followed her, rubbing his hands together, but the motion seemed not so much conniving as uncertain. "You're early. But that's good. Great, really," he added hastily. "You can meet the staff and get a feel for the place."

It was discouraging to realize the door she had entered was the front door. While she scraped the bottoms of her boots clean on a broad mat practically placed across the entire entryway, she stared around the great open room. Someone had once tossed a coat of whitewash on the uneven plaster of the walls. But the freshness had faded years ago, so it did more to highlight cracks and flaws than to disguise them. Thick dark curtains covered the windows, which explained the darkness in the alley.

The floor was crowded with dented, scratched tables and chairs except for a small empty square near the stage she guessed was reserved for dancers. A scrawny, discouraged-looking man moved from table to table checking for empty bottles of hot sauce. Cheerful cursing emanated from the kitchen in the back. The bar on her left gleamed with polish and the mirror behind it reflected a disconsolate looking room through a pristine surface. Although there was a probably permanent funk of ale in the room, the floor looked surprisingly clean. So BangBang might be shabby but it was loved, she decided.

"Want to check out the microphone? The piano player should be in before opening, but lots of times he isn't." The man shrugged with a guilty look. "I'd insist, but he's my younger brother and co-owner so…"

Dilara stared at him, hope glimmering. "What's his name?"

"Rudolph. Why?"

"No reason." She sighed internally. "Then your name must be Stanley."

"It is," he said. "But everyone calls me Porky. I know it doesn't look like much now," he added, gesturing broadly, "but I've got big plans for BangBang. It's about time the hotel's dining room had some competition."

The hotel's dining room was exactly the stuffy, self-important facility she would have expected to serve the executives of a large company like Melchior. If that was the sort of dining experience the upper crust of Sector 1065 aspired to, BangBang couldn't compete, which was unfortunate for Porky but lucky for her.

Still, she nodded politely before striding across the room to inspect the stage. It was small and crudely constructed and the piano took up most of it. She would have to be careful not to trip on the uneven floorboards, but at least there was a microphone, and given the size of the speakers, it was probably a powerful one.

"Excuse me," she said, trying to sound as though she knew what she was doing. "Where could I find a music stand?"

He shook his head and trotted back toward the kitchen. She tried to ignore the tightness in her shoulders. Maybe Rudolph could help her find one if he showed up with enough time to spare. Settling onto the piano stool, she dug into her knapsack and pulled out her music. This, at least, she felt confident about. She'd aced Intergalactic Ethnomusicology, and she knew the origins of every one of the songs.

She pressed a key on the piano and marveled at the tone. She had read about pianos, naturally—Earth Music, 101. But unison and single voice music was preferred on Caron 5, so the rippling tones of multiple instruments playing at once in the recordings she had been assigned to listen to and analyze for homework had been a revelation. Tonight she would be able to hear that tangled mess of beautiful sound in person. She shivered in anticipation.

She looked up quickly as customers began to push their way into the room, arguing in a friendly way about who got which table. Porky and his small crew of waiters were quickly outnumbered, and the noise level rose as drinks were slammed down on the flimsy tables.

"Hey! No touching the piano, friendly! Get off my stage!"

A roar of drunken laughter and a chorus of jeers accompanied the shout. Reflexively Dilara snatched her fingers back from the keyboard. Given the resemblance to his brother, the burly man shoving his way through the packed room had to be Rudolph. But where Porky was kindly, if overworked, Rudolph was simply hostile. He lumbered across the room, brow furrowed as he squeezed between tables. She rose, snatching her music to her breast, her heart in her throat. He had nearly made it to the stage when Porky intercepted him, shoving at his chest and shouting what she assumed was an introduction or, at least, an explanation.

He must have succeeded at communicating at least some of the message since he gave Rudolph's shoulder a slap and headed back to the bar. Rudolph nodded after him and then stomped onto the stage, pointedly ignoring Dilara as she scurried around to the curve of the piano. His hands were huge, but he seemed to have no difficulty playing the thing. As he launched into an energetic number, the crowd joined in, shouting the chorus and slamming their drinks on the tables in rhythm, liquid sloshing over the sides of the mugs with each heavy downbeat. It was catchy but not one of the songs she had researched and learned in school.

Feeling exposed and a little foolish, she tried to look like part of the act, swaying to the music and tapping the top of the piano with her palm. The song ended and Rudolph segued into another. This one got some of the younger audience members gyrating on the dance floor but after a few minutes, Rudolph changed tunes again. The moment the thumping baseline began, the dancers stopped in their tracks with a roar of approval and all the audience members turned their attention to her, cheering and gesticulating. Mystified, she turned to stare at Rudolph, but as his fingers found what had to be familiar patterns, he ignored her and stared across the room at Porky. Porky met his gaze with a horrified look and gestured at Rudolph sharply to stop, but Rudolph just grinned in response and played louder.

Moving with surprising speed, Porky forced his way forward, shoving the remaining dancers aside as he stormed through the crowded dance floor and toward the stairs to the stage. He didn't slow as he reached the stairs but barreled up them putting the force of his momentum into his fist. Rudolph ducked, but not fast enough. Porky's knuckles slammed into his nose and Rudolph fell off the piano stool with a thud.

The crowd noise had subsided into an eager silence as Dilara heard an ominous creak from the wooden platform at the combined weight of two large men and a piano. She inched toward the far corner that wasn't anywhere near as far away as she would have liked and considered where she might jump to if things went any further south than they already had. But Porky seemed unconcerned. Ignoring his brother, he turned to the crowd.

"First act's over. Second act is this here new singer. She's traveled all the way here from Caron 5 to bring us a little culture. Your next drink is on the house, so have a seat and give Dilara Elian a warm Sector 1065 welcome, folks!"

With a mixture of half-hearted cheers and a certain degree of grumbling, the customers left the dance floor and headed for their seats. Rudolph, meanwhile, hauled himself off the floor, settled back at the keyboard and nodded at her politely. If there hadn't been a large splatter of blood on his shirt, she would have thought nothing untoward had happened. She edged back around the piano and slid a sheet of song titles with chord markings in front of him.

No music stand, but she wouldn't need one for this particular set because she had memorized this first bunch of lyrics. The professor in her ethnomusicology class called them characteristic of the primitive settings and lyrics common before the dawn of intergalactic travel back when civilizations were historically isolated and insular. But Dilara had fallen in love with them.

They were nothing like the music she had grown up with, religious poetry and historical sagas set to long sinuous lines of solo melody. Nor did they resemble the sort of upbeat intergalactic pop music from other cultures she had considered a guilty pleasure as a girl. These songs had repetitive structures, verses and recurring refrains. Their topics were, well, about life.

Songs like these didn't feel primitive, they felt personal. From a Caron 5 perspective, that *was* primitive. But Dilara hadn't agreed, and on some microscopic level she thought that disagreement had been yet another hidden tear in her connection to her home planet and family. Because songs ought to touch the heart or else what was the point of them?

She turned toward the microphone but took a moment to breathe before she began. The audience, largely composed of men, with a sprinkling of both male and female friendlies, seemed more interested in each other and in their drinks than in her. At least no one had walked out after seeing her on stage. The shaking in her knees and the tension in her neck were stage fright, but there was something reassuring and elemental about this specific anxiety because the end result would rely on the quality of what she produced rather than something she could not control. She herself might be intrinsically flawed, but what she produced was a different matter, and for the first time in her life she had a chance to get it right. Still, she was glad Poe was not in the audience, in case she didn't.

Just as she finished the first verse, she realized something was badly wrong. The crowd was transfixed, but the expressions on their faces ranged from fierce glee to equally fierce fury with nothing in between. She froze and the words died on her lips. She had the distinct impression she had unwittingly set something large in motion she hadn't anticipated. There was a nightmarish quality to the moment, a sense that no matter what she did now, it would be insufficient to stop what was going to happen next.

She glanced at Rudolph, who was grinning at her while his clever fingers made beautiful figures of music, plucking out the melody line from lush chords even as one of the men near the stage rose and aimed a tremendous punch at a man from the next table. By the time Rudolph stopped playing, the audience was in utter tumult, a writhing mass of humanity. The only sounds remaining were grunts, the sounds of fists hitting flesh, the crunch of furniture under falling combatants and the occasional scream as a blow hit home.

Chapter 16

OUT OF THE BOOKLET OF FIFTY CITATION SLIPS Poe habitually tucked in his pocket at the beginning of every Saturday night shift, twenty-three still remained. Not bad. On Saturdays, Poe often ran out of citation slips and had to write the charges on an individual's hand with strict instructions not to wash until the fine was paid. So far this evening the citations only included minor issues like drinking in public and disturbing the peace—misdemeanors that weren't worth clogging up his two jail cells with. Although there were always problems that taxed definition, and tonight had been no exception.

Ren Handling had abandoned his chevalo and wagon on Main Street in order to relieve himself behind a building. That would have been reasonable had Ren hitched the chevalo to one of the many convenient hitching posts the town had installed all along the entire length of Main Street, but no. Ren had simply stopped his chevalo in the middle of Main Street and ambled off through an alley to Second Street where seduced by the siren call of a poker joint he had gotten caught up in a game and had passed out in the corner after losing most of his week's salary to the house. In the meantime, the chevalo had decided it was time for bed and headed home to its stable. When Ren woke, he accused the poker dealer of being a chevalo thief in addition to running a rigged game, and things had gone south from there.

Poe wiggled his jaw. At least Ren hadn't knocked any of his teeth out. Man could pack a blow, but then he was a blacksmith. It would have been great if Poe had the budget for some extra

89

deputies just for weekends and holidays, but it would take a crisis to open the town councilors' purse strings, and he couldn't bring himself to hope for that sort of catastrophe because given Teamue's opinion of him, a crisis would get Poe fired. So in the meantime, Saturday nights were all three pairs of hands on deck. At least Melchior provided its own security force, so he wasn't directly responsible for managing the miners once they crossed into their own neighborhood. Even so, Emilio manned the roads to the west where the miner's housing crouched, and Zela caught the action to the east of town where the roads snaked toward the historical farm community. Poe took the party zone, Main Street, Second Street and their adjoining alleys.

A lot could go wrong on Saturdays and frequently did, but luckily he didn't have to go far to put out fires when they occurred. The fires weren't always metaphorical, which was why he spent Saturday nights patrolling on foot. Most of the miners and farmers were squeezed into taverns at present, but when the bars closed for the evening, all those drunken customers would stumble out onto the streets spoiling for a fight.

When he reached the last lamppost, he turned back. Growing up, Poe had never seen the point of exercising just to exercise. If you wanted to gain strength and lose weight, there was plenty of work begging to be done. But it was a nice coincidence when work was also a pleasure. Just now, with the soft glow of the streetlamps against the velvet sky and the scent of spring in his nostrils, he could afford to enjoy the moment.

He glanced at the hotel as he passed it. The dining room was full tonight, light pouring from its tall windows onto the verandah. There was some sort of Well-Wed event going on. He stopped to look at the well-dressed crowd and wondered if Dilara Elian was among them. Probably, he thought. She was clearly from an upper crust background no matter what story she had cooked up for herself. He thought about her snooty response to him when he'd told her about BangBang and grinned. She had refused to believe him at the time, but Jenkson, the hotel manager, would have set her straight. Jenkson was a twerp, but Poe would have liked to have been there for that conversation.

He passed through the pool of light from the hotel windows and stepped back into the shadows. It was quiet enough for him to hear the soles of his boots on the street. But as he reached the cross street, the noise level rose and he raced past it, heading down the alley toward BangBang at a run. As he neared the door, it flew open and a pair of men locked in combat fell through the doorway, pummeling each other as they rolled back and forth over the threshold. They ignored his order to clear the way, so he simply planted a boot on the back of the man on top and stepped through into the melee in the tavern.

The noise level inside was extraordinary. Normally tavern owners kept order in their establishments through a combination of threats of violence and actual violence. But tonight something must have overridden the customers' normal respect for Porky's fists because the entire room heaved with men, grunting and shouting as they struggled with each other. In another building, he might have pulled his weapon from its holster and shot a warning round through the ceiling. But it would be counterproductive to accidentally shoot one of the friendlies who entertained their own customers in the shabby rooms upstairs. Poe settled for producing the piercing whistle every farmer's child learned at its mother's breast—as good for being heard over a drunken crowd as it was for calling livestock in from the fields.

He couldn't take complete credit for the hush that suddenly fell over the crowd. Some of it had to do with an enormous tearing sound as the wooden stage floor gave way. The piano's legs poked through first and then, inevitably, the body of the instrument plummeted through the remaining scaffolding with a jarring clash of chords. But it was the scream that shattered him.

A woman. He hurtled toward the remains of the stage. There were always a few friendlies trolling for business opportunities in the taverns, especially on a Saturday night when the pickings were good. Sector 1065 was a relatively safe place to ply that trade, but once in a while a customer got the wrong idea.

He shoved his way through the men on the dance floor, some of whom were still fighting with each other in a halfhearted way and others who had given up on whatever had cued the

disagreement in the first place and had subsided into drunken singing.

At the far corner of what once had been the stage, the woman
was struggling with a customer. Poe considered his options even
as he pushed his way toward them. Saur Fanko was a regular at
BangBang and almost as regular a visitor in the jail cells. But it
usually took two to subdue him. He was broader than Porky, for
one thing. But more to the point, he was vicious.

Nonetheless, the woman was holding her own for the moment.
The blood trickling from Saur's swelling nose meant he hadn't
been prepared for resistance, but now his meaty fist was locked
around her left arm hampering her attempts to kick him where it
would hurt. His face was flushed with fury and his grin at Poe
more a showing of teeth than an expression of pleasure.

"Watchu looking at, pig man?"

The woman didn't look at Poe but focused on trying to kick
Saur with a single-minded intensity that would have been funny if
it had been anyone else gripping her.

"Looking at six to ten years off planet, Saur?" Poe said. "Not
worth it, if you ask me."

The woman whirled around at the sound of Poe's voice. Saur,
surprised by the unexpected motion, lost his grip on her arm and
Poe's jaw dropped. He had envisioned her so clearly against the
backdrop of the elegant environs of the hotel, he was having trouble believing she was here at all, never mind brawling with a career troublemaker. Dilara glared back at him, angry but with a
flicker of fear in her eyes.

"It's not my fault," she said.

Ordinarily he might have wanted to explore that since in his
experience when a person started a conversation that way, it absolutely was that person's fault. But there really wasn't time to argue. Even though the crowd seemed to have calmed somewhat, it
was only a matter of time before it turned back into a mob.

"Do you need me to shut down again?"

Porky's tone was resigned.

"Yep."

Porky stumped over to the wall and pulled the big red lever, plunging the room into darkness. In the moment of silence that ensued, Poe spoke.

"Show's over, folks. Double penalties for anyone still in here in ten minutes."

Porky flicked the lights on again, and grumbling and swearing, the crowd of customers dispersed. Saur shot Poe a murderous look but stalked off in their wake. Without having to be told, the staff and friendlies emerged from the bar behind which they were accustomed to taking refuge during riots and with a resigned air began hauling the still functional tables and chairs back into position. Porky trotted toward the telephone, presumably to call the doctor since his brother was using the remains of the scaffolding to balance on one foot, his face pale. Considering the weight of the piano, and the way it had fallen, it was lucky the damage had only been to Rudolph's foot.

There were often problems at BangBang, but this had been worse than usual, and the only difference Poe was aware of was Dilara. Which begged the question, what was she doing there? She was dressed too well to be working as a server. On the other hand, she hadn't struck him as a friendly. For one thing, a successful friendly had to be affable, and she wasn't. Besides, he suspected the application process for Well-Wed, while flawed in many ways, would have eliminated any candidate who wished to sell her favors. Well-Wed was all about the wedding. Which made Dilara a mystery and Poe detested mysteries. He glanced back at her over his shoulder. Her struggle with Saur had torn her gown, and she stared down at the tear now with a surprisingly forlorn air, considering she had probably arrived on planet with a trunk full of fancy clothing.

Zela, uniform spotless as usual, her black hair neatly braided into a crown, had arrived to check in with Poe just as the crowd was beginning to break up. She finished ushering the last customers out the door and waved to Poe before leaving. Zela wouldn't return to her post right away, Poe knew. She would wait until the last loiterer had left the alley to go home. That was the great thing about having reliable, responsible deputies. In his youth, when farm routine was unavoidable and the essence of predictability, he had yearned for the excitement of the unpredictable. He knew better now—there was no joy there. He turned toward Dilara with an internal sigh.

"I'll escort you back to the hotel."

"No, thank you." If it hadn't been so ridiculous, her wariness would have been insulting.

"It's not optional."

She shrugged and headed toward the remains of the piano. He followed her and watched as she fished around for the loose papers that had made their way into the newly opened space under the piano. When she nearly upset herself leaning too far, he grunted in impatience and reached for the last available sheet not pinned beneath the instrument. He did a double take when he saw the lyrics printed on it.

"You weren't singing this, were you?"

She snatched the sheet from him and looked at it with a frown.

"I was. That's what I do. I sing."

"So this," he gestured at the deserted room, "was in fact your fault."

"It most certainly was not!"

He tapped a finger on the sheet. "Singing this song in Sector 1065 is like dropping a lit match in a barn full of hay. You just don't do it unless you want problems."

She frowned. "That makes no sense. It's just an old ballad about a lover's quarrel. The only thing that makes it distinctive is the implied key change in the second to last cadence."

He shook his head. "See, that's the trouble with people like you."

"People like me?" She looked at him politely enough, but her fingers tightened, crinkling the paper.

"You come from Caron 5 with your airs and graces, thinking you're going to teach us rubes a thing or two about our own culture. Maybe twenty cycles ago when your textbooks were written, this was a simple folk song. But since then, it's become a political anthem for civil discord."

"Oh." She looked crestfallen now, and he liked her more for it. Not enough to let her off the hook, but still, some humility went a long way. Even on short acquaintance it was clear she had a limited supply of that particular characteristic, so he guessed he should appreciate it while he had the opportunity.

She shrugged and tapped her foot, looking away from him as though there were something she was impatient to get to on the other side of the room. He restrained himself from reaching for her shoulders and giving her a shake. The desire alone was worrisome because part of it had to do with wanting to feel the warmth of her under the palm of his hand. And he couldn't afford that risk.

After BangBang, the cool evening air felt like wine. The street was quiet except for a few stragglers, and he could hear her boots crunching on the pavement in rhythm with his own. She shot him a sidelong glance.

"Thank you," she said.

"For?"

She gestured impatiently. "That man. What did you call him? Saur?"

He grinned. "Not sure you needed much help. Saur wasn't good looking to begin with, and a broken nose isn't going to improve things much."

She stopped a moment and stared. "Do you really think I broke it?"

"Yep. You've got yourself a good left hook there."

"I guess that's a good thing." Her tone was doubtful. "At least, next time, I can—"

"Next time?" He stared at her. "You can't seriously be considering going back there."

She stiffened. "Of course I will. It's my job now. I just have to get better at it, so I don't cause any more riots."

Chapter 17

POE SAT FORWARD, HIS ELBOWS ON HIS KNEES and frowned at his hat. He passed the brim from one hand to the other, turning it slightly each time. He had done six full hat revolutions before Rinda Edj, Teamue's aunt, who also served as the mayor's secretary, spoke again.

"I'm sure His Honor will be with you shortly."

Rinda's apologetic smile had a practiced quality. Poe nodded politely and rose.

"Perhaps I'll come back another time."

"Oh dear…" Rinda flicked a look toward the closed door behind him. "Why don't I check? If you'll wait just one more minute?"

Without pausing for Poe's response, Rinda scuttled toward Teamue's office. Poe considered sitting back down but decided since he had already made a stand he would be better off sticking to it. His weekly appointment had been scheduled, just as it always was, for five o'clock. He had arrived promptly, but then he wanted to keep his job. Teamue, on the other hand, hoped Poe would be late and then made sure to keep him cooling his heels when he wasn't.

The door opened wide, and Rinda beckoned to him with a self-important expression now. Poe strode by and waited for her to close the door behind her before he approached Teamue. Teamue sat in his throne-like desk chair, frowning down at the budget Poe had dropped off earlier in the day. The rest of the desk's broad polished surface was clean and empty.

Poe stood, hat in hand, until Teamue looked up and gestured toward one of the two low chairs facing his desk. Rumor had it Teamue had ordered the legs of the guest chairs filed down, so petitioners would be at a slight disadvantage. The ruse wasn't effective in this case since Poe was by far the taller of the two men. But that didn't make it any more comfortable to sit in the guest chairs. They seemed to have been designed to ensure short meetings.

The genial expression Teamue wore in public and when he was asking favors was gone now. His mouth was tight and his eyes hard. He pushed his wire framed spectacles down his nose and tilted his head back to stare at Poe through the thick lenses.

"You've padded this budget and the town can't afford padding."

Poe opened his mouth to deny it categorically but changed his mind mid-thought. "I'd be glad to explain my reasons if you tell me what categories concern you."

Teamue's mouth eased slightly as he tapped at one of the lines of text. "This line, for instance. Why do we have an open line of credit at Glory Ann's Café?"

Poe wanted to say, "So I can feed all my friends at the town's expense," but he suspected Teamue wouldn't get the humor, so he said, "That's for when we have overnight guests in our cells."

"What about this item?" Teamue frowned. "The whole point of creating a budget is to avoid spending money on irrelevancies. For instance, now that you have a mechanical conveyance, why on earth would you continue to need a monthly allotment of hay?"

Mystified, Poe stood and leaned over the desk to see what Teamue was pointing at and struggled not to smile. "HAY is an acronym, sir. It stands for our youth outreach program, Healthy Active Youth."

Teamue reddened. "And this entry? Why are we paying Ansel's Livery and what are dog services anyway? Or is that another acronym?"

"No, sir." Poe sat down again, squirming pointlessly in an attempt to make the seat more comfortable. "Sometimes we need a dog for tracking, and Ansel's lymer is the best in the area for that.

If it's any help, I've been thinking about getting a dog myself. If he ends up being as good a scent hound as Ansel's, I'll be able to eliminate that expense from the budget."

"Humph." Teamue picked up the pages, tapped them on the desk so their edges aligned and added them to his outbox. Poe felt as though he had passed some sort of test, maybe not with flying colors, but well enough to squeak by. But true to form, Teamue didn't allow Poe's sense of success to linger. Rising from his seat, Teamue clasped his hands behind his back and strolled to the window overlooking the green.

"Sven Borin called this morning after you left his place. It took fifteen minutes out of a busy morning just to calm him down enough to speak rationally."

"Vandalism can be upsetting." Poe kept his tone noncommittal.

"It's even more upsetting when the victim tells the marshal who the culprit is, and the marshal refuses to act on that information. Borin was extremely angry and I can understand that. Minimally, by now you should have found the boy. Or do you need to rent Ansel's dog again?"

Poe blinked and raised a hand in an attempt to stop the flow of words without overtly interrupting. Finally Teamue stopped his criticism long enough to allow Poe a chance to speak.

"After I met with Borin, I drove directly to Mnoani Territory and spoke with Chief Manzarin. He told me—"

"Of course Manzarin made excuses for his grandson," Teamue interrupted. "Everyone knows the Mnoani are clannish. But just because the chief had an excuse ready doesn't mean you should be gullible enough to buy it."

There were so many things wrong with Teamue's perspective Poe wasn't sure where to start. There was a longstanding mostly one-sided animosity between the founders and the Mnoani. Statistically the Mnoani committed fewer crimes as a group than farmers or merchants and significantly less than the miners did. But Teamue's parents had made their fortune selling less than perfect goods to needy founders and tribespeople for higher-than-average prices. Poe thought people like that often preferred to think of their customers as dishonest or as fools. It was easier on the conscience than thinking of them as victims.

"Orioldo's alibi is rock solid," Poe said. "There were dozens of witnesses who can vouch for him on the night the vandalism at Borin's farm reportedly took place. Unless Borin changes his story, I have to look elsewhere for a perpetrator. Sir."

"Fine." Teamue huffed. "Just try to get the matter resolved in a reasonable time frame. I can't be bothered constantly by complaints from citizens about the job you're doing. Or not doing, for that matter. I should be able to rely on you to fulfill your responsibilities without my having to keep an eye on you all the time. I have enough to do without being your keeper."

For the next twenty-eight minutes, Teamue detailed exactly how busy and important he was. Poe nodded and made understanding noises while mentally planning the duty roster for the week. At least the budget was off the table now. He was so focused on willing the clock hands to move faster, he nearly missed Teamue's announcement.

"The statue of Mayor Winslett is set on its base now on New Colony Hill, and the board has decided to hold a town wide dedication ceremony Saturday morning. There will be music and speeches, including one from me. The Well-Wed women will attend along with some of the Melchior upper management, and there will be a community picnic to follow. I'll need you to make sure nothing untoward happens that day."

Poe's stomach tightened. His own family, along with many of the other founders, bore little affection for the memory of the harsh and vindictive former mayor. But the newer generation of farmers, who had not known him, saw the past through a rosier lens. And the merchants, who were better represented on the board every year, were always eager to create events that would bring farmers and miners into town to purchase goods and services.

Still, Poe thought placing the statue of Winslett so near to Mnoani Territory was insensitive, to say the least. It was bad enough the Mnoani had been dispossessed of their land. Forcing them to look at the source of their deprivation, glorified in marble, every time they traveled into town was tantamount to incitement.

The Well-Wed women's presence would provide additional chances for conflict. Between Melchior executives, farmers, and merchants, each hoping to outshine the rest to win the attentions of the women, there was bound to be trouble. If he was lucky, it would rain that day, but luck hadn't been his friend for a long time, and except for the sick feeling in his stomach, he felt detached. He knew that wasn't good—it was the kind of numbness that could get a lawman killed, but he couldn't bring himself to care.

Chapter 18

SATURDAY MORNING DAWNED SUNNY AND temperate, proof that the world was unfair. The doctrine of the Higher Power Worship House where Poe had attended religious school as a child had never impressed him. At seven years old, Poe had already felt that if a deity got credit for things going well, it should also get blame when life went awry. His opinion hadn't changed. If there was some kindly being up there, it would have sent rain in buckets.

This morning Poe had learned that Teamue had accepted an offer from Melchior security to help with crowd control. This was not reassuring from Poe's perspective. Melchior security's chief, Zan, was a sensible guy, but his underlings could be overzealous. It was one thing if they were too aggressive on their own turf, Poe felt, but security in the town of Sector 1065 was Poe's responsibility. The set-up potential here didn't escape him. It did annoy him. If the ceremony went smoothly Melchior would get the credit. If it didn't, Poe would be blamed. In either case, he would have to deal with the inevitable fallout.

But there was a larger issue. Over the past year Poe had observed increasing friction between the farmers, the Mnoani and the miners. Even the merchants seemed uneasy and quick to blame others for what in ordinary years would have been considered the cost of doing business. Normally in Poe's experience, merchants found it economically unwise to take sides. But this year, he had observed in uptick in the number of complaints, specifically against the Mnoani.

There was no point in trying to speak with Teamue about it—

the man was a self-absorbed idiot. Poe had made an excuse and gotten out of Teamue's office on Friday before the temptation to deck the guy became overwhelming. And now he was standing on New Colony Hill, sending mental encouragement to the few clouds dangling in the uncooperative blue sky while a crew assembled the portable stage next to the base of the statue. He shook his head and let the hope of a deluge go with a sigh. Maybe Teamue's speech would manage to bore the protesters so thoroughly they would give up out of sheer exhaustion.

The first group of Mnoani arrived just as the crew finished wrestling a large podium up the stairs and into position. Ignoring the white chairs arranged in a tight careful grid in front of the stage, the Mnoani settled around the base of the statue and in the open space between the first row of chairs and the platform. They spread colorful woven blankets on the grass and arranged folding chairs on and around them. Picnic baskets vied for space with drums and signs. The scent of mishec sandwiches wafted across to Poe, and his mouth watered.

The statue itself was covered with a sheet of shiny white fabric that would be raised by means of a pulley system when the moment of the unveiling arrived. A long rope draped across the span from the pulley to the podium, curving over the heads of the picnickers. It swayed in the breeze as a laughing child, perched on her father's shoulders, reached for it unsuccessfully. Poe sighed and headed toward them. Melchior security forces were scheduled to arrive at any moment, and it would be better to preempt the issue.

Three men stood as he approached, and the mood in the group shifted from upbeat good cheer to watchfulness. He knew two of them by sight, but the third was Orioldo, Chief Manzarin's grandson. Over his embroidered tunic, he wore a complex necklace of silver worked into depictions of flowers and vines, a marker of his status. The silver accented his green eyes and contrasted with the gold strands of his long braid.

At seventeen, Orioldo already bore the air of a leader. He was slim and graceful, but Mnoani often were. Didn't mean they were weak. Poe stopped at a respectful distance—close enough to converse, far enough to be unthreatening.

"Marshal."

Orioldo's tone was impassive, but his feet were braced, his fists clenched. His companions moved closer to him, glancing at him as though waiting for a signal.

Poe clasped his own hands behind his back and nodded politely at the trio and at the crowd seated behind them.

"It's a beautiful morning."

"Every morning is a beautiful morning." Several members of the crowd joined Orioldo in the time-honored response.

Poe let out a breath. "If I wasn't on duty, I'd probably ask to sit down and join you. That mishec smells delicious."

"Winslett lovers aren't welcome to eat with us."

One of the old women near a pile of drums shook her head with a click of her tongue. She shot a disapproving look at Orioldo before turning to tend to her infant grandchild.

Poe spoke loud enough so the crowd could hear him. "I'm not a Winslett fan either. But I have to ask you folks to either sit in the chairs we have set out, or if you want to sit on the grass, to move to the sides of the audience area or even to the back behind the seats."

"We can settle anywhere we want," Orioldo said. "This is our land more than it is yours, homesteader. We're ready to fight for it if necessary."

Poe nodded. "You could do that," he acknowledged finally. "But there are a lot of little ones with you here today, and there are likely to be more children arriving from the school any moment now. And my job, when you come down to it, is about trying to keep all citizens from getting hurt. Young Chief, would it be possible to speak with you privately?"

He could see Orioldo was torn between the opportunity to posture some more and the chance to demonstrate to his companions that he was respected as a leader. Poe waited an uncomfortable moment, listening to the rustling and uneasy murmurs among the folks seated on blankets. But in the end, pride won out and Orioldo waved his two second-in-commands away before walking toward Poe. Poe extended his hand and when Orioldo clasped it, Poe gestured toward the center aisle. It would be easier to convince Orioldo to stand down if they were out of hearing distance.

"I'm glad we have a chance to speak alone before the Melchior security forces get here. Once they arrive, I'll have a lot less control over how things transpire. And I think it's important you and I have a plan to ensure no one gets hurt today."

Poe felt his shoulders clench as he waited for Orioldo's response. He remembered being seventeen—heroism had been a lot more attractive back then. The bigger problem was that Orioldo was right to be angry. Hospitality was a bedrock concept for the Mnoani, but it hadn't served them well when the colonists from Earth had arrived with trunks of Earth crop seeds, an entirely different type of currency and a firm belief in Manifest Destiny bolstered by pages of contractual documents from a distant planet the Mnoani had barely heard of.

Still, there had been an uneasy balance between the farmers, the merchants, and the Mnoani until Melchior arrived on the scene. Poe had been seven when the early scouts arrived. At the time, he couldn't imagine anything cooler than surveying for ore. He had even fastened a box to the end of a stick and spent long hours wandering across the pasture with his brothers pretending to discover timony.

Timony was the ultimate find, a self-perpetuating fuel with an eon's long shelf life. A boy who found even a small chunk of it was guaranteed to be rich, or at least rich enough to buy the fancy bicycle in the Mercantile—the one with the spokes that glowed in the dark and the torchlight on the handlebars. Of course even if Poe had found a chunk of timony, it wouldn't have been his to sell. By that time, United Earth Council had already sold the timony rights in Sector 1065 to Melchior and as a result, only Melchior was entitled to harvest it.

Out of the corner of his eye, Poe could see the Melchior security detachment assembling near the road. Townspeople straggled up the hill toward him along with an assortment of farmers, merchants, off duty miners and a few Melchior executives. Even at a distance it was obvious who was who. The townspeople and merchants were dressed in their most elegant clothing and chattered excitedly with each other as they approached. The farmers might have put on clean clothes, but their expressions were more dutiful than joyous. Dressed in their orange coveralls at the end of their shift, the miners looked exhausted but determined to enjoy the entertainment. The bright colors of the Well-Wed women's gowns contrasted with the more subdued hues of the farm women's homespun dresses. Below the chatter of the approaching crowd, the drums from the Mnoani circles rumbled, deep, placid and inexorable.

Orioldo's face hardened at the sight of the Melchior executives. In their fine black wool suits, they resembled a flock of crows stalking across the grass, cocking their heads to stare coldly at the other attendees. Poe's heart sank. But in that instant, a crowd of excited children scrambled around the Melchior group, laughing and chasing each other up the hill toward the viewing platform. The elementary school was scheduled to perform a song to open the program. He glanced again at Orioldo who stared at the children, the muscle in his jaw ticking.

"There will be no trouble from us today," the young man flicked a glance at him, "but perhaps soon."

Orioldo strode back toward the Mnoani, and Poe watched with relief as the Mnoani resettled themselves along the sides of the chairs. Sometimes it felt that his entire job was stamping out sparks. But stamping out sparks wasn't an effective long-term strategy when you were dealing with a mulch fire.

As it turned out, the ceremony itself was anti-climactic. Once the statue was unveiled to a mixture of applause and scattered booing, the Mnoani decamped without incident. Teamue, along with some senior Melchior executives, did the same, presumably to enjoy a meal in more formal surroundings. As the Melchior security team trailed after them, the atmosphere became more relaxed. Poe strolled over to Zela and Emilio who were watching from the other end of the hill.

"Looks like you two can take off," he said.

"Sure you don't need me, boss?" Emilio smiled. "There could be a big fight over coleslaw."

Poe slapped Emilio on the shoulder and shook his head firmly.

"It's your day off, Emilio. Go home now and try to salvage some of it while you can. You go home too, Zela. Your shift's almost done anyway. I'll stay until it's over."

"Okay," Zela said. "I can grab a bite with Glory Ann before I pick up Jebbie, and then I'll check back in at the office to make sure no one's called in with a problem before I head home. I'll leave you a note if there's anything to report."

The two deputies walked down the hill together. They had climbed into Zela's wagon and disappeared around the curve in the road before Poe turned back to check on the crowd. His shoulders eased as he surveyed the picnickers scattered over the hilltop. Sector 1065 had its problems, but in moments like these, he could admit he loved it, even with its flaws. He loved the occasional rough kindness, the persistent ingenuity and the stubborn work ethic of its citizens. A wash of unexpected pleasure filled him as he watched miners, farmers, executives, and merchants gather at the large tables filled with dishes folks always brought to these events—casseroles of every description, sandwich platters, and roasted vegetables. For once they were all getting along, and he suspected if the Mnoani had stayed longer, they too would have enjoyed the momentary truce.

He didn't even feel his usual surge of irritation at the sight of the Well-Wed women mingling with the crowd. He was at no risk of falling in love. He felt like that fortress he had visited once while he was at the Academy in Centra. The great stone structure was in ruins, but it had been built on the top of Mount Minador by a long-gone indigenous tribe. From the vast courtyard, he had been able to see down the craggy mountain on all sides. The sense of remoteness had been vast too, and reassuring.

Chapter 19

A GENTLE BREEZE MADE THE GRASS WAVE, but the sun was warm on Dilara's shoulders, and the effect of a full stomach was to make her sleepy. To be fair, the new routine of working until late every night at BangBang and still maintaining the lively schedule the Onkelsons had created for the Well-Wed women was taking a toll too. During class this morning, she had been hardly able to keep her eyes open.

Mrs. Onkelson had set out blankets for the picnic, but most of the women had taken advantage of the opportunity to socialize with the many single men who attended the ceremony. As a result, Dilara was one of only three women remaining in the Well-Wed women's area. Susanna sat on a blanket several yards away, her nose in a book. Her blonde hair shone in the sun. Ngendo had pulled a square of fabric from a satchel and was engaged in embroidering a brilliantly colored series of flowers around the edges of it.

Kiko had slipped away after the ceremony, purportedly to go back to the hotel. Dilara suspected Kiko had other plans, but the new friendships Dilara was forming with her roommates were still too tentative to bear much pressing, so she hadn't. It was surprising to her how easily the three women had fallen into a companionable threesome, sitting near each other during events. Even more, she was surprised at how much that had mattered to her. She leaned back against a handy boulder and closed her eyes for a moment, enjoying the warmth and the unaccustomed sense of safety. How peculiar, she thought drowsily, that she would feel safer as a fugitive than she had as a resident of her own planet.

She was dreaming when she heard Susanna's voice, and at first she thought the sound was part of her dream. But when Susanna gasped, Dilara's eyes snapped open. Two men stood over Susanna. One of them was the big man who had grabbed Dilara on the night of the riot at BangBang. Although her subsequent performances had been uneventful, she had kept a careful eye out for Saur Fanko since. The other man was smaller, a farmer, she guessed by his clothes, but he was wiry and mean looking. Both were laughing as they tossed Susanna's book back and forth between them, and the little man shouted with pleasure as it tore in his grasp. As it fell to the grass, Susanna scrabbled on all fours between the two men to retrieve it.

Ngendo had dropped her embroidery and was already scrambling to her feet. Dilara did the same, looking around for something she could use as a weapon. Now she wished she hadn't been so diligent about returning her plate and utensils after eating. A fork would have been more effective than the embroidery scissors Ngendo was holding. The tiny blades were unlikely to do much damage, although they might serve as a distraction.

Frantically Dilara glanced back at the crowd. Those who had remained after finishing their meals were engaged in watching and betting on some sort of team game. It involved lots of balls, cheering and jeering. The chances of catching anyone's attention were low. At least the two men looming over Susanna were too focused on shoving each other to notice their quarry was getting away.

The Onkelsons had set up the Well-Wed women's picnic area in the midst of a sea of other picnickers, no doubt with an eye toward increasing the women's exposure to the townspeople. Among the setups was one with a large sun umbrella, now folded closed and lying on the grass next to its owner's goods. The long wooden shaft protruded from beneath a bright red and blue paneled canopy. Without hesitation, she ran for it, grateful the umbrella's owner was nowhere to be seen.

By shoving the canopy end under her left arm and supporting it with her stump, she was able to hold it like a lance, the sharp metal tip forward. As she reached Ngendo's side, Susanna ran toward them, hugging her book to her chest. Her cheeks were flushed and the braids she usually pinned tightly in a crown atop her head had come loose. Ngendo shoved Susanna behind them and Dilara stood her ground. The umbrella was heavy, but she tried not to let the strain of holding it show.

"Hey! That's my umbrella! Stop thief!"

The peevish male cry distracted her, but the two men were distracted as well. They looked up and Saur's eyes met hers. His gaze was an unpleasant mixture of contempt and hostility. But when she flicked her glance to the farmer, she felt a chill. He was looking between her and Ngendo, completely focused on Susanna, and there was a determined set to his mouth. She moved in front of Susanna to block his view and waved the shaft of the umbrella in what she hoped was a threatening fashion.

"Good afternoon, ladies. Dilara." Poe's voice conveyed an air of resignation that would have been insulting if she hadn't been so grateful he'd appeared. "What seems to be the problem here?"

"The problem, Marshal, is that this young woman stole my umbrella." The rotund little man braced his hands on his knees and worked to catch his breath, his cheeks flushed from running, and also she thought, from pique.

"Somehow this does not surprise me," Poe said. He nodded at Saur and the farmer. "Mr. Fanko. Mr. Borin. Anything I can do for you two gentlemen?"

Saur spat to the side and walked past them toward the game, nearly clipping Ngendo with his shoulder as he did so, but the farmer stood his ground.

"You better figure out who your real friends are, Lancaster," he said. "You don't want to be on the wrong side when it comes time to choose."

Dilara glanced up at Poe. Normally she thought of him as a man in motion, but he was completely still now, as though he were listening to something she could not hear.

"That sounds like a threat, Borin," he said.

"Take it any way you want," Borin replied.

Casting one last look at Susanna, he turned and walked away down the hill.

"Excuse me." The little man had caught his breath and seemed even more upset. "Marshal Lancaster, please arrest this woman. She has stolen my umbrella, and there are witnesses to it."

It took effort to loosen her grip, but when she did, she held it out to him.

"I apologize," she said. "I was trying to protect my friend, but it was wrong of me to take your umbrella without permission."

With an indignant air, he pulled the umbrella from her grasp, inspecting it carefully.

"No harm done then, Quence?" Poe said.

"These newcomers think they can come here and run all over us," Quence blustered, "and you do nothing. What kind of marshal are you? The law is clear on stealing. I want to press charges."

Poe sighed. "She returned it to you unharmed."

"This time she did," Quence retorted, "but once a thief, always a thief. And I don't care what her reasons were. Next time she might walk into my bank and decide to make an unauthorized withdrawal. If she tells you she robbed me in order to donate the funds to charity would that also be excusable? Where do we draw the line?

"No, you can't talk me out of it, Lancaster. And if you continue to try, I'll take it up at our next board meeting. I expect you to arrest her immediately. If our own marshal won't enforce the law, perhaps it's time for a new marshal."

Dilara heard Ngendo gasp as Poe nodded. He gripped Dilara firmly by the elbow and walked her through the diminishing crowd until they were out of Quence's sight. She didn't like him, she reminded herself. The only thing that appealed to her about him was a weird sense that she could trust him, probably because he didn't trust her.

"This is not my fault!" she said. "Arresting me would be completely unfair. You didn't arrest those two men."

"Pipe down," he growled.

He was close to her now, his eyes on hers. His smile was wry but there was a glimmer of wariness in his eyes. It so closely mirrored her own feelings she almost smiled back but caught herself just in time. The desire to step closer was a physical thing, but instead she forced herself to back away.

"You're right and I have no plan to arrest you—this time. But consider yourself on notice. You're going to have to stop alienating the taxpayers if you want to stay here. Besides, if I arrest you, you'll lose your work permit and then who will be responsible for creating civic unrest in the bars?"

As Dilara turned to follow the women back to the hotel, she felt it had been a near thing, a dangerous moment. The whole incident had been distressing, which might explain her reaction, but she would have to be more careful in the future. She had no room for error.

Chapter 20

"RUDOLPH WILL BE FINE. HIS ANKLE'S STILL swollen, but he's so happy his hands escaped unscathed, he doesn't care."

Stig sank into the chair next to Poe's desk. Poe handed Stig a cup of coffee and hesitated before picking up his own. His shift was ending in half an hour, but he wanted the boost. He had just made it around his desk, cup in hand, when Dilara slammed into the office and dropped her knapsack on the floor. Her face was flushed, and for a moment he could imagine her as a child—bright, frustrated and fascinating.

"Shouldn't you be tucked into your elegant hotel room for the night?" he said.

Her voice was tight with fury. "The hotel management said I can't stay there anymore."

His eyebrows shot up. "How'd you manage to tick them off that quickly? Usually Jenkson will do about anything for a paying customer. Maybe making people dislike you is your special skill. Too bad you can't turn that into a money-making venture."

Her stare hardened. "It's your fault."

"*My* fault?"

She nodded and did a credible imitation of Jenkson's prissy tone. "We pride ourselves on being an upscale establishment, and you were seen being taken into custody by the marshal."

He blinked. "Huh. Hey, Stig," he said without taking his eyes off Dilara. "Meet Dilara Elian. She's here with the Well-Wed group, and she's already managed to cause more trouble than any other participant in the history of the program."

Stig rose. "Dr. Stig Haugen at your service, Miss Elian. I'm very pleased to meet you. You'll have to forgive the marshal. He's had the manners of a bovoquin since he was a child. I, on the other hand, am about as refined a gentleman as you will find in this..."

Poe felt his shoulders tighten. Stig was tall and slim, blond and blue eyed, in addition to being well educated and charming. He would make some woman a great husband. So there was no good reason why Poe felt an undeniable urge to boot him out of the office.

"Stig," he interrupted, "she's not your type."

Dilara's head whipped round, and she looked ready to give him the same left hook she'd given Saur, but her eyes were suspiciously shiny, and he wondered if she had been crying. Not his fault, he reminded himself. She had brought her troubles on herself the moment she boarded the MacLaren on false pretenses, which didn't explain why he felt guilty or why he found the slight smile lurking on Stig's face irritating.

"Our rabble rouser here needs a place to stay, Stig. You know of any rooms available in town?"

"Tonight? Not likely. An extra shuttle landed today. I heard it's a group of prospectors stopping overnight on their way to Yxil. The ones who can't afford a hotel bed will grab up any available space in the brothel. But you have an extra room at your place, Poe."

Poe glared at his friend who gave him an innocent look before busying himself adding sugar to his coffee.

"Come on, Stig," he said, wishing he sounded less pathetic. "Can't she stay in the clinic just for one night until we figure out an alternative?"

"No can do." There was an undertone of enjoyment in Stig's response that made Poe grit his teeth. "You know the clinic's full up most nights."

Stig drained his cup and rinsed it as he continued. "I've still got a possibly broken arm to set when I get back there, along with a head wound that may need stitching. And that's not counting anyone who might have stopped in while I was visiting with you. So, as long as neither of you need first aid, I'll be on my way."

Picking up his kit, Stig headed for the door. Before he opened it, he turned back and grinned. "Have a nice evening."

Poe growled as the door slammed shut on Stig's laughter. He stared at his untouched coffee, now cool.

"Let's go explain matters to Jenkson. You're irritating, but he should be accustomed to irritating customers by now."

She shook her head and shouldered her knapsack again, tapping her foot as he reached for his duster. He took his time putting it on just to be contrary. Despite the late hour, several hotel guests including some of the Well-Wed women had claimed the rocking chairs on the broad veranda to take advantage of the crisp fresh breeze. They watched silently as Poe followed Dilara up the wide stairs but made no attempt to catch her eye or to greet a fellow guest. Pleasant bunch.

Jenkson stood behind the counter, polishing a brass pen holder with a stained rag. Poe cleared his throat, but Jenkson didn't look up at him until he had finished buffing, had inserted pens into the holder and had placed the item on the countertop. Then he used the rag to give his name tag a swipe. Poe wondered if he went through that process every time a guest touched a pen and decided he probably did.

"Welcome, Marshal Lancaster. How can I help you?"

"There seems to be a mix up. Your guest, Miss Elian, would like her key to room—"

"Room 217," Dilara filled the silence.

Jenkson pursed his lips and raised one brow.

"She can't stay here. No felons allowed."

Dilara stepped forward with a scowl, gesturing at Poe. "I'm not a felon! He didn't arrest me."

"I didn't say you had been arrested, but I have it on good authority you are a thief," Jenkson said primly.

"I am not."

"Did you, or did you not, take Mr. Quence's umbrella without permission?"

"I did, but—"

"I don't know what the laws are wherever you came from, Miss, but here in Sector 1065 taking another's belongings without permission is illegal. Is that not correct, marshal?"

Without waiting for Poe's response, Jenkson continued in his pedantic fashion. "The Alarite Hotel prides itself on being an upscale establishment, and my instructions are clear. You will have to move on."

"I'd like to speak with Lieutenant or Mrs. Onkelson, please," Dilara said.

"Lieutenant and Mrs. Onkelson are in accord with me on this," Jenkson said. "In fact, Mrs. Onkelson was so concerned about the impact your behavior might have on her program's reputation, she was nearly in tears."

"Then tell me who the owner of the hotel is, and I will explain the situation myself," she insisted. Poe could see her lips tremble and his heart sank. He hated knowing what was coming and not being able to stop it.

"Mr. Quence owns the Alarite Hotel," Jenkson said with a triumphant tone.

It was as though the air had gone out of her and much as Poe had wanted to take her down a peg or two initially, there was something painful about seeing her look so defeated. He put a hand on her shoulder.

"Come on. Let's get out of here."

As they stepped onto the sidewall, he mentally flicked through the remaining options, slowly and ever more reluctantly dismissing one after the other. It was patently unfair. Stig had been right several too many times recently. One day soon Stig would blow it, and Poe would have the chance to rub it in his friend's face, but for the moment, he had to deal with the housing issue. At least the expression on Dilara's face mirrored his own frustration, which made it a little easier to proffer an olive branch.

"You can stay with me for the night."

"I'd rather sleep in the street," Dilara muttered. It was petty of him, but he considered offering her a bed in one of the jail cells. On second thought, he decided not to. Someone would find out, the way people always did in Sector 1065, and she would never be able to erase the taint. It was bad enough Quence had made the accusation.

"I don't love the idea either," he said finally. "But it's a perfectly nice room. My wife spent hours decorating it."

"Your wife will not be pleased to have a guest like me," she said.

She gestured toward her right arm as though the implication of the sentence would have been obvious to anyone but him. He wasn't sure how to respond because in a sense, she was correct. Lenette would have been polite on the surface, but she would have been annoyed, not because Dilara was different physically, but because she was unimportant. Social status was the way Lenette measured value, and Dilara didn't have any. But what Lenette thought wasn't his responsibility anymore.

"Not an issue," he said finally. "Should we go back to the hotel for the rest of your luggage?"

"This is all I have." She nudged her knapsack with her toe.

He rolled his eyes. Just one more reason he could be sure Dilara Elian wasn't being honest with him. No one in that group would ever travel with less than a steamer trunk.

Not that it mattered. He was immune to women now—Lenette had made sure of that. But later, after he had settled Dilara into the spare bedroom with its ruffles and lace, he wondered how it might have gone if things had been different, if he had been different.

Initially Lenette had found him appealing enough. He thought now it was because she had seen him as a project. But over the year of their marriage it became clear he was simply unredeemable. Lenette complained he was rough, abrasive, sometimes grouchy, and always crude. No matter how carefully he chose his words before he spoke, he inevitably got it wrong. He was just lousy at relating to women.

Seeing Stig interact so confidently with Dilara had just illustrated the point. Poe had never had that sureness, certainly not with people he barely knew. That was what made his visceral interest in Dilara so peculiar. From the moment he had met her, speaking with her had felt easy. But it was important to remember that was just a feeling, not reality. Just because he enjoyed their exchanges didn't mean she did. Even the fact she had accepted his invitation only meant she needed a place to stay that night. Still, as he fell asleep, there was an unexpected comfort knowing she was breathing in rhythm with him just a room away.

Chapter 21

"KEKKIN' TAPPERHEAD!"

Dilara threw off her covers and was out the door of the tiny bedroom before she even registered the cold on her bare feet. Poe was shaking his fist out the gaping doorway at a rainbow-colored bird swooping away, its long tail feathers waving as it went. So far he had impressed her as being sane, if irritating. Now she wasn't so sure. It was good she had slept fully dressed. She jammed her feet into her boots and grabbed her knapsack.

Poe turned toward her and scowled. "What are you doing up?"

"I should probably head out," she said. "See if I can find any lodging for tonight."

He gave her a long look and sighed. "Sorry. I didn't mean to startle you. Don't leave."

She studied him a moment. He looked rumpled, as though he too had just leaped from bed. She could see a crease from his pillow on his cheek, and his shirt was still unbuttoned. It would have been nice to rest her palm on his chest. She blinked the thought away and forced herself to speak in a light tone.

"Is this a traditional Sector 1065 ritual to greet the new day? Or is that just on Sunday mornings?"

"Only in my cabin," he said. "When it comes to that blasted tapperhead, I lose my temper. He pecks at the cabin wall every morning, but I swear he saves his loudest productions for the days after a late-night shift."

"He's beautiful."

"I guess. But beauty's not much compensation when he's slamming his beak into my wall at sunrise."

"Why does he do it?"

Poe shrugged. "Looking for breakfast, I guess, same as us. Are you hungry?"

"A little."

He brushed by her as he headed toward the kitchen, and she caught a whiff of something unfamiliar, an herb maybe, spicy and a little pungent. She suppressed the urge to follow him and turned away to look at the cabin's main room. She had been too tired to take it in properly last night. Although the two bedrooms were walled off from the main living space, most of the cabin was one large open room with a kitchenette in one corner.

Evidently Poe and his wife liked clutter. Every available surface was covered with knickknacks on knobby, off-white doilies. The walls were crowded too with framed artwork. Not very interesting artwork, she thought. All the pictures seemed to feature little cottages surrounded by overgrown flower gardens. Interspersed between the pictures were framed mottoes—not actually stitched but made to look as if they were. "Home Sweet Home" and "East, West, Home's Best" were the shortest. But one actually listed twenty-six virtues of Home, each beginning with a different letter of the Earther alphabet.

Then there was the furniture. For a large man who made his living catching and subduing law breakers, Poe seemed inordinately fond of spindly chairs, delicate end tables and tall thin glass fronted display cabinets. Most of the cabinets housed collections of porcelain figurines depicting elegant young men and women doing elegant things. But one contained bisque clowns staring at her with their beady little eyes. She shuddered and moved away carefully, trying not to turn her back to them. Once she felt she was at a safe distance, she hurried toward the kitchen.

"We're in luck." His disembodied voice emanated from within a cupboard behind the tiny breakfast bar. "My mother came by while I was at work."

For a moment she wondered whether his mother was actually in the cupboard.

"There's food!" He waved a loaf of bread triumphantly and set it on the countertop next to a bowl of eggs and some stuff she couldn't identify.

"What's that?" She pointed at the most intriguing item. It was knobby and orange and gave off a sharp sweet scent.

"It's a myriad, a hybrid between a myr and a gilead. Never mind. You'll like it. It's good."

"Want help?"

"Nah. Be a guest." He sounded so cheerful at the prospect of eating she nearly smiled until it occurred to her he wasn't simply being hospitable. She glanced at the single stool but didn't sit.

"I *can* help if you want. I mean I know how."

"Sure," he said. "Must be a little complicated though." He gestured with his whisk toward her stump.

She felt a flush of relief. He had misunderstood her, which meant he might not have done a search for her through GalacticPol after she left his office. Or, if he had, he hadn't learned much about her upbringing. Still, she would have to be more careful. She made her glance to her stump overt before shrugging and meeting his gaze.

"Maybe a little. Sometimes."

To her surprise, she felt a certain release in saying it. One didn't consider flaws an inconvenience on Caron 5. They were an insult to the community as a whole. So there was something self-indulgent and therefore a bit illicit in thinking about her stump as a personal difficulty. For the most part, she worked around the challenge, whether embroidering a scapular for the priest, which she was supposed to do, or secretly learning to cook from kitchen staff, which she wasn't. But no amount of skill compensated for the visible mark of shame she had born since birth.

Oddly this didn't seem to be the case in Sector 1065. Poe's gaze was interested, compassionate maybe, but held none of the assessment, judgment and decisive dismissal she considered a normal response. Uneasy, she turned away from him and gestured toward the furniture sale that was his living area.

"Nice place. Was there a sale on breakable stuff when you and your wife were furnishing it?"

He made a sound that might have been a laugh. But when she glanced back he was busy with a griddle. He cleared his throat without looking up.

"That's Lenette's taste."

"Where *is* your wife?"

"Gone." His tone was flat.

"I'm sorry your wife is dead," she said. "On Caron 5 we say your wife will live in your heart as her soul lives with the ancestors."

He turned to stare at her. "Lenette isn't dead. She left. Do you always jump to the worst possible conclusion?"

"You said gone." She shouldn't have had to feel defensive, but she did. "How am I supposed to know what you meant by that?"

He shrugged, scowling. "She left the planet. End of story. End of marriage too."

"Does that happen here? I mean, is it allowed?"

"What? Leaving the planet? Of course it's allowed. If you wanted to get on the next ship out, no one would stop you."

Now he was looking at her as if she were weak-minded, which was insulting but at least she had managed to distract him from his original subject. He shook his head and slid a plate of scrambled eggs, toast and sliced myriad in front of her. Then he took his own meal and rested his hips against the cabinet behind him before forking up a bite. The food was good, delicious, in fact, especially the myriad. It was crisp and cool on her tongue, with a lingering sweetness.

"I know *I* could leave the colony. But you said Lenette was your woman, which is why I asked."

He set his plate in the sink and looked at her, waiting, so she continued.

"Once a ring is linked with another, it cannot be undone."

Now his expression was incredulous.

"Is that how they do things on Caron 5?"

She nodded.

"That's ridiculous," he said. "What if you don't get along?"

It was silly to feel offended when she herself had run from a ring linking she had dreaded. But that didn't mean her whole way of life on Caron 5 had been ridiculous. Still, he wasn't making fun, exactly, so she tried to explain it in a way he might understand.

"Getting along isn't the point. Ring linking signifies destiny and therefore perfection."

He rubbed his face with his hands as he formulated a reply.

"So what happens if someone wants out?"

She paused, unsure, and decided on the safe response. "Want doesn't have much to do with it."

Shaking his head, he took her plate and fork and put them in the sink.

"There must be a lot of murders on Caron 5."

Chapter 22

SUNDAYS WERE GENERALLY DEAD QUIET in Sector 1065, and today was Emilio's shift, so technically Poe wasn't on duty until the evening. Even so, he figured he could get a few things done. He frowned at his bulging satchel he had abandoned near the door last night. He had agreed to update the manual on procedures when Teamue had made it an issue, but when he agreed, Poe hadn't realized how large and outdated the manual was. He turned away to hang the skillet on its hook, wishing he had more utensils to wash. Household chores were a great way to feel virtuous while avoiding the inevitable.

Sunday mornings with Lenette had always been a flurry of activity, without, as he could see it, any discernible results—usually cleaning or rearranging something that had been cleaned and rearranged the previous Sunday. He probably should dust. He glanced at the dust catchers in the living room and winced at the thought. Still, the manual would be worse. It wasn't the work itself, he decided, it was that he had to do it on what should have been a day off.

He considered doing some outside chores, gardening maybe. He stared out the front window toward the patch of sturdy weeds and felt a sense of resistance to that too. A flick of movement caught his eye, and he realized the porch swing was swaying gently. When he had insisted on cleaning the kitchen himself, Dilara had scanned the one set of shelves he had succeeded in allotting to books and was now sitting on the swing absorbed in one of the contemporary romances Lenette had left behind.

He edged closer to the window and watched her read. She pushed the toe of her boot against the floorboards every so often to keep the swing moving, and suddenly he wanted nothing more than to join her there. Just an hour, he thought, and then he would get back into the traces and continue hauling the impossibly heavy wagon that was his life uphill. Maybe if he gave himself a short break, he would have more mental energy.

He slid a book he had been putting off reading from the shelf and joined Dilara on the other end of the swing, shoving some of the excess pillows Lenette had collected onto the wide floorboards to make room. The cushions settled into an uneven heap, some imprinted with wholesome sayings and some decorated with those little hard knots and twists of colored thread that made the person who touched them feel unwelcome, no matter what maxim the embroidery illustrated. The clouds overhead were beginning to clear, and a sunbeam touched the porch floor near his feet in a companionable way. He had barely waded through the first boring chapter when Dilara spoke.

"It's different reading paper books. It's slower and it smells different."

He looked up, surprised. She sounded younger, somehow, or at least as if she had given up sounding superior for the moment.

He nodded. "Yeah, I like it better. Or at least sometimes I do." He scowled at the book in his hand.

"What's yours about?" she asked.

"History of Law Enforcement in Sector 36754 before the Intergalactic Police Force was established. There was a lot of action during that period, so I thought it would be interesting reading. But I guess some writers can even manage to make a revolution sound dull. How's yours?"

"Confusing," she said. "Is this how people in Sector 1065 behave?"

He reached toward her and tipped the book so he could see the title: *The Duke's Surprise Baby's Mother's Christmas Wedding.*

"Maybe parts of it?" he said cautiously.

"You said the ring binding in Sector 1065 is not forever." Her tone was accusing. "But in here it is. See?"

She pointed to the last page.

"You couldn't have read that quickly," he protested.

She didn't take the bait but just watched him with her sharp gaze. He didn't roll his eyes, but he had to work at it.

"Okay," he said finally. "A book like that isn't totally wrong. Everyone hopes their wedding means forever when they get married. But sometimes, later, it just doesn't work out."

"Like you and Lenette."

He nodded.

"Because you were autocratic and distant like this duke. And you did not believe her child was yours."

"What? No! No, that's not..."

Dilara gestured toward the living room. "Perhaps she did not enjoy so many figurines and so much furniture. It is quite crowded in there."

Poe was proud he put his book aside without slamming it. He walked toward the front door, but once he had opened it, the urge to enter passed. What was the point after all? He couldn't outrun history. But he could put this young woman in her place. He turned to stare at the weeping willow leaning at an angle in his yard, anger pulsing in his arms, whooshing in his ears. He had a sudden desire to say something cutting, anything to get her to back off.

But the expression on her face told him she hadn't intended to hurt him, at least not in the way she had. So he held his tongue and for the first time since Lenette had left, he allowed himself to assess the cabin he called home the way a stranger might. More than the stupid knickknacks with their dust laden doilies, more than those God-awful clowns, he hated the stupid pillows and framed mottoes with their smug sayings. Forever Love. What an idiot he had been.

For the past year he had hoped he was wrong. Lenette would come back. She would tell him she had been foolish and that she had never meant to hurt him. She would tell him she had simply forgotten to take her wedding ring with her when she left. She would explain about the contraceptive pills he had found hidden in the back of her night table drawer one day months after she had left when he was looking for a sewing kit to tighten a loose button.

But she hadn't meant any of it. Not her wedding vows, not her exclamations of pleasure in being part of his family, certainly not her often professed desire for children. And now, as he gazed at the relics of his marriage crowding him from every side, his stomach tightened with revulsion, and it was all he could do to stop from slamming the door shut and fleeing to his office.

"Did I say something wrong?" Dilara seemed curious, maybe a little surprised, but not in the least apologetic.

He shook his head as though that would clear his brain.

"No. Well, yes." He gestured broadly at the room. "Lenette and I didn't have children. Turned out she didn't want them. And she decided to leave Sector 1065 because she wanted a different life than I could provide her."

Dilara's brows shot up, and she gave him an incredulous look. But he cut her off before she had the chance to try to soothe him with some sort of platitude. Although, to be fair, soothing him didn't seem to be her style. Instead, she changed the subject.

"Want to tell me why you're really here?" he asked.

"You invited—oh, you mean why I'm in Sector 1065?"

"And don't say you came here to work at BangBang," he continued. "No one in their right mind would make that mistake."

He wasn't proud of it, but he enjoyed her sudden wariness. Anything that kept her off the topic of his life or the lack of it was okay with him. He could practically see the gears turning as she worked to formulate a response, and he couldn't resist goading her.

"Trying to avoid the ring linking of destiny?"

He hadn't expected to score a hit, but her sudden pallor showed him he had. She swallowed and stood, stacking the two books before turning to face him. He had seen condemned prisoners who looked less uneasy.

"I, um," she stopped and started again. "It's complicated."

"I have time." He walked back to the swing and patted the space next to him.

She ignored the gesture. "Were you telling me the truth, before, about not having to stay linked here?" she asked.

"Yes. It's called divorce."

"Divorce," she pronounced the word carefully. "What if you don't wish to be betrothed in the first place?"

"You mean getting engaged? Well, it's not obligatory. I always thought of engagement as more of a trial run, but some folks don't bother with an engagement. What are we talking about exactly?"

She took a deep breath and let it out as she sank down to sit beside him. Instead of looking at him as she spoke, she picked up the novel and set it on her lap, staring at it as she absently smoothed the cover. She held it in position with her stump, and something in him loosened at the knowledge she felt comfortable enough with him to forget about hiding it.

"My parents betrothed me to a man named Mart Henkelor. It was so my younger sister Saskia could...marry." She said the word tentatively and then continued with more sureness when he didn't speak. "I am the eldest, so Saskia cannot be betrothed until I am, but of course there was no one who wanted me."

He turned to look at her, but her delivery was so matter of fact, he wondered if he had misheard.

"Why not?"

With an impatient expression, she gestured toward her right arm and continued.

"My parents were correct in their actions. And if I were a more obedient daughter, I would have bowed to their gracious offer. But I will not link rings with anyone, and rather than stain the family reputation more than I already had, I left."

He sat back and thought a moment. Given the stiffness of her delivery, he figured the parts of her story she was telling him were likely true. But there were some gaping holes there too, and from the way she was gripping that book, she didn't want to fill any of them in.

Okay with him, he decided. Sector 1065 had always been a landing spot for fugitives in one way or another. The founders were farmers fleeing what they considered the commercialization of agriculture on Earth. Many of the men who worked for Melchior, even some of the executives, were vague about their own histories and it was considered socially inappropriate to delve too deeply. Some of the merchants along with most of the friendlies had sheets. Dilara would fit right in.

"Wanna go catch some geithers?"

Her grip on the book suddenly loosened, and he cupped his hand under hers in time to catch it before it hit the floor. His fingers brushed hers as he curled his hand around the spine of the book. The smooth surface was warm from her palm, and suddenly he felt freer than he had in months.

"What's a geither?" she said.

"I'll show you," he replied, heading down the porch stairs. "Come on."

He hadn't been to the brook in over twenty years, hadn't thought about catching geithers in about that long. But when he and his brothers, Emmer, Lindo and Hawt, had been boys, there had been nothing they loved more. Even Mindin, their big sister, had always found an excuse to join in on geither days.

He wasn't sure what had brought the memory to mind today except that for a moment, when he watched Dilara turning that stupid novel, he had wondered what sort of childhood she had. It seemed to him there would not have been much laughter, or mischief in it. Some of it was her missing hand, maybe. But he guessed it probably had more to do with that family honor she had alluded to.

His own family was the closest thing to old nobility Sector 1065 had. The Lancasters were founders, one of six original homesteading families who had established the original settlement, so there was a kind of honor there too and a reputation to uphold. And there had been plenty of pressure on him and on his sister and brothers to live up to the family creed. But even back then, he hadn't felt the weight of social responsibility Dilara had expressed.

"What do you do with geithers when you catch them? And what are these buckets for?"

It was the second time she had asked, he realized.

"You'll see."

"Can you eat them?"

"Not unless you want a stomachache."

Chapter 23

THE SUN WAS HOT ON DILARA'S SHOULDERS as she followed Poe. The scent of freshly turned soil from the fields to her left mingled with the dust brushed up as her boots scuffed along the dirt road. There was a large messiness to it all, a kind of glorious haphazardness. Not the fields, themselves—they were orderly enough. But flowering vines draped themselves over the stone walls, bird songs she didn't recognize overlapped with those she did and the woods to her right were overgrown with weeds and fallen timber in various states of rot.

This was nothing like Caron 5 with its pruned hedgerows, manicured lawns and strict gardening procedures. Discipline reigned on her parents' properties. No leaf dared reach for the sun if it meant ruining the cubic cut of its parent plant. Saskia had once suggested that Dilara's flaw must have been a result of being pruned as a baby. It had been a joke, of course, if a cruel one. But Dilara had since wondered if there had been a hidden truth there. She forced herself to look up and blinked. The road ahead was empty. Puzzled, she stopped in her tracks, wondering if she had wandered past Poe while she was lost in thought.

"Are you coming?"

Startled, she whipped around. His clothes blended with the forest colors so well, if he hadn't beckoned, she might not have seen him. Gingerly she stepped forward. There was a winding path through the trees, but some sort of clinging vine with tiny thorns had grown across much of the entrance from the road. She managed to squeeze through without scratching herself too badly and trotted to catch up with Poe. Despite its hidden air, the path was well trodden and mostly smooth.

Even so, as the path wound its way downward, she had to concentrate on her footing. There were several tricky root networks to negotiate as well as a large boulder. At one point, Poe paused, ostensibly to tighten his boot laces. But he took a long time about it, and she wondered if he had stopped to give her a chance to catch her breath. The idea was irritating, all the more so because he was right. Two weeks on the MacLaren hadn't done her stamina any favors. She looked up at the canopy of new leaves far above and some of her irritation dissipated.

"I can see why you like coming here," she said.

"Yeah." He nodded, stretching. "It makes you feel small and unimportant. Sometimes that's a good thing."

"And it's quiet." It wasn't that there was no noise. The leaves rustled, birds sang far above and there were mysterious rustles in the undergrowth that might have made her uneasy if she hadn't been pretty sure Poe didn't intend to have her actually eaten by geithers, whatever they were. And somewhere below, she could hear water flowing. But there was an overarching hush, the magnitude of which seemed to have a weight in itself.

He came to a stop at a brook sunk deep between its banks. The water swirled gently, lapping at the shore with tiny splashes. It was shallow enough she could see the rocks under the rippling surface, rounded and mottled in shades of brown. Without speaking, Poe handed her one of his buckets and squatted to scoop handfuls of pebbles and water into his own.

Following his lead, she slid down too, her boots landing ankle deep in the water. After considering her options, she angled her bucket so the water would flow into it and then wedged it in position with her foot while dipping her cupped hand into the brook to roll pebbles into it. The stones rolled smoothly through her fingers until the bottom of her bucket was filled with a miniature version of the brook itself. Getting the bucket out turned out to be more of a challenge. It was heavy and there was no good way to get it up the bank to level ground without spilling it or falling into the brook herself. Before she had to ask, Poe's hand grasped the bucket handle and hauled it up, leaving her to scramble up the bank behind him.

"Where are we going now?"

She gasped as her boot caught on a root and she nearly went down.

"Here."

He settled onto a patch of moss in the deep shadow under a wide gnarled tree and patted the space next to him. Mystified, Dilara sat down beside him. With a sigh he pulled the still dripping pail onto his lap and leaned back against the broad trunk behind them, adjusting his shoulders until he found a comfortable spot and closed his eyes. Feeling foolish but unsure what her options were at this point, she imitated him and waited for something to happen. Or for him to start laughing at what was probably some sort of "make fun of the foreigner" practical joke. But he didn't laugh. Instead he just sat there silently, so she did too, until she felt the bucket move.

At first it was just a sort of shiver, the merest tremor, so slight she thought she had imagined it. But when she glanced at Poe, the corners of his lips were curved upward and she knew she hadn't. Her hand tightened on the edge of the bucket, and she decided if she had to she would throw the pail and its contents as far as she could and scramble in the other direction. If Poe thought she was a coward, so be it. He was a jerk for—she stopped mid thought and stared.

On the surface of the water in the pail, she suddenly saw motion. She looked closer and startled when she realized the pebbles at the bottom were subdividing, glowing as they did so. A minuscule light flew out from the top of her bucket, and then another until there was a disorganized swirl of thousands of tiny sparks dancing and flickering in the air. When there were no more left to emerge from her bucket, they twisted into a loose spiral, arcing high and flitting through the air as they streamed back toward the brook and disappeared into the water. She glanced at Poe. He was grinning, as much she thought at her reaction as at the event itself. Despite herself, she laughed.

"How did you ever discover this?"

"My brother, Emmer, showed me. We practically lived in the woods as kids. It was our favorite place to play."

"And your parents allowed you to do this—to run in the woods by yourselves?"

"It was perfectly safe," he said. "Sector 1065 was a great place to grow up and it still is. Out here in the farming community, crime is rare and people look out for each other. Mind you, we kids were always tracking brook mud into the house back then. It drove Ma crazy. And when it came to bringing geithers home as pets, she put her foot down."

Dilara felt envy touch her. She had seen other children running and jumping, shouting for the sheer pleasure of being able to, but Dilara had learned early on that an Elian didn't play. Even casting wishful looks at those children would occasion a reprimand. She pushed the thought away. More than the missed opportunities of her childhood, knowing a parent could be like that stung.

"How many brothers do you have?"

"Three brothers, one older than me and two younger. And we have a big sister too. That's Minden. She's married now with kids and a farm of her own. Emmer is next. He lives just outside of town. He's a baker and he lives over his store. Then there's me. Lindo and Hawt are the babies, twins. They still live with Ma and Pop and work the farm. Pop's training them to take it over when the time's right."

She felt that lick of envy again but this time accompanied by disbelief.

"And your father accepts this?"

He blinked. "Why wouldn't he?"

"Two of his children have rejected his way of life and everything he has worked for."

Poe cleared his throat. "That's an interesting way to look at it. Is that how it works on Caron 5?"

She opened her mouth and then closed it again, abashed. It seemed she was constantly making errors in judgment when it came to manners and mores in Sector 1065. But how was she to know that parents here were so lax with their children? Or maybe lax was the wrong word. She turned the thought over in her mind.

"What do you call it," she asked finally, "when you let someone do what they want even if you aren't happy about it? Like your mother did. Or like your father does with you and Emmer. Is there a word for that?"

"First of all, Pop isn't unhappy with me and Emmer. Even if none of us had chosen farming life, he would have been okay with it. He and Ma just wanted us all to be happy in our own ways. That's just love. Wouldn't you want your children to chase their dreams?"

She shrugged and didn't respond. The concept was so foreign it was hard to know what to say. Children didn't have dreams, their parents had them. A child's obligation was to fulfill those dreams, which was why she had failed so spectacularly since the day of her birth. Still, when she had stared out the porthole at Caron 5 growing smaller in the distance as the MacLaren catapulted from its dock into the star-spangled darkness, she had experienced a moment of such overwhelming relief even now she could feel the remnants of it. It was as though she had been living with a boulder on her chest her entire life without realizing it.

She didn't notice he was standing until he reached down to grab her bucket. Clambering down to the brook, he emptied both buckets and nested them together before striding back to join her.

· "Ready to go?" he asked.

She nodded, surprised to see that the sun was already high overhead. He wiped his free hand on his jacket and reached down to her, palm extended. She hesitated and then put her hand on his, scrambling to her feet in the epitome of ungainliness. It shouldn't matter what he thought of her, she reminded herself, but somehow it did. He didn't let go of her hand right away and when he did, she missed the warmth and solidity of it.

To cover her sudden embarrassment, she asked, "Was being a marshal your dream?"

He laughed. "Not by a long shot. For a while my family despaired of my ever making anything of myself. When I wasn't in the principal's office, I spent most of my time in school in the back row of my classroom coming up with ways to get myself in trouble. How about you? Did you always want to sing for drunken farmers and miners in a rundown tavern?"

She flicked a glance on him, but he wasn't making fun of her. He waited for her response, his gaze intent and oddly warm. There was a seductive quality to being the focus of his attention. She would have to be careful about that, she decided. It would be easy to confuse interest with affection. Easier still to like him more than she should.

"Not exactly. I wanted to sing since, I think, forever, but it wasn't possible for obvious reasons."

"Because?"

She felt her cheeks redden and she pulled her hand from his.

"I am flawed."

"I don't see why that should stop you." His tone was mild.

She took a deep breath and let it out, holding on to her patience.

"That's because you grew up here, so you are used to mediocrity."

His brows shot up.

"You are a perfect example," she continued. "You were a troublesome child who did not value law and order. On Caron 5, the thought of someone like you imposing rules would be laughable. Our courses are set at birth."

"You don't believe that," he said. "You came here. So you changed your course."

He was right, but he was also wrong. Just because she had revolted on her own behalf didn't mean the whole system was incorrect. And she had additional reasons, painfully private ones, for leaving Caron 5, which were none of his business. The entire conversation felt dangerous, as though she had stepped onto a lily pad and any additional movement would result in disaster. Still, it felt important to make him understand.

"It's not that change is impossible or discouraged on Caron 5. But the goal, as it should be in life, is excellence. Naturally, every citizen can stand some improvement. But in most cases it's more a matter of refinement and polishing over time. A brilliant mind can become more learned. A talented artist can hone his skill.

"In my case, it's more of a challenge. Symmetry and aesthetics are signs of inner worth as well as measures of divine favor. So if one is born flawed, one is accorded greater responsibility, which is a blessing as well as a burden. Refinement, in my case, is simply a more difficult and painful process than it would be for someone like my sister."

"She's perfect, is she?"

"Of course not, but Saskia lives up to parental and societal expectations and in some cases exceeds them. I do not."

"That's an insane standard. No wonder you left."

Oddly he was looking at her with a kind of respect. She scuffed the toe of her boot against a lump of vegetation and then smoothed the leaves back into position. It was the conclusion she had come to also, but it was different hearing that harsh assessment from an off-planet person. Her throat was tight, and she made a conscious effort to ease the muscles there before trying to get him to understand.

"I didn't leave because the expectations were unreasonable. I left because I was weak and failed in my responsibility to my parents and to the community. The longer I stayed the more damage I would have caused them."

"Damage?"

She nodded. "Socially, absolutely. The Elian clan is second only to the Leader clan, and Saskia's match will strengthen the family's position considerably."

"I still don't understand why you couldn't sing professionally there. It would have been a way to make your family proud."

She shook her head, smiling at the idea. "No one with an obvious flaw like mine would be allowed to perform in front of citizens. Flaws are a curse on a family and an insult to society."

"And you believe that?"

"I, I don't know anymore. I did believe in it once. Everyone around me did."

"And now?"

"Now I think maybe it was a wrong way to think. But I don't know what the right way is yet."

He stood for a moment, watching her, and then nodded.

"I think Ma left some cheese for sandwiches. Are you

hungry?"

She nodded and followed him through the trees, and when they reached the road, he draped his arm over her shoulder as they turned toward the cabin. Her heart warmed a little at his touch. Or perhaps it was the sunshine on her shoulder. In any case, it felt right. Not good. She knew where falling in love with a man led. It led to pretending he loved you back and ultimately to being party to breaking your own heart. She wasn't going that route ever again.

Chapter 24

THE RAIN ON MONDAY WAS TORRENTIAL. After Poe left the cabin, Dilara spent the morning and much of the afternoon reading the remaining books of any interest on Poe's shelves and was now facing the unpleasant probability that she would have to read the uninteresting ones. To avoid making that decision, she went into her bedroom and unpacked her few belongings. She was unlikely to be staying with Poe long, but it seemed sensible to hang her clothing before the wrinkles became permanent.

She was going to have to buy another gown as soon as she could afford one. She hadn't had time yet to mend the burgundy, still torn from the night of the riot and the remaining two she owned were hardly eye catching. There was only so much an artistically draped shawl could accomplish. She had noticed a tailor shop in the center of town, but pay day was five days away so until then the plain gown would have to suffice. The one she was wearing now, her second best, was made of a dull yellowish-brown fabric, chosen by Wraya for durability rather than style. In retrospect, this was puzzling.

Dilara didn't expect to dress beautifully or in a way that would draw attention—her flaw made that impractical. But there was a difference between serviceable and downright ugly. She eyed herself in the long mirror that stood in the corner of the crowded guest room. The jagged hair didn't help.

She swallowed and sank down onto the edge of the bed. She had been so sure she was resigned to the necessity of a life lived alone she hadn't accounted for longing. But on Sunday morning as she and Poe sat companionably reading on the porch swing, a treacherous yearning had tugged at her, whispering of things that were, on their face, impossible. Resentment was unreasonable, she knew. Especially it was unfair to resent Poe for being what he was—attractive, generous, and most of all kind under his gruff veneer. Still, as she rose, she nearly slipped on a nubby throw rug embroidered with the phrase "Truly Toasty Toesies" and her desire to kick it across the room was surprisingly strong.

She liked Poe, she acknowledged. As a friend, she amended quickly. She hadn't had friends on Caron 5, per se, but she was pretty sure that the way she felt about Poe was the definition of friendship. The thought it might be something more was worrisome because what she felt toward him was quite different than anything she had ever felt for Alexandr—stronger and more visceral.

Her knapsack would be lighter now, she realized. Slowly she wrapped her sheets of music in a scrap of cloth to keep them dry and tucked them into the very bottom of the bag. In a sense, now that she was working, she felt lighter too. It was disconcerting to think of herself as an independent woman, the sort of person who could make her own decisions and who could afford mistakes. She shivered and went into the kitchen to heat the kettle.

The rain had slowed by the time Poe arrived home, shaking droplets from his duster as he draped it over a hook behind the door. As she finished rinsing her cup, he paused to watch her. She had noticed this before about him, the way he stopped completely to assess a situation. He nearly missed putting his hat on its hook, but his focus was completely on her. In other circumstances, it might have been flattering.

"Want me to heat up yesterday's casserole for dinner?" he asked.

She shook her head. "Thank you for your kind invitation, but I want to get to BangBang early this evening to go over a few new pieces."

He gave his hat a shake and hung it on the hook next to his duster.

"Once we've eaten, I'll drive you into town."

"Thank you for your kind invitation," she repeated, "but—"

"Would you stop that?"

He looked annoyed, and she glanced to the floor as she mentally replayed the conversation, searching for what she might have done wrong. Mystified, she looked at him and her confusion must have been evident to him as well, although it seemed to make him no less annoyed.

"Stop thanking me all the time," he growled. "And I wasn't *inviting* you for a drive. Nothing wrong with walking into town alone in daylight, but it's a bad idea at night. Just like working at BangBang is a bad idea." He scowled and turned away from her toward the stove.

"I have to be back at the office this evening," he continued as he moved the pot from the refrigeration to the stove, "so I'm going in that direction anyway. I'll be working late, but I'll speak to Porky about escorting you back here when you are done creating havoc for the night. What's on this evening's program—civil insurrection?"

She satisfied herself by sticking her tongue out at his back and had a childish sense of delight when she managed to force her expression into an adult one just as he turned toward her again. He was right, she guessed. Well, not about the civil insurrection thing, but about traveling alone at night. Most of the individuals she had met in Sector 1065 were polite enough in a rough sort of way, when they weren't riled up. But there had been a few, like Saur and Borin, who were more worrisome. And the idea of meeting either of them alone on a deserted road at night didn't bear thinking about.

"I'm running all my selections by Mr. Lummon before I add them to the list," she said.

"Good idea. I'm surprised Rudolph didn't catch the problem song in the first place."

She had her own suspicions on that matter, which was why she was planning to show the songs to Porky ahead of time, not Rudolph. But she didn't clarify. Poe had solved several problems for her since she had met him, and she didn't want relying on his good will to become a dangerous habit. She had a poor record when it came to judging character, and now that she had become aware of that weakness in the most painful way possible, she wasn't planning to forget it.

"I will also ask Mr. Lummon if he has any suggestions for lodging closer to town," she said.

He frowned. "There's no rush. You're welcome to stay here as long as you need."

The wash of guilt stung. She hadn't meant to be discourteous. In many ways Poe had been kinder to her than anyone else in her life. Still, she wondered whether kindness came with its own dangers. Her mother had ordered a small ivy plant included in the garden once against the advice of the gardener. Wraya had delighted in the tiny perfection of the leaves and delicate tendrils until the plant wrapped itself around a nearby tree and nearly killed it. Wraya had fired the gardener.

"Perhaps when Mr. Lummon pays me, I can give some of the money to you."

The corner if his lips twitched. "If it makes you feel better, you can. But it's not necessary. The room is just sitting empty."

Still, she thought it would make her feel better. Independence was even sweeter now that she had experienced it, and she didn't want to let go of it for the sake of a new gown. She would make do with the ones she had until she could afford a better option.

Chapter 25

"SOME WOMAN'S ASKING FOR YOU, DILARA."

Titch had risen from the staff table at dinnertime the next day to answer the polite but insistent knocking on BangBang's door, but Dilara hadn't even bothered to look up from the exceptional stew in her bowl. The only person likely to look for her was Poe, who had dropped her off earlier that afternoon, and he wouldn't have bothered to knock. Now she rose uncertainly. A searcher wouldn't have found her this quickly, she reassured herself, and a searcher would have no need to disguise himself as a woman. She considered asking Titch for a description but decided that would draw too much attention. Better to just handle it. The cavernous public area felt chilly after the warmth of the kitchen, and her heart sank when she recognized Mrs. Onkelson in the dim light.

"Oh, thank goodness." Mrs. Onkelson fluttered a hand against her ample bosom. "Ngendo and Kiko said you never returned to the room after the picnic and then Jenkson told me you had moved out of the hotel, and I've been beside myself with worry. The lieutenant and I asked at the marshal's office and Emilio, the deputy there, said he hadn't seen you but that he thought you worked here. Are you all right, dear?"

Dilara edged closer so their conversation need not be overheard by curious staff, but not too close. She was at a loss. She had expected recriminations, a demand for payment in arrears perhaps, certainly not concern. Mrs. Onkelson looked alarmingly likely to hug her.

Dilara took a step back. "I apologize for having worried you and the lieutenant. I am safe and healthy and, as you see, I have found a method to earn a living."

Mrs. Onkelson's eyes widened.

"Mr. Lummon hired me to sing here every night," Dilara added hastily.

She swallowed a grin as relief flooded Mrs. Onkelson's face. Dilara knew some people thought poorly of the sex worker profession. Guerenne had made a pointed comment during one of the tours. But the friendlies Dilara had met at BangBang had lived up to their job title. And they were uniformly far more physically attractive than Dilara would ever be, so it was hard to know whether to feel insulted or flattered at Mrs. Onkelson's assumption.

"Well, you can't stay here, dear. People will get the wrong idea. Run and get your bag, and we'll get you settled in at the hotel again. All the women miss you."

A bit of an exaggeration, Dilara thought, but still a kindly sentiment and well meant. Unfortunately it was also a dangerous idea. Initially staying among the other women had seemed the best strategy—the group provided a camouflage of sorts. But in Poe's cabin she felt truly safe.

"I thank you for your kind invitation," she said, "but I have found suitable lodging elsewhere."

Mrs. Onkelson blanched. "Not up there?" She gestured toward the brothel above. "Your reputation would be ruined, my dear."

With some effort Dilara forced a bubble of hysterical laughter back down. The thought of having any reputation left to salvage was ludicrous.

"No. The lodging I have found is exceptionally respectable."

"Excellent! I know several of the locals provide bed and board." Curiosity sparked in Mrs. Onkelson's eyes. "Who is it, dear?"

Stalling, Dilara busied herself straightening some chairs. One could hardly get more respectable and law abiding than the town marshal. Still, Mrs. Onkelson might not approve of a Well-Wed woman living with a single man she had no intention of marrying.

The bigger issue was other people knowing. A competent searcher, and Wraya would have hired the best, would ask questions. Poe knew, of course. And Stig did too. But neither of them was likely to volunteer the information to anyone else. Poe hadn't even told his family she was living in his cabin.

Despite Mrs. Onkelson's chattiness, she wasn't a gossip. But once Mrs. Onkelson knew, her husband would know. She might, for instance tell Ngendo or Kiko to reassure them, or Jenkson, as a way to chide him. The dangerous circle of people who knew where Dilara was would spread even wider with each well-meant conversation. Heart sinking, she grasped for the best distraction she could think of.

"I hope this will not exclude me from the wonderful activities you have planned for our group, Mrs. Onkelson."

Clapping her hands together, Mrs. Onkelson beamed.

"Never, dear. I have a copy of our schedule of events right here in my bag. I do hope you enter the talent show."

Five endless minutes later, as the door closed behind Mrs. Onkelson, Dilara sank into a chair. She had managed not to lie outright. Still, refraining from telling the truth was also cause for punishment, and the penalty was on the crisp square of paper in her hand.

The list of programmed events she had agreed to attend was painfully long. It included lectures on local history that did sound interesting along with varied opportunities to mix and mingle with Melchior executives, which she suspected would be mortifying. The worst was a formal dance scheduled for the Saturday night after next. After having promised she would attend, she could hardly back out of it now. Then there was the talent show. She didn't love the idea, but at least she knew what her talent was.

Unfortunately, she couldn't use work as an excuse to avoid either event. As recently as that afternoon, Porky had reminded her she was due for a vacation day. She hadn't taken an evening off since she had begun at BangBang a month ago, as much because she enjoyed the work as because she needed the money. But if she used BangBang as an excuse to avoid Well-Wed events people would start asking questions.

At least she wouldn't have to worry about keeping a low profile at the dance. Compared to the other Well-Wed women, who would be dressed in their most elegant gowns, she would be nearly invisible. Perhaps once the dancing began she would be able to slip away, having fulfilled the letter of the obligation if not the spirit of it.

She folded up the list and walked back into the kitchen to put it into her knapsack. Most of the staff and friendlies had scattered to begin their preparations for the evening, but Rudolph remained at the long table, scowling into a steaming mug of tea. She almost backed out again, but he looked up and his scowl deepened.

"What do you want?"

Without responding, she marched to her knapsack and shoved the paper in before turning to meet his gaze. But he had already lost interest and was staring into the depths of his mug as though the unpleasant answer to a vexing question lurked there.

"What is it that you dislike about me?"

The question popped out almost without her volition, and the moment it did she wished she could pull it back. She could not afford to look weak, here of all places. He flicked a glance at her and shrugged.

"You are not important enough to dislike," he said.

Shaking her head, she left the kitchen, closing the door quietly behind her as she had been taught. He was right. She wasn't important to him or to anyone else. But it would have been nice to have the answer to her question anyway.

Chapter 26

POE REACHED FOR HIS PENCIL, BUT THE TIPS of his fingers were a fraction off, and it rolled off the edge and under the desk. Sighing, he rose to pick it up but instead of settling back into his seat, he slotted the pencil into its cup and grabbed his hat. There was no point in trying to focus on paperwork when he was this restless. Nothing much ever happened in Sector 1065 in the early morning quiet on a weekday after the bars were shut. He would do one more patrol and then he would go home. He felt a tingle of anticipation. It was always interesting going back to the cabin now that Dilara was there.

He just enjoyed her company, he reassured himself. There was nothing wrong with that. It was easy to relax with Dilara, probably because she had no agenda. In that sense, he found her restful. Well, not always restful, he grinned. Still, there was a kind of advantage in knowing she would be leaving the planet as soon as she could scrape together the money to do so. It meant he could like her as much as he wanted without any real risk.

He strode down the middle of the moonlit street, enjoying the nip in the air and the sense that he was the only one awake. But as he turned, he saw a flicker of light in the deserted farmers market between Rank's General Store and the Mercantile. It disappeared so quickly he wasn't sure whether his eyes were playing tricks on him. Then in the darkness near the Mercantile, a darker shadow moved.

There was no reasonable excuse for anyone to be in that alley at this time of the night, and the alley shouldn't have been dark. The farmers often left debris when they broke down their stalls at the end of the day so Darius, who ran the Mercantile, always left a light on over the door at night. That way he could enter through the alley door in the pre-dawn hours all year long without having to worry about tripping. The bulb might have simply gone out, but the hairs prickled on the back of Poe's neck, and he had learned to pay attention to that sensation.

Quickly, but quietly, he approached. Using the porch of the Mercantile for cover, he peeped around the corner. Nothing moved. Still he waited a silent moment before slipping around the corner and into the dark of the alley. Now that his eyes had adjusted, he could see a faint light glowing around the edges of the door to the Mercantile where it was propped open a finger's width. Silently he scanned the ground and reached for a thick bit of planking someone had conveniently abandoned. Then he edged closer to the door, but before he could make his move, the door swung open. The shadow he had seen earlier had been large and broad, but this man, hunched over to accommodate the weight of a large sack on his back, was smaller.

"Drop it," Poe said.

Without a word, the man let the sack slide off his back and sprinted toward Second Street. Poe left the sack where it was and took off after him, but the sound of hoof beats fading into the distance told him he was too late. Curious, he headed back to the abandoned sack of loot. He reached up to the light fixture and was not surprised to find the bulb had been loosened. In the pool of gentle light, he opened the scrap of rope holding the sack shut. He stepped back and stared at the contents. This made no sense.

Carefully he stepped around the sack and walked into the Mercantile. The door opened directly into the back area of the store. Darius' office hugged the wall of a cavernous storage area. Here he kept all the bulky items too big to house in the crowded main room of the store. Also he had stacked ceiling-high piles of gardening supplies in preparation for sowing time, which would arrive any week now. Despite the size of the space it was filled to capacity, but it was tidy nonetheless. The sacks of seed bags and potting soil were neat and square. But one pallet had been decimated.

Poe called Darius from the office, telling him only that there had been a break-in, and wasn't surprised when the store owner met him at the front of the Mercantile ten minutes later, rumpled and furious.

"These Mnoani kids are outrageous!" he said. "Something ought to be done about them—first Borin's farm and now this. Where will it end?"

Poe saw no reason to respond to the assumption just yet. Pop called it reflex bias based on ignorance. Poe just called it hatred. But no amount of arguing about unjust accusations was going to solve the problem. Besides, Darius had a right to be angry, he was just aiming his anger at whatever target was simplest.

"This wasn't a kid," Poe said mildly. "I saw two grown men. Can you look through your inventory and tell me what's missing?"

Darius threw his hands up. "Didn't you see the sign outside, *1001 Items Every Day*? I can't inspect the entire store at a glance."

Grumbling, Darius unlocked the front door of the Mercantile. First he checked the safe embedded in the wall behind the counter. Once he found that undisturbed he calmed a bit and began a methodic scan of the shelves and display cabinets. The door between the customer area and the storeroom didn't appear to have been tampered with either. As they entered the storeroom Darius looked mystified and, to his credit, embarrassed.

"Sorry for losing my temper," he said. "I know I shouldn't leap to conclusions. But just last week your lady deputy arrested a Mnoani boy who tried to lift one of my Replica 2020 Pocket Knives. He stuck it in his pocket and tried to walk out the door as jaunty as you please. If I hadn't caught him, he would have told all his friends, and my store would have been a target for every light-fingered kid in the colony. But I can't imagine what anyone would want to steal back here."

Poe nodded. "Zela told me about that incident," he said. "But tonight's robber wasn't a kid, and I don't think you had a whole lot of replica pocketknives on that pallet."

He pointed toward the far corner. Darius wheeled around to stare at the depleted pallet, his eyes wide.

"Well, that takes the cake," he said. "Why the heck would

anyone steal all my bovoquin manure?"

Chapter 27

DILARA FINISHED DRYING THE PLATE AND PUT IT on the stack in the cupboard. She liked tidiness, but Poe's living space was so cluttered as a whole, even if she had dusted every knickknack, the cabin would have felt a mess. The kitchen was the only place where there was no superfluity. Every item had a purpose and a place.

The guest bedroom where she slept was no better than the living area. By daylight, the flounced bed coverings, cutesy porcelain figurines and fussy skirts around things that shouldn't have skirts were hard to ignore. Even the wallpaper was overwhelmed with flowers. Altogether, it was a more pleasant space when one's eyes were closed.

There were hours left before she had to leave for BangBang, and she had already finished planning her music set for the evening. She only needed one for weekday nights. She had just decided to spend a pleasant hour taking a walk in the sunshine when she heard footsteps on the porch. For a moment she stiffened. Poe wasn't due back until later, and this step sounded lighter than his. As the door swung open, she grabbed the frying pan from its hook.

A young woman bustled in, one arm draped with laden bags and the other wrapped around a toddler on her hip. Dilara turned to put the frying pan back and took the moment to fix a polite smile on her face. This was not a searcher. The woman hoisted the bags onto the counter and hiked the boy higher on her hip.

"What are you doing here?" she asked.
Dilara stiffened. "Poe invited me."
The woman's hair was a joyous explosion of copper curls, but

her gaze was assessing and not particularly warm.

"I'm his sister, Minden. You must be one of those Well-Wedders."

Dilara gestured toward the smaller bedroom in case Minden had the wrong idea.

"He's letting me stay in the guest room."

Minden sniffed and began removing jars of preserves from the bags while pointedly ignoring Dilara. The baby however, intrigued by a new face, gurgled and then burst into a radiant smile. Dilara carefully looked away. The child was so enchanting she had almost forgotten her manners.

"You don't like babies?" Minden sounded offended, but there was a note of triumph there too, as though her suspicions had been proved correct.

"No, I do." Dilara, shocked at the injustice of it, met Minden's eyes. "Of course I do. How could one not…your child is beautiful."

The habitual Caron 5 greeting felt both reassuring and painful as it popped out—the words flowed easily, but the aftertaste was bitter. Mollified, Minden gestured at the child. "Then hold him for a moment while I put these jars away. There are so many knick-knacks in this cabin, there's no way I can set him loose."

Dilara froze. Children of five or older were strong enough to withstand the risk of seeing a flaw—they had already been schooled in the importance of beauty, wholeness and perfection. But everyone on Caron 5 knew that an infant could be permanently damaged by looking into the eyes of a flawed one. Minden seemed to be an attentive mother. Did she not understand the danger to her child, or had she simply forgotten?

Still, it seemed important not to offend Minden. She was Poe's sister after all. The question of *how* to not offend her was the problem. Perhaps, Dilara thought, she could manage to hold the child and still keep him safe from the danger she presented if she kept her eyes from meeting his. With her eyes fixed on Minden's face, she sidled forward cautiously.

"He doesn't bite." Minden's tone was sarcastic. "Haven't you ever held a kid before?"

Dilara shook her head. The mothering courses, which had been obligatory for Saskia, had been unnecessary for Dilara.

"Oh, for heaven's sake. Don't they teach you anything in those stupid Well-Wed classes? Just pretend he's a sack of grain and try not to drop him."

Minden thrust the child toward Dilara and Dilara grabbed him reflexively, pulling him to her hip. He was heavy, solid, warm. His hands patted her back and shoulder. His breath smelled sweet. There had to be consequences for this feeling. When she was sure he was looking away from her, she risked a glance at him. His cheeks were soft, pudgy. There was a dimple on his chin and his curly ringlets fluffed out, brushing against her shoulder with the lightest of touches.

Rising from stowing the preserves, Minden brushed her hands on her skirt and reached for the boy. Reluctantly Dilara surrendered him. She was lucky to have had the chance to hold a baby once, she reminded herself firmly. The opportunity was unlikely to arise again.

"Would you like a cool drink?" she asked. "I made some iced tea."

Minden shot her a doubtful look but then nodded. "I can spare a few minutes. Let's sit on the porch so Henry can run around on the grass."

A few minutes later, settled in the rocking chairs, Minden stirred sugar into her tea.

"It is kind of you to bring your brother food."

Minden snorted. "We have more myriads than we know what to do with this week. If I don't preserve them, they'll go to waste. Besides, Poe will return the favor when his ola tree bears fruit. What do you want from Poe?" Minden asked, shooting Dilara a piercing glance.

"I..." Dilara paused, at a loss.

Minden looked impatient. "He already had one bad experience with a Well-Wed woman, and he sure doesn't need another. There are plenty of fine girls from founding families who are willing to give him a chance if he just nods at them. Any one of them would be a better match for him than someone from away, especially a woman who expects to make her fortune by marrying him."

Henry shrieked in delight at a beetle he had found and then, in his excitement he accidentally stepped on it. By the time Minden had comforted him with a toy from her pocket, Dilara couldn't contain her curiosity.

"Is that what happened with Lenette?"

Minden took a slow sip of her tea and nodded approvingly at it before she spoke again.

"Lenette thought Poe was her ticket to the big time."

Dilara shook her head. "I don't understand why that would be. A marshal is an important person, but ultimately he is a civil employee and serves at the pleasure of others. If Lenette had wanted prestige, or power, a top-level Melchior executive would have been the obvious choice. In addition, the things she left behind imply she was not a person who likes getting dirty. But as you say, Poe comes from a farming family. So he is an odd choice, unless she loved him."

"She didn't." Minden waved a dismissive hand. "Lenette loved the idea of getting married. But when it came to the day to day of being married—well, no matter how great the match, sometimes marriage is boring and irritating and just plain messy. Reality didn't live up to Lenette's expectations. And neither did Poe."

"This puzzles me," Dilara said finally. "Ring linking is for always on Caron 5, so simply leaving a mate is not an option, even if he is hateful or unpleasant. Not that your brother—"

She broke off at the sudden sensory echo of Poe's hand in hers. It was hard to imagine linking rings with Poe would not surpass expectations. She thought of him standing in the doorway of his bedroom and hoped Minden did not see the slight flush she knew had tinged her cheeks at the memory.

She cleared her throat. "But I understand it is different here. Poe told me in Sector 1065, things are more…flexible."

"Sure," Minden said. "Lenette was entitled to leave if she wasn't happy. But she could have talked with him about it instead of just leaving a note and skipping out. Now he thinks the only reason why anyone would marry him is to get to his family."

Dilara blinked. "I don't understand."

"Don't play the fool," Minden snapped. "The Lancasters are a founding family. We don't flaunt it, but anyone who did a modicum of research would know we have both power and influence in Sector 1065. Lenette wanted the advantages that influence could buy. So she used Poe. And he fell for it.

"And I get it, I do," Minden added. "I understand what falling in love is like…all you see is what you want to see. But marrying an outsider almost destroyed my brother, and I'm not going to let that happen to him again. That's why I hope you understand that Poe is not a good target for you."

"Target?" Dilara stared at her, mystification morphing into cold understanding. It would have been funny if it hadn't been so annoying. "I'm not interested in marrying anyone. But even if I were, it wouldn't be Poe."

And as she said it, she knew it was a lie. At least Minden was unlikely to challenge it. Here, in Sector 1065, Dilara was of no social value whatsoever. When one combined that deficit with her stump, no one would believe that a relationship with any man was a possibility, certainly not with a man like Poe. Guerenne and her friends in the Well-Wed class might have been nasty, but they hadn't been wrong.

Chapter 28

EMILIO STACKED THE FILES SCATTERED ON THE TABLE and trans-
ferred them to the floor before nudging the box of pastries Poe
always provided for their weekly afternoon staff meeting toward
Zela. She looked as if she might refuse, but when she saw the bear
claw, she sighed with defeat and reached for it. Poe grinned and
reached for a chocolate croissant. Glory Ann's breakfasts were
lousy, but her pastries were a different story, probably because she
bought them from Emmer.

"I don't see how we are supposed to trace the manure," Zela
said. "All a thieving farmer has to do is mix the stolen stuff in with
his own heap of cow manure and get rid of the bags. It's not as
though bovoquin manure is a different color."

"It would be convenient," Emilio said, "if bovoquin manure
were blue." He reached for a cinnamon bun and took a large bite
before continuing. "Maybe we could wait until fall. Some farmer
has an unusually abundant harvest, we'll just arrest him."

Poe dry scrubbed his face. "Joking aside, it's going to take
time to visit every farm in Sector 1065, to check every barn and
utility shed. A pallet of stolen manure could even be tucked away
in an abandoned outbuilding. We'll have to fit those visits in between our other duties."

"I'll make a list of farms," Zela said. "We can split it up between us."

"Darius is sure Mnoani kids did it. He's wrong—the suspects
weren't built like Mnoani men. Still, I'll go through the motions
and interview Orioldo right after our meeting. I figure the sooner

we get him off the list of suspects, the sooner we can concentrate on finding the thieves."

Emilio licked icing off his thumb. "I'll bet you a kvin Darius won't even be willing to wait a week without complaining to the mayor."

"I wouldn't take that bet," Zela said. "Any luck on the graffiti? Borin thinks it was Mnoani kids, right?"

"He's wrong," Poe said. "Chief Mazarin says the three kids who asked Borin for work ended up getting hired to paint the newly renovated Mnoani community building."

"What color paint?" Emilio asked.

"Red," Poe said. "But they were at the community building helping out most of the night too. Lots of folks saw them. The kids didn't do it."

He rose to refresh his coffee, and his gaze flicked to the window as he circled the spoon in the dark liquid. He wondered what Dilara was doing now, and a part of him wished he were doing it with her. She had managed to slide into his life nearly seamlessly—even bickering with her was a companionable activity. He could feel his lips beginning to curve into a smile as he thought about continuing their most recent conversation when he got home. There was no question she was wrong about the relative merits of forks and spoons. For one thing, no one stirred his coffee with a fork. He forced his attention back to the conversation.

"—eminent domain."

Poe returned to his seat. "Sorry. I tuned out there. What did you say?"

Zela frowned but repeated herself.

"At the farmer's market yesterday, there was a lot of angry talk about Teamue and eminent domain. People were really pissed. Some guy stood up on a vegetable crate and started a harangue about settlers' rights and said since the Mnoani are unproductive members of society, his words not mine, they should be the ones giving up land. Then another guy started yelling about homesteading law and how that should take precedence over eminent domain. I stuck around because I was concerned there was going to be some sort of melee, but mostly there was just a lot of shouting."

Emilio put down his coffee cup. "Eminent domain is that thing where the government takes privately owned land, right? Seems like bad timing just before planting season. What does Teamue need other peoples' land for anyway?"

"Maybe not Teamue..." Poe paused in thought. "Teamue is all about staying in office. If he could glue himself to his desk, he would do it. So I can't see him voluntarily doing something so unpopular. On the other hand maybe Melchior found a way to persuade him."

As far as Poe knew, the vein Melchior had been mining for the last few years was still producing, but a big corporation like Melchior was always thinking five steps ahead. Or maybe there were signs the vein they were currently mining was petering out. Either way, there would be problems. Melchior had enormous power, and historically the corporation hadn't hesitated to flex its muscle when necessary, whether through bribes or political pressure.

"It would have to be a pretty sweet deal," Zela said. "It's not just farmers who are upset. The Mnoani are already unhappy. Between being treated like second class citizens and dealing with constant attempts at encroachment from neighboring farmers, it wouldn't take much to bring that community to a boil either."

"So who benefits from chaos?" Emilio asked.

Poe stared at him. His deputy was normally so laid back and cheerful Poe sometimes forgot what a sharp mind was hiding behind Emilio's mild exterior.

"That's a good question," Zela said after a moment of thought. "Not Teamue, maybe, but lots of other folks might. Farmers who'd like to grab some of the Mnoani territory, for instance. Once a farmer got his crops into Mnoani land it would be harder for the Mnoani to maintain title."

"Right." Emilio nodded. "There was a case when we were kids. The Mnoani had to take their plea up the ladder to an intergalactic court to resolve it, and even then all the tribe got was reparations. They couldn't get the actual land back."

"I remember that," Poe said. "But didn't the tribe appeal the ruling?"

"Sure. But you know what appeals are like in superior

intergalactic courts. It can take decades to get a judge assigned, never mind a ruling. So in the abstract, any activists among the Mnoani might see unrest as an opportunity to take back what was theirs."

"I don't see the miners benefiting," Zela said. "And merchants never win during conflict."

"Unless they are selling torches, pitchforks and banners," Emilio said. "Then they make out like bandits."

Zela laughed as the phone on Poe's desk rang. Poe strode toward it, grinning, but his smile faded as he listened to Minden.

"I met your houseguest. You should bring her to Ma and Pop's for Sunday dinner."

"This Sunday? That can't be right, the last family dinner was only…"

"Four weeks ago, Poe," she said. "Don't you even think of missing it. And bring Dilara. This time Ma and Pop should meet the girl before you get serious, don't you think?"

The irony didn't escape him. He had been wishing he was back at the cabin spending time with Dilara and now, as though created by some malign god, his idle wish had morphed into an unpleasant reality. His shoulders sagged and his voice came out as a croak.

"She's just a lodger. She'll probably be busy that day anyhow."

"Convince her," Minden said. "I like her."

Chapter 29

IT WAS AFTERNOON BY THE TIME HE MANAGED to visit Mnoani territory again. The soil under his boots was dry, but Poe scrubbed them on the mat anyway. There wasn't any point in giving Pretie more work to do. He raised his hand to knock on the door, but it opened before his knuckles made contact.

"Marshal." Manzarin stood in the opening, the wrinkles at his eyes crinkling as he smiled. He stood back and gestured Poe in.

"Welcome. Pretie just left to visit a friend, but I'm sure I can find something you would like in the kitchen."

Poe raised his hand. "I apologize, Chief, but I cannot stop to enjoy your hospitality. Is Orioldo here?"

A shadow crossed Manzarin's eyes and his expression, while remaining polite, seemed more distant.

"He is."

"I need to speak with him, please."

"Certainly." Manzarin gestured toward a couch. "Please make yourself comfortable while I tell him you are here."

The guilt was tangible but Poe remained standing. He knew that couch, and he'd never manage to squirm out of the cushions in time if Orioldo decided to make a run for it. He looked up as Orioldo shambled into the room, Manzarin close behind him. Orioldo yawned and rubbed his eyes.

"Late night?" Poe asked.

Orioldo stopped in his tracks and his gaze narrowed.

"Why? What crime am I accused of committing last night?"

"Where were you?" Poe asked.

"Out with friends," Orioldo snapped. "If this is just another attempt to play Pin the Crime on the Mnoani—"

"Where?"

Orioldo flicked a glance toward his father and shook his head. Poe sighed.

"Chief, with your permission, I'd like to speak with Orioldo privately."

Manzarin's brow was furrowed, but he nodded assent and Poe gestured toward the door. Orioldo strode past him leaving the door open, a rudeness Poe knew would bother Manzarin. Poe closed the door gently as he left the house.

"Walk with me," he said. Striding past Orioldo, he headed down the pathway into the forest. When they reached a clearing, he stopped and turned to face the young man.

"Last night," he snapped. "Tell me where you were and who you were with."

"I was out. With a girl." Orioldo scowled at Poe's sudden grin. "You can't tell him. My grandfather thinks I was out talking politics with friends."

Poe shrugged easily. "No reason to tell the chief unless he needs to know. When did you get home?"

"I came back to the house just as the sun was rising. Everyone was still sleeping." Orioldo's defiant glance made him look younger, and Poe had a flash of sympathy for him. It couldn't be easy carrying the weight of expectation Orioldo carried every day as sole grandson of Chief Manzarin.

"Okay. I'll need the girl's name to confirm your story. If she backs you up, you're off the hook."

"She—" Orioldo flicked a glance backward. "Her parents don't know either. They won't like it that she's spending time with me."

Poe nodded. "I'll be discreet."

An hour later, after an embarrassed but vigorous confirmation from Senndra Quence, Poe was satisfied Orioldo had not personally been present at Darius' store the night before. Orioldo had friends, of course, but Poe thought they were unlikely to act without Orioldo's express instructions. In any case, except as a way to give Darius a well-deserved poke, there would be little purpose to the theft from a Mnoani perspective. Bovoquin had been introduced to Valora by an enterprising homesteader several decades back, but the Mnoani preferred the gentler native cattle and had their own agricultural methods. Teamue would not be happy.

Chapter 30

POE LIKED THAT DILARA WAS NEAR TO HIS HEIGHT. He had always felt, with Lenette, that he was awkward and a bit bumbling when compared to her delicate mannerisms. It was one of the things that had troubled him about their relationship—the idea Lenette expected him to work on improving himself but that she simultaneously knew it was beyond him.

But Dilara was solid, big boned like Ma. The sort of woman who wouldn't feel that physical labor was beneath her. And he liked the way Dilara smelled too. Not fussy, just soap with a little sweat and dirt from helping him rake up the leaves in the front yard. Minden had been right. Dilara would fit right in at Ma and Pop's table, so that was where they were headed.

A monthly Sunday lunch was a tradition on the Lancaster farm—had been since the first generation had settled there. And now that spring had officially begun, the long tables were set up in the side yard under the ancient maples grown with seeds brought from Earth by Poe's great-grandfather. Cousins chattered as they laid place settings, poured water into Ma's prized blue glasses and set out the contributions they had brought on the buffet table.

Pop emerged from the house carrying a tray of sandwiches and was nearly bowled over by a trio of shrieking children playing tag. Ma followed behind with a bowl of fruit salad. She called out some sort of rebuke to the children. He couldn't hear the words, but her tone was so cheerful, he doubted the comment would have any impact.

Dilara shifted out from under his arm. It was a subtle but purposeful separation. She looked as if she were preparing for battle. He was sorry for it—he had enjoyed how she had felt beside him as they walked.

"Hey, Poe. Who's your friend?" Emmer's shout was cheerful.

"She's a new arrival from Caron 5," Poe replied as they approached. "Her name is Dilara Elian."

Emmer eyed Dilara with more interest than Poe liked. Poe saw his brother's flicker of surprise as he noted Dilara's empty right cuff and then quick understanding as he extended his own left hand to shake hers.

"Hope you like cake. I brought enough for an army." He gestured at the milling guests. "Apparently I guessed right."

Some of the tension in her face eased, although her expression was still somber as she nodded. "I do like cake. Thank you."

"I'll save you out a piece," he responded, winking. "The crowd around the dessert table can be pretty competitive. Wouldn't want you to get trampled trying for a piece of my world-famous Ginger Layer Cake."

Emmer was a lady's man, so Poe decided to cut in before his brother got the wrong impression. He gave Emmer an affectionate slap on the back. It was a little harder than necessary, but Emmer must have gotten the message. Instead of scowling at Poe, he grinned at him. That alone was suspicious, Poe felt, but this wasn't the time to explore it.

"You make sure Poe introduces you to Pop, Dilara," Emmer said. "He's going to love meeting you."

Dilara gazed after Emmer as he strode away and then turned to Poe with a puzzled expression.

"He seems happy."

"Sure. He lives for this stuff." Poe gestured toward the tables of food where his brother was rearranging trays of pastries. "And he's good at it. Best baker in Sector 1065."

He could afford to be magnanimous, he decided. And besides, it was true. Against all odds, Emmer had made his bakery thrive by building a loyal clientele across social boundaries. He had learned to bake the beloved specialties of most of the cultures that made up Sector 1065, wheedling culinary secrets even from the Mnoani who were notoriously closemouthed about their recipes. But Pop always said Emmer could talk a bird from a tree, and Poe had to admit it was a useful social skill.

He and Emmer hadn't always agreed, but whatever friction they had sharing a room as boys had morphed into something better as they grew. It was the same with Lindo and Rawt and to a lesser degree with Minden. More of an age gap there. The siblings were still competitive with each other, but they were friends now in a way he thought only brothers and sisters could be. And they had a depth of shared history that meant they understood each other in a visceral way. He wondered fleetingly whether that would have been the case if they had been forced into constant competition throughout their youth. Probably not, he thought.

Dilara stood watching the crowd, silent. She looked surprisingly lonely, almost lost. It made his heart stutter for a moment. So he took her hand in his and led her toward the tables, nodding and chatting with relatives as they passed but not letting her go until he had seated her next to him, near Pop's seat at the head of the table. It was where he often sat, but now it occurred to him he might have been better off choosing something a little less conspicuous.

Minden and her husband, Sen, were occupied settling their children and supplying them with food at the far end of the table, but between chores she shot curious glances at Dilara. Lindo and Rawt, hair wet from cleaning up after their morning chores, slid into the seats opposite Poe and Dilara. Rawt winked at her and Lindo nodded politely, but both shot Poe questioning looks. There was no point in putting off the inevitable, so the moment Pop sat down, Poe stood and beckoned Dilara to join him.

"For those of you who haven't met her, this is Dilara Elian. She's a new arrival from Caron 5. Join me in wishing her bonvenon varmeta to Sector 1065."

Shouts of "welcome" and "bonvenon" rippled down the table and he and Dilara sat again, her cheeks flushed.

"What was that you said?" she whispered as he unfolded his napkin.

"It's a traditional Sector 1065 greeting for a new arrival. It means a warm welcome. When the founders came here, they used Esperanto. It's a combination of lots of earth languages. Eventually everyone just shifted to English, but some of the farming families still use Esperanto at home."

She nodded and fumbled for her fork, but it bounced off the edge of the table and fell to the grass. He pushed his chair back and reached for it, but she did the same and their heads collided with a solid impact. Wincing, he sat up without the fork.

"You okay?"

She nodded but blinked hard and looked away for a moment.

"Let me see."

She shook her head sharply. "It's fine," she hissed.

He could see the bruise forming on her forehead near her hair line and cursed quietly. Grabbing his glass of water, he scooped out the ice cubes and folded them into his napkin. He shifted his chair closer to hers and encircled her with one arm while pressing the compress to her head. She startled but sighed as the cool eased the pain.

"Is she okay? Want me to call Stig?" Rawt, ever observant, watched the two of them speculatively. Poe considered. It was probably just a bump, but having Stig take a look couldn't hurt. He opened his mouth to say so when Dilara spoke up.

"Not necessary. I'm fine. I have a hard head."

She was probably right, but having Stig confirm it would have gone a long way toward alleviating the guilt he felt at having caused her pain in the first place.

"Let me look," Ma said, pulling the ice pack away from Dilara's brow. She cupped Dilara's chin and looked her in the eyes. "She's right. Her pupils are fine. It's painful, probably, but not dangerous."

Poe felt marginally better. Ma probably had as much experience assessing head injuries and potential concussions as Stig did. Still, he shot an apologetic look at Dilara, whose embarrassment had clearly eclipsed her discomfort. She flushed and refused to meet his glance.

Lindo had gotten up to reload his plate and Pop grabbed the

opening. He pulled the empty seat next to Dilara, sat in it, and patted her shoulder.

"Try to eat something," he urged her gently. "I brought you a clean fork."

Her lips trembled, and for a moment, Poe thought she might cry. But then she took a deep breath and asked Pop to tell her about the farm. Pop took care to keep the stories light, and by the time he had finished, she'd cleaned her plate and had even smiled a few times.

Later, Poe carried a bag of leftovers in each hand as he and Dilara strolled back to the cabin after the usual noisy leave taking. Dilara was quiet, and he wondered if the good-natured tumult had overwhelmed her. He was used to it, but he could see how it might be off-putting to someone who didn't grow up in a large extended family. Still, he wasn't getting an uncomfortable vibe.

Not like Lenette. His ex had never enjoyed family gatherings, or at least not gatherings with his family. She liked the cachet of marrying into a founding family, but the realities of farm life left her cold. He had only met Lenette's family once, at the wedding. She had told him she wasn't close with her parents, and he had tried to compensate for that by making sure his own family made her feel welcome. Still, for all her attempts to convey a sense of ease and warmth with his family, she had always been more comfortable when it had been just the two of them.

But he didn't get that sense with Dilara. She had smiled shyly back at Minden's five-year-old son, Ako, and by the time they got to dessert, Ako was standing at her shoulder and regaling her with the sort of riddles five-year-olds thought were hilarious. Dilara had noticed when Rawt's glass was empty and had refilled it automatically. So she wasn't awkward, exactly. It was more that she seemed reserved, as though she was standing back waiting for the other shoe to drop.

His family seemed to have not noticed her reticence. Pop had pressed leftovers on them, and Emmer had lived up to his promise to save Dilara a large piece of cake to bring back with her. Rawt had given Poe a thumbs-up when Dilara hadn't been looking. Lindo slapped Poe on the shoulder. And Ma had checked Dilara's head one more time before they left.

"My family likes you," he said.

She shot him a mystified look. "Why?"

"Why shouldn't they? You didn't throw food or break a bowl over anyone's head."

"Not a high bar, then." She looked relieved, which deserved exploring. But he didn't pursue it. He pushed down the tiny whisper of resentment at the memory of his family's interactions with Lenette. Pop had been courtly, and Lenette had appeared to be charmed as she did whenever men paid her attention. Ma had offered her wedding dress to Lenette. Lenette had just as politely refused. Minden had invited her to play with the babies, and somehow Lenette had never found the time. Poe had convinced himself the rough edges would smooth over in time. Now he thought they would never have smoothed. The knowledge that his parents and siblings had realized that and he hadn't was irritating in a way he didn't care to examine too closely.

Chapter 31

"YOU DIDN'T NEED TO LEAVE WORK FOR THIS PURPOSE," Dilara protested. "You could have just told me where to look for the sewing kit."

"No, I couldn't have."

He looked like a thundercloud, and for some inexplicable reason it made her feel tender toward him for a moment. But then he shoved a fussy looking work basket at her and turned on his heel, stomping off to his bedroom. She scowled at his retreating back. It wasn't her fault her only good dress had been torn her first night at BangBang. For that matter, it was only because she had offered to pay him rent that she couldn't afford to replace it. But there was no point in dwelling on it, she reminded herself. It was her own fault she had procrastinated dealing with the torn garment for weeks. Now it was Saturday, the Melchior dinner dance was two hours away and all the other women would be dressed in their best gowns.

She set the basket down on her bed and gave it a dubious look. Anything with that many bows and ribbons decorating it was unlikely to be of any practical use. But to her relief, it had the basics—a packet of needles, several snarled spools of thread in surprising shades and a pair of flimsy scissors. It took time to untangle the threads, but she always found the process of solving tangles soothing, and it was pleasant to see the spools once they were tidy and smooth. She had just threaded a needle and was pulling the knot tight with her teeth when she heard the floorboard creak.

"Need any help?"

"No, thank you."

He filled the doorway and she felt a tiny shiver at the thought of that, so she looked down at the fabric and concentrated on aligning the torn seam until he left. It was odd, the way he had offered help—too late to be useful, but still odd. Or maybe that was the way things were done around here. Certainly his family at last week's gathering had been welcoming, which was surprising under the circumstances.

As she held the gown down against the mattress with one bare foot, she tugged the needle through a thick section of seam, remembering how Tok's hands had guided hers. Dilara had been seven when Tok had given in to her pleading, teaching her how to mend, how to cook, how to use a hammer. Now, with the benefit of hindsight, she understood how much of a risk Tok had taken. If Dilara's parents had found out, it would have meant punishment for Dilara, but Tok would have lost her position and without a reference would have been unlikely to find another at her age.

Now she wondered why Tok had done it. The housekeeper had worked for the family since both Tok and Wraya were in their teens, and Tok bought into the social strictures of Caron 5 as much, if not more so, than Dilara's parents. So, even as she had given in to Dilara's pleading, Tok had still reflexively held the tips of her fingers to her thumbs whenever Dilara walked into the room. It was a protective gesture, an ancient guard against sharing the fate of one who was born flawed. Seeing Tok do that, even unconscious as the habit was, had always stung, as had the inescapable knowledge that Tok considered Dilara useless.

Perhaps Tok had taught her because as an adult, Dilara would have no other role in Caron 5 society except as a household servant, like Tok herself. And if Dilara were so lucky as to be married, it would be to a husband who would put up with her flaw in exchange for years of labor and a copious dowry to make up for the shame she would bring his household. There would be no children, naturally—or at least none Dilara had born. Carefully she tied the thread into a finishing knot, and just as Tok had taught her, drew the needle through the fabric one more time to hide the ends in the seam before clipping the thread off.

In Sector 1065 it was different, although Dilara wasn't sure yet the difference was better. The intoxicating sense of freedom she had tasted when she watched Caron 5 fade into the distance had dissipated quickly once she realized she had simply traded a set of stringent but predictable rules for an unpredictable and almost chaotic system. There were no clear-cut social guidelines here, and the lack of social rules created its own set of problems, which meant she was never quite sure where she stood.

Poe didn't seem to think anything of her flaw. If it bothered him, he had given no sign of it, and she suspected he wasn't courteous enough to hide true disdain. But maybe it wasn't a matter of courtesy. Likely he just didn't care enough about her one way or the other.

Still, others who had even less stake in her were more obvious in their opinions. At the family luncheon, Poe's mother had been kindly, but there was a skeptical quality to her gaze. And then there were the customers at BangBang. Last night someone in the crowd had yelled "One-Handed Tess" as she climbed onto the stage, and even though several other audience members had shouted him down, the epithet had rung in her head later as she tossed in her bed. Still, in a sense, overt commentary was better than unspoken contempt. She spread the dress on and eyed the mended seam. She hadn't done as good a job as Tok would have, but it would do until she could afford to buy another gown.

Physical objects were unimportant so it was silly to long for them. She had reminded herself of this fact whenever Saskia had expressed satisfaction in one of her many clothing purchases. Saskia had needed to make many such purchases in order to complete her trousseau once she reached a marriageable age.

But an additional dress in this case was simply a matter of practicality, Dilara reminded herself. There was a blue gown the color of a peacock feather in the window of one of the shops in town. If it was still there tomorrow, she would put a deposit down on it. Pleasure didn't enter into it, Dilara reminded herself. This was a simple purchase, no different than buying any other tool of one's trade. Still, a little thrill of excitement tingled up her spine at the thought. She had never actually bought herself an article of clothing, and she had never owned anything in blue.

She eyed her hair with some satisfaction. Over the three weeks since she'd arrived in Sector 1065 it had grown out, and some of the worst thin spots had filled in. So now, although she would never be attractive, at least she didn't look unkempt. She turned away from the mirror before her eyes could come to rest on her flaw in the reflection. There was no point in tempting fate—she wanted all the good luck she could get this evening.

When she went to return the sewing kit to Poe, she found him in his bedroom. He was perched on a spindly chair, rubbing polish onto a pair of dress shoes. She cleared her throat and he looked up. She felt a click as his eyes met hers.

She held up the sewing kit and looked the question. He grunted and gestured toward the little table on the far side of the room next to his bed. Poe's bedroom room stretched across the length of the rear of the cabin. There were so many windows it might have been built as a sleeping porch. As the afternoon cooled, a breeze puffed through, making the lace curtains bell away from the windows.

It must be his table, Dilara thought. It was the only clear surface in the room. The white lacy spread on his four-poster bed was festooned with pompoms, lace and ribbons. A small mountain of embroidered pillows filled the opposite side of the mattress, giving the bed a forlorn air, like a lopsided wedding cake. She edged by him and set the sewing kit down.

"The carving on your headboard is beautiful." She snapped her mouth shut so quickly she nearly bit her tongue. What had she been thinking? Well, she knew what she had been thinking, and that didn't make it any better. She could feel the blood rush to her cheeks.

He stood and looked at her, the corner of his hard lips quirked slightly. For a moment she wasn't sure she was breathing. There was a small scar on his cheek. It took willpower to keep her hand down, to keep from reaching up one finger to trace it. It was curved like a tiny crescent moon. For a moment she wondered whether it was the result of his job. But the indentation was white, and she thought it might have been from a childhood injury. She wondered if his mother had kissed it.

She could feel heat radiating from him. But that had to be wrong because he was too far away to affect her that way. Maybe she was coming down with a cold. Trying to be casual about it, she rubbed her eye and slid her palm over her forehead. It was cool. Besides, it wasn't her own touch she wanted, it was his. She glanced at his hand now, and looked away, tapping her foot and then abruptly stilling it.

"The dinner dance isn't anything to worry about," he said. "All you have to do is avoid singing any more Mnoani protest songs and you should be fine."

She let out a breath she didn't know she had been holding. He was right—she had nothing to worry about. She might be slipping perilously closer to loving him, but at least he wouldn't reciprocate. There was no way he was interested in a one-handed woman for anything more than a polite friendship and an occasional rent payment. And despite their warm manner and kind hospitality, she would be foolish to think his family would ever encourage anything beyond friendship between their son and a flawed outsider. She was a novelty in the small town, nothing more.

Among the knickknacks in the living area, she had noticed a pair of portrait photos, small, in delicate silver frames hinged together. One image was of Poe, a younger Poe than she was looking at now, but still with the same impatience at sitting. She had smiled at the image—he looked as though he couldn't wait to leap from the photographer's stool. But the other portrait was of a woman, delicate and small. She looked as if she had been modeled after the fragile figurines that dominated the living room. Lenette was perfect.

"How would you know?" Dilara tried to sound jocular, but a tinge of anger seeped through.

"They're probably going to try to set me up with the least popular executive," she added. "They'll pair us up as a joke on him. I've changed my mind. I'm not going. If I have to compensate Melchior, I'll find more work and pay them off over time."

"No way," Poe said promptly. "You owe me."

Her jaw dropped.

"Maybe I do, but I don't see how going to this stupid event

would—oh!"

The significance of the polished shoes and the dress uniform draped over the closet door sank in.

"You have to go too?"

Chapter 32

POE TIMED THEIR ARRIVAL AT THE MELCHIOR dinner dance with precision. He was still within the accepted time frame for a guest, but just barely. The milling crowd of expectant arrivals had inhaled the appetizers, which he knew from painful experience were platters of thin stale slices of bread topped with anemic slices of meat. The other possibility was trays of no-longer-crisp vegetable sticks arranged in mounds around bowls of a white dip of indeterminate age and contents. The food at Melchior events was inevitably an embarrassment for a farming community. He supposed it took a certain skill to make good produce taste like the city stuff. That was why he had insisted they eat before leaving the cabin.

A crowd milled throughout the lobby, chattering with the raucous good cheer of people who were trying desperately to convince each other they were enjoying themselves. He kept his hand cupped around Dilara's elbow, not only because he enjoyed the feel of her, but because something about her expression made him think she might bolt given the opportunity. Damned if he was going to let her get away with that, or at least, not alone. If she got to leave, he wanted an excuse to leave too.

He saw a Melchior executive look Dilara up and down appreciatively and understood, even as he caught the man's eye and stared him down. The contrast between Dilara's cropped hair and sophisticated gown accentuated her eyes and made her look like a child playing dress up, although, she didn't behave like a person who had ever played much as a child. That bubbling laughter she had given in to when she saw the geithers take flight had sounded rusty from disuse, as though the laugh itself had taken her by surprise.

If she had been honest with Poe, and that was open to question, she had grown up in a powerful family and had experienced many occasions more elegant than this one. So he wondered about the flicker of excitement he caught in her face as she glanced toward the far end of the room where a group of musicians were tuning up to provide background music for the dinner. Maybe there were aspects to the high life she missed even if the local talent couldn't come anywhere near providing what she was used to.

The musicians began to play, and the guests milled about with more purpose now. Seating was not assigned, except for the head table. Some Melchior executives made it their mission to sit as close as possible to the head table while others, for reasons he could only guess at, wanted to be as far away from the CEO and the mayor as possible. That left a pair of chairs halfway down one of the long tables in easy reach for him and Dilara. He caught her eye and she nodded, sliding into one of them quickly just as he saw Mrs. Onkelson waving frantically from across the room.

The ratio of men to women at any Melchior event was always lopsided, but especially so tonight. Unlike many of Melchior's big events, the dinner dance was strictly a corporate event, which meant Melchior executives would have first crack at the Well-Wed women. As a result, the room looked like a sea of dark suits with a small pool of color surrounding Mrs. Onkelson.

The chairs were squeezed as close as possible in order to maximize seating. Poe managed to wedge himself into the seat next to Dilara and wondered whether he would have room to move his arms in order to pick up his fork and knife without elbowing his neighbors. The long tables were preset with food because once everyone was seated there would no room for a waiter to walk in order to serve the meal.

The man on Dilara's right seemed pleased at the unexpected proximity to one of the special guests and edged toward her. In response, Dilara turned toward Poe. Her shoulder pressed against his, which would have felt companionable if he hadn't been sure she had only moved to get away from her neighbor.

Poe leaned forward and caught the guy's eye over her shoulder. He knew Dith Roben, although not well. He guessed that said something. For one thing, it meant he hadn't booked Roben for anything. Still, Poe kept his stare menacing until Roben returned his chair to its original position. Dilara flushed red.

"You didn't have to do that. I'm perfectly capable of protecting myself," she whispered.

He crooked his brow. "And you don't have to sit next to me. Want to go sit next to Mrs. Onkelson? She's waving at you."

She shot him a mutinous look and shook her head. It occurred to him belatedly that she probably hadn't read the sign in the lobby detailing the evening's events. He leaned forward to explain, but his breath caught at the way the back of her neck curved, elegant and vulnerable under her chopped hair. He cleared his throat.

"There's a ceremony during dinner, like the one at the dock. All the women march up on stage to be formally introduced. That's why the rest of your group is seated over there just below the dais."

She sat up for a moment and peered toward the front of the room. But then she turned back quickly, her face white, and sank low into her seat. He glanced toward the stage, trying to identify what had frightened her, but there was only Roland Cross fiddling with his camera on its tripod. Roland filled in for the Gazette when necessary, and the Gazette always ran a feature on the women of Well-Wed.

Roland was no threat, so Poe couldn't figure out what was frightening Dilara so badly. He wanted to pull her close, to make her feel safe, but there was no room to maneuver from side to side without drawing unwanted attention. Instead he too slid down on his seat so his face was on her level.

"What is it? What's wrong?"

She was shaking now. "He's got a camera. I can't have an image taken. They'll find me and I won't be able to get away again. Please."

Without stopping to consider, he slid all the way under the table and pulled her with him. He had questions, lots of them, but now was not the time. So he pushed her in front of him and followed her as they crawled between the lines of dark pant legs heading toward the back of the room. At the end of the table, they scrambled to their feet and in silent agreement, headed out the service door.

Poe could hear pans clanking in the kitchen down the hall, but the corridor itself was deserted for the moment. He pulled the door shut behind them and leaned against it.

"I'll help you, but I need to know why you are running."

She shrugged, shooting him a miserable glance. "Mart Henkelor is wealthy enough to hire help, and the people he hires will scour whatever sources they can find for my image because they'll assume I'm traveling under a false name."

"Dilara," he said, "I need you to be honest. Are you married to him?"

"No. But my parents promised me to him." Her face was a portrait of misery, but this was not the time to comfort her. He kept his tone impassive, but his hand on the knob of the door behind him tightened as he spoke.

"On Caron 5, do your parents have the right to betroth you without your permission?"

"Historically the groom and the bride's parents had six months to enforce the promise. That law was changed a decade ago, so legally it's no longer enforceable. But in practice, my parents are old fashioned, Poe, and Mart is determined."

"He can be as determined as he wants." Poe shrugged, relieved. "He'll have no more right to kidnap you in Sector 1065 than anyone else does. We don't hold with that kind of behavior here."

Her expression of relief was palpable, her eyes alight with joy.

"Thank you," she whispered. She stepped toward him now and reached up to cup his cheek. "You are a good man, Marshal Poe Lancaster."

His cheek tingled and he inclined his head a little toward her palm. It had been a long time since he had wanted a woman's touch. Slowly he reached for her, placing his hands on her waist and drawing her close.

"Do you want to go back into the dinner?" His voice was

hoarse.

"No," she whispered, her face luminous in the dim light of the corridor.

"Good," he said. He only meant to brush his lips to hers, a reassuring affectionate kiss between casual acquaintances. But this was something different because he had assumed she would pull back, maybe reprove him or be a little shocked. Instead she sighed and leaned in, and suddenly the heat level shot up from impromptu to purposeful.

The hallway felt disconnected from anywhere real, the air stuffy and the noise from the banquet hall muffled compared to the sound of their breathing. But then someone opened the door to the kitchen, and Poe raised his lips from hers. She looked dazed, and there was a pucker of confusion between her eyebrows.

He raised his hand before she could say it. "I'm sorry. That was out of line and I apologize. It won't happen again."

She pulled away now, shaking her head. He could hear the tightness in her throat as she spoke, and he wanted to kick himself for being the cause of it. "No, it won't happen again. And there's no need to apologize. It's my fault."

A pair of servers trundled a cart down the hall toward them, and Dilara backed away from him to the other side of the corridor to let them pass. It was probably a good plan. Distance—that was the ticket. But she looked just as appealing a few paces away. He frowned as he replayed her response.

"It's not a question of fault, exactly," he said. "We're both adults."

"We are." She was sober now. "But our differences are too great to ignore."

"Aren't differences the whole point? If I wanted to kiss myself, I'd buy a mirror."

She snorted at the image, and he felt the tension in his shoulders ease in response. It was so much easier spending time with a woman who let him console her. He had almost forgotten what that could be like. Somehow with Lenette, he had never been enough. Maybe he wouldn't be enough for Dilara either, but it sure would be interesting to find out. Two paces brought him to her side of the corridor, and he leaned back against the wall next to her.

"I liked kissing you. It felt good. Did it feel good to you?"

She flushed and he felt like pumping his fist. It was a small victory, but he would take what he could get. He had lied. The kiss hadn't been good, it had been amazing, at least if his past experience was any measure. It occurred to him now she might not have anything to compare it to. It hadn't struck him as a virginal kiss, but maybe.

"Besides old Mart, is anyone else on Caron 5 interested in marrying you?"

She watched the toe of her boot trace the pattern on the carpet for a moment before responding.

"I had a boyfriend for a time. Alexandr Lekin. But Alexandr was ambitious, and my little sister is perfect and therefore will inherit leadership of the family in time. So he pretended to love me as a way to get closer to Saskia."

Poe rubbed his forehead. "Let me get this straight, this yenxer used you as a ticket into your sister's bed?"

"What's a yenxer?"

"I guess the exact translation of it in Caronite would be Alexandr."

"It wasn't all his responsibility." She glanced at him, her eyes serious. "In essence, I colluded with him. I knew Alexandr was driven to succeed, so befriending me was a natural and reasonable strategy for him, given his goals. But I told myself he loved me because that is what he said and because I wanted to believe the impossible. That was my fault. I should have realized I was deluding myself."

"And Saskia? What kind of sister is that? Didn't she owe you some loyalty?"

She shrugged and he wanted to shake her.

"Alexandr and Saskia came to me together in secret and asked for my blessing. They intend to marry as soon as I marry Mart."

"But you're not going to—oh. Clever. How long will they have to wait?"

"They are betrothed," she responded. "But they will not be free to marry until Mart breaks his betrothal to me or until the six months have passed. In the meantime, Saskia may have second thoughts. She can be flighty."

"It sounds like they deserve each other."

He looked at her with new respect. Maybe she hadn't gotten a fair deal in life, but she had made good use of the tools she had. She would fit in to Sector 1065 well, at least for as long as she intended to stay. The Well-Wed program would end at harvest time. Come winter, Dilara would have moved on and life would get a lot duller.

He had a flash of what winter would look like—dark days and darker nights melding into each other with sameness. Crime slowed down in winter and what there was didn't tax the brain much, so Emilio and Zela were on half duty. Zela devoted her free time to taking care of Jebbie, and Emilio took part-time work as a night watchman at Melchior, so Poe would spend hours in his office alone. And then, in the cabin every night, he would be even more alone among the remnants of his life with Lenette.

It wasn't that he missed Lenette. Even if she showed up tomorrow, all politeness and meaningless apologies, he wouldn't have wanted her back. Some days during their marriage, he had been lonelier with Lenette than without her. But since she had left, he had felt frozen, brittle—as though any sudden motion might crack him to pieces.

He glanced at Dilara. She was fiddling with her gown, trying to brush off a bit of food that had gotten ground in as they crawled under the tables. She would leave, just as Lenette had. He couldn't rely on her for anything else but some temporary companionship. Still, the sense of liberation at the notion of that friendship was intoxicating.

Another server came down the hall and entered the banquet hall. As the door opened, Poe caught a fragment of Teamue's speech. It was the same material as always, stuffy and dull, so carefully worded it could not offend even the most sensitive of listeners.

He turned to Dilara. "Want to get out of here?"

Chapter 33

IT WAS FULL DARK OUTSIDE, COOL AFTER THE WARMTH of the day. Dilara could see tiny insects flinging themselves optimistically at the gas chandelier dangling from the portico high above. The scent of lilansen buds hung heavy in the air. If it hadn't been for the low hum of the Melchior pumps in the distance, it would have felt like the beginning of another garden party on Caron 5. There had been so many during the summer before Dilara left. She tried not to let her visceral recoil at the memory keep her from enjoying the beauty of the evening, but it wasn't easy.

"Want to sit for a while before we go home? I'd offer a walk, but…" Poe gestured at his shoes with a rueful look. At her nod, he laced his fingers between hers and led her around the building into a gated garden. One moon was nearly full and the other at the half, so the edges of the flowers were distinct even if their colors were not. And then an employee opened the drapes on the floor to ceiling windows to the ballroom that overlooked the garden.

Light spilled out onto the lawn, but she and Poe were in the dark shadows outside the yellow rectangles on the grass. There was something cozy and a little illicit about being able to observe the staff preparing the dance hall without being seen oneself. She sat on a stone bench and watched as Poe toed off his shoes. His sigh of relief made her smile. It felt good being alone with him. And even if the kiss hadn't meant anything, it had felt good too— it had felt right, somehow, although that made no sense.

Muffled notes filtered out of the building now as the band began to warm up. She had caught a glimpse of the musicians earlier and had been interested to note that Rudolph had also taken the night off to perform with the ensemble. A pair of crutches leaned against the wall behind him, but he no longer relied on them as much as he had. He appeared to be playing with his usual brilliance. She wondered what Porky was doing for entertainment that night without either of his musicians.

She looked at Poe's shoes and then at his feet wiggling in relief. "Why did you choose such narrow shoes?"

"They were for my wedding. Lenette chose them."

She turned so she could see his face in profile. His expression had that frozen look it had when he talked about Lenette—his jaw tight, his lips in a straight line. Violence was not a solution. Dilara had been taught that from girlhood. But in the moment, Dilara wished Lenette would appear just so she could punch her.

"I thought you said ring linking was not permanent in Sector 1065."

He acknowledged the hit with a nod. When he spoke, it was so quietly she had to lean toward him to hear what he was saying.

"At first I couldn't believe she would leave me like that. She seemed so invested in making me into someone I wasn't. But I guess she decided I would never be what she wanted."

"She wanted you to have narrow feet?"

He barked a humorless laugh. "That's about it."

He turned to look at her now.

"Don't get me wrong, I wasn't a perfect husband. On nights I managed to make it home in time for dinner, I was tired and often irritable. The last thing I wanted to do when work slowed down was to go out dancing or to some improving type lecture. But Lenette kept telling me I could be better, more sophisticated.

"And she talked about the cabin as though it were a stepping-stone to bigger things. She decorated the hell out of it so it could be the sort of place where she could hold dinner parties. But every time I walked in the door, I ruined the look. Lenette was trying to lay the groundwork for me to be mayor, not because she thought I had anything important to contribute, but because she wanted to be a mayor's wife. Then we would move into the mayor's mansion, and she could entertain in the style she wanted. She was like you, you know."

He saw her incredulous stare and shook his head.

"Not like that. You're not a climber. But Lenette was also a Well-Wedder. She came here looking to make a difference in her own way, I guess. But I screwed that dream up for her by refusing to run for mayor—it was the last straw for Lenette. She was on the next ship back to Earth. She always said I was the biggest improvement project ever, and I guess I was just too much of a screw up even for her to fix."

Dilara cleared her throat and gently poked her toe at a blade of grass sticking out a little above the others.

"I'm not sure what she was trying to improve."

It popped out before she could hold her tongue. And now she was grateful for the dark because it covered the blush she could feel warming her cheeks. How stupid could she be? He would think she was some sort of mooning adolescent, or worse a flatterer. But he looked at her with a non-committal expression, and she realized she hadn't been explicit enough to be clear, which made things worse because now she would have to elaborate.

"You loved her," she said. "That should have been enough. It would have been enough for…"

She clamped her mouth shut and turned her head away from him, blinking hard. The vision of Lenette cavalierly tossing away the opportunity for a lifetime of love with Poe was exquisitely painful. And not just on Poe's behalf, although her heart hurt at the thought of his pain.

She hated the flash of envy that jabbed at her, resented it too. She couldn't afford the luxury of self-pity for at least another five months and probably not even then. The lump in her throat grew, and she forced herself to swallow hard. She would not cry.

The side of her leg that had been warm from pressing against his was cool now. She looked up, and he stood before her with his hand held out. He would be ready to walk to the automobile now. They would go back to the cabin, and it would be as if nothing had changed. The knickknacks would have accumulated another day's worth of dust, the pillows would sit smugly on the couch and Poe would continue on, like a beetle in amber if that beetle had been alive.

She placed her hand on his, her heart heavy. But instead of turning to walk out of the garden, he pulled her close and wrapped his arms around her, swaying gently to the music.

"I thought you hated dancing." Her voice was muffled against his shoulder, but she didn't want to move her face away from the scent of him.

"I hate those stupid shoes," he corrected. "I like dancing okay. Do you?"

"I think so," she said. "I mean I've only watched other people do it. So tell me if I get it wrong."

She could hear the smile in his voice as he spoke. "You're definitely getting it right."

He held her to him and pivoted, and to her surprise she didn't stumble but moved with him. He was signaling her, she realized with a flash of gratitude, telegraphing his moves an instant before he made them so she had a chance to keep pace. The music changed tempos from an upbeat melody to a more contemplative one, and they swayed gently in rhythm, his hand warm on the small of her back.

Then he loosened his grip and pushed her inward, spinning her in a slow circle under the arch of their raised arms. She had seen other people doing this, but she hadn't realized how exposed she would feel beneath the gaze of a dance partner. It was a relief when he pulled her back into his arms.

Deception was wrong, of course, her mother had said, but there was a fine line between deception and rubbing someone's nose in the unpleasantness of life. So at social events, Dilara always kept to the background, choosing her location carefully so her flaw faced toward a wall, was hidden behind a houseplant or was covered by a shawl.

Still, now, in front of a man she was beginning to like a great deal, she could not bear knowing that he would look at her in that assessing way a man looked at a woman. He was kind, she thought, so he would try to cover his distaste with kindness. And because it was too dark to see his eyes from a distance in the shadows, she would not know when that moment occurred. She wasn't sure whether that was a blessing or a curse.

Chapter 34

SHE WAS BEAUTIFUL. HE SWEPT HER INTO HIS arms again, enjoying the feel of her body next to his as they swayed and turned to the music. As the music slowed he could feel her pulling back, and he loosened his hold and let his hands slid gently down her arms toward her wrists. He wanted to kiss her again, but before he could act on the desire, he heard a hoarse whisper from behind him. He dropped his grip and spun to find the source.

The wall of bushes bordering the garden hid a service door, and staff members often took their breaks under the lamplight there. So quiet conversation was not unexpected, but this whisper had a fierce urgency to it.

"You're not paying me enough to go to prison for murder."

Poe stiffened and held up a finger to Dilara as a signal before edging closer to the bush. The second man's voice was higher.

"Don't be a fool. No one will be seriously hurt unless you screw up. But I trust that you know what you're doing. At least that's what you told me."

Something about the tempo of the words was familiar, but Poe couldn't identify the speaker.

"I do," the deeper voice responded. "When it comes to controlled explosions I'm the best you'll find in the sector. But this is different. There are variables I can't control."

"You saying you won't do it?" The higher voice grew menacing now, and there was an uncomfortable pause.

"Sure I will," the deeper voice responded in an appeasing tone.

"I said I would. I'm just saying, it won't be easy, is all. Long as I get my chance, you'll get yours."

The conversation moved out of hearing range, and Poe ran toward the gate, hoping to catch a glimpse, but he was too late.

"Poe?" Dilara sounded so bewildered he wanted to kick himself.

He could have sworn she was enjoying dancing with him. She had stood close as they swayed, and she had gasped when they spun together, but it had been the good kind of gasp. And then he had twisted her outward so she could pivot under their raised arms. Lenette had always loved that move. She had said it made her feel beautiful. But the brief glimpse he caught of Dilara's expression before she backed into the shadows was unsettling.

There was a quicksilver quality to interacting with her, which made no sense on a physical level. Her body was muscular and sturdy, solid. But every time he thought he might have a handle on her, he was wrong.

He intended to go to her, to say something light and reassuring, to make her laugh—anything to take that haunted look from her eyes. Instead he hustled her toward the marshal mobile and gave her a quick summary of what he had overheard once they were on the road.

"I need to get back to the cabin so I can call my deputies and bring them up to date."

She shot him a troubled look. "Do you know who those men were?"

He shook his head. "One sounded familiar, but I must be wrong because they were speaking in Mnoani."

"I thought the Mnoani were peaceful."

"In the abstract, they are," he said. "But there is a lot of justifiable anger there too. The entire planet was theirs before earth colonized it. And now that Melchior is involved, the tribe is feeling even more pressed. On top of it is that stupid statue. Insult to injury. Not that any of this justifies crime," he added.

"Maybe not," she said. "Do they have other options besides committing a crime?"

He stopped the vehicle in the middle of the deserted street and turned to stare at her.

"Of course they do," he said. "Everyone has options they can exercise instead of breaking the law. They might not like the options but they have them."

"Yes." She nodded thoughtfully. "I can see why you might think that. I mean," she added hastily, "there is never an excuse to hurt someone, especially not purposefully. But sometimes when there are two bad choices, a person might have to choose the least bad one, even if it breaks the law."

She watched him intently now, and he wasn't sure what sort of dispensation she expected from him. He sighed.

"You're right in a sense. As marshal I have discretion over which offenses I choose to prosecute, and sometimes I do let citizens off with a warning when they could have gotten worse. But those are minor infractions. Violence or the threat of violence is another matter. I can't just let that go no matter how pure the cause or how right the perpetrator thinks he is."

He pulled into the road leading to the cabin and stopped where the path to the porch began. She looked puzzled when he followed her out of the automobile and pushed past her on the narrow walkway, so his body stood between hers and any threat that might be waiting behind the front door. As a boy, Poe had thought the concept of door locks was hilarious, and he hadn't even seen one installed in a home until he was in his teens. Among the farming community, they were considered more of a novelty than a necessity. But now, to his disbelief, he wished he had one, at least for those times when Dilara was alone in the cabin.

He was being irrational, he decided, spooked by the conversation he had overheard. There was no reason to worry about Dilara's safety any more than he had ever worried about Lenette's. Maybe less, in fact. Dilara had been doing a decent job of defending herself against Saur Fanko the other night at BangBang, and she had been effective at doing whatever she needed to do in order to flee Caron 5. But there was an essential guilelessness to Dilara that worried him. Lenette had never been that young, even when she was the same age Dilara was now.

Chapter 35

EVEN FOR A TUESDAY, POE WAS GRUMPIER than usual, for no good reason that he could understand. Except that when he had asked Dilara what she was doing with her day, she said she planned to spend it preparing for her program at Bang Bang's that evening. And when he had suggested she might want to rethink that, she had pointed out that of the two of them his job was more danger-ous, and she hadn't suggested he should quit.

"It's been a month now and I'm beginning to get the hang of it," she had added. "After what happened the first time, I knew I needed a different type of music."

After what happened the first time? A normal woman would have decided to go into another line of work after nearly causing a riot in a bar. He opened his mouth to tell her so, but the expres-sion on her face was so stubborn, he changed his mind. There was no point in fighting about it. She would do what she wanted no matter what he said and in five months she would leave.

He picked up the file of papers he would need for his weekly meeting with Teamue and set out down Main Street. Clouds mat-ted above him as though someone had spread an unfriendly quilt across the sky. Sunday morning after the Melchior dance, for the first time ever, Poe had requested a meeting with his boss. And naturally the request had been turned down. Teamue had been in Central City attending the annual mayors' conference.

Today was Teamue's first day back in town, and Poe was anx-ious to update his boss. An overheard conversation was easy to misinterpret, but Poe's gut kept insisting something was wrong, and he was finding that feeling impossible to ignore. He nodded at Rinda and took his seat on the wooden chair. Thirty minutes later he wished he was still sitting there.

"The most useful lecture at the conference was about managing staff. You would have benefitted from it, Poe. This instructor really got it. He talked about how easy it is to feel overwhelmed by responsibility. You know how spaceships steer by using their propulsion system? He said successful leaders think of themselves not as that propulsion system, but as the igniter that sparks the fuel. As a leader, it's not my job to steer my staff, just to inspire them to act by lighting that spark."

Poe nodded politely, hoping he looked sufficiently enlightened.

"So," Teamue continued, smiling beatifically, "anything new?"

"I discovered a robbery in progress at the Farmers' Mercantile last Tuesday night. But even more concerning—"

Teamue stopped him with a raised hand.

"Another thing the instructor talked about was encouraging staff to focus on one challenge at a time. So. I heard about the robbery. What progress have you made?"

"We'll get the guys," Poe said. "We have a few leads."

"Among the Mnoani, I assume." Teamue nodded with a sage expression.

"Well, that relates to the second thing I wanted to talk with you about. I overheard a conversation on Saturday night. I couldn't see the two men, but they were speaking Mnoani. They seemed to be talking about explosives."

Frowning, Teamue leaned back in his chair.

"That makes no sense. Melchior doesn't hire Mnoani men because it's common knowledge they are thieves, and lazy to boot. So they would have no access to explosives. I fail to see what this conversation you say you overheard has to do with the robbery. Maybe you misunderstood."

Poe contained his impatience. "Melchior isn't the only source of explosives on the planet. The bovoquin manure stolen from the Mercantile is highly flammable."

Teamue tapped the tips of his fingers together and then looked at Poe over them with an expression of sudden understanding.

"Ah. I think I understand the real issue here. It all makes sense now that I have taken that course. Let me assure you, Poe, that I understand and validate the importance of your job. There is no need to inflate that importance in my eyes by creating a false emergency. The best way you can gain my approval is to do your daily tasks. In this case, concentrate on finding the robber. Mark my words, you'll find the perpetrator in the Mnoani territories."

Poe kept his mouth firmly shut as he rose, nodded to Teamue and strode out of the office. His jaw ached by the time he reached Main Street. It wasn't so much fury, although that was certainly a factor. The selective logic of prejudice never failed to surprise him. No one who had seen a Mnoani settlement could ever think the tribespeople were lazy. The thievery accusation was so common it was more rule than exception, but as marshal he had seen little to justify the belief. In fact, a disproportionate amount of the theft in Sector 1065 was committed by miners. But Teamue wouldn't know that because incidents involving Melchior employees were automatically referred to Melchior security to be handled in house. Worse, Teamue wouldn't believe it. That was the problem with belief—it was rarely swayed by fact.

Chapter 36

POE'S STOMACH GROWLED. LUNCH HAD BEEN a hurried and scant affair jammed between his meeting with Teamue and a backlog of paperwork. But his shift wasn't over until ten so going home to eat dinner would be foolish. He rose from his desk and jammed his hat onto his head before stalking out the door. The street was quiet as he strode toward BangBang.

There was plenty of standing room in the bar that evening and not every table was in use, but it was still surprisingly crowded for a Tuesday. Obviously some of the changes Porky had made when he took ownership of the tavern had been good ones. For one thing, the food actually smelled edible.

A server walked by with a laden tray. The scent of meat pastries, roasted weggels and generous slabs of noodle pudding tantalized Poe, and his mouth watered. He chose a table toward the back of the room where the light was weak. No point in Dilara seeing him. Not that it mattered, he decided, pushing his chair back a little farther into the shadows.

The replacement stage didn't look much sturdier than the original. It still sagged in the middle and inclined where it shouldn't, but Porky had managed to salvage the piano. It had a new leg made of a four-by-four strip of raw wood, and the top looked the worse for wear, but Rudolph, just settling back into his seat after a break was managing to play a tolerable version of some old song Poe couldn't remember the words to.

As the server set Poe's meal before him, Dilara walked onto the stage from the back door. The chatter of the crowd subsided somewhat, and to Poe's surprise there was a smattering of applause. One customer called out a vulgar suggestion, but the troublemaker was shouted down by several other men and the noise subsided before Poe finished rising from his seat. In his haste, Poe had nearly knocked his table over. He snatched his glass just before it tipped and sat again feeling a bit foolish.

Dilara didn't seem affected by the crowd's behavior. She stood there a moment, scanning the room, as though waiting for a signal only she could hear, her feet sturdy beneath her. Then she began to sing. He wasn't sure what he had expected, but it wasn't this.

The song was nothing special, some old ballad about love. He would have normally considered it insipid and a little dull, but she presented it with a combination of simplicity and kindness that made the words fresh, important even. Even given the political issues, he'd been surprised the Mnoani song had caused a riot, but now he understood. If she had sung that protest anthem the way she was singing now, even the most hardened of farmers might have felt a twinge of sympathy for the Mnoani cause. And there was nothing like an unexpected and unwelcome surge of compassion to irritate a person.

He let his gaze roam across the crowd, farmers in worn denim, miners just off their shift, coarse orange coveralls bleaching their faces of whatever color they had left after a long day underground. One customer didn't fit in, a slim man with a sharp gaze. He dressed like a Melchior executive, which made his presence in the downscale tavern even odder.

Poe sliced off a piece of noodle pudding with his fork and took a tentative bite. It was surprisingly good, excellent even. He wondered fleetingly whether Porky had hired away a cook from the MacLaren. He hoped not. It wouldn't be the first time that sort of thing had happened, but since the colony relied on the goods passing ships provided, it was better not to alienate the shipping companies by poaching their staff. On the other hand, people were free to choose where they worked, and if a chef wanted to work at BangBang, Poe wouldn't stand in his way. He took a bite of roasted weggel and sighed appreciatively.

He glanced back at the Melchior guy who had waved off any

attempt by his server to take an order. Except for an untouched mug of ale, his table was empty. Dilara was singing a livelier song now, smiling as the crowd joined in on the chorus. Her hips swayed to the rhythm, but the catcalling Poe would have expected didn't happen. Instead there was good-natured laughter at a particularly on point lyric as the song came to an end and some loud suggestions for the next number. They weren't treating her like an import, he realized, but like a local girl made good.

There wasn't going to be a riot tonight. Dilara had demonstrated more talent than Sector 1065 had seen in some time, and the crowd appeared fonder of her by the minute. If Porky played his cards right, he would get a good six-month bump up in business just for having hired her. Poe took the last remaining bite of his food and drained his glass, leaving a generous tip for the server who was probably going to get stiffed by the Melchior guy. Sure enough, the suit left his drink behind and pushed toward the stage. There was no good reason to follow, Poe told himself. Dilara's business was none of his business.

He pushed his chair back and stood to leave. It wasn't as though he could offer Dilara anything permanent, even if she had wanted it. In any case, given her performance tonight Poe thought she would be crazy to stay. Once she left for one of the larger planets she could have a real career—the sort that didn't involve singing in bars. On the other hand, maybe the suit was looking for a wife. And if the Melchior executive thought he was going to keep her on planet, well good luck to him.

It was none of Poe's business of course, but still he waited and watched anyway as the man in the suit approached her. Whatever he said seemed to please her because she signaled to Rudolph and left the stage to settle at an empty table with her admirer. Poe felt his lip curl and chided himself. He had kissed her once. He had no rights to her fidelity or even reason to care. If she wanted to spend her nights vetting potential husbands, it was her choice.

He headed toward the door, smacking his palm against it as he pushed his way out into the cool darkness. Stupid door. Stupid Melchior guy. Stupid him for letting his guard down for that moment when he had held her in his arms and allowed himself to pretend the impossible. He kicked at a piece of trash.

"Hey!" The complainer, drunk and nearly comatose on the floor of the alley, was all but invisible in the deep shadows.

Poe knew he should arrest the man. Loitering was an offense as was public drunkenness, but he couldn't summon the energy. Instead he muttered an apology and headed for his office. There were forms to fill out and filing to do and then, when his shift was over, he would go back to his cabin and sleep. Alone.

Later, when he had finished writing up the report, Poe drove home and sat in the marshal mobile for a moment listening to the spring crickets' rusty fiddles. The porch light was on but the cabin was dark. Dilara would be in her room, although she was probably still awake. Once she had told Poe that singing made her too wired up to fall asleep easily. Not surprising since she had spent the evening enthralling crowds of men, he thought sourly. She smiled with such intensity when she was onstage it was as though she was making a distinct connection with each customer. So he couldn't blame the increasing crowd of farmers and miners who thronged to BangBang every night for wanting more of what she had to offer. And he could hardly blame her for being good at what she did.

He got out of the car and stood for a moment. He wasn't accustomed to feeling indecisive, and he didn't like the sensation. He should go to bed too, he knew, but he couldn't bring himself to enter the silent cabin. He compromised by climbing up the porch stairs and sitting on the bench swing. It squeaked a bit as he swayed in concert with the chorus of insect hums and chirps. Nothing sadder than a man alone on a porch swing, Emmer had once quipped. But then, Emmer didn't have that situation often. Scratch that. Emmer *never* had that problem. The only time Emmer was alone was when he wanted to be.

Poe scowled and pushed against the floor with his boot, so the bench swayed unevenly. No one understood why he hadn't just found another woman after Lenette. It wasn't for lack of opportunity. It was true there were far fewer women in Sector 1065 than men, but in the farming community there were plenty of women who would love the idea of marrying into the Lancaster family.

But he didn't want to be a rung on the ladder again, a

convenient foothold for someone on her way to the top. What was the point? Once the shine wore off, that same woman who had thought she would love him forever would look past the uniform and the connected family and see him for what he really was when you stripped it all away—a failure.

He had been careful to avoid the relationship-y types of things a woman might read as a sign of an impending commitment. That kiss had been a mistake, he realized now. It was just that in the moment, it had seemed totally right, perfect. Clearly his judgment was off.

He pulled off his hat and ran his fingers through his hair. Maybe marriage shouldn't be off the table for him in the long run. He could see committing to a woman in a few years. She would be from a farming family, someone he had gone to school with. It wouldn't be romantic, but real-life marriages weren't. Affection would be fine—respect too. Just not love because love could destroy a guy.

And that was the problem with Dilara. Unfortunately even with all her defensive prickliness, maybe even because of it, she was the kind of woman he could fall in love with. She was sharp, bright, and incisive. It didn't escape him that these were also the characteristics of a knife blade, a great instrument when used as intended, but lethal if misused, even unintentionally.

She was kind too. So she wouldn't mean to hurt him—it would just happen. The tip of his thumb rubbed the sharp edge of his badge. She was nothing like Lenette personality-wise. But that didn't change the end result. A woman like Dilara, whether she knew it or not, was destined for bigger places than a backwash like Sector 1065. And when that day came, she would leave him behind just as Lenette had, standing in a cloud of dust, his heart in his hand.

He stood and dragged himself into the cabin, trudging straight to his bedroom without stopping. He didn't want to disturb her, not because he was considerate, but because he didn't want to face her. It didn't work completely. He heard her door open after his had shut, but he resisted the urge to check in with her.

There was a tightness in his chest he hadn't felt since a drunken farmer's fist had collided with his ribs a year ago. Dully he sank to the bed and began to loosen his boot laces. Who was he kidding? He thought about her all the time. He couldn't get enough of her, the way she moved, her rare precious laugh, her sharp intelligence. He loved her. So he was going to have to get a grip because she could never know. She wasn't responsible for his messed-up heart.

As he drifted into an uneasy sleep, it occurred to him that he might not even be able to maintain a friendship with Dilara. A friendship might be too confusing for both of them. Surprisingly that thought was even more painful than the idea that a romance with her was off limits.

Chapter 37

DILARA LOVED "THE GOLDEN SPOOL SONG." The melody was sweet but the lyrics were sly. It was a risky choice because it relied on the audience actually listening. On the upside, if the customers were too focused on food and drink to pay attention to the music, they were less likely to riot. So there was that. Besides, Tuesday nights tended to be calm. Mostly.

The lighting was designed to draw audience attention to the stage. As a result, she couldn't see clearly beyond the first few rows of tables. But as she slid into the chorus, her breath caught in her throat. Poe was here. She couldn't see his face because he was in the shadows near the back wall, but the way he sat, relaxed but fully alert, was unmistakable.

She felt a flush of warmth at the thought he had come to hear her sing. That might not be the case, she reminded herself. He might have simply been hungry. For that matter, he might have wanted to check to make sure she hadn't caused another disturbance. There was no point in assigning more meaning to his presence than it merited, she decided.

At least the stage fright wasn't bad tonight. Since her first ever performance at BangBang or anywhere outside her bedroom for that matter had ended in catastrophe, she had assumed she would be fired the moment she returned for her next shift. But Porky had been so solicitous of her, offering her food and drink and even to escort her home at the end of each evening, that despite Rudolph's persistent glare, she had felt much better about standing onstage again.

In fact, recently she had been relieved to find that her stage fright was beginning to morph into more of a stimulant than a handicap. She was able to think about the music and the words as she sang them and most intriguing of all, she was able to feel the audience was paying attention. It had never occurred to her that a critical part of live performance was the intangible connection between performer and audience.

Better still, for the first time she could remember, her stump didn't matter. All that seemed to matter to the audience was the music and whether she was transmitting it in the best way she could. It wasn't that the customers couldn't see her flaw. But they didn't seem to care about it as long as it didn't get in the way of providing what they were paying for. The sensation was almost frighteningly liberating.

She took a breath and the air, filled with the tang of sweaty bodies, dirty clothes and spilled liquor, smelled sweet. This was the last song of the last set and when she was done, she would find Poe and maybe they would celebrate. The thought was so delicious, her heels bounced in anticipation.

After the final cadence, she nodded to Rudolph, whose grimace was marginally less irritable than it had been at the beginning of the evening. It was progress of a sort.

A man in a suit approached her, looking up at her on stage with a speculative stare. He wasn't dressed like a searcher. Still, she felt a chill between her shoulder blades at the thought.

Rudolph was still riffing on the keyboard behind her. Though he didn't like her, he was unlikely to let her get kidnapped right under his nose. She flicked a glance toward where she had seen Poe, but there were so many people milling about she couldn't catch a glimpse of him.

"I'm Manx Spinner, Ms. Elian. I've got a proposition for you."

Dilara's heart sank. This was exactly the opportunity Mrs. Onkelson had spoken of so glowingly and which Dilara had done all she could to avoid. She would have to be careful to be clear in her refusal of his advances all the while making sure she didn't provoke him. She smiled politely, stepped off the stage and joined him at the table he chose.

"First, I wanted to welcome you to Sector 1065."

"Thank you." She nodded politely, hoping he would get to the point soon.

"I didn't see you at the Welcome Banquet." He waited a moment and when she didn't respond, he shrugged and continued.

"I'm the entertainment resource director for Melchior, and I'm always looking for talent like yours. I imagine you've heard of our cultural ambassador program?"

She blinked and shook her head.

"Perhaps you've heard of Phae?"

"Everyone's heard of Phae." Her pulse quickened. Phae was a multi-planetary singing phenomenon, the sort of star who only came along once in a generation.

"Phae got her start in the Melchior cultural ambassador program. I'm here to offer you a similar position. We have a corporate presence in hundreds of colonies and settlements like Sector 1065, and not just on Valora. Our ambassadors are tasked with providing cultural enrichment to our employees on planets from Fornax to Nebulara and even to Earth. The company provides travel, lodging and expenses, of course, and a generous salary as well. It's an opportunity to do some good while getting paid for it. But from your perspective, I would think the primary draw would be exposure. It's a great way to build a loyal audience of fans."

She kept her smile courteous but cool as he continued to describe what he probably thought she wanted to hear. She couldn't afford to alienate a Melchior executive, at least not for another five months. She glanced toward the back of the room. She could see Poe clearly now that the room was nearly empty and the lights had been turned up. She had pictured a glance of approval from him, maybe even admiration. Instead he looked disgusted. He turned and pushed his way out the door, the door hinge squealing as he shoved it and then banging closed behind him. Her heart sank. Dully she turned her attention back to Spinner. He waited politely for her response without even a flicker of inappropriate interest, and for the first time she wondered if what he was offering was real.

"I'm contracted with Well-Wed to stay in Sector 1065 for six months."

"Naturally, we would release you from that commitment if you wanted to start your tour immediately. Or if you prefer to stay out the six months here, that could work too. In any case, no need to make a decision right away," he added. "You have plenty of time to think about it."

He pulled a sheaf of papers from his jacket pocket and placed it on the table. "Here is some additional information about our program. I've included a blank contract for your signature should you choose to agree to it. My contact information is on the top sheet. I hope you'll consider coming onboard. You're wasted here."

After he left, she stared at the papers unseeingly. If she took the offer, she might be harder for a searcher to capture. She wasn't exactly sure how these things worked, but she suspected her parents would balk at significant travel expenses for a searcher, especially if they felt funds were tight. So Spinner was offering her a kind of security Sector 1065 couldn't. She should jump at it. But even after he left, she couldn't bring herself to touch the papers.

"Is that yenxer bothering you?"

Porky stood in front of her, broom in hand, next to the pile of trash he had been pushing. There was something endearing about the big man. He was red and sweating from the effort of cleaning, and his anxious expression only added to his vulnerable look.

"He's from Melchior," she said. "He offered me a job."

"Oh, no. Are you going to take it?"

He had been kind and she owed him honesty.

"I don't know," she said. "Why'd you call him a yenxer?"

"It's an old habit." He shrugged and sank into a nearby chair with a sigh. "People from founding families like me and Rudolph and your friend Poe, for that matter, tend to have a poor opinion of Melchior folks. It's not completely fair. The company feeds a lot of mouths and that's hard to argue with.

"But farmers look at the long game, it's the nature of farming. And some of the changes Melchior is proposing…" He shook his head. "Anyway, that's not your problem. But it's important for you to know that Melchior can be a lousy work environment."

"Did you ever work for the company?"

"Just long enough to earn enough to buy BangBang. I would

offer to match what Melchior's offering you, but my guess is they've already calculated what I can afford and are proposing to give you a little more than that."

"I haven't looked at the amount yet. Besides, I promised you I would stay here for the six months. That is, if you want me to stay."

His shaggy brows rose. "Are you kidding? This was a record crowd for a weeknight, and it's been two weeks in a row. Now I'm thinking maybe we should stop closing early on Mondays—and that's all because of you. So of course I want you to stay. But I'll also understand if you take the offer. Just be careful. I know from personal experience you only succeed at Melchior if you're willing to step on a lot of other people on your way up."

Porky had offered to escort her home, but she told him she had plans to meet Poe. That had been true until Poe walked out. Now she just wanted the opportunity to be alone. Grabbing her knapsack she strode out the door, neatly avoiding a snoring heap of clothing in the alley on her way to Main Street. The houses and businesses sat dark and still and the road was deserted, so it was safe enough to head back to the cabin on her own. Besides, she needed to think.

She didn't want to consider the implications of Poe's behavior. She could feel herself flinching away from the prospect. But that wasn't how the new Dilara did things, she reminded herself. The new Dilara, the one she had become when she had walked up the gangplank of the MacLaren and changed the direction of her life, didn't shy away from accepting truth no matter how painful. And the truth was Poe was a distraction and a problem.

She glanced to her left as she passed the marshal's station and paused. The light glowed warm from the big window overlooking the street. She edged closer. He hunched over his desk, one hand clamped around a pencil, the other raking his hair. For a moment she let herself consider an alternate universe in which she walked into the room. He would lean back in his chair and fix her with those assessing eyes. But there her vision cracked and shattered.

She had felt his hesitation, slight but still there, as he had drawn her into his arms in the garden. And the way his hand had paused when it reached her wrist. She hadn't imagined his sigh of relief when they were interrupted by the two men whispering behind the hedge. That had hurt.

And once he was absorbed in dealing with the implications of that whispered conversation, it was as though the kiss had never happened. At least now she understood why. His expression before he had stalked out of BangBang said it all. She was so repugnant to him he couldn't even enjoy her music.

She shivered in the balmy warmth of the quiet night. She had never wanted anything, anyone, more than she wanted Poe. Her jaw tightened reflexively. Other people had many desires—fame, wealth, power. She only wanted one thing, which made it even more unfair that she couldn't have it. And the worst part was that her need for him had ambushed her. She had been so careful, she thought mournfully, and still she had fallen in love. Stupid, stupid heart.

She stepped back into the pool of darkness between the circles of light cast by the streetlamps and took one last look. It wasn't that she blamed him for his revulsion. Everyone found her flaw revolting—that was normal. But she had promised herself on the day she watched Caron 5 receding in the porthole, she'd never again fall prey to the urge to pretend otherwise. And now she had allowed herself to slip up in regard to Poe.

She would have to be careful not to be fooled again. He was courteous, that was all. But that was what was so confusing. As hurtful as growing up had been on Caron 5, at least she had been in no doubt as to her social position. Sector 1065 had seemed an improvement initially, but this way of living had the potential of being much more painful. How was anyone supposed to know where they stood? Deflated, she turned away from Poe's window and headed into the darkness. Tomorrow would be better, she told herself. But the promise felt hollow.

Chapter 38

WEDNESDAY HAD BEEN A PRODUCTIVE DAY SO FAR. Poe looked around the empty office with satisfaction. Emilio was off planet, escorting Lendo Hastings to serve as a witness in Galactic court, and Zela wasn't due in until late afternoon. All three had spent several days interviewing citizens, and while they had yet to find the manure thieves, at least he could defend himself to Teamue at their next meeting. The raindrops slapping against the window-panes meant there was unlikely to be a lot of activity in town be-yond business as usual. Anyone planning trouble would likely wait for tonight.

He poured himself a cup of coffee and gave his tidily stacked outbox a smug look. Over the rim of his mug, he caught a glimpse of the bulletin board. It was crammed with old wanted posters, aged notices of long past town events, and obligatory postings from GalacticPol, the newer layered over the older so thickly it would soon be necessary to find tacks with longer points.

In an unwonted burst of tidiness, he put his coffee down on his desk and reached for his wastebasket. Five minutes later, the bas-ket was nearly full and the board oddly uncluttered. He stood back and surveyed it. Strange how such a small act could make one feel triumphant. Shaking his head, he sat behind his desk and turned on his tablet. It had been at least a month since he had seen the bottom of his e-inbox. Since he was on a roll, maybe he could give that a go too.

GalacticPol communications came in on a daily basis, some-times several per day, and most of them didn't apply to Sector 1065. Still, as marshal, he was obligated to skim them before clicking delete. He started with the most recent. Anything older than three weeks was likely too outdated to matter anymore. Methodically he worked his way through the dozens of communications, enjoying the little ringtone each time he eliminated one.

When he reached the three-week mark, he stopped and stretched to release his shoulders. He clicked to select the rest of the posts, figuring he would just trash them and call it good, when one header caught his eye. His finger froze and he felt a slow seep of unease. GalacticPol was notable for its slow response time—there was no way the drones at Central would have gotten back so quickly on his request for Dilara's criminal check. Besides, he knew her now and she was no criminal. Scoffing at his own foolishness, he clicked it open.

Interplanetary Criminal and Offense Report
Re: DILARA ELIAN
DOB: 10-1-3052
Galactic Identification Number (GIN): Caron5-67839472043984
Jurisdictions Searched: All, interplanetary registries
Report Dated: 4-2-3080
Order ID: 591-24963
Reported by Caron 5
WRAYA ELIAN
Case No: 48-67384-SE-5666049-G
Charge: FUGITIVE FROM JUSTICE
Charge class: FELONY - LARCENY WITH INTENT TO STEAL AN AMOUNT LARGER THAN 500 ZILS
Statute: 11-569
Offense date: 3-31-3080
OFFENDER ACCUSED OF THEFT OF 500 ZILS AND ONE PENCE. OFFENDER REMAINS AT LARGE. IF FUGITIVE IDENTIFIED, APPREHEND AND CONTACT GALACTICPOL FOR TRANSFER WARRANT.

He sank back in his chair and let out the breath he had been holding. Raking his fingers through his hair, he stared unseeing at the screen. Dilara was a lot of things, but he would have sworn she wasn't a thief. On the other hand, GalacticPol might be slow, but they were undeniably thorough and rarely mistaken.

Caron 5 courts assumed defendants were guilty until proven otherwise. This had been a sticking point with GalacticPol since the policy didn't accord with Intergalactic standards, but in the end GalacticPol had caved.

He guessed Dilara knew nothing about her new felonious status, and he found himself reluctant to enlighten her. She was safe enough in Sector 1065 for the moment. He tapped the tips of his fingers against the top of the desk as he thought. Just having asked for the report was unlikely to alert anyone at GalacticPol. In the unlikely event anyone did follow up, he could just say he had been mistaken. People made mistakes all the time, right? Like the mistake he was about to make right now. He reached for the keyboard and clicked delete.

DILARA LEANED THE BROOM IN ITS CORNER AND SANK into the couch with a sigh. The rain seemed to be abating, but until it did there wasn't much to do in the cabin since she had read all the fiction and even some of the non-fiction. She was finding it increasingly difficult to stay upbeat and not all of that was because of the weather. It didn't help that she now saw herself through Poe's eyes and it hurt. She had promised herself when she boarded the MacLaren that she would love herself the way she was—the way no one in her family ever had. She had thought that promise would be easier to keep away from Caron 5, but it wasn't. She wasn't sure how other people managed it.

Poe was a perfect example. He was so sure of himself and his view of the universe. The way he strode into a room, the way he spoke, careless of the consequences, demonstrated a breathtaking sense of entitlement. Not financial entitlement, she amended the thought. If his cabin was any measure, he wasn't rich. It was more that he felt entitled to respect just for being himself.

She kicked off her boots and curled her legs under her. On the table next to her stood a framed portrait of Poe and Lenette, an engagement photo, maybe. She reached for it and cradled it in her lap, running her thumb over the embossing on the frame. Surprisingly given the formality of the pose, the photographer seemed to have caught them in an unguarded moment. Lenette smiled at the camera, a triumphant gleam to her eyes, but Poe looked as if his collar was too tight.

It was the only example she had seen of Poe looking anything but self-confident. Well, that and the way his face had frozen when she had brought up the profusion of knickknacks in the cabin. In that moment, he had withdrawn somewhere deep inside himself. She guessed it was good to know he had a weakness, but it bothered her that his sole weakness seemed to be a woman who had left him.

Not that it mattered. It wasn't as though she was in the running to be the next Mrs. Lancaster. Poe had made that perfectly clear the night they had kissed and had reinforced it when he had listened to her sing. She winced at the memory of his expression, angry and remote. It hadn't been the lyrics, she thought. It had been she herself who had displeased him.

Nonetheless, she did not want to forget the way he had kissed her. Alexandr had kissed her once, but Alexandr's lips had just brushed hers, a reluctant contact, as clinical as it was brief. Of course now she had a better idea why that had been the case. Still, she hadn't thought a kiss *could* be a memory worth treasuring until Poe had kissed her, which made falling for Poe all the more dangerous.

The depths of Alexandr's duplicity still pained her, but it felt more like a wound to her pride than actual damage to her heart. It was a bit embarrassing to realize she hadn't actually loved Alexandr. Saskia's betrayal had more staying power. The two sisters had never been close, Saskia's competitive streak had seen to that, but the ease with which Saskia had thrown away their lifelong bond had been a shock, and seeing Poe with his siblings and parents had driven the difference home. Dilara didn't like the way watching him with his family made her feel.

She reached back and returned the framed picture to its position on the end table. It was easy to do this correctly because there was a sharp dust outline where the picture frame had originally stood. Dilara had considered dusting, but the risk of accidentally breaking something had seemed high, and she wasn't sure what that might have done to Poe, so she hadn't. As she pulled her hand back, her knuckle brushed against a figurine of a shepherdess and nearly knocked it off the table. It teetered and she held her breath, but then it settled into place again.

Lenette was beautiful. She was small, curvy, and wore the knowledge of her own attractiveness like a crown. She was every-thing Dilara was not, and clearly this was what had attracted Poe. This was reasonable, she reminded herself. She tried to feel mature in her assessment but instead felt an unexpected flash of anger. It wasn't that she had expected to find love in Sector 1065 once she had found herself with no other choice but to stay. That would have been unrealistic. But everything she had read about Sector 1065 had contained the promise of a new way of life, the sort of place where her flaw might be, if not insignificant, at least less of an impediment.

And now there was this offer from Melchior, an opportunity she would never have dreamt of on Caron 5. So she hadn't been wrong, exactly, to think of Sector 1065 as a place of possibilities. But maybe she had been greedy in thinking that one opportunity might open the door to another, that her skill might also increase her value in Poe's eyes. Since he had left BangBang that night, they hadn't seen much of each other. He spent even more time than usual at work, and when she knew he would be home, she made a point to be busy elsewhere. It was already Thursday, and she hadn't even told him about Spinner's offer yet—she wanted to hug the compliment of it close for a little longer. But she would tell him tonight, she decided. He might not approve of what she did for a living, but she owed it to him to be honest. It wasn't Poe's fault she had hoped for the impossible, but the fact was that she felt a kind of constant ache now. It was a weird empty gnawing feeling and nothing seemed to help.

Chapter 39

JUST AFTER NOON, TEAMUE'S SECRETARY CALLED to order Poe to the docks to supervise the arrival of Melchior Intergalactic's CEO, Jandar Holyand. Poe pointed out Melchior's security detail was more than capable of escorting Holyand to headquarters safely without Poe's help, but Teamue had broken into the conversation and insisted. That meant the staff meeting got pushed forward by another hour and then they had all gone out to dig for gossip about stolen manure. It was sunset by the time Poe was back in the office. He was just about to leave when the phone rang.

"When are you making an arrest?" Darius began. "How hard can it be to find one or two Mnoani kids? I pay just as much taxes as the next guy."

Poe rolled his eyes, grateful Darius had used the phone instead of walking across the street—this way Poe was free to scowl unobserved. Since Darius had called daily since the robbery, everyone in the office had been on the receiving end of his litany of complaints. Emilio did a bang-up job of imitating it. To be fair, Darius had a point. It was reasonable to expect results, and Poe was a bit surprised that neither he nor his deputies had heard any usable rumors about the theft yet.

On the other hand, the more often Darius called, the more curious Poe became because stolen manure shouldn't have been the crime of the century from a store owner's perspective. Darius would have insurance after all, and theft was a common problem for store owners, even in Sector 1065. Or maybe the Mercantile didn't actually own the manure.

"Darius," he said, "was the manure on consignment?"

"What difference would that make?" Darius sputtered. He sounded even more annoyed at having his litany of complaints interrupted than at the actual list of perceived wrongs he had been delineating in such loving detail.

"Whose manure was it?" Poe pressed.

"It was Borin's," Darius said. "But I still don't see—"

"Thanks." Poe hung up before Darius could regain momentum. He wasn't sure why the information mattered, but he was pretty sure it did. Still, no matter how he turned the matter over on the way home, he couldn't make sense of it. Even then, he might have managed to salvage his mood if it hadn't been for the tarnots. Black and knobby, they rested on a pile near the cutting board on the kitchen counter.

Dilara turned back from the pot she was tending on the stove and picked up a carving knife before realizing he was there. Her cheeks were flushed from the steam and for a moment he was lost in her eyes. But then she wedged a tarnot under her stump and began slicing the vegetable into thin discs. She scooped the discs into a bowl and smiled up at him.

"We had these on Caron 5 too, but I haven't tasted them in years."

He could feel the accumulated irritation of the day coalesce into something bigger. He turned away for a moment, just long enough to get a grip on his annoyance.

"I didn't know you had gone to the market today," he said. "I'm always glad to save you the walk and pick stuff up when I'm in town."

"No need," she said in a self-satisfied tone. "I dug them up from your garden patch."

He knew he should have been complimentary or grateful, should have said something polite, anything but what wanted to come out of his mouth. She was still talking, so at least he had a moment to regroup.

"It's a big patch," she said. "I think you could get a good crop out of it, but it needs a lot of weeding. I'm only about a quarter done, but it looks like you have a bunch of next generation plants from last year you could already begin to harvest. There are lettuces, jinhin, flower herb, pepper and these tarnots."

"I hate tarnots." It sounded angrier than he'd intended, and it wasn't true. In fact, since she had found them in his garden patch, it sounded completely irrational.

"And I hate that garden patch," he added, completely truthfully. "You had no business meddling with it."

She flushed and he felt like a bovoquin, surly and clumsy now, which made him angrier still because he was right, damn it. More than the stupid figurines, the framed insipid sayings, it had been the garden that had been the mortal blow. Lenette had known how to hurt him without leaving bruises, and it seemed Dilara had an unerring instinct for doing the same. He closed his eyes and saw the image of Lenette, her pretty face disgusted when she saw the garden patch he had dug and planted in neat rows.

"How could you think I wanted this?" she had cried. "How could you think I would want to be married to a dirty sweaty farm worker?"

"I'm sorry." Dilara put the paring knife down on the cutting board and backed away from the counter. "I didn't know."

"Well, that's just it, isn't it? You don't know but then you do what you like anyway. Which would be fine if it didn't also mean I had to bend over backwards to fulfill your ridiculous plans."

Her jaw tightened as she picked up a dishcloth. "I don't have ridiculous plans."

"Oh, no?"

He felt a rush of gladness now, a kind of joy in combat. The mincing around a topic, not saying what one meant or wanted, was a game for elegant people but he wasn't elegant. He never would be. And if she thought he would consent to being made into the sort of man she had grown up with, she had another think coming. She was in his battleground now. One didn't take prisoners here.

"That yenxer from Melchior will be a perfect match for you— a bloodless, gutless, moneymaking machine. I wish you the joy of him, but don't ask me to congratulate you."

She shook her head. "You don't understand."

The laugh scraped his throat. "I may come from uneducated

farmer stock, but I understand the basics," he said. "You have an offer on the table. It's likely the best you are going to get here. I recommend you take it."

Blood rushed from her cheeks. When she spoke, her voice was low and tight. "He doesn't want to marry me. He offered me a job singing on tour for Melchior."

"Sure he did. That's just a come on." He sneered. "I bet he told you the story about Phae. Am I right?"

She stared at him silently, her eyes hot, lips tight.

"You're no Phae. You'll never be Phae," he said.

"I know that. But I—"

"No. That man knows exactly what you are." He bulled on, knowing how stupid, how cruel he sounded and not caring. "And he's taking advantage of your ignorance and even more of your illusions about yourself."

There was an air of finality in the way she set the dishcloth down onto the counter. Her expression was set now, polite but distant.

"To be clear," she said, "that is your opinion of me—that I am easily fooled because I am deluded about my worth."

He felt a creeping sense of unease as he nodded. It wasn't what he had meant, exactly, but the momentum of the conversation seemed out of his control now. It was like the time he had ignored Pop's warning and sneaked out to try his wheeled sled on Whittecomb Hill. It had been glorious at first—the wind tearing through his hair, the sense of invincibility, until he lost control of the sled. He could still hear the sound of the axles straining before they wrenched apart, could still feel the snap of the bone in his arm as he hit the dirt, the burn of the cut on his cheek. The arm had healed, but the scar remained.

She shook her head and walked past him toward her bedroom, her feet placed carefully, head high as though she were balancing something heavy on it. When she came out, her knapsack on her shoulder, she nodded to him. He nodded back without comment. He should have guessed she would walk out just when things were getting interesting. He looked at the clock.

"It's too early for BangBang."

"I'm going there to rehearse some new material for tomorrow night," she said. "Porky says Saturday nights are getting so crowded he needs to have two shows."

"I'll take you."

She gave him a long look, and then shook her head.

"I'd rather go on my own. I'm sorry about the tarnots and I'm sorry about the garden."

"I'll pick you up after your shift," he said.

"That won't be necessary," she replied. "I'll stay in town."

After she left, he swept the tarnots off the counter and into the trash. She had no right to interfere with his space, his garden, his life, his heart. No right at all.

Chapter 40

IT WAS MIDNIGHT WHEN DILARA FOLLOWED PORKY up the stairs outside the building leading to the second floor, the treads creaking under Porky's bulk. She kept the tips of her fingers hovering above the railing as they ascended, hoping she would not need to grasp the splintery wood. The door opened to a long corridor stretching down the center of the building. Every few paces they passed another door, and she wondered how many of the rooms were already inhabited.

"You sure you want to stay here?" Porky's forehead was crinkled with concern. "It's safe enough, but it's not exactly elegant."

He had been surprised at her request but was too polite to argue. She nodded and forced her lips into a semblance of a smile. She kept replaying the argument with Poe and filling in his words the way she wished they had happened. But there was no point. Poe hadn't asked her to stay. He didn't really want her there, whether he realized it or not.

Porky patted her shoulder gently with a sympathetic air and looked as if he wanted to say something kind, but at the last moment he shoved his hands in his pockets and cleared his throat. She braced herself. Being the object of sympathy was an unfamiliar and not entirely welcome sensation. To her relief, he just nodded toward the end of the hall where the shared conveniences were located before opening the door to a vacant room.

She nodded back at Porky and watched him shamble away before she closed the door behind her and turned to assess her new home. She hadn't expected much and she wasn't disappointed.

The room was cramped and dingy, the floor space mostly filled with a sagging bed, a rickety looking chair and a chest of drawers with a wash basin and pitcher on it. The sheets and coverlet spread on the bed hadn't seen a washtub in some time, but when she peeked at the mattress underneath them, she decided the sheets were the lesser of the two evils. A discouraged looking set of curtains had been a previous tenant's attempt at sprucing up the room, but they did little to distract from the large water stain spreading across the ceiling and down one wall.

The dusty window looked out onto Main Street. She used her elbow to rub a circular spot clean so she could look out into the deserted roadway. Most of the storefronts were dark, but there, on the far right, she could see a lighted window. It would be one of the deputies. Poe would still be at the cabin, probably asleep by now. He snored sometimes. She had heard him when she woke at night and had been soothed enough by the sound to sink back into sleep.

Here the noises were different and not nearly as comforting. The aged headboard rattled, and her bed vibrated in duet with the thumping from next door. Creaking sounds emanated from the opposite wall in a different rhythm. A man down the hall whooped occasionally. Whoever it was, the whooping sounded more pro forma than enthusiastic.

Dilara's eyes widened, and she could feel a hysterical laugh trying to bubble up. This was what Porky had meant when he said he hadn't thought she would like living upstairs, why he had shaken his head dubiously before leading her to her room. She had known many of her neighbors would be friendlies plying their trade, but it hadn't occurred to her it would be noisy.

There was nothing wrong with deciding to do friendly work for a living, but she was hardly a candidate for it. You had to have training and she didn't. She had been approached about it on Caron 5 once. Friendlies even worked in the court there, so it could be both a lucrative and upscale profession. The recruiter had assured her there were always men and women who were interested in variety, so flaws like Dilara's could have even been an advantage of sorts. Her parents would have accepted it. Saskia would have been delighted. But in the interest of self-preservation, Dilara had refused the offer. Love for her was improbable, certainly, so unlikely as to be laughable, but accepting it as impossible would have broken her.

She gave the bureau a dubious look and decided not to unpack just yet. She wasn't up to dealing with spiders, and she guessed there might be some inhabiting the drawers. Instead she carefully balanced her knapsack on the chair and turned back to the bed. Maybe she would sleep on top of the covers tonight.

She might have managed it if her bed hadn't collapsed. To be fair, the chair collapsed first. Evidently the knapsack was a final insult in a life of degradation, and the chair had decided it couldn't take it anymore. But then when Dilara sat up, startled at the noise, the entire bed frame gave out beneath her and the mattress hit the floor with a crash. It was lucky the bed frame was flimsy or the falling headboard might have caused her more damage than a bruised shoulder.

Someone down the hall shouted a curse in response to the noise, a different voice than the whooping man, but no one came to see what had happened. The lack of response was a relief of sorts. Anonymity was a new and delectable experience after the tight social circles she had grown up in.

But even as she prized the novel sensation, it also reinforced how alone she was here. On Caron 5, her solitary life had been an obligation, a civic duty. There had been a kind of pride in that until she realized no one except her actually valued her contribution. But here there was no inherent virtue in being alone, and it occurred to her for the first time there might even be danger.

There was no lock on the door, nothing to prevent a person from walking in and taking everything she owned, except that a burglar was likely to be noticed because evidently traffic in and out of the other rooms was regular and showed no signs of abating. Trying not to trip over the debris on the floor, she made her way to the bureau and shoved it, creaking but intact, against the door. She stacked the remains of the bed frame and the chair in the space the bureau had once inhabited. Then she curled up on top of the coverlet again, hugging her knapsack close, staring wide eyed out the window at the stars in the distance.

It was better this way. She had thought she could manage living with Poe, that going through the motions of living together would be sufficient to feed the intensity of her yearning for him. But she had been wrong. It was like being hungry and watching someone else eat a meal. If anything, living with Poe made her heartache worse.

She couldn't have him, and the sooner her heart accepted that, the better. Pretending otherwise wasn't fair to him and was dangerous to her. She knew this was the most sensible solution—a quick, sharp, decisive pain designed to prevent a fatal event—a kind of amputation. But for all the practicality of it, the anguish was breathtaking.

Chapter 41

"YOU PUT HER WHERE? YOU KEKKIN' YENXER!" Poe pounded a clenched fist on the bar so hard the glass bowl of salted qnoks on the polished surface jumped.

"I offered to put her up on our couch, but she refused." Porky shrugged, snagging the bowl and moving it out of harm's way. "It was the best I could do on short notice."

Poe shook his head, although what he wanted to do was shake Porky. The thought of Dilara in a brothel, the idea that she would *let* herself live in a brothel rather than stay in his spare room, was infuriating. He scowled at Porky who glared back at him with a defiant air.

"It's not my fault Dilara doesn't want to be with you anymore, Poe." Porky sounded uncharacteristically firm. "If you wanted to have a say in her living arrangements, you should have either given her a ring or arrested her. She's my employee and a friend, so when she came to me for help last night, I did what I could. You want to be mad at anyone, be mad at yourself."

Poe felt the air seep out of him. Rubbing a hand over his face, he sank onto the barstool. Porky picked up another damp glass and began to polish it.

"You're right," Poe said. "I'm an idiot. But still, a kekkin' brothel?"

"She has her own room. No one'll bother her unless she wants them to. I told her I'd walk her to her door every night at the end of her set. She said it wasn't necessary, but I'm doing it anyway." Porky shot him a defiant look.

Poe felt a prickle of jealousy and then quashed it. "Thanks," he said.

Porky set down the glass and picked up another. "Not doing it for you," he replied.

DILARA SAT ALONE AT THE LONG TABLE IN THE deserted kitchen. Understandably friendlies didn't prioritize breakfast. Idly she stirred her porridge. Even with the addition of fresh milk and fruit, it didn't appeal. Nonetheless she forced herself to finish it.

She had just risen, empty bowl in hand, when Poe appeared in the doorway. Loomed in it would have been more accurate, she thought. His broad shoulders nearly filled the narrow opening. She nodded at him coolly and then turned away toward the sink to wash her bowl and spoon, but her shoulder blades itched as though his gaze was palpable.

"You didn't have to move out," he said. "We could have made it work."

She nodded as she rinsed the spoon. "I know that's what you think. But I did have to leave."

"I was in a bad mood and I took it out on you. It wasn't fair. I'm sorry."

She turned to face him, dishtowel in hand. He looked so appealing she had to steal herself against giving in. Moving back with him, resuming their relationship, whatever it was, would be a mistake she wasn't willing to make. She had ignored her misgivings when it came to Alexandr, and that had led to disastrous consequences. Still, there was no reason to be rude.

"I can accept your apology. What you said wasn't fair, but sometimes I also am not fair or in a bad mood, so I understand that happens. I hope you will accept my apology for any hurt I caused you."

There was a flicker of relief on his face, and he stepped forward, sliding carefully onto the nearest bench.

"I didn't leave because of our argument," she said.

His jaw tightened and the momentary relaxation in his eyes slipped away.

"Then what is the issue?"

She sighed and put the dishtowel back down on the drain board. There was no avoiding this conversation, but still she wished she was somewhere, anywhere else. She could feel her heart pounding, and she tucked her hand in her pocket so he wouldn't see it tremble.

"I'm not like Lenette."

"That's for sure." He snorted.

Suddenly feeling more certain, she held her hand up to stop him interrupting.

"Given what you have said about Lenette, I'm not sure I'd want to be like her. Still you probably couldn't have found a woman more different. For you I'm the anti-Lenette."

"An excellent thing, from my perspective," he said. His grin was tight, and she felt even surer she had made the right decision.

"That may work for you," she added, "or you may think it does. But it won't work for me."

Confusion warred with impatience on his face. The exhaustion of her own sleepless night suddenly seemed too heavy for her to carry. Sighing, she sank onto the bench opposite him. He didn't understand, and he was unlikely to understand ever. Still, she owed him a debt of friendship, and she didn't want there to be any misunderstanding between them.

Frowning, he shook his head. "You're not making sense. Why would you want to be like Lenette?"

"I don't," she said. "But I also don't want to be defined in contrast to her. Can you understand that?"

He stared at his tightly clasped hands and then met her gaze.

"You're wrong. I don't compare you to Lenette and you shouldn't compare yourself to her either. It's not even close to a competition. You win."

She stared at him. How was it possible that such an intelligent man could be so stupid? She stood quickly, nearly upsetting the bench.

"You're wrong. I lose. Or maybe it's just that we are playing two different games, you and I."

POE FELT THE BRUSH OF HER GOWN AS SHE PASSED HIM on her way out the door, a whisper of a tug, and then she was gone. He unclasped his fingers and stared at them unseeingly. He knew better than to try to hold onto a handful of sand. No matter how tightly one grasped, the grains slipped through the cracks.

She was wrong, of course, not that it was any comfort. Being right wasn't making him feel too good right now either. He pushed himself up from the bench and wondered if this was what feeling old was like—as though the most normal of activities sapped one's energy and focus. He scowled and forced himself to walk with purpose out the front door, along the sidewalk.

He tried to shake the conversation off as he strode along. He should be relieved, he reminded himself. Taking Dilara in had been a time-consuming obligation and had flown in the face of all his well-considered decisions about interacting with women after Lenette, which made it hard to understand why he wasn't feeling better about her moving on. Losing her had been inevitable. She wouldn't leave the way Lenette had, but still, she would leave. He had always known that. And when she did leave, he ought to be glad for her, he instructed himself.

Dilara had always been too upscale for Sector 1065 and for him, for that matter. For that reason she had known better than to try to change him. Unlike Lenette, Dilara had recognized a lost cause when she saw it. So, score one for her.

As the day wore on, his sour mood got worse, not better. He found himself wishing it was Saturday so he could look forward to releasing some of his frustration by enforcing the peace at a bar brawl. Instead he forced himself to catch up on paperwork so he would have something productive to show at the end of the day, but by evening, the little he had accomplished was poorly done, and he knew he would have to redo it the following day.

Back at the cabin, he made a point of closing the door to the spare room, so he would stop glancing into the room every time he walked by it. And then he opened it again because when it was closed he kept imagining she was in there, and that was worse. Then he stripped the bedclothes off her bed because they needed washing in case he were to have another guest sometime, but when he held them in his arms, he caught the remnants of her scent and for a moment he considered not washing them after all. Suddenly furious, he jammed them into a ball and loaded them into the back of the marshal mobile. He would drop them off at the laundry tomorrow and then there would be nothing left to trigger the memory of her. But removing the last trace of Dilara made no difference because when he tossed in his own bed that night, the memory of her scent lingered, and he dreamed she was leaving Sector 1065 and he was too far away to stop her.

Chapter 42

UNCERTAIN, DILARA STOPPED WALKING AND SHIFTED her knap-sack to the other shoulder. At the dance the Melchior executive complex had reminded her of a fairy tale castle, but in the prosaic light of a Monday afternoon, without the strings of twinkling lights and the kindly cover of darkness, the hulking building seemed util-itarian and even a bit threatening.

The four stone towers, one rising from each corner, loomed above the base. Porky had told her the vast multi-story rectangular base of the complex was the only public area, used for large events like the Welcome Ball, conferences and orientation activities for new executives. According to Porky, one tower was divided into lavishly appointed apartments for the executives who preferred to live on campus. The remaining three contained offices, laborato-ries and guest suites for visiting dignitaries.

It had been overcast when she set out from town, but the bank of clouds she had thought were comfortably far away had moved surprisingly quickly, and now the purple bruise-colored clouds filled the sky. The spires looked less like castle turrets and more like the corner towers of a fortress belonging to a sullen despot. She flicked a glance over her shoulder. The road behind her was deserted save for a farmer's wagon disappearing into the distance.

There was no going back and fairy tales, like love, weren't true anyway. Until she was off planet, a fortress was the safest place for her to be, she reminded herself. She shot the building another dubious look and tried to think of it as a refuge. It didn't work—the brothel was beginning to feel homey by comparison. The image of her cramped room in Poe's cabin flashed unbidden, and she blinked fiercely before hitching her knapsack higher on her shoulder.

As she strode down the long driveway, the first drops of rain began to fall, plopping sullenly between the branches of the trees and splattering as they hit the dry earth at her feet. By the time she reached the portico, her hair was plastered to her head and the hem of her dress was caked with mud. She made a futile attempt to brush it clean, but she only succeeded in making it worse. Belatedly it occurred to her that Spinner might have changed his mind about the offer. Or might change it now, given her bedraggled appearance.

She paused as she stepped into the lobby. While the room was not as crowded as it had been the first time she'd entered it, it was still busy enough with employees scurrying to and fro that no one seemed to notice her entrance. Heartened, she asked directions to the restroom. She couldn't do much about her hair, but she did manage to rinse the mud off her dress and squeeze it until it was merely extremely damp. Then, feeling marginally more confident, she made her way to the information desk.

Manx Spinner's office was situated on the fifty-fifth floor of Tower 2. It was spacious and expensively appointed from the thick dark green carpeting to the ivory and tan upholstered armchairs in the small seating area near the large window. On a clear day, she thought, he would look down on the company housing and farther away, the town itself. But now rain beat against the pane and mist obscured all but the nearest buildings. He was reading a portfolio behind a vast slab of timber formed into a desk but put it aside and rose, smiling as she entered.

"How lovely to see you again," he said. "I hadn't been sure I would."

Coming around his desk, he cupped her elbow and guided her toward a small sitting area. She glanced at the pristine upholstery and winced at the thought of sitting on it with her sodden clothing. Instead she removed her knapsack, setting it on her boots so as not to leave a puddle on the carpet, and pulled out the contract.

"I signed it," she said.

"Wonderful." He took it from her and flipped to the back page. "I'll have a copy made and get it to you right away. Will you be staying with us?"

She nodded. "I'd like that."

He smiled. "Then I'll have someone escort you to a guest suite. You can arrange to have your clothing delivered there."

She tried to look like the sort of person who might have a trunk or two of fashionable clothing just waiting to be delivered and felt a little deflated when he saw through her.

"And we will need to arrange for a proper wardrobe before you begin your tour. Perhaps I could send up a designer later today, after you have settled in."

Settling in seemed the wrong term, she thought a few minutes later when the door had closed behind her escort and she was alone in the suite. Slowly she lowered her knapsack to the entry mat and stared. Her parents' home had been luxurious, but Dilara herself had had little access to the most elegant rooms. Some of them had even been off limits for dusting. She hugged herself to try to keep from shivering, but her clothes were still too damp to be comfortable.

Suddenly impatient, she yanked open her knapsack and pulled out her few remaining dry garments. When she was warm again, her damp clothes hung neatly in the entry closet above her boots, she explored, her stocking feet sinking into the thick pile of sea green carpet. There was a dining table big enough for a party with a long narrow arrangement of fresh flowers down the middle. A sunken area held a puffy gray couch embellished with fat squishy looking pillows in shades of blue.

A double door to her right opened to a lavish bedroom. The bed, resplendent on a platform, was about the same size as the room she had left behind in Poe's cabin. The walk-in closet was embarrassingly large, and the opulent bathroom contained a bathtub big enough for ten of her. She knew she should feel relieved, joyous and even exultant. From here it was just a short step into the career she had only been able to dream of a few short weeks ago. She caught a glimpse of her face in the mirror and turned away. If she couldn't rejoice, at least she could work.

The couch was exactly as soft as it looked. She sank into it with her sheet music in hand, figuring she could tweak some of her compositions while she waited, but she couldn't get comfortable. Poe's couch was worn and in some places, the springs poked, but it had become familiar. Annoyed, she ignored the papers before her and stared out the broad window. The fury part of the storm had passed, and now the rain fell almost without purpose.

She was being foolish, she scolded herself. It was true Poe hadn't used her the way Alexsandr had, or at least not intentionally. Still, that didn't mean he loved her. Given her conversation with Minden, it seemed likely Poe was using his friendship with her as a way to avoid a relationship with one of the local women. Dilara had been a fool to imagine even for a moment Poe might consider a ring ceremony with a one handed, penniless outsider when he could have his pick of eligible women in town, any one of whom would have met with his family's approval. She felt like kicking something, but since she wasn't wearing her boots she contented herself with slapping the papers onto the table beside her.

She had just hauled herself out of the pit of softness that was the couch when she heard a polite knock on the door. For a moment she considered just not answering. The thought of dealing with a designer who would no doubt take one look at her and depart in disgust felt like more than she could cope with. Still, beggars couldn't be choosers. She had a momentary flash of shimmying across a stage in one of the black suits that seemed to be the only acceptable outfit for a mid-level Melchior employee and grimaced as she reached for the door handle.

But the tiny old man with the measuring tape dangling from his neck seemed so delighted to meet her she could hardly refuse to let him in. He introduced himself as Izak and quickly beckoned to the flock of assistants behind him. They pushed carts laden with bolts of cloth in a variety of hues and a hanging rack filled with gowns. Reluctantly she agreed to try on a few things, feeling like a fraud as she let him pin, prod and poke, fitting the loose shapes into body skimming perfection. When, upon his request, she showed him the clothing she owned, he clicked his tongue dismissively.

"Caron 5 has never been in the forefront of fashion, so I suppose it can't be helped. I will leave you with some basics as soon as we finish here. They will do you for a start. And then in a few days, we'll have another fitting."

After she was alone, she returned to the walk-in closet, less empty than before. She now had several choices of elegant casual wear along with more formal options. There was even a gown in nearly the same shade of blue as the one she had asked the manager of Rank's General Store to put aside for her. But the gown in the store was made of a sturdy linen wool mix, suitable to withstand years of wear in a hardworking farming community.

The fabric on the dress Isak had left her felt like gossamer, and it shimmered when she touched it. She had never owned anything so exquisite in her life, and she was a bit frightened of it. Carefully she closed the closet door and walked back to pick up her music. This, at least, she knew how to handle. And maybe later she would wear one of the new outfits to the rehearsal and pretend to be someone else—a person who matched those elegant clothes, who knew how to become what Isak mistakenly thought she already was.

The rain had stopped and a watery sun peeked through the clouds. She stood near the window and forced herself to concentrate on the song. There was something not quite right in the third stanza. She stared blindly toward the window as she considered tweaking the bass line.

The collision between bird and windowpane was quick and loud. So much so that it took Dilara a moment to realize what had happened and another to spring forward to watch the bird's colorful body pin-wheeling downward. It was a tapperhead, she thought. The suite was too high to see whether the bird survived the fall.

Her heart sank. It was not logical to see any connection between the fate of a bird that had been blinded by the sun's reflection and her own situation. So the tears stinging her eyes made no sense.

She knuckled them away impatiently, but a few fell on the sheet music and where they landed they left tiny pucker marks.

Chapter 43

POE DRY SCRUBBED HIS FACE AND TRIED TO concentrate, but the figures on the ledger in front of him kept blurring. Bookkeeping had never been his strong point, but exhaustion didn't help. He hadn't been sleeping well. Scratch that, he had barely slept at all since Dilara had moved out. He had never minded being alone until recently. Even when Lenette left, despite his pain and anger, there had been a tiny treacherous whisper of relief.

So it had come as a shock to realize he enjoyed living with Dilara. He liked the way she was always too busy doing her own projects to spend time correcting him on his. There was something restful in feeling he was enough the way he was. He hadn't trusted the sensation at first because she wasn't a fool, so she surely could see what a mess she was living with. But it hadn't seemed to affect her. She puttered around the cabin, humming to herself, as though she was perfectly satisfied with it, with her life, with him.

He guessed he knew better now and that was good, he reminded himself, because he wasn't going to change for anyone. So it was important for her to understand that—important for him to remind himself of that too. No. Dilara was better off without him, and he was better off without her. Everyone was getting what they needed.

It should have been a satisfying thought, so there was no good explanation for the savagery of his desire to hit something. He slapped the ledger shut and jammed it into his desk drawer. Rising to grab his coat, he strode toward the door. He would go on patrol. Maybe the good cheer that flooded through the downtown on a

Friday afternoon would be contagious. Minimally it would give him a chance to clear his head and distract him from thinking about things he couldn't change.

His hand was on the doorknob when the telephone rang. For a split second he considered ignoring it, but it occurred to him it might be Dilara calling. He would be cool and professional, he decided. He picked up the phone.

"Marshal," the nasal tone grated. "Mayor Teamue would like to meet with you immediately."

Poe's jaw muscles clenched. This was a perfect time to meet with Teamue because the day wasn't already miserable enough. Ten minutes later he was ensconced once again in the uncomfortable little chair. Rinda shot him a cryptic look and then returned to her filing with the enthusiasm of a zealot.

The telephone buzzed and the secretary, without turning from her task, said, "He's ready for you now."

To Poe's surprise, Teamue wasn't alone. Darius rose from the visitor's seat as Poe strode into the room, the shopkeeper's expression an uneasy mixture of guilt and triumph. Borin remained in the other chair but turned to watch Poe approach. There was a flicker of malice in Borin's eyes, but there was no time to consider the ramifications because Teamue began to speak.

"Thank you for joining us, Marshal Lancaster."

Teamue's tone was formal and something in Poe stilled. He could hear his own pulse, the blood rushing in his veins. The pounding was almost loud enough to drown out what Teamue was saying.

"…substandard performance…temporary leave of absence while the Board discusses our options…I will notify you of our decision after our monthly meeting…"

Poe opened his mouth to say something, anything, but his throat was clenched tight. Instead he nodded, tipped his hat to Darius and Borin and walked out. The sunshine rested palely on the storefronts. Songbirds flitted from branch to branch of the trees lining the town green. But all he could hear was the pounding of his pulse, and the sun's warmth made no inroads into the chill at his core. For the first time in his life, he did not respond to greetings from passersby, and he ignored their curious glances as he passed.

He needed Dilara. She would know what to do, he thought dimly. But as he neared his office, his steps slowed until he stopped. She didn't want to see him. She didn't want to be with him. And really, what did a broken man who couldn't even hold onto his job have to offer? Slowly he trudged into the office, closing the door behind him before pulling down the window shade. Amid the flood of professional phrases there had been something about clearing out his desk. Wearily he pulled a flattened box from behind a set of shelves and set about refolding it.

He picked up his coffee mug and put it in the box and then thought the better of it. He had never liked that mug much. He took it out and put it back on the tray near the others. He tugged open a desk drawer and had just begun to sort out his personal items when he heard a knock. He guessed he was still marshal until the end of the shift, so he tucked the box under his desk before heading toward the door.

He had been too absorbed in his own situation to look out the window until now, so he hadn't noticed the storm clouds roll in. As he swung the door open, a breeze filled the room with the scent of ozone. The first fat drops began to plop onto the dusty boards of the sidewalk at his feet in what was likely to be the opening salvo of a major storm if the ominous clouds overhead were any measure. The visitor had impeccable timing.

On a smaller individual, the black hooded robe might have looked ridiculous, but this man was taller and lankier than Poe. The robe's sleeves fell just short of his wrists, and his large hands looked strong from use. An odd pendant dangled from a thick silver chain around his neck, an eye shaped medallion. He pushed back his hood as he entered the office revealing golden hair was cut close to his head. It reminded Poe incongruously of the fuzz on a baby chick.

His cheeks were gaunt, his eye sockets deep. But it was the brilliant blue eyes that held Poe's attention—they fixed on his with a steady implacable gaze. It was a trick searchers employed, Poe reminded himself, and took care to avoid thinking about Dilara.

Searchers couldn't read minds, but they were selected for their intuition and predatory instincts. It would be a mistake to underestimate this man.

"I'm looking for Marshal Poe Lancaster," the man said. His voice sounded rusty, as though he did not use it often. "Are you he?"

"I am he." Now he sounded stilted too. "And you are?"

"I am Searcher Jens." He reached into his cloak and plucked a rolled parchment from an interior pocket. "I carry a warrant from the Grand Leader of Leaders of Caron 5 for one Dilara Elian."

GalacticPol frowned on self-help when it came to law enforcement and for that reason had an uneasy relationship with searchers. There was a tinge of the vigilante in the searcher industry that had been a useful, if occasionally a violent, tool of law enforcement during settlement times but was increasingly unnecessary and even dangerous now that homesteading colonies in the area had united under a centralized code of law. A searcher like Jens worked for a bounty, usually for courts or even for GalacticPol on occasion. On the other hand, sometimes less particular searchers worked for private parties following personal agendas.

Poe took the document and squinted at it, mouthing the words as he read. It was a standard form for interplanetary extraction, but he needed a moment to think, and it wouldn't hurt if Jens thought him a fool. Sometimes appearing stupid was an excellent weapon. He put the document on the pile of paperwork on his desk and slid a ledger on top of it before sitting and gesturing Jens into the visitor chair.

"Well, now." Poe drew it out, mimicking the drawl of his predecessor. He leaned back, balancing the chair on its back legs, his boots crossed on the desk, his hands clasped behind his head. All he needed was a stalk of linna grass between his teeth to look like the image of a folksy sheriff.

"You have a seat, sir, and we'll see what we can do to help you out."

Jens hesitated, but he was clearly too professional to appear impatient. After checking the surface of the wooden seat carefully, he sat. Apparently at least some people from Caron 5 had learned it was better not to alienate a person one wanted a favor from, Poe thought sourly.

"I imagine you'll find the folks a bit more welcoming here than on Caron 5," he said.

"Perhaps."

"Sector 1065 is a small, friendly type of place. We would have noticed if there was a stranger in town. What makes you think she's here?"

Jens shrugged.

Poe tried for a congenial chuckle. "Tricks of the trade, eh?"

Jens gave him an impassive stare.

"Working on behalf of GalacticPol then?"

"No."

Poe nodded. "So who is your boss?"

"The Elian family hired me."

Poe whistled and tried to look properly impressed. "They must have some funds. I can't imagine you come cheap."

The Searcher inclined his head as though a nod would reveal too much. Poe thought quickly and put on a concerned frown.

"There any risk to our population from this woman? Elian, you said her name was?"

"Unlikely," the searcher replied.

"Well, that's good," Poe said. He didn't have to pretend relief. Neither the document nor the searcher had mentioned larceny, and since the searcher wasn't working for GalacticPol he wouldn't be privy to Poe's criminal check. But experienced searchers checked for warrants as part of preparing for a hunt. It was interesting that Jens hadn't. Or maybe he had checked, but the warrant wasn't pertinent to his pursuit.

"It may take a while to locate your quarry," Poe continued. "Do you have a place to stay while you're in town? I can recommend a good hotel."

Jens stared at him for a moment, those unsettling blue eyes boring into his. "A hotel will not be necessary," he responded. "I do not rest until my search is complete. In any case, I do not anticipate any difficulty. Sector 1065 is not a metropolis. It's unlikely there are many one-handed women from Caron 5 here."

Poe gestured toward the map of Sector 1065 tacked to the wall. "Sector 1065 is a small colony in terms of population, but between farms, Melchior's property and the Mnoani territory, you can see there's a lot of land to cover. That's assuming she's even here on Valora. I've only got your word on that."

Jens just looked at him.

"Right." Poe continued. "If this woman you are looking for found work on one of the farms, for instance, it might take a week for you to locate her. And that's if she even stayed in Sector 1065. Once a person heads past the mountains yonder," he gestured vaguely toward the north, "they can be near impossible to find."

Chapter 44

AS SOON AS THE DOOR SHUT BEHIND THE SEARCHER, Poe snatched up his phone and called BangBang, but Porky was out running an errand and Titch, who picked up the call, didn't know when Porky would return or where Dilara was. Gossip was a popular sport in Sector 1065, but folks tended to be closemouthed around outsiders, so it would probably be a day or two before Jens managed to get a lead. Still, as much as Poe wanted to reassure himself Dilara was safe, it would be imprudent to walk to BangBang in person to look for her. Jens was no fool, and Poe didn't want to lead the searcher to his prey.

It was only an hour until his shift was over, but it was a long hour. When Zela arrived, Poe was looking into the box, bemused at how little there was in it. He explained the situation briefly. Her shocked and barbed comments about Teamue's likely ancestry, most of which involved barnyard animals, were amusing and surprisingly touching, and when Poe tried to hand her his weapon, she shook her head.

"Might as well hold onto it," she said. "He didn't fire you. You're on suspension. I can't see this lasting for more than a day or two. Even if it does drag on, Emilio and I can manage until you're back on duty. The Mnoani community center dedication is the only big crowd event coming up this month, and it should be peaceful. It's nowhere near as controversial as the Winslett statue installation and we managed that okay."

Poe just shrugged, picked up his box and headed for the door. Zela offered to drive him home, but instead he suggested she take

234

the marshal mobile and head up toward the outer farms to see if there had been any additional instances of vandalism. It would be good if she and Emilio could find the culprit. There was no point in all of them losing their jobs. And as a side bonus, if Jens was watching the office, Zela would provide a useful false lead.

Once she had driven off, Poe slipped out the back of the building, taking back routes and shortcuts to drop the box off at the cabin before heading back to town by an even more circuitous route. He worked his way to BangBang from the north end of town and felt fairly confident he hadn't been seen. Poe walked in the door and found Porky sorting items in the storeroom. When he looked up at Poe, he scowled, but the expression didn't seem at home on his normally amiable face.

"If you're looking for Dilara, you can take a hike."

"Where is she?"

"Not here, thanks to you."

"Porky, I need to speak with her. It's important. She may be in trouble."

Porky set a crate of apples aside with a sigh.

"She left. She's signing up with Melchior on that kekkin' ambassador program. Rudolph's tearing his hair out."

"What are you talking about? Rudolph hates Dilara."

"Rudolph hates everyone," Porky said with a sigh. "But he hates Dilara less."

"When did she leave?"

"She left on foot this morning. Hope she made it to Melchior before the rain came. That was a hell of a storm, and now the alley's a swamp. Folks'll be tracking mud in all night long." He stared pointedly at the floor.

Poe looked behind him at the trail of mud from his boots to the door.

"Sorry, Porky. For the mud, but also for Dilara leaving. I know she was a popular draw."

But he knew he sounded less sincere than he should have because underneath he felt a swell of relief. As long as she was on the Melchior campus, the searcher didn't have a chance. Besides, he was going to head over to Melchior himself next. Kindal Zan, the head of security, had mentioned once that security at Melchior always had job openings and unlike Zela, Poe had zero faith Tea-mue was going to change his mind. Dilara might not want to be with him anymore, but at least he could be sure she was safe.

A couple of hours later he walked home again, this time pleas-antly tired from the exercise and feeling a mild sense of triumph at having solved his income problem so quickly. Not only was Zan eager to hire him, the position would pay a little better than the salary he had been earning as an interim marshal, and there was room to move up if he was willing to transfer off planet. He tried not to think about that possibility too closely. He should be pleased, he told himself firmly. This was the beginning of a new chapter for him. It was the sort of lateral move Lenette would have approved of. He had told Zan he could start in two weeks when his paid suspension was up. In the meantime, Zan would keep an extra watch on Dilara.

Poe trudged up the porch steps to his cabin, pushed the door open and flicked the light switch. He had seen these rooms every day for years, but now he looked. Shaking his head, he walked into the back entry to grab an armful of empty crates left over from last year's harvest. At first he considered wrapping the figurines, but as the sheer quantity of them became more apparent he stopped worrying about preserving them. If Lenette had wanted them, she would have taken them with her. If Lenette had wanted him—well, she hadn't.

He began tossing the statuettes into the crates more quickly now, feeling a surreptitious sense of glee at the crack and crunch of them as they struck each other. When those crates were brim-ming over, he carried them out back to the trash pit, poured the contents out and returned to fill them again. He thought he should feel something, pain maybe, or sorrow, but nope, just relief and an odd sense of lightness. It took fifteen trips to the trash pit before the surfaces in the living room and the bedrooms were clear of all detritus, the walls empty of mottoes and pockmarked with nail holes he could take time to plaster now that he had nothing to do during the workday. The only things he kept were the photo-graphs. He plucked them from their frames and packed them away in a shoe box. He wasn't sure what he wanted to do with them, but keeping them on display was definitely off the menu. Then he got rid of the frames too.

The piles of decorative pillows went into some empty feed sacks. Minden could probably find some use for them. He stacked them on the porch along with half a dozen of the more rickety knickknack tables and shelves. Now that he had finished, the rooms sounded different, hollow. But for the first time since Lenette had moved in, he felt as though he had room to move, to breathe. He stared at the pile of detritus on the porch. It was odd that none of it carried the essence of Lenette. In contrast, Dilara had left nothing behind. It seemed unfair that nonetheless, he could still sense her presence in every room.

Chapter 45

DILARA CHECKED HER BAG FOR HER MUSIC one more time before she stepped into the elevator. This was a normal Friday afternoon, she reminded herself. There was no good reason for her to be nervous heading into a rehearsal. Rudolph would be there. That wasn't a comfort, exactly, since Rudolph could hardly be called sympathetic. She wondered if his look had always been disdainful and then suppressed a grin at the thought of such a surly baby. Still, he was an excellent pianist, and he hadn't let his dislike of her color his musicianship. And if she did well at the talent show tomorrow night, her ambassadorship would be even more secure than Manx Spinner had promised.

She was early for her assigned rehearsal slot, so she peeked in the door from the lobby to see if Rudolph was ready for her yet. The talent show would be held in the same hall that had been filled with tables for the dinner dance. But now it was jammed with rows and rows of chairs and looked even more cavernous than before. Rudolph was seated at floor level, plinking at the keyboard with a dubious expression. He looked up as she climbed the stairs to the stage.

"Oh. It's you."

She might have been offended if she hadn't known this was Rudolph's equivalent of an enthusiastic welcome.

"Everything okay with…" she gestured down toward the piano.

"I told them to tune it," he growled. "But did they listen?"

She winced in sympathy. She didn't have perfect pitch but she

238

knew Rudolph did.

"You got music for me?"

She reached down to hand him a sheaf of sheets.

He shuffled through them and glared up at her. "What's this?"

"It's something new," she said.

"I can see that," he snapped. "Why?"

"I just—" but he began to play, and she didn't have to stammer through the explanation she had planned.

"Where'd you get this?" he asked as his fingers came to rest.

"I…wrote it."

She swallowed suddenly and wished she could take the words back. She turned to fumble in her bag for her alternate song, keeping her face averted until she had blinked away the sudden stinging in her eyes. It had been a stupid idea, she realized now.

"I brought some of our regular stuff too, in case—"

"Shut up." He ignored her and began playing the piece again from the beginning, slower this time and with more care, filling in the bass underlay with spare chords. "Okay. Run it," he said.

She blinked and scrambled into position at the center of the stage. She had written what she had heard in her head, but it was a different thing altogether to hear it, to sing it in front of another person. It wasn't that she liked Rudolph exactly, but his opinion as a musician mattered to her. When she finished the song, she took a deep breath and looked at him.

He shrugged. "It doesn't suck."

She let out her breath and grinned, the surge of pleasure taking her by surprise. Before she could respond the door at the back of the hall opened, and several of the Well-Wed women ambled in. They were talking but Dilara couldn't hear what they were saying, and in any case none of them seemed interested in including her in their conversation even if they noticed her. With a mental shrug, she picked up her knapsack and nodded to Rudolph before heading past the women on her way back to the lobby. She intended to return to her suite to fiddle with the lyrics one more time, but the concierge waved to her as she passed. The envelope was sealed, but she recognized Poe's handwriting, as though his energy had been imprinted on the paper along with the ink from his pen.

She rubbed her thumb along the letters and remembered the tips of his fingers, calloused but gentle. Her skin warmed at the memory of his lips on hers, the hardness of his arms as they encircled her. He had been careful not to alarm her, she realized, moving slow and steady. Maybe he thought kissing was new to her. She wished it had been. It would have been good to have Poe as her first kiss memory instead of Alexandr. But ultimately it was best to remember the two men were similar in one respect—they were dangerous.

Perhaps Poe was not looking to gain from relating to Dilara, and she was hard put to come up with any conceivable gain for him, there was still the matter of her stump. Even in Sector 1065, a man could not want a woman with such an obvious visible flaw, and she knew from her experience with Alexandr that any man who said it didn't matter was a liar. She refused to be a fool twice, so she had done the right thing, the smart thing for both Poe and herself by walking away. Which made the sense of betrayal she felt now completely unreasonable.

Unbidden, the image of Poe's angry face popped into her head. He didn't owe her anything, she reminded herself, not love, nor friendship, nor even courtesy, although he had been courteous, more than courteous. He had invited her into his home, a gesture that far surpassed his societal responsibilities to a stranger. He had treated her more like an honored guest than an interloper, introducing her to his family, protecting her from harm, dancing with her, kissing her. It was an astounding degree of hospitality, even if for a brief foolish moment, she had allowed herself to pretend it could be something more.

It would be better to do the kind thing, the right thing, she decided. There was no hope for either of them if she stayed in a dream. Without allowing herself to weaken, she held the envelope back out to the concierge.

"I don't want this," she lied. "Please dispose of it."

Chapter 46

THE PREP ROOM ALLOCATED TO THE WELL-WED women performing in the talent show was cramped, but Dilara did not need to
compete for a mirrored table or a changing booth. She had warmed
up and dressed in her suite, expecting to arrive in the prep room
only a few minutes before the show was scheduled to begin since
Mrs. Onkelson had been insistent on the importance of prompt-
ness. But given the flurry of activity, Dilara suspected the concert
wasn't going to start on time after all.

She found a square of empty bench to sit on and watched the
other women prepare. Guerenne had commandeered the largest
mirror and was absorbed in unpinning a mountain of pin curls.
Ricki, never short of self-confidence, spun on her toe tips, waving
her arms overhead. With each pivot, she snapped quick kicks, apparently heedless of her neighbors' unprotected shins.

Susanna sat on a stool on the other end of the room, lacing on
tap shoes. Susanna had been in near constant communication with
her distant boyfriend during the journey to Sector 1065, and Dilara
wondered whether she still was. If Susanna's worn but determined
expression was any measure, missing a boyfriend who loved you
was harder than never having had one to miss. One of Guerenne's
acolytes, Reba, struggled to untangle the strings to a gangly mari-
onette. Dilara watched her a moment, idly wondering whether
Reba was even aware of the irony of demonstrating puppetry skills
when she let her own strings get pulled by Guerenne so often.

Dilara was surprised to see Kiko stretching her hamstrings
with an intense focus that implied, if not professional chops, at

least a dedicated amateur status. On Caron 5, professional dance was an exercise in conveying languid tranquility, or on occasion, serene joy. The dance performances she had watched as a child had been invariably tedious. But there was a banked fury in Kiko, a purposeful driven kind of anger that would necessarily infuse her choreography. Dilara hoped she would have the opportunity to observe Kiko's performance—it would be interesting to watch a different sort of dance.

She had assumed since she had gotten over her initial stage fright at BangBang that performance nerves would no longer be an issue. But apparently she was mistaken. The combination of a different venue and the mingled excitement and anticipation among the other women was making her jittery. She pulled out her music and forced herself to concentrate on the lyrics and on whether the third line of text in the second verse was the very best she could do. She had rewritten it several times already, but now she wondered whether she would have been better leaving it as it was originally. She had just pulled out a pencil to tweak some words yet again when Mrs. Onkelson scurried into the room, clipboard tucked under one arm, and clapped her hands sharply.

"Ladies, I have an announcement. I didn't want to say anything ahead of time in case of disappointment, but we have a special guest in the house tonight. The CEO of Melchior Intergalactic arrived in the auditorium just now and is sitting in the front row of the audience. This is an enormous honor for all of us!"

She spoke with such awe Dilara barely managed to swallow a laugh and then immediately felt a flash of guilt. Luckily Mrs. Onkelson had been too involved with her clipboard to register the sound, but Kiko shot Dilara a glance from across the room, a flash of companionable humor in her eyes that took Dilara by surprise. She forced her attention back to Mrs. Onkelson as a sort of penance. Mrs. Onkelson might be overly reverential when it came to the Melchior hierarchy, but she had been kind to Dilara. For that matter, Dilara herself was indebted to Melchior—the company was offering her an opportunity she could never have hoped for on Caron 5.

"I'm going to read the order of the program now. Listen

carefully because I will only read it once. Please make a note of the name of the woman performing just before you. When she begins to perform, you must be standing with me in the wings stage right so you can be prepared to take your place immediately once she has finished acknowledging her applause. When you finish your performance, you should wait in the wings stage left until I signal all of you to come out for your final group bow."

She paused and scanned the group, smiling at no one in particular and everyone in general before continuing. "This is an excellent opportunity for each of you to draw the eye of a Melchior executive. I don't need to tell you what an advantageous match that could be. So do your very best. Remember, this is the very first talent show we have run in the history of the Well-Wed program, so the lieutenant and I are depending on all of you ladies to make us proud."

Dilara was scheduled to perform at the end of the first half, just after Kiko. Mrs. Onkelson wanted to precede intermission with an announcement about Dilara's new position as a Melchior ambassador. Dilara didn't love the idea, but there had been something about Mrs. Onkelson's delight in the opportunity to make that announcement that had made it impossible for Dilara to reject the plan even as she dreaded the embarrassment of being made the center of attention. She didn't mind it when she was singing but having to just stand there was a different matter.

Slowly the prep room emptied out as performers took the stage. Guerenne, dressed in a crisp white confection of a dress, her golden ringlets cascading down her back, looked paler every time another woman left the room. She had prepared a dramatic reading of a poem and clutched the book of verse so tightly her knuckles were white. Dilara couldn't help feeling just a little sympathetic.

"I'm sure your reading will be eloquent," she said. "I look forward to hearing your interpretation."

Guerenne shot her a contemptuous look. "No one cares what you look forward to."

"I do," Kiko said. "Besides, I'm sure Dilara was just being polite. There's no competition here."

"Definitely not," Guerenne huffed. "I happen to know the

CEO of Melchior Intergalactic loves this poem. I expect he'll want a private audience after the performance."

Dilara opened her mouth and then closed it. There was no good response, and in any case it was Guerenne's turn to leave the room and head toward the stage. Kiko followed her and Dilara decided to do the same. There was little point in waiting in the green room—it would only make her more nervous.

Mrs. Onkelson nodded at her when she arrived at the stage wings and checked Dilara's name off her list before turning to embrace Guerenne who received vigorous applause for her rendition of "The Wreck of the Hesperus." Kiko was next. Dilara edged closer to the stage to watch. One had to notice an audience, acknowledge them in a way, but then dismiss them from one's consciousness in order to perform in Dilara's experience. But when Kiko danced, it was as if she was alone, and because Kiko was so sure in her movements, it was as though they were the only possible movements that *could* have come from those musical phrases. Rudolph must have liked what she was doing too. He was playing with real emotional delicacy.

The piece neared its climax, and Kiko leaped toward the back of the stage in preparation for what Dilara presumed would be a big finish. But as Kiko pivoted to face the audience, a fireball exploded at the front of the stage and billowed toward the front row of seats. For a split second, fragments of fire seemed to hang in the air like stars. But then the screaming started, and it seemed impossible to believe that anything so horrible could also be even momentarily beautiful.

Everywhere the fragments landed, fire spread. Kiko backed into the wings across the stage looking as shocked as Dilara felt. But there was no time to react because Mrs. Onkelson was screaming and slapping at the sparks attaching themselves to the long skirts of her dress. Dilara saw a rolled-up carpet along with an armchair and table nearby used for a skit earlier in the program. The armchair was smoldering and the table was no use. But Dilara kicked the carpet roll open, urgency lending her strength.

There wasn't time to watch the carpet unroll—she just prayed it had as she hurtled toward Mrs. Onkelson, slamming into her so both women fell to the floor. Scrambling nearer, Dilara jammed her shoulder against Mrs. Onkelson's torso, forcing her to roll onto the carpet. Then it was a matter of suffocating the sparks before they got more of a hold of the thick fabric of Mrs. Onkelson's gown.

The shock might have subdued Mrs. Onkelson's normal officiousness, but it did not prevent her from exercising her organizational skills. Once she had scrambled out of the carpet cocoon, somewhat charred but otherwise uninjured, she set to work rounding up her charges, most of whom had been just far enough out of range to have avoided being injured by the blast. But Dilara ran toward the edge of the stage, her heart in her throat as she stared at the upended piano.

In the wake of the explosion, the silence in the room was eerie, punctuated only by groans and sobs. The swath of destruction was centered at the front of the stage. She would have been standing there singing when the fireball exploded had the concert begun on time. The people who had been sitting in the first few rows of seats were mostly on the floor now, many of them badly burned. At least one she could see was likely dead. She had never seen a battlefield, only read about them. But this scene reminded her of the etching in a book she had read about Earth history. Survivors staggered upright, their faces blank with shock. Rudolph was one—the force of the explosion had tipped the upright piano, but a nearby podium had caught it. The piano balanced perilously on its edge, but the thick iron plate must have protected Rudolph to a degree. As she stared, he managed to crawl out from underneath. The flash of relief she felt at the sight was followed closely by the knowledge there were others who would not be so lucky. And even though many would have avoided physical injury, no one who had experienced that evening would be unscathed. The stench alone would be hard to forget—smoke, burned flesh and fabric, some sort of organic material she couldn't identify, and overriding those, the scent of fear, anger and helplessness.

She blocked it out as best she could and got to work. There was water in the wings intended for the performers, and she offered sips to those of the injured who wanted it. For others, a hand clasp or words of encouragement were the best she could do. The security guards arrived and imposed a kind of order, ushering anyone who was able to walk outside to the gardens. Then a man who clung to Dilara's hand wouldn't let go so they allowed her to stay with him.

She kept her gaze on the man's face as much because she didn't want him to look down at his legs as because she didn't want to see them herself. She suspected it was only the shock that kept him from realizing how badly burned they were. He was about her age, she guessed, one of the up-and-coming executives who had been part of the welcoming committee for Melchior's Intergalactic CEO. Not a big shot. His suit cuff was frayed and the fabric was smooth at the elbow. He would have wanted, even expected, to be a big shot eventually, she thought, but right now his trusting look reminded her of a little boy.

Chapter 47

LATER, POE COULD NOT REMEMBER THE RIDE in Stig's wagon except it did not seem fast enough despite Stig keeping the chevalo at a gallop. It was the moment they neared the compound and Poe heard the alarm bell that stayed with him. The harsh ringing contrasted with the unnatural hush of the huddled observers standing under the grove of flowering trees nearby. The white petals overhead stood out in the darkness, beautiful and remote. He leaped from the wagon before it stopped, forcing down his desperate need to run toward the furious activity in the lobby. Zan strode toward him, a look of contained fury flickering in his eyes.

"The building is fine. The fire is out now," he said. "But there was an explosion and some of the injuries are serious."

"Poe!"

Stig came round the back of the wagon, two med supply bags banging at his sides, their shoulder straps crossed over his chest like bandoliers. His arms were wrapped around a hefty box. Poe took it from him, grateful for a chance to do something, anything to take his mind away from where it kept going.

"I brought all the burn salve I have," Stig said. "What the hell happened here?"

Poe strode past his friend and led the way toward the doorway to the hall. "Nobody knows anything yet. It was supposed to be a talent show. Then the stage exploded."

Stig grabbed his elbow. "Did you see Dilara?"

Poe shook his head and tightened his grip on the box.

"Looks like the women are outside," Stig said, gesturing toward the grove of trees. "We'll find her after. Right now you need to focus on doing what you can."

Poe recognized the soothing tones of a professional, but he was too wired to resent it. Maybe Stig was right about the focus part, but he was wrong about Dilara. Increasingly Poe figured he would have sensed it if she was in the crowd he had passed on his way in. He hadn't, so she was inside—injured, maybe even dead. His heart stuttered at the thought.

He forced himself to walk forward, into the room. Someone had turned up the big chandeliers, which would have been dimmed for the performance. Their twinkling gaiety lent an even more surreal quality to the scene.

Scorch marks were everywhere. A few security officers worked with volunteer firefighters to disassemble the piles of upended chairs as they searched for remaining hot spots. But the center of activity was near the stage. The explosive must have been small—the worst of the damage was within a thirty-foot radius, but within that circle the damage had been devastating.

Poe set Stig's carton down on the edge of the stage and set to work. His training had included basic medical instruction, and he had taken a refresher course whenever it was offered. Most of the townspeople, especially those in farm families, had accumulated some minor doctoring skills if only to stabilize the injured person until the doctor could arrive at whatever rural location he was needed at.

But the sheer number of injuries was daunting—mostly men, their black suits hiding the extent of their injuries, a few women, likely wives of the most successful farmers, dressed for an evening out. There were lots of burns, of course, so Stig would need all of that salve, Poe guessed. But there were other injuries too. Some folks had been thrown by the force of the blast. A man to Poe's right cradled an arm that looked broken. Another victim stared around the room, his eyes wide and confused, but did not get up from his seat on the floor.

Poe nearly missed seeing Dilara. She crouched, curved over a man protectively, her hand in his. Her blue gown was smeared in ash and filth and her hair fell forward, so he could see the vulnerable line of the vertebrae of her neck. Relief slammed him. He could feel his ribs release as he inhaled what felt like the first full breath he had taken since he picked up the call from Stig. His eyes stung, and he blinked hard before turning to reassure a man who looked to be about his Pop's age.

"My son." The man's whisper was hoarse, strained. "He isn't moving."

To Poe's relief, the unconscious man was breathing and his pulse was steady. As soon as Poe had bound a stretch bandage around the older man's ankle so he could hobble alongside his son's stretcher, Poe turned to the next victim and the next. Once he looked up and saw Stig near Dilara. But he kept his focus on what he was doing and didn't interfere.

A man at his feet moaned, and Poe opened another jar of ointment before crouching to see where the damage was worst. It would have been useful to have had a salve to apply to his own heart's wounds when Lenette had left. But it occurred to him as he began methodically applying the ointment to the man's face, that the wounds Lenette had inflicted had been notable more for their number than for their depth. With Dilara it would be different, more dangerous. With Dilara he might sustain only one wound, but it would be deep—fatal, maybe.

It was odd. He had thought after Lenette that he hadn't any emotions left to destroy. Maybe the stupid things grew back like the weeds in a garden. Didn't matter how many times you yanked them out, there was always a spore or two left to sprout again.

All of which went toward the argument that walking away from Dilara was the only smart thing to do. She had been bound to leave sooner or later, sooner now that Melchior yenxer had gotten her to sign the contract. At least when she did leave, she wouldn't be taking Poe's heart with her.

He glanced back toward her and flinched. Something was wrong. She had let go of the victim's hand and stood now, swaying slightly as Stig helped lift the man onto a gurney. Then Stig turned and pulled Dilara into his arms. Her body shuddered and for the first time ever, Poe felt like punching his best friend.

It should have been Poe holding her, comforting her. But he couldn't have it both ways, he reminded himself bitterly, and just because he couldn't have her didn't mean no one else could. He had no right to impose boundaries on her or on Stig for that matter.

Stig would be a better fit for her anyway—it was surprising Poe hadn't thought of that already. Dilara was an upper crust type of person, and Stig was smooth and charming and talented. More to the point, Stig knew better than to fall in love with a woman who could break him.

Scowling, Poe turned away and scanned the room. In the chaotic aftermath of the explosion, the hall was filled with emergency workers, upended chairs and stretchers, but he thought he saw something move under a pile of rubble near the far end of the stage. Weaving between obstacles he kept his gaze fixed on the place he had detected movement, but the closer he got the more he thought he must have been wrong. Still, once he had climbed around the upended piano, he began to pull detritus away, carefully at first and then more urgently as he heard a moan.

Under a slab of wallboard, Teamue lay curled on his side, one arm at an unnatural angle. Blood oozed from his temple. He was pale and shivering—from shock, Poe assumed. Poe glanced back, shouting for an EMT, but in the meantime he knelt and yanked off his duster, draping it around Teamue as snugly as possible without jostling him. Teamue reached out with his functioning arm and gripped Poe's hand.

"You were right." Teamue's voice was strained, a harsh whisper.

"I wish I hadn't been," Poe responded after a pause. There was no sense of triumph in Teamue's capitulation. Instead he just felt hollow.

"I'll get you the doctor." Poe started to stand up so he would have a better chance of getting an EMT's attention, but Teamue's grip on his hand tightened for a moment.

"I can wait," Teamue said. "Go see to the others."

Poe blinked. In a sense, Teamue was right. His injuries didn't appear to be life threatening. But for the first time since Teamue had taken office, Poe felt a whisper of respect for him. They would probably never like each other, but still, he had to give Teamue credit. At that angle, Teamue's shoulder had to be causing him excruciating pain.

"Gonna have to overrule you, Your Honor."

Later, after he had seen Teamue into the bed of Stig's wagon and exchanged a clean warm blanket for his rumpled duster, Poe turned back to see if he could catch another glimpse of Dilara, but she had disappeared. She would be in her suite now, living the life she was meant to live. He should be glad for her. He should move on with his life, content in knowing she was happy. All he needed to do was to see her one more time—just to warn her about the searcher in person. Then he would go home to his silent cabin and try to remember how it had been to breathe before his rib cage had become so unaccountably heavy.

Chapter 48

DILARA COULDN'T BRING HERSELF TO STEP INTO the elevator. After the horror of the explosion, the thought of indulging herself in the luxury of her suite, of sinking into a bath and choosing from her shiny new wardrobe felt wrong. She was pretty sure none of her classmates had been hurt, but the urge to check on them was surprisingly strong, so she turned on her heel and strode toward the exit. She would just see that they had all made it out safely.

She turned to watch as Mrs. Onkelson's gurney rumbled out the door, Mrs. Onkelson protesting she was unhurt while the lieutenant walked by her side, doggedly refusing to concede. Dilara's breath caught in her throat. That was love—the kind Poe deserved. The kind she couldn't give him. She had no right to grieve, she reminded herself—her choices were her own. Her eyes stung and she stared down at her feet, blinking the tears away so they would not fall.

The carpet beneath her shoes was likely irreparable too. There were lines pressed into it from stretcher tires and the entire surface was smudged and speckled with cinders. The ash had been ground in by the shoes of audience members running away from the explosion and by the boots of people like Poe who had run toward it. The smell of smoke and fear felt sharp in her throat, and she suddenly needed to be outside with an urgency that nearly overwhelmed her.

After the pungent odor inside the building, the clean night air felt decadent. She inhaled greedily, savoring the slight touch of damp on her cheeks. Gaslights at the portico illuminated the circular driveway crowded with wagons and a few automobiles. As soon as each vehicle was loaded, it raced away and new ones arrived. In the dimness outside the glow of the gaslights, she could make out crowds of people milling about under the trees. She wove her way between the wagons, searching for familiar faces in the shadows.

The crowd was an unlikely mishmash of Melchior executives, curious townspeople and catering and cleaning staff. Men in suits lounged on boulders alongside workers in chefs' jackets. It looked like an upside-down version of a community picnic. She could feel a bubble of hysteria rising inside her, and she swallowed hard. The yearning to see someone, anyone, she actually knew was almost physical in its intensity. Systematically she began scanning faces.

In the distance, she caught a glance of Kiko and headed in that direction. But there was a thicket between them, and in the process of circling around it Dilara lost sight of her. She had paused to get her bearings when she felt a tingle between her shoulder blades. She spun to look behind her, and her breath caught in her throat. Moonlight broke through the mass of branches above, and for a moment there was only Poe.

She meant to speak, but when she opened her mouth she couldn't think of what to say and then it didn't matter because his lips were on hers, his arms tight around her. He smelled like ash and smoke, and underneath there was that indefinable scent that was Poe and which she had missed so much since she walked out of his life. If there was a smell of home, this was it.

She knew doing what was right was its own solace. This was a commonly accepted truth that did not explain why the pain in her heart was a kind of howl as she carefully pulled back. In the split second it took him to register her motion, she could see his expression harden again, and for a moment she wondered whether in fact what she was doing was the right thing.

"I apologize," he said.

"No," she said hastily. "I…it was…I liked it."

His jaw tightened, and she thought she might have said the wrong thing. She was quite sure of it when he grabbed her elbow in an iron grip and marched her back toward the building. The entrance under the portico was quiet now the wounded had been carted off, but hastily scrawled signs tacked to the doors warned staff to leave the premises undisturbed until security completed its investigation of the bombing. Any of the evacuated crowd who wished to re-enter the building could only do so through alternate entrances. Poe seemed unaffected by the restrictions though and the elevator cab was still waiting, open and empty in the deserted lobby.

A part of her hoped he would get into the elevator with her, come into the suite. It would be foolish, she knew, even hurtful in the long run to pretend they could be anything more than friends. She couldn't do that to him, but that didn't change the wanting of it. So he was protecting both of them when he pushed her into the elevator but stayed outside it himself. She could feel the sense of hurt rise inside her and tamped it down fiercely. It wasn't fair to blame him for being self-disciplined. Still, he didn't walk away but stood in the open doorway, holding one big hand against the tongue of the door so it would not close.

"I liked it too." His eyes locked with hers, his expression somber. "Too much."

She felt a wash of relief. At least on this they were on the same page. The last thing Poe needed was another outsider woman in his life, one who would never fit into the tight community he loved so much. She looked down at her boots quickly to hide the stinging in her eyes.

He cleared his throat. "You got my note, I assume."

"I—" she stopped and could feel her cheeks flushing. "No."

"You should stay here at the compound until you leave on your tour," he said. "I ran into a searcher yesterday."

Chapter 49

THE BLOOD DRAINED FROM HER FACE AND SHE backed farther into the safety of the elevator, her eyes skittering from side to side as though the threat was imminent.

"Are you sure he was here for me?"

It came out in a hoarse whisper. One of the things that attracted him to Dilara was her height, but just now she looked small, fragile. He wanted to take her back into his arms, hold her close, but that would be exactly the wrong thing to do. Instead he would tell her the truth quickly and leave.

"He told me he was," Poe said. "And it's not just him. There is an interplanetary warrant for your capture because you were convicted of thievery. Apparently you stole five hundred zils and one pence."

"That's not true!" she snapped. "I had two zils hidden away after years of saving, and it was only enough to buy paper for my music and passage to the dock. You searched my bag. You saw everything I had. With five hundred zils, I could have traveled to the next galaxy in style."

He nodded. It had bothered him when he had seen the figure. Five hundred zils and one pence was just exactly enough to bump a theft up to major crime, to justify a searcher. He wondered how much her parents had spent to pay off the judge. At least Dilara didn't seem wounded so much as infuriated, and he felt a measure of relief at that, although he suspected her fury wouldn't last.

He envisioned the table at his parents' house crowded with siblings, in-laws, and Pop and Ma, and his chest tightened at the certainty that they loved him, wanted the best for him. That knowledge was such a basic building block of his life, it was hard to conceive of the alternative. He couldn't imagine how he would have felt if his own family had turned on him or how he could have become the man he was without their support. And yet here stood Dilara before him—strong, capable, and loving. He shook his head.

"I assume your parents have the funds or the power to buy a judge, and the judge assigned a searcher. Unfortunately the guy I met struck me as competent. I gave him the 'aw, shucks' routine and sent him on a tour of the more distant farms. It should take him a while to visit them all since he's on foot, so you should have wiggle room for the next few days. You should be safe as long as you are cautious and stay in the Melchior compound until your ship leaves. When is that?"

To his surprise, she looked stricken at the question. "I don't...ten days from now."

Not great. Even allowing for less cooperative farmers, Sector 1065 was small. It would only take the searcher a few days to visit all of them. And not all the farmers would be unwelcoming. Someone would be bursting to share the news about the one-handed woman who sang at BangBang and who had been plucked out of obscurity to launch an intergalactic career as a Melchior ambassador. That kind of sensational gossip didn't come along often.

If Poe was lucky, the searcher would be walking from farm to farm for a week. But more likely he would be back in Poe's office tomorrow. Still, while a marshal had an obligation to honor intergalactic law, big businesses were a law unto themselves. Security on the Melchior compound would be unusually tight now, so it was unlikely the searcher would have access to Dilara as long as she stayed on company grounds.

His hand tightened on the elevator door lip again as it tried to close. Her eyes were wide, the pupils large. He recognized the signs of shock, but he knew the best thing he could do for her now was to let her go. So he released the elevator door and watched as it cut off his view of her.

He turned to leave and nearly made it to the exit but then, swallowing a curse, he strode back to the elevator and jabbed at the button after all. It would be better if she were not alone, at least until she recovered from the shock. The toneless quality to her voice had made his chest tighten.

He waited in silence as the car sped smoothly upward. He had been prepared for opulence, but when the doors slid open, he was still taken aback at the lushly appointed circular foyer. After the destruction below, the tranquility of the space seemed almost jarring, as did the pristinely dressed attendant who sat behind a thin legged carved desk. The attendant seemed so suited to the place it was hard to imagine he ever left his post, although surely he had been evacuated along with the rest of the staff.

"May I help you, sir?"

The man's tone was so distinctly unhelpful Poe had to resist punching him. Instead he flicked his duster open, flashing his marshal's badge. It might not be worth anything now, but the attendant wouldn't know that.

"Dilara Elian."

"I just arrived back at my desk," the attendant said. "She went down to prepare for the performance and then…I haven't seen her since the explosion. I hope she isn't hurt."

The man's perfect brow furrowed slightly, and Poe liked him a little better for it.

"She came up just a moment ago," he said.

"I see," the attendant responded. "If you would care to wait, I'll check to see if she's receiving visitors."

The door swung open at the attendant's knock, and Dilara met Poe's gaze before turning back into the room. He followed her and closed the door behind him. The living area was opulent, the view from the floor to ceiling windows dramatic. The surroundings were much closer to the wealthy accoutrements she had grown up with than the crude furnishings in his cabin. Her gown was smudged from smoke and ash, but it was elegant too. She glanced at him, her expression remote, and then turned her head to stare out the window.

"Was there something you needed from me?" She spoke without looking at him.

He paused, suddenly unsure. What he had wanted was to be of

some use, to be a comfort perhaps, but now he felt foolish. How could he have thought he was what she needed? It wasn't that she was like Lenette. Lenette had wanted things she had never had access to. But Dilara just fit in here, at ease with a kind of luxury he could never provide her with.

"I just wanted to see that you got to your room safe," he said finally.

He thought he saw her flinch, but if anything, her expression appeared even more remote when her eyes met his.

"Thank you."

The dismissal in her tone was unmistakable. As he walked away, he made an effort to stand erect as he had when he took his oath as interim marshal. That too had been a moment of wrenching pain and loss. But then at least he had had the badge and the pride and responsibility that went with it. Now there was just the pain.

The elevator ride back down to the lobby took longer. Every floor or so, there were stops to let passengers on or off. Poe stood in the back corner, his arms folded across his chest. It was good he was tall since it meant he could stare over peoples' heads without appearing rude. When the interminable ride came to an end, he strode past the milling crowd in the lobby and shoved the door with his shoulder as he exited into the good clean air. It wasn't any easier to breathe outside, but at least it smelled better.

Chapter 50

DILARA STARED OUT THE WINDOW. It was two days after the explosion, and she hadn't had the heart to leave her suite. She could see an overview of Sector 1065. From above, under overcast skies, the town looked gloomy. Considering the size of the Melchior compound, there was no good reason to feel trapped. She supposed the feeling of restlessness had more to do with Poe recommending she not leave the compound than anything else. Still, she found herself desperately wanting to move, so she headed down to the lobby. At least there she could watch other people without fear of being captured.

The lobby looked weirdly normal. She thought there ought to be at least some sign of the hurried exodus from the night of the concert, smoke streaks on the ceiling, perhaps. But the room was immaculate. Even the crystals dangling from the massive chandeliers above appeared to have been polished. Their reflections twinkled in the ornate rectangular mirrors that lined the walls and formed little prisms on the floor.

She settled onto one of the elegant, padded benches and stared at the vast patterned carpet. Here too there was no sign of the ashes and grooves she had noticed on the night of the bombing. She thought about what Kiko had said, and she wondered how many people and how many hours it had taken to knot the complex design. And whether children had been involved.

Uneasily she scanned the room. Staff people scurried in and out and minor executives trotted by on their way to executive meetings, their customary air of self-importance firmly in place.

No one nodded to Dilara, but that was normal and was probably a good thing, she decided. Living with Poe, meeting his family and friends, had weakened her defenses. It wasn't Poe's fault, and it hadn't been intentional on his part, she assured herself hastily. He just didn't know any better. But she did.

Friendship wasn't a good strategy for her, especially since the searcher had arrived. Love would be even more dangerous. She would be a fool to allow a mad and fantastical desire for Poe Lancaster to overrule her good sense. Maybe Poe hadn't even realized he was essentially lying to her with those kisses. Worse, he was misleading himself because she could never be what he needed.

She dug her toe into the carpet. Nothing in the universe had actually changed since she had fled Caron 5, and in eight days she would be leaving Valora. Her heart clenched at the thought. How odd that in the few weeks since she had arrived, she'd become so attached to the town and to the people in it.

A familiar voice caught her attention and she looked up, her mouth already curving in a smile. It was hard not to smile at Porky. He looked out of place in the elegant setting, his rough apparel contrasting with the finely woven fabric of the executives' suits, and there was a stain on his shirt she suspected had been there since breakfast. She walked forward to greet him. If she hadn't known it would mortify him, she would have reached up to comb his hair back from his forehead with her fingertips.

"Rudolph said you were okay, but I wanted to see for myself," he said.

She had appreciated the smooth care provided by Melchior in the wake of the bombing, but something in Porky's gruff kindness undid her. It occurred to her that this was what people saw in friendship, a kindness that overrode manners. She turned her face away on the pretext of stroking the petals of flowers in a nearby vase until the risk of tears had passed.

"I was lucky," she said when she could speak again. "A lot of people were hurt, although at least no one was killed."
Porky nodded. His shoulders were hunched, and his hands were jammed into his pockets. She guessed it was what he must have looked like as a little boy in a store when he'd been cautioned not

to touch anything.

"Poe was pretty scared for you. I mean," he stammered after glancing at her, "everyone was. But Stig said Poe was crazy with worry. It wasn't like that with Lenette, you know. He's never been so—"

Porky broke off and added hastily, "Not that you should change any of your plans. An ambassadorship is an amazing opportunity, and you're wasted here in Sector 1065. Still, we sure are going to miss you."

Dilara could feel herself flushing and when she opened her mouth to speak, at first nothing came out. She wondered if this was what a pane of glass experienced when it shattered—a sudden crack and then all its sharp and dangerous parts rearranged and scattered.

"How's business at BangBang?" she finally asked.

"Could be better," he admitted. "Rudolph hasn't been this grouchy in months."

"I'm not due to leave for another eight days," she said on impulse. "I could take another shift this week, if you want."

Porky's face lit up. "Would you? That would be great! We can make it a special event and get everyone in to give you a big send-off."

As she watched Porky walk away with a newfound spring in his step, she couldn't bring herself to regret the impulse even though she knew Poe would be displeased when he learned of it. She could feel her jaw set in the kind of stubborn position she had occasionally seen in others but had never had the freedom to allow herself. Once she set foot on the ship she would be bound to the Melchior ambassador program, but right now she still had the freedom to make her own decisions. She had denied herself pleasure for much of her life, but she refused to deny herself this one.

The searcher wouldn't dare try to take her in the middle of her farewell performance in front of a crowd of miners and farmers, even if he happened to figure out she was there that night. And maybe, just maybe, Poe would be there too. The thought of Poe, the way his eyes darkened when he kissed her, made her shiver. It would be worth the risk to see him just one more time.

Chapter 51

"I THOUGHT YOU WERE TAKING YOUR PAID LEAVE as vacation time," Zan said.

"This is my home," Poe said. "And Teamue was injured along with a lot of other townsfolk."

Zan gave him a long look and then nodded. "You'll be on staff here soon enough, so I'll bring you up to speed. We didn't formally check in everyone who came into the building Saturday. Unless they were going into the laboratory or office towers, there wasn't a need. Or there hadn't been up until the explosion." Zan shook his head. "That'll change now, of course. Corporate is sending a ship's worth of security workers, some of whom specialize in anti-terrorism, so we should have a tighter perimeter by the end of the week."

Poe kept his face expressionless. He respected Zan, but Zan's responsibility was to focus on the wellbeing and safety of Melchior operations only. In Poe's experience, bad acts were rarely about just one thing. Maybe Zan was right and the bomb was intended as a statement about only Melchior, which would make follow up Zan's responsibility.

But Poe's gut was telling him this was more personal. Feuds were a common part of Sector 1065 life, primarily because the community was so inbred. But while fistfights and even brawls were not uncommon, mostly the friction was kept at a slow simmer. He couldn't remember a time when conflict in the sector had boiled over into this level of violence, but that didn't mean it couldn't, given the right reasons and participants.

"You said there was a timer," he said.

"We found bits of one," Zan responded, "but maybe it didn't work as planned. There are also signs of a receiver for a remote detonator, and that's what actually triggered the explosion. In that sense, the UNSUB got lucky, if you can call it that."

Poe nodded. Remote control devices were iffy at best on Valora, so a timer would have been the most reliable option. It was odd that someone who had the capacity to wire a remote detonator to work successfully would have messed up on the timer.

"I'd like to look at the site again," he said.

"It's mostly cleaned up by now." Zan had the grace to look apologetic. "Orders from the top. But we have diagrams of the scene and witness reports."

"That would be helpful," Poe said. "But I'd like to walk through the auditorium anyway."

Zan looked at him sharply. "Is something bothering you?"

Poe shrugged. "It's probably nothing."

They rode the elevator in silence and when they reached the lobby, Zan handed him a copy of the crime report but stayed behind to speak with one of his men while Poe headed into the deserted auditorium. The walls had been repainted, ruined chairs replaced and the damaged parts of the floor sanded in preparation for refinishing. Poe flashed on the scene he had walked into two nights before, and his nostril's flared at the memory of the acrid odor.

He opened the crime report. It was bound in a textured burgundy cover, tastefully embossed with the company's emblem in gold. Poe rolled his eyes. Trust Melchior to have its own bespoke portfolios for crime reports. He flipped through the pages until he reached Rudolph's witness statement.

Rudolph had run a rehearsal on the morning of the concert. Appended to his statement was a handwritten list of participants, presumably in the order the women were expected to perform. Poe reached into his pocket for a copy of the program he had absently tucked there the day before and unfolded it. For the most part the lists were the same—many of the women had planned to play instruments, sing or dance. Even those who had preferred reciting poetry and a lone comedienne had been scheduled to rehearse with Rudolph so they could specify what sorts of musical support they needed. But there was one inconsistency. Dilara's name was in the wrong place. On Rudolph's list, she was scheduled second to last. On the program, she was listed just before the intermission.

Maybe there had been a simple scheduling conflict for the rehearsal. Still, something about the discrepancy was niggling at him. He took another look around the room, but he thought now there wasn't any more it would be able to tell him after all. Instead he would go talk to Rudolph.

Like every morning BangBang was closed up tight, but the Lummon brothers lived in a cramped apartment above the bar. Poe pounded on the door and when he got no response, he grabbed a fistful of pebbles and tossed them at the second story window above it.

"What the—" Rudolph pushed the casement open and stuck his head out. His eyes widened when he saw Poe. "Is Dilara okay?"

Porky edged his head into the frame next to Rudolph's. "What's wrong?"

"Dilara's fine. She's at Melchior." His heart squeezed a little at the knowledge she was absolutely fine without him. He cleared his throat and continued hastily. "This is about the bombing. Can I come in?"

Several minutes later he was ensconced at their kitchen table. The mug in his hands was stained and had a chip in its lip, but the coffee smelled delicious and the scent from the fry-up Porky was pushing around the skillet made Poe's stomach rumble. Rudolph plunked a platter mounded with toast and a crock of jam in the middle of the table and then limped back with a handful of silverware.

Poe had just reached for a piece of toast when he heard footsteps ascending the staircase. Stig's head appeared and then the rest of him. Poe let out the breath he had been holding and slid his weapon back into his holster. Stig raised a brow but didn't comment. Instead he gestured to Rudolph who rolled his eyes but raised the leg of his trousers so Stig could inspect the wound.

"You're lucky," Stig said once he had finished rewrapping the dressing.

Rudolph snorted. "That's me—lucky. At least the piano didn't land on my other leg. Then I would have a matched set."

"Thanks, Stig," Porky said, shooting his brother an annoyed look. "Want to join us for breakfast?"

"I wouldn't say no." Stig sank into the chair next to Poe with a sigh and turned to look at him. "What are you doing here?"

"I had some questions for Rudolph," Poe said.

"It's not as though the day's going to get any better, so you might as well get started," Rudolph said. He grimaced and plucked a piece of toast from the pile, eying it with a dubious expression before he took a bite. Poe pulled the rehearsal list and the program from his pocket and shoved them across the table.

"Dilara's placement in the program changed."

Rudolph frowned. "That was a last-minute decision. She ran through her piece with me at the original time she had been scheduled for at rehearsal—second to last. But afterward the organizers decided to move her earlier on the roster so they could announce her new position as Melchior ambassador just before intermission. That's why they had to reprint the programs in a hurry before the concert."

"Who knew about the change?"

"What, you think the guy who had to reprint the program was so aggravated he blew the place up just for spite?"

"I think the person who detonated the bomb overrode a timer in favor of a remote detonator."

Porky's fork stopped halfway to his mouth. "That makes no sense. A remote detonator would be completely unreliable."

Stig set his mug down on the table. "You think this was personal? That it was some sort of crazy vendetta against one of the women?"

Poe shrugged. "I don't think a personal vendetta was the primary reason for the bomb because there are plenty of other less showy ways to kill an individual. But using the remote detonator implies a sudden change in plan to accommodate a new circumstance. It bothers me."

"Because the only new circumstance we know about is the change in the program," Porky said, nodding. He reached for the crime report and leafed through it as Poe went to the stove to pour himself another cup of coffee. "Hey, that's weird."

Poe looked over Porky's shoulder at the photograph. Zan was right—there wasn't much left of the timer. Little gears were scattered across the field of the image. But in the left upper corner next to Porky's index finger was what remained of the timer's clock. The hands were gone, but a fine ash had settled onto the white clock face leaving a clear silhouette of where they had been at the moment of impact.

Rudolph and Stig rose to look too.

"Nine forty-five," Rudolph said. "But the explosion was an hour earlier. You think whoever pulled the trigger was in the audience?"

"No," Poe said. "Zan showed me a detailed map of timony veins under the compound. The only possibility for a direct signal path to that location would have been from behind the backstage wall outside the building. So either the bomber was incredibly lucky, or he had access to detailed information about timony deposits. Then all he'd have to do was stand outside and push the button. Worst case, it wouldn't override the timer and the bomb would go off later."

Rudolph frowned. "But wouldn't that point toward a Melchior employee? Who else would know where those veins run?"

Poe could feel his jaw tighten. He knew he was being stubborn, even unreasonable, but ignoring intuition would be stupid too.

"The concert should have started at eight," Stig said slowly. "So nine forty-five would have been close to the end of the program. But instead the bomber overrode the plan and detonated at eight forty-five. Who was performing then?"

"A dancer. The only reason she wasn't killed or maimed was because at the moment of the explosion, she was all the way at the back of the stage. But the concert started fifteen minutes behind schedule. If it had started on time, Dilara would have been standing center stage to sing, right in the sweet spot."

"But that makes no sense," Porky said. "Dilara hasn't been

here long enough to have made any true enemies. You have to hate someone a lot to do something like this."

Poe nodded in acknowledgment, but he was pretty sure Porky was wrong. He raked his fingers through his hair and resisted the urge to yank. "Rudolph, was there anyone else in the room besides you and the performers during the rehearsal?"

"Sure. There were tons of guys. A bunch of them were setting up chairs when I arrived. Someone had already checked the sound system. A couple of workmen even lowered one of the big chandeliers to replace a few bulbs. Oh, and they checked the trap door center stage. One of the women was planning to perform a series of magic tricks, and she wanted to vanish in a puff of smoke by using the trap door, but they told her it was all spiders down there so she changed her mind."

"You recognize any of the workmen, maybe from the bar?"

Rudolph made a non-committal gesture. "I might have seen some of them around. We get a good crowd most nights. But usually I'm too busy to notice, and I wasn't paying attention to the workers that day either."

Poe shot Stig a look. "In marshal training, I learned a technique for helping witnesses remember things. Would you mind me seeing if I can jog your memory a little?"

Rudolph's brows shot up, but he didn't object.

"Close your eyes," Poe said. "Now set your hands on the table as though it were a keyboard. Can you tell me what you played for the first performer?"

"'Love Me Sweet,'" Rudolph responded immediately. "Key of C."

"Good," Poe said. "What was the singer wearing?"

"Blue top, black skirt," Rudolph said.

Quietly Poe pulled the handwritten rehearsal list closer.

"Who else was in the room just then?"

"Onkelson popped in for a minute. Two Melchior maintenance guys came in to fix the chandelier like I said."

"Were the men tall or short?"

"One was kind of scrawny and the other was taller and heavier. They wore orange coveralls. I didn't see their faces."

"That's okay. You're doing great, Rudolph. What did you play next?"

By the time they reached the fifth performer on the program, Poe had settled into a rhythm. But at this point the process was beginning to feel more like an exercise in futility than a clever idea. All he had learned so far was the concert program would have been dull and Melchior maintenance workers were diligent.

"This one was a poetry reading. I was just supposed to play an introduction and exit music. The woman who was going to recite just handed me the music and left. She wanted 'The Swan' in G and then 'Floating Gently' in B minor."

"And what did you do then?"

"I sat and played them while I waited for the next performer. She was late."

"Was anyone else in the room while you waited?"

"The chandelier guys were still there. Except now they were up on the stage checking out the trap door."

Poe felt a little tingle.

"So they were in front of you. What could you see?"

"They had a couple bags with them. They looked heavy."

"Then what did you see?"

"The big one climbed into the hole and out again and then they left."

The tingle increased. Poe kept his tone even.

"Were they carrying anything when they left?"

"The big guy was carrying a bag." Rudolph's eyes popped open. "It was Saur. I couldn't see the smaller guy's face, but the big one was Saur Fanko."

Chapter 52

BORN TO HOMESTEADERS, SAUR HAD FALLEN OUT with his family and now worked for Melchior and lived in a small house in the miners' section of town. His neighbors had made some attempt to keep their dwellings in order, but Saur's tiny plot was overgrown. The weeds stood waist high except for a narrow path that ran along the side of the house, presumably trodden down by Saur on a daily basis. The roof sagged and several broken windowpanes facing the street had been stuffed with rags rather than replaced.

It was unlikely Saur would be home on a weekday morning if he wanted to keep his job. Still, Poe was careful as he approached the house. He followed the beaten path around the side and stepped quietly up onto the stoop. The kitchen door was ajar. Poe's pulse picked up a notch as he gently widened the opening. The odor of unwashed clothing and overripe food mingled with other more elemental smells.

Saur was sprawled on the floor in a pool of blood, an expression of vacant surprise on his face. When Poe reached for him, turned him, he saw the puncture marks on the big man's back. Only bovoquin knives made that kind of mark and every farmer who raised them had one, which meant unless the killer had left the weapon behind with a thoughtfully placed set of prints on its bloody handle, Poe was back to square one.

He washed his hands at the sink piled high with encrusted dishes and then headed toward the front of the cottage to begin a systematic search. But systematic, as it turned out, was unnecessary. In what normally would have been a living room, Saur had created a lab of sorts. A workbench took up most of the floor space. It was littered with wires, timers and tools in no particular semblance of order.

The stench was even stronger here, and Poe recognized it now. He found the burlap manure sack crumpled in a corner and swept the detritus on the workbench aside so he could spread the fabric out on the flat surface. The Mercantile stamp was front and center, but there was a reference number stamped in the lower right corner Darius used to keep track of what farm the manure came from.

As Poe stepped away from the table, a bit of color caught his eye. In the corner near a stack of rags was a can of red paint. For a moment, he flashed on the image of the graffiti on Borin's barn. He took one of the rags and wrapped the can with it. Zela could check it for prints.

Then he left the house, making sure to close the door behind him. It was unlikely anyone who lived nearby would risk entering Saur's house uninvited—even among the miners he would have been considered too big and too mean to mess with. Still, it would be better to preserve the scene a bit longer, at least until he had a clear sense of who else was involved.

Sunlight made the store windows sparkle as he walked down Main Street, and the sun's heat pressing on his shoulders reminded him of Pop's hand, but he couldn't *feel* the warmth of it. His pulse seemed sluggish—a constant reminder that any chance of real happiness would be leaving on a Melchior tour any day now. He stopped in his tracks, irritated. Maybe happiness was out, but minimally he ought to be satisfied with what he had. If a sense of purpose was the best he could do, maybe that would have to be enough. He pulled his notepad from his pocket, entered the Mercantile and found Darius behind the register.

"I have some additional questions," Poe said.

Darius glared at him. "I thought you were on leave."

Poe shrugged.

"Well, you shouldn't blame me for that." Darius stared at him with a defiant air. "I pay your salary with my taxes. It's been over a month since my store was robbed, and I told you who the likely culprits were. But did you listen? If you had taken me seriously, those Mnoani kids would already be in the lockup, and I would have my goods back. But you..."

Poe's patient expression must have finally sunk in because Darius' querulous voice trailed off. Poe handed him the scrap of paper.

"Is this reference number from one of the stolen bags?"

Darius pushed out his lips as he studied the paper. "It could be. I'll have to check."

Poe followed him back into his office. It was cramped and crowded with piles of ledgers and papers on every flat surface but Darius' chair. Poe resigned himself to a long wait, but Darius seemed to have a system, no matter how opaque it appeared to Poe. Within a few minutes, Darius had found the ledger he needed and was running an ink-stained finger down the column.

"There." He tapped an entry. "That's one of mine. I guess it's too much to hope you found the rest of the bags?"

"Just the one," Poe said.

Darius sank into his chair and stared unseeingly at the ledger in front of him. "I don't normally front the money. But this time Borin insisted. His product is reliably top of the line, and I knew I'd be able to turn it over in a day or two for an excellent price, so it didn't seem like a big risk. Now I'm out the money and the product. And probably that off planet customer won't come back either," he added gloomily. "Those Mnoani kids will have sold them off already for half the price I would have gotten."

Poe was surprised to feel a flicker of sympathy for Darius, even as he disagreed with his theory as to the culprits. Historically homesteaders and merchants in Sector 1065 had an uneasy relationship. It was hard to feel friendly toward a merchant when your farm was having a bad season and you couldn't afford the things you needed. But the Mercantile had been in business since early in the colony's history, and even though the cost of shipping farming equipment from off planet had always been too high for Darius' family to make much of a profit, they had continued to carry them out of a sense of civic duty. Losing thousands of credits was bad for his bottom line, but Poe could tell Darius also felt personally hurt.

Poe turned to leave and then paused in the doorway. "You ever sell a bag of Borin's manure to Saur?"

Darius frowned. "No. Saur doesn't farm, and besides, Borin's manure is a luxury item. Saur couldn't afford to buy it even if he wanted to."

Chapter 53

IT WAS MID-AFTERNOON WHEN POE HEADED toward the foothills. Since he was no longer officially on duty, he had decided he could drive what he liked. Zela and Emilio were back at the office dickering over who would drive the marshal mobile today, so Poe had headed toward the livery stable with a lightness to his step he hadn't felt in a while. He didn't miss farming per se, but there was nothing to compare to the peace of driving a chevalo and wagon on a spring day.

The chevalo's hooves clopping on the hard packed surface of the road formed a sleepy counterpoint to the regular creaking of the wagon. Birds twittered and fussed over their nestlings, frogs chirped, and Poe could hear whistling from the farmer plowing in the distance. The lines from the plow blades curved around the base of a gentle slope, reminding Poe of an ink drawing he had seen once of ocean waves.

It was hard to believe that amid such peace and beauty, there could form the kind of hatred required to create a bomb and maybe even more, to kill a man face to face. But it had, and now he was going to find out why. Instead of driving up to the front of Borin's house, he pulled the wagon into a clearing at the side of the access road about two thirds of the way up. He would walk the rest of the way in. Shaking his head, he unsnapped his holster.

Arresting Borin would create a scandal. It had always been easier to blame the Mnoani, drunken miners and marauding Raiders for whatever went wrong in Sector 1065. No one in the farming community would believe, would want to believe, that a founder, even an unpleasant one like Borin, would do such a thing. The Homesteader's Grange would cause a stink. Strings would be pulled.

Of course they would have a readymade scapegoat in Poe. And Teamue would be all to ready to take advantage of it. This was the perfect opportunity for Teamue to fire Poe, and maybe he would be right to do so. It wasn't as if Poe had any clear authority at this point.

Poe stood for a moment in the soaking warmth of the sun, staring at his right hand as he opened and closed it slowly. He had raised that hand when he had taken his oath, *to serve and protect, without fear or favor*. There was no avoiding it. In order to live up to that oath, he would have to risk losing his job altogether.

Poe expelled the breath he had been holding and headed up the slope toward Borin's farm. He knocked sharply on the front door, but there was no response. So he strode past the house and headed for the barn. The red paint had dulled over the weeks since he had seen it last, but it still stood out starkly against the worn wood. The main breezeway was shut, but the side door was wedged open just enough to allow a man Borin's size to enter. Poe paused and stood a moment listening. The bovoquin would be out to pasture at this time of day, and since that was the only time one could safely muck out the stalls, he suspected Borin was within. But the clicking noise Poe heard was not the sound of a rake or shovel. He yanked the door wide, allowing sunlight to stream into the wide space.

Borin was perched on a barrel. His right hand clutched an aged blaster. His left flicked the load check lever in a slow rhythmic pattern. Across from him stood a heap of aging manure, the beginnings of his next sale to Darius. It would be dry in another week—just as volatile but easier to package.

"Hi, Sven." Poe tried for casual.

Borin kept his eyes fixed on the pile and clicked the lever again. Poe took a step closer. From a distance it was impossible to tell if the weapon was loaded.

"I came to update you on what I've found out about the writing on your barn."

Slowly Borin turned his head until his vacant blue eyes met Poe's.

"The Mnoani did it." His voice was without affect. "They are the root, the cancer. Stay where you are."

Poe, who had edged closer, stopped. One blast toward the manure heap and there wouldn't be enough left of either of them to identify. He lifted his hands in a gesture of acquiescence.

"You seem pretty sure of that."

"They are born to evil." Borin rocked back and forth as he spoke. "They take and take what is not theirs."

There seemed no point in reminding Borin that from the Mnoani perspective, the original thieves were the Earther homesteaders. He took a minute step forward.

"I'm still looking for the person who vandalized your barn. Has there been a theft too?"

"You could call it that." Borin's eyes were alive now, sparking as he spat out the words. "They steal your heart. The best thing you ever had. They steal it and defile it."

He was clicking the lever faster now.

Poe kept his tone calm and edged a little closer. "I'm going to reach into my pocket to take out my notebook. Sounds like you have a crime to report."

"You could say that." The old man forced the words through gritted teeth. "You could definitely say that."

Poe fingered his duster open. "What got stolen?"

"My wife, you fool."

Poe froze. For a moment there was no sound save the clicking of the lever and the lowing of a distant bovoquin. To the best of Poe's knowledge, Borin's wife had left the planet of her own volition. At least that had been the story Borin had circulated. According to him, she had gone back to care for her parents on Yaro.

"Your wife," Poe said.

"They pulled her in with their foolishness. They made her think life is all music and dancing. She was a sensible woman when I married her. She worked the farm, bore my sons. She knew her place. But the Mnoani cast a spell on her and stole her in the night. I woke up and she was gone, and I knew."

It took effort for Poe to stay expressionless. "How did you know?"

Borin shook his head. "She left a note filled with lies. I gave her everything a woman could want. She was a fool and they lured her with foolish dreams. But you don't need to take out your notebook. I've made sure they'll pay for what they did, and so will she."

Even in the warmth of the sun pouring into the barn, Poe felt chilled.

"What do you mean by that? How are you going to make sure they'll pay?"

He shook his head as he watched Poe, his eyes opaque now. "Not telling you. No sir. Not telling no yenxer. A man takes care of his own, he does." He chuckled and then began to laugh, a manic sound devoid of joy.

In one swift move, Poe reached for Borin's blaster. Borin managed to get a stream off, but it missed the pile of manure and just barely missed Poe's boot. Poe pulled the weapon from Borin's hand, dropped it onto a nearby bale of hay and pivoted to stomp out the scorched smoldering straw on the floor where the blast had made contact.

As he did so, Borin took off running out the door of the barn. Poe swore, stomped out the remaining embers and headed after him. When Poe caught up with him, Borin whipped around to face him, a well-used bovoquin knife in hand. The handle was aged, but the blade had been honed fine and it shone in the sunlight as Borin flicked it back and forth.

Poe's fingers tingled the way they had when he was a boy pushing off the top of Whittecomb Hill. There was probably something wrong with enjoying the prospect of a knife fight, especially when he didn't have a knife to bring to it, but maybe now wasn't the time to think about that. He grinned and crouched, circling so he stayed just out of Borin's reach.

The old man had experience on his side, but he was also breathing hard and limping a bit. Borin lunged forward, jabbing at him, and Poe feinted left. His arms were a little longer than Borin's, so as he did, the tips of his fingers tapped Borin's right shoulder. Borin lunged again, missing by a breath, and Poe tapped the farmer's bony shoulder again. The third time, Poe didn't dodge left, but grabbed for Borin's wrist and wrested the knife from his grip with minimal damage, considering. Borin's wrist was probably going to hurt for a while, but under the circumstances, Poe didn't much care.

Chapter 54

FRA KYR RANDALL LEANED FORWARD AND TAPPED on Poe's desk for emphasis. "My client refuses to answer on the grounds he may incriminate himself."

Normally Poe would have waited for the Galactic Police convoy and shipped Borin off to Central on their secure shuttle. Major crimes were automatically moved up the ladder. If you did your questioning on planet, you could make mistakes and screw up the prosecution. But there was the small matter of not being technically on duty as marshal.

Randall, who had studied law on Earth, but for reasons he refused to divulge, had never graduated, was a popular choice for defense attorney in Sector 1065. Because law was an avocation—most of the time he ran the worship center—he didn't charge his clients much. Borin, cuffed to Poe's visitor chair, glanced at Fra Randall now and again with a triumphant grin. Poe sighed.

"You and Saur planted the bomb at the Melchior auditorium. There's an eyewitness, so you're not getting out of that."

After a whispered conversation, Fra Randall said, "my client saw Saur set the bomb but did not know what Saur was doing until later. My client was shocked to learn his friend had committed a violent act."

"That's not what Saur says."

Borin's grin faded fast.

"You'll be glad to know your partner in crime survived the stabbing you treated him to—just barely—so that means you're on the hook for assault, not murder. But the Melchior bombing?" Poe shook his head gravely. "Galactic will consider that corporate terrorism. That's life in prison. Off planet."

Randall's conversation with Borin now involved gesticulating on Randall's part, which Poe considered an encouraging sign.

"My client would like to make a statement."

Poe leaned back. "Always glad to hear from our fine citizens."

"In exchange for which he wants a pardon for any involvement in the Melchior bombing."

Poe scowled, pretending to think about it. "I think I can persuade Galactic to consider clemency if the information on Saur is accurate."

"It was all his idea," Borin said. "He had a hard-on for that girl with the one hand. He kept talking about her, how she had to be taught a lesson. So he made sure we were on duty when the rehearsal was scheduled. That way he could figure out where it would be best to set the explosive and what time to set the timer for."

Poe could feel the fury now—not hot, but cold, implacable. He clenched his clasped fingers until the joints ached below the desktop so Borin would not see.

"Pretty high-grade materials for a working stiff," he commented. "He used your manure."

"It's the best," Borin said, his eyes flicking toward Randall.

"That's what everyone says." Poe nodded. "Did you give it to him?"

"Don't answer that," Randall said sharply.

"I don't know where he got the manure," Borin said. The grin flickered again. "Maybe he saved up."

"I think my client has met his obligation," Randall began. "Under the circumstances, I think personal recognizance—"

"Saur died," Poe interrupted. "Your client will be charged with murder."

Borin leaped to his feet and leaned over Poe's desk, glaring at him. "You lied! You lied like the Mnoani!" Spittle flew from his mouth as he gathered steam. "But they will die and you will too. There is nothing you can do to stop it. They will gather there, she and her downfall, and there will be a mighty reckoning."

Poe stared sightlessly as Borin ranted on, no longer listening. He had a sudden image of Pretie gardening. There would have been plantings around the new community center too, flowers and shrubs that would have gone in last when the painting was done, just in time for tonight's dedication. Without bothering to explain himself, he took Borin's arm and forced him into the cell. Randall stared but didn't attempt to stop him. Poe guessed maybe it had occurred to Randall his client was a bit out of his league.

Stig's clinic was quiet and empty, so Poe had no trouble convincing Stig to come for the ride in the likely event his services were needed. Borin's sanity was so shaky, Poe wasn't convinced he could manage to set a timer correctly, which meant an explosion at the community center could occur at any time, even accidentally. He had called Chief Manzarin already, but he wanted to see for himself that the Mnoani were all safely away from the building before trying to defuse any explosives.

He pushed the chevalo to a gallop and when the path narrowed too much to allow a wagon to pass, he left the animal to recover while he and Stig headed into the woods. Poe had asked Manzarin to evacuate the tribe until the danger had passed, and to his relief, the village appeared deserted. Clothes snapped unattended on a wash line, and a child's toy lay on the edge of the path as though it had been dropped mid-flight. But as Poe and Stig approached the community center, they heard angry voices.

"Lancaster's no better than the rest of them. A drop of Mnoani blood does not make him one of us."

"Your grandfather trusts him."

"My grandfather sees what he wants to see. But we know better. Earther law will never be fair to the Mnoani people."

Orioldo and his comrade turned to stare as Poe and Stig stepped into the clearing.

"Perfect," Orioldo said. "Did you come to arrest us for staying in our own village?"

"You see a bomb here, Earther?" Orioldo's companion sneered. "You're just looking for a way to keep our people from celebrating in unity. Chief Manzarin may have fallen for it, but we're not stupid."

"Maybe you are stupid," Stig snapped with the authority of a man who had vaccinated every child on the colony whether they liked it or not. "Answer the marshal's questions."

"I've got it, Stig," Poe said mildly. He turned to the two youths. "Where'd you get the manure for the plantings?"

They stared at him and then at each other, confused.

"It was donated," Orioldo said finally. "The Mercantile had it delivered. A big guy brought it. Saur, I think his name was. He insisted on putting it down himself, a good thick layer too. I didn't expect a gift like that from Darius. He doesn't think much of us."

Poe bit back an oath. "We need to search through the plantings," he said tersely. "Since you're here, you can help. We're looking for a timer with an incendiary device. It'll be small."

Orioldo studied him. "You're serious."

"As a heart attack," Poe said. "Are you helping or leaving?"

Orioldo looked at his friend and then nodded.

"Helping."

In the end, it was Orioldo's companion who found the devices tucked between the roots of the newly planted shrubs. There were three, and they each had the same signature construction as the one that had caused the explosion at Melchior. Tiny clock faces ticked away the minutes until nine twenty, twenty minutes into what would have been a well-attended community event. Once any one of the detonators created a spark, the manure Saur had carefully raked into the soil would have burst into flame, surrounding the entire building and the celebrants inside in a wall of fire.

Chapter 55

RINDA SMILED AT POE WHEN HE STRODE INTO the mayor's office late Wednesday morning, and he had to restrain himself from looking over his shoulder to see who the secretary was greeting so warmly. Maybe Rinda had forgotten who Poe was.

"Marshal, good to see you!" she said. "Can I get you a glass of water? Or a cup of coffee?"

"Thanks, but no." On the many occasions he had been summoned to Teamue's office, not once had Rinda smiled at him, not to mention offering coffee. Mystified, he headed toward the wooden chair. By rights, his backside should have worn it into a more comfortable shape by now, but he didn't have a chance to prove that theory wrong once again by sitting in it for the requisite half hour.

"No need to wait, Marshal," the secretary continued. "The mayor is ready to see you now."

Surreptitiously Poe dug his nails into his palm to see if he was dreaming. Nope, not dreaming. The delusion grew even weirder when he stepped into Teamue's office and saw the man himself standing behind the big desk, one arm in a sling, the other extended and a huge grin on his face.

"I hope you don't mind," Teamue gestured behind Poe. "I took the liberty of inviting a few folks."

So—more of a nightmare then if Teamue needed witnesses. Poe turned to scan the small crowd. His whole family was there, even Minden's little ones. This was either an attempt to embarrass him by firing him in front of everyone who mattered, or maybe

282

Teamue thought Poe would fall apart at the idea of losing his job and wanted witnesses.

Poe flicked a look at his father. Pop met his gaze with a calm expression, which made no sense. Poe looked away, removed his tin badge from his coat pocket and set it on Teamue's desk. Then he reached for his holster so he could do the same with his weapon.

"No need for that," Teamue said.

Stiffly the mayor walked around the desk until he faced Poe. From Teamue's wince, Poe guessed he was still feeling the after-effects of the explosion.

"About time you turned that shield in, Interim Marshal Lancaster. As of today, you are officially Marshal of Sector 1065."

Teamue slid a smoothly polished wooden box from his pocket and held it out to him. Poe froze and mentally replayed the sentence to be sure he had heard it correctly, but as he did Pop rose to help him. Inside the box, wrapped in a strip of silk, a bronze medallion nestled, a five-pointed star with rounded points, thick and made to last. The fibulin tree in the center stood out in relief and Poe's name was etched beneath it, the edges of the letters new and sharp looking. Pop plucked the badge out and pinned it on Poe's duster.

"And Marshal Lancaster," Teamue said, gesturing toward his sling, "thank you."

Poe knew he should have said something gracious in return, but the lump in his throat was too large. And then his brothers were slapping him on the back and Minden came in for a hug and the little ones tugged on his duster as they jumped and hopped in excitement and Ma hugged him and Pop slung an arm around him and whispered, "I'm proud of you, son."

It seemed that everyone at Glory Ann's had heard the news too. Glory Ann had set aside a long table for Poe and his family, and as they entered the crowded room a cheer rose up. Stig joined them, and even Porky and Rudolph made an appearance. The mood at lunch was celebratory, convivial, and Poe thought mostly he succeeded at looking like he was enjoying himself. It would have been churlish not to after all the trouble his family and friends had gone to. Still, he felt as if he was watching someone else's celebration through glass. He could see the joy, hear it, but he couldn't feel it.

When the family began to disperse, Poe made an excuse and slipped away. He didn't want to see the glint of sympathy in Emmer's gaze, to know that Minden's pat to his shoulder was as much kindness as pride. He headed toward home, striding at first, but after the first mile he slowed to a stroll. Clouds were gathering over the foothills. In another hour it would rain, but for the moment the sun shone overhead as though determined to have its chance before darkness took control. The demarcation of the clouds' shadow on the mountains was clean, as defined as a pen and ink drawing—this side dark, that side light. It would be nice if life were clear-cut like that. Instead it was more like the dust cloud his boots were making on the dry dirt road. He could barely see the pebbles at his feet, but the cloud didn't extend higher than his boots, which made it difficult to explain why his eyes were stinging.

Chapter 56

THERE WAS AN EDGY ATMOSPHERE ON MAIN STREET Thursday evening, and the conversations were all about the Melchior bombing, a combination of shock at the event itself and pleasure in speculation about the cause. Most folks had opinions about Borin's guilt, but there was an undercurrent of unease among the farmers in particular. There was no love lost between the farming community and the Mnoani even if they had reached a kind of détente over the decades since Earthers had first arrived in the sector.

There was no good reason for farmers to be in town again today, but everyone seemed to have come up with an excuse to drive a wagon by the Melchior building and then to drop by the taverns to chat about what they had seen—not much as it turned out since the bulk of the structural damage had been internal. And of course Dilara would be giving a farewell performance at BangBang that night. Since Porky had papered every vertical object with notices, there was no avoiding the fact of it, although Poe had no intention of attending. The searcher couldn't be back yet—there would have been chatter about a tall, pale stranger in a weird cloak, and in any case, Porky would have planned to escort Dilara to and from the bar.

Poe stood at the entrance to the Mercantile in a moment of unaccustomed indecision and stared across the street at the pool of light pouring from his office windows. It looked like Zela had arrested Ren Handling again. Poe could see Ren gesticulating and Zela nodding as she filled in the paperwork. A group of miners strolled by, joking and shoving each other. One of them grinned at him in passing, and he made an attempt to smile back, but it took effort. Despite having nailed the culprit, he felt a notable lack of triumph.

So instead of heading back to the office, he veered across the street to Stig's clinic. The waiting room was surprisingly quiet. Stig's office help was Mrs. Tompkins. She looked like a gnome and was as tough as they came. Woe betide the person who tried to mess with Stig's schedule. But she had a soft spot for Poe, so when he caught her eye, she smiled at him and waved him through to the back.

Stig was just finishing up with a five-year-old boy. The child had tears running down his cheeks and shot Stig a betrayed look before following his mother out of the room.

"Beating up little kids again?" Poe asked.

"Splinter," Stig replied. "His mother told him it wouldn't hurt if he let me pull it out. Cost me two sugar candies and the boy still hates me."

"I don't understand why people tell kids things won't hurt." Poe shook his head. "Life hurts. Kids should get used to it early."

"That's going to be a popular philosophy. You should write a book. No one would buy it."

Poe stared. Stig was rarely sarcastic. You needed an undercurrent of anger to make sarcasm work, and Stig rarely got mad.

Poe watched his friend cautiously and waited a beat before asking, "Something wrong?"

"You mean besides the aftermath of a catastrophic explosion, lots of pain and suffering and finding out my best friend is a first-class idiot? No, nothing. Nothing at all."

Stig reached into a cupboard, grabbed a handful of tongue depressors and replenished the supply in the canister on his desk, his movements accurate but unnecessarily vigorous.

"You got a new best friend? Because last I checked I was brilliant."

Stig shook his head and held up a mug. "Nope. You're it, more's the pity. Coffee?"

Poe figured if he drank any more coffee now, he'd be ready to do a tap dance number on Main Street. He nodded anyway, took the mug and sat in one of the visitor chairs.

"Why am I an idiot?" he asked.

"Dilara is the best thing that ever happened to you," Stig said, "and you're letting her get away, which makes you a Grade A fool in my book."

"It's not that simple," Poe said.

"Sure it is." Stig's tone was sharp. "In fact, I thought you were quite capable of figuring it out on your own. But as it turns out, you're too much of a coward."

"Right," Poe said. Well, that wasn't true. He felt his shoulders release in the certainty of it.

Stig waved his hand dismissively. "I know, I know. You were the first kid in school to climb the Elkenor Tree, the first to try bullfighting with a bovoquin, the first to swim across Lake Moortan. But that's not bravery. That's just foolhardiness. You knew you might get hurt, but you were betting you wouldn't. Bravery is when you risk getting hurt again in the same way you got hurt before."

"Big talk from the guy who hasn't ever made that commitment," Poe said.

Stig nodded. "You're right. But I don't have a Dilara yet."

"She likes you," Poe said.

"Yeah. Well, that's where the fool part comes in," Stig snapped. "She doesn't want me. She doesn't want that Melchior yenxer who offered her the world on a spoon. She wants you. And you're too bullheaded to see it."

Poe looked at his hand wrapped around the mug and was surprised to see it tremble. He set the cup down before he dropped it.

"Stig, even if she *thinks* she wants me, she's wrong. Why would she want a washed-up dead end? I'm a living embodiment of disappointment."

Stig stared at him. "That's ridiculous. You're a perfectly competent marshal, a good son, and when you're not being an idiot, you're a good friend. What's wrong with you?"

"Being marshal doesn't matter anymore."

Poe's chest felt tight, as though there was a metal band curved around his ribs. Stig put down his half-drunk coffee.

"What are you talking about?"

"I thought it was everything I wanted. It *was* everything I wanted. But now I have it…" He shrugged.

"Forget the coffee. I'll buy you a whiskey."

DILARA SIGNALED TO RUDOLPH AND SLIPPED OUT THE door into the alley for a breath of air before her next set. BangBang was packed, and after the pungent odor of food, drink and sweat, the clean night air felt decadent. She inhaled greedily, savoring the slight air of damp on her cheeks. At the far end of the alley in the glow of the gaslights, she could make out a group of people milling about in the street. She glanced about her, and deciding it was safe enough, walked toward them, trying to pretend she didn't care if Poe might be there. The yearning to see him was almost physical in its intensity. Systematically she began scanning faces.

On the other side of a wagon, she caught a glimpse of Stig and headed in that direction. But by the time she made her way around the wagon, there was no sign of him, and she wondered if she had been mistaken. Disappointed, she turned to go back to the tavern, but the hairs on the back of her neck stood up. She spun to look behind her, and her breath caught in her throat.

The man stood beside her. His black cloak melted into the pool of darkness at his feet. His hood drooped low over his brow, casting his face into shadow. But there could be no question of his identity. A ray of moonlight glinted off the dangling medallion hanging from the thick silver chain around his neck. It was a round silver disk inscribed with an eye, cold and empty except for its ruby center.

Frantically she looked from side to side, but the milling strangers she had considered a hindrance before seemed to have melted away into the tavern. She didn't expect the townspeople to interfere, especially once they understood the situation, but it would have been good to have witnesses, to know someone at least had seen her before she disappeared. Because just at the moment it felt as if all of it, the journey, the singing, Poe, had been a dream. She would wake up and find her life exactly as her parents and sister had planned it.

She looked at the searcher's weapon. His hand was relaxed around the handle, but his finger was poised over the trigger. Running was pointless. He would dose her before she took a second step. So she let out the breath she had been holding and forced her lips into a smile. Shrugging her shoulders, she spread her arms in a gesture of defeat. He paused, assessing her, his finger tightening ever so slightly on the trigger.

"I'll come peacefully," she said, "so there's no need to dose me. Besides, if you do, I will make sure everyone on Caron 5 knows you were afraid of a one-handed woman."

His lips twitched but he remained silent. She waited until the finger relaxed again and tried not to let her relief show. She still had a chance. He was encumbered by his cloak, so if the opportunity arose to run, she might be able to evade him. The thought must have shown on her face because he tossed her the looped end of his rope sash. She picked it up, ruefully wishing she had made her move the moment it had occurred to her. Now it was too late.

Wordlessly he gestured toward her neck and mimed tightening the loop. Searchers rarely spoke—it was one way to engender fear in the hunted. In this case though, it might be to her advantage, she decided. Instead of draping the loop around her neck, she slid first one arm and then the other through it so it fit snug around her waist. She flicked a glance at him, but he simply turned away and began walking. Maybe it didn't matter to him. He probably didn't consider her a threat, and it would be advantageous to her to keep it that way.

Chapter 57

BANGBANG WAS THE LAST PLACE POE HAD PLANNED to be that night, but here he was. Stig had insisted on buying them both dinner to go with the promised whiskey and then pointed out there had been complaints of food poisoning at the other two bars in town. Poe thought there was likely something flawed in Stig's argument, but he was too tired to argue. He claimed the one remaining vacant table and sank into the chair while Stig went to order their food.

According to the poster behind him, Dilara was due to start her second set ten minutes ago. The crowd was growing increasingly restless at the delay, and despite his knowing it was foolish, he felt a sense of disquiet too. He was being ridiculous. She was probably grabbing a bite to eat herself.

He forced himself to scan the crowd carefully, even as his heart slammed urgently against his ribs. Marshal Jackson's maxim about panic getting in the way of intelligent thought had always seemed superfluous until now. This wasn't panic, Poe assured himself. He was probably just dying of a heart attack. He caught a glimpse of Porky across the room and abandoned the table to squeeze through the crowd.

"Have you seen Dilara?"

Porky frowned. He gestured to his brother who broke off a conversation with a woman Poe vaguely remembered from the Well-Wed group and stumped toward them, waving his cane irritably.

"Where'd she go?" Rudolph asked. "Crowd's gonna lose it if she doesn't start soon."

Poe could feel the blood drain from his cheeks.

"Could she be ill?"

"She seemed fine during the first set," Rudolph said, "great, actually, considering someone tried to blow her up last time she was supposed to sing. I finally got someone with musical talent, and now she's going to fly off and leave us all behind. It figures."

Rudolph peered at Poe more closely and cut off his plaint mid-stride. "You're saying she's missing?"

"Probably not. Maybe. I'm not sure."

"But you're worried," Porky said.

"Someone was looking for her a few days back," Poe replied. "A searcher."

Rudolph's eyebrows shot up. "I find that hard to believe. What'd she do? *Nice* someone to death?"

"Her parents were forcing her into a marriage with someone she didn't like."

Stig reappeared, loaded plates in hand just as the woman Rudolph had been speaking to edged closer.

"I saw Dilara speaking with someone."

Poe snapped his gaze toward her. "And you are?"

"Guerenne Ynax. I'm with the Well-Wed group. Dilara was standing with a man just at the end of the alley." Guerenne pointed toward the door, her expression a mingling of self-righteousness and faux concern. "I happened to see her when I stepped out for some air. They stood close together the way people do when they are in an intimate relationship. I came here tonight because I suspected all along she was up to no good. I'm planning to report her to Mrs. Onkelson. We're forbidden to have lovers from our previous homes. That would defeat the whole purpose of being a Well-Wedder. But if Dilara was doing something illegal, that's even worse."

"What did the man look like?" Stig asked.

"Tall and gaunt," she said promptly, shooting Stig a fawning look. "He was a little frightening." She shivered delicately to illustrate her point before continuing. "He wore a hooded black cloak and a silver pendant. He gave Dilara something, a belt, I think, and then they left together."

"Were they on foot?" Poe spoke sharply. "Which direction did they go?"

She shrugged. "I only saw them turn south down Main Street. It's not as though they let me in on their plans. For all I know they were going to find a quiet place to consummate their relationship. In fact, I suspect..."

Poe's fingers were tingling now. If he ran, he could catch up with them. Of course there was always a chance he might miss them. Or that the searcher had had a wagon waiting. Or even just a chevalo. Blindly he turned away from Guerenne.

"Kekk that yenxer," Porky said. "He's not taking away my entertainer. Come on, Rudolph, move it. We'll take one of the wagons outside and make excuses later. You coming, Poe?"

Stig slid the plates in front of two nearby customers and slapped Poe's shoulder.

"We both are," Stig said.

The wagon was roomy enough to accommodate the four of them, but the rusty brackets holding it together moaned when they climbed in, and Poe wondered whether he might not be better off on his own. The old chevalo seemed to share his misgivings. Still, it set a steady pace down Main Street.

Poe cleared his throat and tried to force his brain into some semblance of order. Today's shuttle wasn't leaving until tomorrow morning, but Jens would want to secure his quarry on the ship as soon as possible. His voice was hoarse.

"They'll be headed to the docks.

Porky clicked at the chevalo, and it settled into a rocking shamble that was probably as close to a trot as it could manage at its advanced age. As they passed the miners' housing and the surroundings became farmland again, Poe studied the undergrowth on the sides of the road, hoping for a miracle. Once Dilara was on the ship, international nautical law applied. But even then, if he could catch the ship before it left colony territory, he might stand a chance. Not a chance of marrying her. Dilara had made it clear that wasn't on the table. But if he managed to free her, she might want to stay on planet, at least for a little while longer.

The moon was full, the night cloudless. Male clickers sang in the trees overhead, a kind of clickety-whirr designed to sound attractive to female clickers. It seemed deeply unfair that every male creature in nature came equipped with a lure tailor-made to appeal to the female of the species. Bovoquin sported vast horns. Even the damned tapperhead had found a mate, although for the life of him Poe couldn't imagine what she found appealing about him. Still, he had seen the couple flying together, swooping and diving companionably at twilight as they hunted insects. Maybe in a tapperhead's case, the attraction was in proportion to how annoying he was.

Rudolph sat on the bench in front of Poe, rocking to some internal beat as the wagon jolted along.

"Is she as good as they are telling her?" Poe asked. "I mean, *I* think she's good. But is she Phae good?"

Rudolph looked back at him. "Not yet. She doesn't have the polish yet. But once she does, better probably. Phae doesn't write her own material."

Poe's heart sank. He couldn't ask Dilara to stay. In fact, even if she had wanted to stay, he would be selfish to encourage her to do so. This was different than Lenette. Lenette's desertion had been painful, a kind of social wounding as well as a personal one. But worst of all, Lenette had always made it clear that it wasn't Sector 1065 that was the essential problem. The essential problem was that *Poe* wasn't enough. Would never, could never be enough.

With Dilara it had been different. There had been realness to Dilara's regard for him that had felt certain, sure—solid, like the packed earth road below the wagon's wheels. Even when they had fought, that sense she saw him as he was and still thought him sufficient in his essence had been a constant. So until she had walked away that last time, he had thought the friction between them would all somehow blow over. It had to. Packed earth didn't melt away with a rainstorm. It might re-form itself into something new, but its essence didn't change.

He wished he could tell himself that she had changed, that the opportunity to become famous had morphed the woman he had come to love into a thrill-seeking self-serving creature. The problem was it didn't ring true. He knew her too, her essence. She couldn't have changed so radically. And if he was right, he had made the worst mistake of his life when he let her walk away.

Chapter 58

THE SEARCHER STRODE QUICKLY AND DILARA stumbled along behind, sometimes by accident, sometimes on purpose. She couldn't
figure out a way to escape yet, but there was still a chance, no
matter how minute, she might be able to. She would only get one
chance though, so it would have to be successful.

She guessed he was planning to lead her to the docks. Once
they were onboard whatever ship he had made arrangements with,
he could ensure she would have no opportunity to escape. She
would have to make her move soon. Carefully, so he wouldn't feel
the motion in the rope connecting them, she pressed the cord
against her with her stump while she ran the tips of her fingers
over the knot at her waist. It was a well tied hitch, but not unfamiliar, and there was one spot that wiggled slightly.

Fortunately in the short time since she had arrived on planet,
she had gotten to know Sector 1065 well. It helped to know the
walk from downtown to the docks would take about two hours,
even at the searcher's mile eating clip. And she was glad she had
resisted wearing the pretty sandals or delicate dance slippers Melchior had generously provided her. Her sturdy boots would be
more helpful.

"How far will we be walking?"

She tried for a balance between plaintive and complaining. If
he thought she was likely to collapse, he would simply dose her
and carry her as far as necessary. Although he did not answer her
question, to her surprise, he slowed his pace slightly. She slowed
her own in response, keeping the rope between them as taut as

before so he would not feel the need to look back. Still, the slower pace meant she could concentrate on loosening the weak link in the knot a bit more. It wasn't much, but at least it was a plan. It occurred to her she had become careless during her stay in Sector 1065. There was something about living here, about working at BangBang, about falling in love with Poe especially, that had encouraged an illogical sense of security. This had been a mistake.

The searcher walked down the center of the street, a move calculated to shame a prisoner. But since it was dark, and since most of the businesses were shut for the evening, there weren't any observers about. Realistically it no longer mattered what the residents of Sector 1065 thought of her. After tonight, Dilara would be just a memory to them. Still, she was glad none of the townspeople would see her shuffling behind the searcher, her head bowed low. Porky and Rudolph would wonder where she had gone. Her eyes stung at the thought. They would think she had left them in the lurch, had just walked away from her responsibilities and her promise to them.

The searcher led her across the intersection and past Glory Ann's Café. Poe ate there regularly. She turned her face from it and stared at the Mercantile instead. Then she kept her gaze to her right as they passed the Mercantile but just before it would have been too late, she couldn't bear to miss her last glimpse of Poe's office.

The window was dark. It was better this way, she reminded herself. Even if she did manage to escape her captor, there was no point in dreaming about Poe. She felt the knot loosen a little more.

The lights from the hotel dining room windows bathed the street. Inside, she could see staff bustling about as they set up for another Well-Wed event. The annual eclipse was tonight, and Melchior was sponsoring a midnight viewing party. Given the catastrophic nature of the last event, Dilara doubted the evening would be the joyful celebration Mrs. Onkelson had intended. Still, Guerenne and her group would chatter about the men they had met, Kiko would stare down potential suitors, Ngendo would smile politely, and Susanna would likely disappear into a quiet nook to write a letter to whoever she wrote to. Dilara didn't even like parties, but she still felt a pang at the thought of missing it.

The contrast between the light from the windows pooling on the road and the dark around it was striking. As the searcher stepped into the light, two things happened. The knot finally gave way, and a peevish voice called out.

"Excuse me." Jenkson came bustling down from the porch. Glancing at Dilara dismissively he trotted toward the searcher and planted himself in front of him. "How much longer will it be before the Melchior executives arrive? We've already held the hot dishes for over an hour."

The searcher halted and Dilara didn't wait. She dropped the rope and ran. She raced through the narrow alley between the hotel and Roland's Photography Studio, shoved through a hedge into someone's backyard and fled across the perimeter road and into the woods. It would be slower among the trees, but at least she would be harder to see. It was lucky she had chosen a dark shawl to wear over her blue dress. The trick would be moving silently. Searchers were famed for their hearing.

She focused so intently on avoiding snapping branches and working her way around thickets that by the time she decided to rest on a fallen tree trunk for a few minutes, she was completely turned around and could no longer see the road. The forest was surprisingly noisy at night. The birds were asleep, but the insects clicked and chirped with abandon. And there were other, less reassuring sounds—shuffling in the bracken and a brief slithering sound uncomfortably close by. She drew her feet up and hugged her knees close.

Her mind raced, leaping from one perceived threat to the next. Every twig snap, every flicker in the shadows made her startle. But as the night wore on and became morning, she began to think the searcher might not find her after all. She curled on her side and let herself slip into a light doze. It was the closest to sleep she had come since she left Poe.

She woke as the sun rose, chilled and cramped from hours curled on top of the rough-barked trunk. She hadn't expected to sleep, but the combination of exhaustion and shock had eventually overwhelmed her fear. Stretching, she cast a cautious look around her. In the daylight, the forest seemed less threatening than it had at night. Birds fluttered through the fresh leaves far above, involved in their bird world. The rustling she heard in the nearby undergrowth was more likely a small hare than a snake. But as long as the searcher was hunting her, she was still in danger.

She wasn't sure what the rule was about searchers and escaped captives. He had to bring her back alive to Caron 5, preferably uninjured, although she guessed the rules were flexible if a captive fought back. Her stomach growled. Yesterday's midday meal was long gone. There were berries on the thicket, but she had no idea if they were safe to eat, so it would be foolish to risk it unless she had no choice. She licked her dry lips. Thirst was a bigger issue.

Slowly she lowered her feet to the ground and turned carefully, trying to catch a glimpse of the road, a farmhouse, the openness of a field, but all she could see were trees in every direction. When Poe had taken her geither hunting, the stream had been at the bottom of a slope. It stood to reason that if she were going to find running water anywhere, it would be downhill. Maybe it was foolish to have developed a fondness for a tree trunk just because she had slept on it safely. Still, she tried to mark its location in her mind before turning to walk away.

The sun was high by the time she found the stream. She heard it first, splashing gently over around the smooth stones that studded its bed. As she crept closer the wavelets sparkled in the sunbeams that slid between the branches above. Carefully she slid down the steep slope and didn't care that her boots landed right in the water. She cupped her hand and brought it to her mouth. The water tasted a little like minerals, but she was so grateful for it, she gulped great mouthfuls. The cold damp seeped into her boots, and she welcomed the refreshing chill.

When she had drunk as much as she could, she washed her face and took a moment to appreciate the sensation before splashing out of the water. She could make her way back to Melchior in an hour or so, she thought. The water ran in that direction so all she had to do was follow it. Or the searcher might find her before she got there. Either way, she would likely never see Poe again. She felt dizzy at the thought and sank to sit on the mossy bank. It was probably hunger, she assured herself. All she had to do was get up and start walking. But she couldn't persuade herself to do so. For the first time in weeks she had no plan. The sensation was frightening, as though she had become suddenly purposeless, untethered.

She flashed on her conversation with Kiko the first night in the hotel.

"The worst thing about poverty is it limits your dreams," Kiko had said.

Dilara hadn't understood that when Kiko said it, but she did now. She had never experienced the sort of monetary poverty Kiko described, but it occurred to her as she turned the stone over in her hand, that there were other types of deprivation. One could be starved for warmth, for instance, and not realize it.

She had read a book in school about explorers from Earth who had died on Dilphin before anyone understood the vast swings in temperature on that planet. The book had been written by a Caronite and detailed the explorers' foolish lack of planning with loving precision. But Dilara remembered most the description of their deaths. The explorers got so cold, they suffered delusions. They thought they were hot, so they took off their coats and clothing in the frigid air. Rescue came just hours too late, but if they had kept their protective gear, the explorers might have survived. Dilara hadn't understood how the explorers could have fallen prey to such a delusion when she first read the book, but now she did. It was perfectly possible to believe one was burning up when one was in fact freezing.

It had been like that with Poe, she realized—whether he knew it or not, he needed her. Something tight in her chest loosened as she turned the idea over. It might not matter whether he could ever love her. She loved him. Maybe that would be enough. It would have to be.

She wouldn't allow the searcher to take her without a fight. She scrambled to her feet and looked about her for anything she could use as a weapon. Most of the downed limbs were too large to use as clubs, but there was a fist-sized sharp rock she thought might work. She pried it from the soil and felt marginally better with it cupped in her hand. It was good to feel the hum of anger in her sinews.

Then she stood and headed downstream, picking her way around the occasional bramble patch but always finding her way back to the water. The rock was heavy, and her fingers ached a bit over time, but she kept it clenched in her fist.

Chapter 59

POE AND WHAT HE WAS BEGINNING TO PRIVATELY call his posse had checked the docks thoroughly. The captain of the shuttle, the ISS Xendal, had no record of a searcher boarding either with or without his captive. Even so, the four men searched the vessel and the docks for hours.

By late morning, Poe had sent Porky, Rudolph and Stig home to catch a few hours sleep. He knew he should do the same, but he couldn't envision actually sleeping without knowing Dilara was safe. Instead he had waved his thanks and trudged down the sidewalk to his office.

The lights were out, which meant Emilio was out somewhere, probably patrolling. Emilio had a good eye for the unusual. It was even possible he might catch a glimpse of the searcher. Waiting for Emilio to return felt pointless, but Poe figured he would leave a note.

As he pushed the door open, the hairs on the back of his neck stood up. He pulled out his stunner and held it ready as he flicked on the light. The searcher was tipped back in a chair so his shoulders rested against the wall, his feet propped on one of the other chairs. The hood of his cloak covered his face and fluttered lightly with each snore. In two strides Poe kicked the chair out from under Jens' feet, grabbed a fistful of his cloak and slammed him against the wall.

"Where is she?"

The searcher made no attempt to get away, but his lips twitched, and too late Poe felt the tip of a blade against his belly. Slowly Poe released his grip and stepped back, keeping his stunner aimed at Jens.

"Dilara Elian. Where is she?"

The searcher removed his cloak, folded it carefully before resuming his seat. He placed the cloak on his lap, hooked the other chair closer with his boot and made himself comfortable again before responding.

"No idea," he said finally. "She is likely somewhere on this planet, which should please you."

Poe sank into his own chair and rubbed his forehead.

"Is she hurt?"

"If she is, it is not my doing. She ran off into the woods off the perimeter road behind the hotel. I did not see her after that, so I cannot say what condition she finds herself in now."

Poe let go the breath he hadn't realized he'd been holding.

"You wonder why I did not pursue her," the searcher said.

Poe nodded. If the searcher had chosen to pursue Dilara, he would have caught her. "Be good to know."

Jens stared at the wall behind Poe as he considered his response.

"For your purposes my reasons do not matter. It suffices for you to know that I will no longer search for her."

Good seemed too small a word, but Poe said it anyway. "But won't other searchers follow in your place?"

"I think that unlikely," the searcher said. "The parents hired me as a face-saving measure. Word will spread if they have to send two searchers, and they will become a topic of speculation. This will not appeal to them."

Poe stared. From a guy who had been barely willing to scrape two words together during their last conversation, this was practically a flood of information.

"What will you tell them?"

"Since they are unlikely to pay me for my trouble, I see no need to communicate with my employers further," the searcher said.

He rose, pulled the silver necklace with its eye shaped medallion over his head and placed it and the folded cloak on Poe's desk with an air of finality.

"Where are you headed next?"

"Inland. I hear the land beyond the mountain range is beautiful and wild."

Poe's brows shot up. "Here? On Valora? If you take a searching job on this planet, you will need to notify local law enforcement before you begin hunting again."

"Yes. I would need a license transfer. But that circumstance is unlikely."

Poe watched as the searcher opened the door.

"You want me to keep this gear for you? In case you change your mind?" He gestured toward the cloak.

"No."

"I'd still like to know why," Poe said.

The searcher turned back and shrugged.

"Your desire to know is not relevant to me. But even if it were, I could not tell you. I don't know why."

Poe watched the door click shut and stared at the folded cloak, mystified. Pop believed in miracles, but in Poe's experience, miracles didn't happen. Trade-offs did. Still, while searchers might be selective in the information they shared, they generally told the unvarnished truth. That was probably the main reason they didn't marry. Although it occurred to him the truth thing might have been specific to Lenette. Dilara seemed to thrive on honesty.

Without thinking, he reached for the coat tree and then remembered he already had his duster on. He turned and ran. The sun was high overhead now, the road empty and waiting. He raced past the hotel and then turned onto the perimeter road. His breath rasped as he stared along the stretch of growth bordering the edge. He could feel a wisp of panic and forced it down, forced himself to wait until he could think properly before he began a systematic search.

He considered going back into town to raise a search party, but as soon as the idea came, he dismissed it. The more people involved in a search, the more likely her tracks would be trampled by accident. He couldn't afford the risk.

He had been skilled at tracking once, but he hadn't gone

hunting since his youth, and most of the people he pursued on behalf of the marshal's office were town folk. Even miscreant farmers and Mnoani usually just ran back to hide in their own homes. So it was a relief to find he hadn't lost the skill entirely.

He found the place she had entered the woods easily. She was wearing boots, he noted approvingly—easy to track but also easier and safer to run through the woods in. Just seeing the first boot print had a calming effect, and he settled into a contemplative rhythm as he systematically checked for prints and bent twigs, never leaving one sign of her passing until he located the next. He stroked the edge of a bent twig and froze.

He loved her. He knew it now. He had loved Lenette, or at least he had tried, but this love for Dilara was a different animal entirely, not a kitten but a cougar—fierce and focused. He needed her with a gut-wrenching intensity and he was pretty sure she needed him. If that meant just being a friend, he would keep his inconvenient emotions under wraps as long as necessary, forever if need be.

He stopped for a moment to trace the outline of her boot with his finger and knew he was sunk. She didn't want him, she had made that clear. And she was leaving forever in a few more days. Still, the thought of seeing her one more time filled him with a disturbing sense of need, a yearning even. He had been so frightened at the thought of her being captured, taken against her will to the home she no longer considered a home. Maybe just seeing her well and safe would be enough. It might have to be if that was what she wanted.

She had stayed on the tree trunk a while, he thought, perhaps even had slept there. Here too she had clearly decided on a course of action. Her wandering path straightened and she had headed downhill. She would be thirsty, and he was glad she had the sense to look for running water, but if she had walked any distance in a stream bed, it would complicate tracking.

The noon sunlight filtered through the tree cover above, and he could see her tracks more clearly so he was able to move faster. But it still didn't feel fast enough. Spring was mountain bear season, and while most of the critters were shy, occasionally one wasn't. He could see where she had slid a bit on her way down to the stream and then, to his relief, where she had scrambled back onto the bank. He still didn't know what he was going to say to her when he found her, or if she would be willing to hear it. She would listen of course—she was too polite not to—but it was that polite listening he dreaded.

Chapter 60

BY MID-AFTERNOON HE HAD LOST HER TRAIL AT THE edge of the road, but at that point it didn't matter. It was clear she had been heading toward Melchior. He felt a surge of pride at her self-sufficiency. It was good she was strong. She would need that where she was going.

The lobby of the Melchior had been set up for a reception. Executives milled about the room, swooping down on the trays of food carried by harried waiters and laughing obsequiously at jokes told by their bosses. Poe made a beeline for the information desk to ask for today's elevator code. But before he could catch the attendant's attention, Zan slapped him on the back.

"Nice work catching our bombers, Marshal, and congratulations on your promotion. Our loss. Anytime you want to jump ship and join the Melchior team, we'd be glad to have you onboard."

"Glad I could help," Poe replied, shaking the hand Zan proffered. "I'm hoping to meet with Melchior's new cultural ambassador. Do you have any idea if she's in?"

"She'd better be. This reception's for her. She's leaving on the SS Centaur tomorrow on the first leg of her tour. Any safety or security problems I should know about?"

"Not at all," Poe assured him. "I just wanted to talk with her."

He scanned the milling celebrants for Dilara without success. It seemed that in the few minutes since he had entered the room, the crowd had doubled.

"Don't these people have anything better to do?" he grumbled.

Zan grinned and held his hands out like uneven scales. "Let's see. Input endless digits into the monthly financial report or..." the lower hand rose slowly, "go to a party with free food in the middle of the workday. I know what I'd choose."

Poe smiled his agreement, but he could feel his throat tightening, a sense of urgency growing, which was ridiculous. Turning away, he stared at the crowd, more to avoid Zan's gaze than out of any hope of seeing Dilara.

"She's in the green room. She's due to perform in about fifteen minutes, and then there's a meet and greet," Zan said. "I can take you back if you want."

"I remember where it is, thanks."

The corridor led past utility rooms and a laundry. As Poe passed, cheerful chatter and a puff of steam came from the open doors. He edged past several wheeled bins filled with tangled linens, moving even faster now as he caught sight of the green door. But when he reached it, he slowed again, uncertain now. He raised a hand to knock but couldn't bring himself to do so. He had just jammed his hands into his pockets and turned away when the door opened.

She was magnificent. Her dress clung to her curves, its burnished copper hue picking up the flecks of gold in her eyes. She had done something with her hair too. Or someone had. It fell smooth and sleek, the sort of fall that looked accidental and was anything but. She might have looked intimidating if he hadn't noticed the tremble in the hand holding the doorknob, her swift intake of breath at the sight of him.

"I didn't expect you to come," she said.

"I had to." It wasn't the right thing to say, he knew, but it was the true thing. "I needed to..."

He waited for a look of understanding from her, a nod, anything that would allow him not to say it. He missed the flicker of anger that had lived in his heart for so long now. It would have helped to have that shield. Anything would be better than this feeling of bareness, as though he were going into battle unarmed, unprotected.

She gave him a long look and then stepped backward, a tacit invitation to enter the room. When he did, she shut the door and turned to face him. She looked, if not exactly unwelcoming, guarded. He was only going to get one chance at this—only one chance to do it right. He took his hands from his pockets and then shoved them back again.

"You grew up rich. In a big city." It tumbled from him. "I can't give you that. I won't be able to. And you can't stay here. I know that. You have your own dream to follow. But I wanted you to know, before you leave, that no one compares to you. It's not that you are better or worse than Lenette, it's that you aren't even in the same category."

She nodded in acknowledgment, but the wary look was still there.

"And I wanted to say too, I love you more than I've ever loved anyone in my life, and it's terrifying. It's not that I can't live without you. I can because I'll have to. But I've been doing that since you moved out, and it's like winter every day. I hate winter. It's cold and miserable, and it seems like it's dark all the time."

She didn't smile, but the corner of her mouth quirked up, and he felt a glimmer of hope.

"I have lots of sweaters now, courtesy of Melchior," she said. "I could lend you one if you're cold."

"I'll probably have to keep it on my pillow to help me sleep at night." He rolled his eyes and she stifled a laugh, turning it into a cough at the last minute. His heart leaped at the sound, and he felt stupid for wanting to kick up his heels, but there it was. He was just going to have to resign himself to feeling stupid.

He stepped close to her now and cupped her cheek, soft and warm, in his palm. It would be just one kiss, he reminded himself, an affectionate goodbye and good luck kiss, the sort one might exchange with a close friend. At least that was the plan. But as he lowered his lips to hers he understood, too late, that this was an altogether different kiss than he had anticipated. Because she gave a minute sigh and leaned in toward him, and he was lost.

And then she reached up and wrapped her arms around his neck, the motion pulling her closer. And his hands were on her back, sliding down that long slope from her shoulders to her narrow waist. The scent he had come to associate with her and with only her—that warm dusky amalgam of cloves, clean and something distinctly Dilara. He held her tight and then buried his face in her hair, trying without success to stop the shudders that ran through him. He hadn't cried since he was a boy.

He thought she would step away then—probably a good decision on her part. He didn't want her to think he was trying to influence her to stay—some sort of emotional manipulation—that wasn't his intent. So when she led him over to the couch and shoved a pile of costumes aside so there was room for both of them to sit, he already knew what he was going to hear. He didn't blame her. She was too kind to do anything but let him down gently. But he hoped she would also do so quickly, decisively, so there was no room for him to pretend she meant something other than total rejection. He didn't let go of her hand though. He thought he might need the solidity of it to get through the next few minutes.

"It's awful, isn't it?" she said. Her eyes met his in a kind of wry acknowledgment, her voice doleful. "When we were first together, I thought I might ask you to do a ring ceremony with me," she said. "But that was when you didn't love me and I didn't love you. It would have been perfect. I wouldn't have had to worry about searchers. And because we did not love each other, neither of us would care if we were apart, so I would have been able to take the Melchior offer without a moment's hesitation. But then I had to go ruin it by falling in love with you."

She looked so disgruntled, he couldn't help grinning, a tiny sense of triumph flaring in him amid the wash of disbelieving relief.

"You love me," he repeated, wanting to be sure he had gotten it right, that he hadn't just heard what his heart wanted to hear.

"Of course." She gave him an impatient look. "And now you love me, which means we are both unhappy. Love is a terrible inconvenience."

He threw his head back and laughed, and after a momentary scowl, she joined him.

When he could speak again, he wiped his eyes and said, "Dilara Elian, I have loved you since the moment I first laid eyes on you, even if I was too stupid to realize it. And I know you're going away for at least a year. But—"

She shook her head and his heart stopped. It took so much

concentration to keep breathing he almost didn't hear her speak.

"I'm not leaving."

He shook his head. "What did you say?"

"I resigned the ambassadorship."

He gestured at the vases of flowers filling the dressing table. "But Zan said you were performing."

"I am," she said. "I'll still perform for the company, and I'm performing today. But it's in honor of Kiko since she is taking the ambassadorship."

"You're not leaving Valora."

"No." She shook her head. "And Manx said Melchior will use my first paycheck to resolve the warrant on Caron 5 on my behalf, which is a great relief even though technically I would be considered guilty."

"Marry me."

She stared at him reprovingly.

"A marshal should not marry a convicted thief. I will always love you, but marriage would be a foolish decision. Besides, I bring no dowry."

He rolled his eyes, put his hands on her shoulders and turned her toward him.

"None of it matters without you. Do you love me, Dilara?"

"More than I love breathing," she said.

"Then say, yes."

"Yes. Oh, yes."

And she was in his arms then and he in hers and when the knock came to warn Dilara of the curtain rise, she was slightly rumpled, but the joy in her eyes was all the audience remembered.

Epilogue

"STOP WORRYING. POE IS HEAD OVER HEELS. You are head over heels. It's going to be fine. If you need anything, I'll be right there in the front row with Pop and the rest of the family."

Minden gave Dilara a quick hug and left, shutting the door firmly behind her.

"Sit still," Ngendo ordered. Carefully she clipped the garland to Dilara's head and stood back with a critical look. "What do you think?"

Kiko, who had arranged to delay her tour for the occasion, nodded judiciously.

"That'll work for now," Kiko replied. "But it won't stay in place for long. Try not to shake your head if you can avoid it," she advised Dilara.

The little room adjacent to the sanctuary had been used for out of season worship items before being abruptly repurposed for the wedding. It still bore the comforting musty smell of old books, but Porky had supplied a table and chair and a mirror borrowed from the brothel, and Fra Randall had piled the storage crates into precarious stacks along the other three walls.

Dilara stared into the mirror now, her eyes meeting her own reflected gaze. Her hair had grown out some since the cropping she had given herself on the SS MacLaren. On that day too, she had stared at her reflection before leaping into another world. Then the image that stared back at her had been pale and determined. Today her cheeks were flushed, her eyes bright with anticipation combined with a sinking sense of panic.

It was the gown. Wedding garb on Caron 5 had been robes of purest white, emblematic of the perfection the bride and groom would aspire to throughout their married lives. But she had no such garment, nor could she afford to squander her limited funds on such an impractical item. So when Poe's mother had offered a wedding dress, the one her own mother, Poe's grandmother had handed down to her and that Minden too had worn, Dilara had been glad to accept.

But in Sector 1065, a wedding dress was a different matter entirely, and Dilara had fallen in love with the gown at first sight. A simple peasant blouse with lace inserts was topped with a rich blue floor length dirndl, lavishly embroidered with colorful flowers of every description. It was unabashedly joyous, bursting with a sure confidence in the wearer's value. When she put it on, it felt as though optimism had been incorporated into the seams, as though the thread was a generational fiber. And the garland crown that wouldn't stay put on her head was the final touch. But the crown's resistance struck her as a kind of sign.

Mrs. Onkelson poked her head in the door and clasped hands over an ample bosom as she inspected Dilara from head to toe. "Oh my dear, you look lovely! A perfect vision! We'll be ready to begin any moment now. We're just waiting for everyone to settle down."

Dilara smiled, trying to look like the fairytale bride Mrs. Onkelson wanted to believe she was. There was a kind of novelty in being cosseted, as though she were a favorite relative. It was a pleasant although slightly peculiar sensation. Since the evening of the explosion, Mrs. Onkelson had been different toward her, warmer, as had many of the women from Dilara's class. Not Guerenne, naturally. But there was a shy friendliness from the others that made Dilara wonder if they might one day become friends.

Because weddings were a relative rarity in the colony, the entire community was invited to attend as a matter of course. She could hear the hum of conversation in the sanctuary when Mrs. Onkelson opened the door to leave. Two days hadn't been much time to plan a ring ceremony, but Mrs. Onkelson had demonstrated her usual dogged persistence, cheerfully wrangling merchants,

Melchior catering and even Mayor Teamue into submission. The last had not been difficult. The mayor too had undergone a change in perspective since the bombing.

"Are you having second thoughts?" Ngendo spoke the moment Mrs. Onkelson left. "If you are, you wouldn't be the first."

Dilara shook her head and blinked her suddenly stinging eyes. "No. I'm ready."

"Great," Kiko said. "Then you shouldn't look as though you are expecting a firing squad out there."

Dilara wanted to laugh but pushed the impulse down. Hysteria wouldn't be good just now, especially since Mrs. Onkelson had reappeared, beckoning urgently. It was time to go.

The walk up the aisle, escorted by Lieutenant Onkelson, seemed to take forever. And when she looked up at the stage ahead, the expression on Poe's face cut like a knife. He looked so in love. And the worst part was he was in love with someone who didn't exist. She only had one chance to make it right, one chance to protect him from a terrible error.

At the halfway mark Lieutenant Onkelson slowed to a stop, and they waited as Poe walked down the aisle toward them. She could see the moment Poe registered her reluctance and for a moment she considered just going through with the ceremony. It would be easier to do what she so yearned to do, easier to pretend just a little longer. Lieutenant Onkelson passed Dilara's hand to Poe's and turned back to sit by his already weeping wife.

"You okay?" Poe kept the pace slow, as though they were strolling through the fields on their way to nowhere in particular, his hand warm and comforting in hers.

"No," she whispered.

"Too much pressure?"

The look of understanding in his eyes was enough to make the tears come. She nodded, biting her lip. If she spoke, she would sob. To her surprise, instead of heading up the stairs to the stage as planned, he took a turn to the left and led her out the exit into the tiny cemetery.

"Want to visit my grandparents?" he asked. "They're right over here."

They stood a moment, staring down at the lichen-covered stones.

"They would have been happy to know you were wearing Grandmother's dress today," he said. "She would have loved you too."

"I can't be perfect." Dilara blurted it out, the words burning like acid as they exited. "I'm not even close and I never will be. What's worse, I'm not even sure I want to be perfect anymore."

In the silence that followed, she didn't dare look at him. He would be thinking about his options, considering how best to back out of the arrangement. He had been kind to try—it was the sort of person he was—honorable. But it wouldn't be fair to hold him to an offer made as a courtesy. Or perhaps he would be angry. That would be reasonable too. Dashed expectations often led to anger. She heard an unexpected snort and risked a glance at him.

"That's your issue? You have got to be kidding. Look at me. I'm not perfect."

He seemed nearly perfect to her, but she knew that wasn't the point. "Maybe," she said. "But it's something you can hope to achieve. That's not a possibility for me."

"No, I can't—is this about your stump?"

"Not about mine," she said. "But if we were to have a child, the imperfection might recur. I don't think I could bear to see you look at our child the way my parents looked at me.

He turned her to face him with a roughness that surprised her.

"Is that what you think of me? That I would reject my child for something she couldn't help, for something he was born with?"

His eyes blazed with fury, and she was filled with an over-whelming joy.

"No. No, I don't. You would never do that."

"Fine," he snapped. "Are we still getting married?"

"Yes, please."

Shaking his head, he led her back toward the worship center, muttering under his breath the whole way. Just as they reached the door, he stopped suddenly.

"You drive me crazy, you know that? I can't get enough of you. It wouldn't matter if you had three hands and no feet. You're all I want."

He rested his hands on her shoulders and looked down at her. "You are perfect for me—do you understand?"

And when his lips met hers, when his arms pulled her close, it was as close to perfect imperfection as she could ever have dreamed.

Free Story!

Join over seven hundred smart readers who have signed up to my free newsletter at **www.rosegreybooks.com/newsletter** and get your FREE copy of "*Baci – A First Kiss Short Story*" plus other exclusive bonus content!

About The Author

Rose's idea of an emergency is realizing that a long weekend is coming and that the library is closing in an hour. She loves finding cool seashells, knitting sweaters which start out right but inevitably turn out too large, and petting stray dogs. She lives with her husband, the love of her life, and suffers from the sin of boundless pride when it comes to her four grown children. Her favorite stories involve unexpected love and the characters who are doing everything in their power to avoid it. Find out more about her stories at **https://rosegreybooks.com**.

Rose strongly recommends joining over seven hundred readers who have signed up to her newsletter. You get a free copy of *Baci - A First Kiss Short Story* as a bonus, as well as exclusive bonus content. Sign up and join the fun here: https://rosegreybooks.com/newsletter.

Please Review This Book

Reviews help authors more than you might think. If you enjoyed *The Heart Thief*, please consider leaving a review on the site where you purchased it or, if you prefer, on Goodreads or Bookbub. It would be greatly appreciated!

Author Note

The Heart Thief is my sixth novel. I had to stop to breathe a bit after writing that sentence because ten years ago I would not have considered it possible.

And this book would not have *been* possible without a lot of help, namely:

The members of Rhode Island Romance Writers, who are both honest and kind. I am proud to be part of this supportive group of authors.

Judy Roth, who edits with gentle precision. If there are errors in this book, they aren't hers.

Izabela Novoselec of izabeladesign who exercised the graphic skills I definitely don't have, to design a cover for a genre blend I could provide no examples of.

Indie Authors who share their guidance with other writers out of sheer generosity of spirit. I am in awe of David Gaughran, Kristine Kathryn Rusch, and Alexandra Sokoloff.

Sam, who opened my eyes to sci-fi and fantasy by introducing me to fabulous writers and their fully imagined worlds of the mind.

Abe, whose distinctive and sharp perspective leads me to look at plots and characters from angles I would not have considered otherwise. And, let me not forget, is a webmaster par excellence.

My extended family, who give me endless reasons for gratitude.

Finally, my biggest thanks of all to David. Sometimes in life, you get supremely lucky. I did when I met you.